William Wordsworth, W. T. Webb

Selections from Wordworth

Edited with Introduction and Notes

William Wordsworth, W. T. Webb

Selections from Wordworth
Edited with Introduction and Notes

ISBN/EAN: 9783337275303

Printed in Europe, USA, Canada, Australia, Japan

Cover: Foto ©Andreas Hilbeck / pixelio.de

More available books at **www.hansebooks.com**

SELECTIONS

FROM

WORDSWORTH

EDITED WITH INTRODUCTION AND NOTES

BY

W. T. WEBB, M.A.

LATE PROFESSOR OF ENGLISH LITERATURE, PRESIDENCY COLLEGE, CALCUTTA ;
EDITOR OF "COWPER, THE TASK, BOOK IV.," "COWPER'S SHORTER POEMS," ETC.

𝔏𝔬𝔫𝔡𝔬𝔫

MACMILLAN AND CO., LIMITED

NEW YORK : THE MACMILLAN COMPANY

1897

All rights reserved

GLASGOW : PRINTED AT THE UNIVERSITY PRESS
BY ROBERT MACLEHOSE AND CO.

PREFACE.

IN editing the present volume my aim has been to
provide the student with a *representative* selection of
Wordsworth's poetry, as far as was possible within the
limits assigned. The book is divided into two parts;
Part I. being intended to break the ground, so to speak,
and lead up to Part II. The poems of the separate
parts are arranged in chronological order of composition
—with one exception, the Ode *Intimations of Immortality*,
which closes the volume in accordance with the poet's
own arrangement, to which he steadily adhered in all
the editions of his works published during his lifetime.

In the preparation of these Selections I have consulted
Wordsworth, by F. W. H. Myers; the Introductions to
Wordsworth's poetry by John Morley, Matthew Arnold,
and R. W. Church; *Appreciations*, by Walter Pater;
The Age of Wordsworth, by Professor C. H. Herford;
and *Selections from Wordsworth*, by Hawes Turner; to
all of whom I wish to express my grateful acknowledg-
ments. I am under special obligation to Professor

William Knight, whose recent valuable edition of *The Poetical Works of William Wordsworth* I have freely made use of, particularly in drawing up the Introductions to the several poems. For the historical portion of the Note to line 68 of *Influence of Natural Objects*, in Part II., I am indebted to the kindness of Professor W. W. Skeat. Lastly, my cordial thanks are due to my friend, Mr. James A. Aldis, Headmaster of Queen Mary's School, Walsall, who kindly reviewed the whole of the proofs, and gave me much valuable assistance in the preparation of the General Introduction.

W. T. W.

CONTENTS.

	PAGE
PREFACE,	iii
GENERAL INTRODUCTION,	ix
POEMS—	
Lines written in Early Spring,	1
"There was a Boy,"	2
Nutting,	3
Lucy,	5
Hart-leap Well,	6
The Sparrow's Nest,	12
To the Cuckoo,	13
The Redbreast chasing the Butterfly,	14
To a Butterfly,	15
To the Small Celandine,	16
Composed upon Westminster Bridge,	18
On the Extinction of the Venetian Republic,	18
London, 1802,	19
To the Daisy,	19
Stepping Westward,	21
The Solitary Reaper,	22
Rob Roy's Grave,	23
To the Men of Kent,	27

POEMS—*Cont.*

	PAGE
The Daffodils,	27
The Affliction of Margaret,	28
Fidelity,	31
To Sleep,	33
Thought of a Briton on the Subjugation of Switzerland,	34
To a Sky-lark,	34
A Morning Exercise,	35
The Primrose of the Rock,	36
"Calm is the Fragrant Air,"	38
Composed by the Sea-shore,	39
On Revisiting the Wye above Tintern Abbey,	41
Influence of Natural Objects,	46
The Rainbow,	49
Resolution and Independence,	50
"It is a Beauteous Evening,"	55
"When I have borne in Memory,"	55
To H. C.,	56
Yew-Trees,	57
At the Grave of Burns,	58
"She was a Phantom of Delight,"	60
Ode to Duty,	61
On a Picture of Peele Castle in a Storm,	63
Character of the Happy Warrior,	65
The Sonnet,	68
Personal Talk,	68
Admonition,	70
"The World is too much with us,"	71
Song at the Feast of Brougham Castle,	71
Laodamia,	76
Composed upon an Evening of Extraordinary Splendour and Beauty,	82

CONTENTS. vii

POEMS—*Cont.*

PAGE

Inside of King's College Chapel, Cambridge,   - -   84

"Scorn not the Sonnet," - · · · · -   85

On the Departure of Sir Walter Scott from Abbotsford, for Naples, - - · · · - -   85

Ode. Intimations of Immortality from Recollections
of Early Childhood, - · · · - -   86

NOTES,   · - · - · · · · · -   93

INDEX TO NOTES,   · - · · · · · -   209

GENERAL INTRODUCTION.

WILLIAM WORDSWORTH was born on April 7th, 1770, at Cockermouth, on the Derwent, in an agricultural district of Cumberland, about six miles from the sea-coast, ten miles to the west of Skiddaw, and fifteen miles north-west of Helvellyn. Thus he lived from his infancy in the immediate neighbourhood of that romantic lake scenery which will evermore be associated with, as it was consecrated by, his genius.

On both his father's and mother's side he came of an Childhood. old north-country stock of good social standing. His mother died when he was eight years old; and five years later he lost his father. As a child he was stubborn, moody, and of a violent temper; the only one of his family for whom the mother had ever felt any anxious forebodings. On one occasion, when he was staying with his mother's father at Penrith, having as he thought been unfairly treated, he went up into an attic determined to kill himself with one of the foils kept there; but, as he says, "his heart failed him."

At eight years old he was sent to school at Hawks- School-days. head, on Esthwaite Lake, a few miles west of Winder-mere. Here he was allowed to read whatever books he

b   ix

liked, Fielding's novels, *Don Quixote*, *Gulliver's Travels*, and the *Tale of A Tub* being among his favourites. But Wordsworth's real education, from his earliest childhood, was received in Dame Nature's open-air school, among river-side meadows, and wooded hills, or, later, amid the solemn silences of mountain and lake. In the *Prelude* (i. 274 *et seq.*) he has given us his inner autobiography :

> " For this, didst thou,
> O Derwent, winding among grassy holms
>
> .   .   .   .
>
> Make ceaseless music that composed my thoughts
> To more than infant softness, giving me
> Amid the fretful dwellings of mankind
> A foretaste, a dim earnest, of the calm
> That Nature breathes among the hills and groves?
>
> .   .   .   .
>
> Fair seed-time had my soul, and I grew up
> Fostered alike by beauty and by fear."

Even his moral nature was disciplined by the same silent teacher. It was not by learning the Decalogue in the class-room ; it was in lonely midnight wanderings over the frost-bound heights of Esthwaite in search of snared woodcocks, when he had unfairly taken a schoolfellow's bird, that "low breathings" from the "solitary hills" came after him, and "steps almost as silent as the turf they trod" taught him the lesson *Thou shalt not steal.*

University career. In 1787 he entered the University of Cambridge, as a student at St. John's College. He troubled himself but little with the University curriculum ; his education was chiefly carried on by self-chosen reading—by communing with Nature—by the conscious equality of brotherhood in the free social life of University men, which matured that sense of man's innate dignity and worth learned in childhood among the sturdy self-respecting peasant proprietors of Cumberland.

In his first summer long vacation he found himself again among his boyish haunts at Esthwaite Lake ; a centre of admiring interest to his former schoolfellows and friends, above all to the kindly dame who had been as a mother to him during his school-boy days. His self-wrapt contemplative love of Nature now began to grow more "human-hearted." He mixed freely in the rustic society of his Cumberland friends, and took a kindly pleasure in the light-hearted talk of their dancing parties, with

> "Here and there
> Slight shocks of young love-liking interspersed,
> Whose transient pleasure mounted to the head,
> And tingled through the veins." (*Prelude*, iv. 316-319.)

Returning to his lodging on one occasion, after a night spent in these innocent gaieties, he was confronted with the calm splendour of sunrise :

> "The sea lay laughing at a distance ; near,
> The solid mountains shone, bright as the clouds,
> Grain-tinctured, drenched in empyrean light ;
> And in the meadows and the lower grounds
> Was all the sweetness of a common dawn—
> Dews, vapours, and the melody of birds,
> And labourers going forth to till the fields."
> (*Ib.* iv. 326-332.)

At that hour the mystic hand of Nature was laid upon him in consecration ; and he felt himself to be thenceforward " a dedicated Spirit," the Poet Priest of Nature and of Man.

Yorkshire tour.

His second summer vacation was spent in a tour among "romantic Dovedale's spiry rocks," through the Yorkshire dales, and the banks of the river Emont, near Penrith, at that time "unnamed in song," but eighteen years later celebrated in the *Song at the Feast of Brougham Castle*. The chief interest of this tour lies in the fact that it was made in the company of his sister Dorothy and of Mary Hutchinson, a friend and companion of his childhood, towards whom his feelings now began to deepen into that steadfast love which thirteen years afterwards culminated in an ideally perfect marriage.

Continental tour; French Revolution.

In his third summer vacation he joined a college friend in a tour through France and Switzerland. They landed at Calais on the "eve of that great federal day" when Trees of Liberty were planted all over France; and on their journey down the Rhone fraternised enthusiastically with delegates returning from the festivities in Paris. To Wordsworth, with his ideal fervour for the dignity of man, the French Revolution seemed a matter of course:

> "Europe at that time was thrilled with joy,
> France standing on the top of golden hours,
> And human nature seeming born again."
>
> (*Ib.* vi. 339-341.)

This tour bore poetic fruit in the *Descriptive Sketches*, which, with the *Evening Walk*, were published in 1792, constituting Wordsworth's first appearance as an author.

In London.

He took his B.A. degree at Cambridge in January 1791, and then settled in London, with no definite plans for his future career. *The Reverie of Poor Susan* (1797) vividly illustrates his own habitual feelings while thus living a stranger in that wilderness of sombre streets and hurrying, pre-occupied crowds.   She hears in the early morning, at the corner of Wood Street, the song of a caged thrush :

> "'Tis a note of enchantment ; what ails her? she sees
> A mountain ascending, a vision of trees ;
> Bright volumes of vapour through Lothbury glide,
> And a river flows on through the vale of Cheapside."

In November 1791 Wordsworth paid a second visit to France.   At Orleans he formed an intimate friendship with the nobly-born republican general Beaupuis.   He returned to Paris in October 1792, a month after the September massacres.   So filled was he with republican enthusiasm that he seriously contemplated coming forward as a leader of the Girondist party.   His friends at home saved him from a course which could only have ended in the guillotine by the prosaic expedient of stopping his allowances.   He was thus compelled to return to England. *Second visit to France.*

But his dreams of a new-born world of Liberty and Progress were rudely shattered by the execution of Louis XVI., and the subsequent declaration of war against England by the French Republic in 1793.   A period of gloom and despondency followed, in which for a time he lost faith in Nature, in Art, and in his own mission—almost indeed lost all belief in God.   His poem entitled *Guilt and Sorrow* (1791-4) reflects something of the darkness that now enwrapped him.   He had no settled home, but lived chiefly in London, with occasional excursions into the country.

About this time, 1795, a young friend and admirer, Raisley Calvert, dying of consumption, left him a legacy of £900, for the express purpose of setting him free to devote his life to his poetic mission.   Wordsworth *Settles at Racedown ; then at Alfoxden. Coleridge.*

accordingly settled with his sister Dorothy, at Racedown near Crewkerne, in the south-east of Somersetshire. Here he wrote his only dramatic attempt, the tragedy of *The Borderers*, and a poem of high merit entitled *The Ruined Cottage*, which was subsequently incorporated in the First Book of *The Excursion*. In 1797 Wordsworth with his sister removed to Alfoxden in Somersetshire near the Quantock Hills, and thus became neighbours of the elder Coleridge, his lifelong friend, who was then residing at Nether Stowey.

Lyrical Ballads.

In 1798, in conjunction with that poet, who contributed *The Ancient Mariner* and two or three other pieces, Wordsworth published at Bristol the *Lyrical Ballads*. These were republished in 1800 with a Preface in which Wordsworth formally defended the theory of the poetic art in accordance with which they had been written. The volume ended with the verses written in July 1798, during a five days' ramble with his sister through the Wye valley—a poem which strikes the characteristic keynote of Wordsworth's genius :

> "For I have learned
> To look on Nature, not as in the hour
> Of thoughtless youth ; but hearing oftentimes
> The still sad music of humanity,
> Nor harsh, nor grating, though of ample power
> To chasten and subdue.   And I have felt
> .   .   .   .   .   a sense sublime
> Of something far more deeply interfused,
> Whose dwelling is the light of setting suns,
> And the round ocean, and the living air,
> And the blue sky, and in the mind of man ;
> A motion and a spirit, that impels
> All thinking things, all objects of all thought,
> And rolls through all things."

(*Tintern Abbey*, 88-102.)

After the publication of this volume Wordsworth and Winter at Goslar, in Dorothy sailed for Hamburg, intending to learn German Germany. during a winter spent at Goslar in Hanover, near the northern slopes of the Harz Mountains. Here he composed some of his best pieces, *Lucy Gray, Ruth, The Poet's Epitaph, Nutting,* and the exquisite group of love-poems on "Lucy." In none of his poetry have the tender grace of English scenery and English girlhood been painted more delicately than in the lines which came to him as he paced the frozen gardens of that winter city, with no companion but a wild king-fisher that used to glance about his steps. Here too he planned, and on the day of his leaving the town he began the autobiographical *Prelude, or, Growth of a Poet's Mind,* a poem addressed and dedicated to Coleridge.

Towards the close of 1799 Wordsworth settled with Settles at Grasmere; his sister at Townend, in Grasmere, and on the 4th of marriage. October, 1802, he married Mary Hutchinson of Penrith. Thenceforward Wordsworth lived an ideal poet's life, consecrated to "plain living and high thinking"; surrounded by congenial friends; inspired by the familiar voices of mountain, lake, and stream, and, above all, blest by the constant home companionship of a devoted sister and an equally devoted wife. Here he planned and deliberately pursued the scheme for which all his antecedents, experiences, and natural talents had predestined him; to write a poem of lofty philosophical aims, such as posterity should not willingly let die.

That poem in its integrity was to have been *The* The Excursion and The Recluse, to consist of three parts; of which, however, Prelude. only the second part was actually finished and published under the title of *The Excursion*. The *Prelude* was intended as an introduction to *The Recluse*; Wordsworth himself comparing the *Prelude* to the antechapel, and the *Recluse* to the body of a Gothic Church; while his smaller poems he regarded as "the little cells, oratories, and sepulchral recesses ordinarily included in those edifices." The *Prelude* was finished in 1805; perhaps on the whole his most interesting and characteristic work. In 1807 he published two fresh volumes of poetry, and in the following year the Wordsworths removed to Allan Bank at the north end of Grasmere. The great bulk of the poems included in these Selections were written between Wordsworth's settlement at Alfoxden and his removal to Allan Bank. Later, in 1811, he took up his residence at the Parsonage House, Grasmere.

Family life. Wordsworth, like Southey, and unlike Coleridge, was a model husband and a most affectionate father. He had five children—John the eldest, born 1803; Dora, born 1804; Thomas, born 1806; Catherine, born 1808; and William, born 1810. Of these, Catherine (described in the little poem composed in 1811—"*Loving she is, and tractable, though wild*") died in 1812, and was soon followed by her brother Thomas. Wordsworth felt the loss of these children profoundly, and nearly forty years afterwards, in speaking of the details of their last illness to a friend, seemed as much overcome by emotion as if the events had only occurred a few weeks previously. So deeply did he feel his loss, that he could not bear to remain at the Parsonage, where the adjoining churchyard constantly reminded him of it; and at the earliest opportunity he removed, in the spring of 1813, to Rydal Mount, his

favourite and last abode. Here he was surrounded
by a small circle of distinguished friends—Southey,
De Quincey, Coleridge, and Dr. Arnold of Rugby
School.

Wordsworth's favourite, indeed his only luxury was Tours in
France, Scot-
travelling; and his tours almost always bore poetic fruit. land, Wales,
etc.
In August 1802, shortly before his marriage, he, with
his sister, paid a short visit to France ; a journey which
gave birth to two of his noblest sonnets, *Westminster
Bridge,* and "*It is a beauteous evening,*" composed on the
Calais sands.

During a tour in Scotland (August 1803), made in
company with Coleridge, Wordsworth and his sister were
greatly struck with two Highland girls whom they met
on the shore of Loch Lomond. "One of them," Miss
Wordsworth writes, "was exceedingly beautiful. . . .
They answered us so sweetly that we were quite
delighted, at the same time that they stared at us with
an innocent look of wonder. I think I never heard the
English language sound more sweetly than from the
elder of these girls, . . . her face flushed with the rain ;
her pronunciation clear and distinct, yet slow, as if like
a foreign speech." This encounter Wordsworth immor-
talised in his lines *To a Highland Girl,* which originated
the opening of the poem to his own wife, "*She was a
phantom of delight.*" This tour also gave rise to *At the
Grave of Burns, Stepping Westward, The Solitary Reaper,* and
Rob Roy's Grave. A second tour in Scotland in 1814,
produced *The Brownie's Cell,* and a few other pieces of no
great note. Other tours, on the Continent, in North
Wales, and in Ireland, followed. In the summer of 1807
Wordsworth visited, for the first time, the beautiful

country that surrounds Bolton Priory, in Yorkshire—a visit of which the striking poem, *The White Doe of Rylstone*, was the outcome. In 1831 he paid, with his daughter, a visit to Sir Walter Scott at Abbotsford before the departure of the latter for Italy. *Yarrow Revisited*, and the touching sonnet, "*A trouble not of clouds nor weeping rain*," are memorials of that excursion.

Revival of classical studies; Laodamia,

Between 1814 and 1816 Wordsworth's thoughts were directed into a fresh channel, while superintending his eldest son John's preparation for the University. For this purpose he read again with him some of the standard Latin poets; and was deeply influenced by the magic of Vergil's verse. *Laodamia* and its companion poem *Dion* (1816) form stately memorials of this classical *renaissance* in Wordsworth's poetic career.

and other poems.

The exquisite poem *Composed upon an Evening of Extraordinary Splendour and Beauty*; a series of sonnets on the River Duddon (1820); the sonnet on King's College Chapel; *To the Skylark, A Morning Exercise*, and *Scorn not the Sonnet; The Primrose of the Rock*, a didactic poem on immortality; and two Evening Voluntaries, *Calm is the Fragrant Air* and *By the Seashore*, with other poems and sonnets chiefly didactic, bring us to the close of Wordsworth's poetical career.

Latter days.

The death by shipwreck of his deeply loved and venerated brother John (1805), and, later on, the serious illness of his sister Dorothy (1832); the death of his bosom friend Coleridge (1834), and of his wife's sister, Sarah Hutchinson, for many years an inmate of Wordsworth's household; the illness and subsequent death in 1847 of his daughter Dora, who had married a Mr. Quillinan, threw a shadow over the poet's later years, though these sorrows were met with dignified fortitude and deepening religious resignation.   On the other hand, these years were brightened by the evergrowing reverence with which the public had begun to cherish a name which for so long had been the butt of reviewers' ridicule and the object of contemptuous neglect.   In the summer of 1839 Keble, the author of *The Christian Year*, and Professor of Poetry in the University, welcomed him, amidst a scene of unprecedented enthusiasm, to receive from the University of Oxford the honorary degree of Doctor of Common Law.   In October 1842 Sir Robert Peel conferred upon him an annuity of £300 per annum from the Civil List in recognition of his distinguished literary merit.   In March 1843, upon the death of Southey, he accepted with some reluctance the office of Poet Laureate.

He closed a long and, on the whole, a happy life at Death. Rydal Mount, April 23, 1850, and was buried in Grasmere churchyard.

The most remarkable feature of Wordsworth's Wordsworth's character was its singular combination of the man's Character. lofty and austere self-control, an habitual consecration of (a) Austerity and suscep-all the energies to the highest moral and spiritual aims, tivity com-with the responsive, self-forgetful susceptivity of the bined. child.   His habits were almost ascetic in their simplicity. Like Milton, the revered subject of his sonnet, *London, 1802*, he lived through youth and manhood a life of flawless purity ; like Milton, too, he lived in stirring times, and showed a capacity for taking a prominent part in public affairs ; like Milton, lastly, he spent his whole life with an abiding sense that heaven had called him to

write something which should be one of humanity's
landmarks; so that his whole-hearted self-dedication to
this great work compelled him to live, like his prototype,
hour by hour and day by day,

"As ever in the great Taskmaster's eye."

(b) Sympathy
with woman-
hood and
childhood.

But he was deservedly happier and morally greater
than Milton in his relations with womanhood and childhood.   He had nothing of that half-contemptuous
assumption of woman's inferiority which marks the poet
of *Paradise Lost* and *Samson Agonistes*.   Milton turned
his daughters into literary drudges; Wordsworth lived
on terms of frank intellectual equality with his sister and
his wife, and habitually sought their sympathetic criticism
of his writings.   He was forward to own that one of
the brightest gems of his poetry (*The Daffodils*, 21, 22)
was contributed by his wife; and that he owed some
of his most characteristic gifts to his sister's early
influence :

"She gave me eyes, she gave me ears ;
   And humble cares, and delicate fears ;
   A heart, the fountain of sweet tears ;
   And love, and thought, and joy."

The depth of his love as a father has been already
noted; while his sympathy with childhood is beautifully
expressed in such well-known poems as *We are Seven*,
Lucy Gray, and *Alice Fell*.   And perhaps an even stronger
proof of that sympathy was his inclusion among his own
poems of two beautiful lyrics by his sister Dorothy,
entitled *Address to a Child* and *The Mother's Return*.   Of
Wordsworth's own deep-seated childlikeness of soul, that
divine weakness which is the secret of genius, perhaps

the best illustration is to be found in *The Poet's Epitaph* :

> " But who is he, with modest looks,
>   And clad in homely russet brown ?
> He murmurs near the running brooks
>   A music sweeter than their own.
>
> He is retired as noontide dew,
>   Or fountain in a noon-day grove ;
> And you must love him, ere to you
>   He will seem worthy of your love.
>
> .   .   .   .
>
> But he is weak ; both Man and Boy,
>   Hath been an idler in the land ;
> Contented if he might enjoy
>   The things which others understand. "

Lastly, a prominent feature of Wordsworth's character *(c)* His love of law and was his intense constitutional love of Order, Custom, and custom. Law. This may seem strange in one who was at one time so ardent an advocate of the French Revolution. Plainly it was rooted in his sense of the abiding calm of Nature, as seen in the Cumbrian lakes and mountains. That there was an element of fierce revolt latent in him is shown by the incident of his one attempt at suicide ; and doubtless that element co-operated with his enthusiasm for the dignity of Man as Man, in his brief fever-fit of Revolutionary zeal. But it is clear that the subsequent history of France proved for him an impressive and never-to-be-forgotten object lesson on the moral worthlessness of lawless revolt. In the period of depression that followed, he seems to have anchored his soul in the conception of God as Eternal Law. And later, when the French Revolution merged itself in the military despotism of Napoleon, the whole force of his inborn patriotism fired with a passionate ardour some of his noblest sonnets, such as *To the Men of Kent, On the Subjugation of Switzerland*, and "*When I have borne in memory*." It would appear too from his *Ode to Duty*, written in 1805, that all these influences combined had wrought within him a distinct consciousness of his need for the guidance of external law; a deepened sense of the kinship which the unbroken order of nature holds with the moral order within the soul of man :

> "Stern Lawgiver ! yet thou dost wear
>   The Godhead's most benignant grace ;
> Nor know we anything so fair
>   As is the smile upon thy face :
> Flowers laugh before thee in their beds
> And fragrance in thy footing treads ;
> Thou dost preserve the stars from wrong ;
> And the most ancient heavens, through thee, are
>   fresh and strong."

Certain it is that from this time onwards Wordsworth steadily grew in attachment to the Church of England as the embodiment of social order and moral law, and in a steady political conservatism. He was to the last a staunch, though never a bitter opponent of the Reform Bill and of Catholic Emancipation ; and a fanatical opponent of the extension of the railway system to the Lakes.

Wordsworth's Poetry.
(a) Its defects :
(1) Inequality.
From Wordsworth's character as a man we pass on to note the distinctive characteristics of his poetic work. The most obvious of these is its great inequality ; its perplexing mixture of the sublimest or tenderest poetry with the baldest and, at times, the most trivial prose.
Unfortunately for himself Wordsworth had theories of

poetry, which he dogmatically set forth in the prefaces referred to above.] In his revulsion from the artificial "poetic diction" of the school of Pope he insisted too strenuously on the half-truth that there is no difference between the language of poetry and that of prose.   He deliberately set to work to portray the elementary passions of human nature as found in their native simplicity among the unsophisticated poor who live in perpetual contact with the abiding grandeur and calm of nature ; and he strove to describe these "situations from common life" in the language actually used by the poor, purified from its accidental defects.   He held that every poem must have a "purpose"; he said of himself, "I wish to be considered as a teacher or as nothing."   And his lifelong sense of having been set apart for a lofty poetic mission impelled him to look on every detail of his own life, on every thought that flashed across his own mind, with an exaggerated seriousness. This, with his severe habit of accuracy, led to those little trivialities of prosaic detail which crop out now and then even in these Selections :

> "On summer evenings, *I believe*, that there
> A long half-hour together I have stood
> Mute."   ("*There was a boy*," 32.)

> "Unless I now
> Confound my present feelings with the past."
>   (*Nutting*, 48, 49.)

> "Though changed, *no doubt*, from what I was."
>   (*Tintern Abbey*, 66.)

What true poetry is Tennyson has unconsciously defined in two lines of *In Memoriam* :

> "I do but sing because I must,
> And pipe but as the linnets sing."

Wordsworth himself, when criticising Goethe, expressed
the same thought in one word—"inevitable." All true
poetry is "inevitable." When we read it we feel that
the poet said it because "he must." He did not labori-
ously make it—it "came to him"; he was "inspired."
Poetry is thus Life at its best—made immortal through
Beauty and Pleasure.

But Wordsworth, owing to his cut-and-dried theories
and his chronic self-consciousness, often fell away from
this ideal; and we find, as the result, that a considerable
percentage of his smaller poems, a large number of the
sonnets, some of *The Prelude*, and much of *The Excursion*,
are little better than metrical prose. Thus it was that in
one sense Wordsworth wholly failed to realise his life's
ambition. His immortal work is to be found chiefly in
his shorter poems, or in scattered passages of *The Prelude*.
The Excursion is like a conglomerate rock of fossilized
mud and pebbles—but a rock that sparkles everywhere
with gems of priceless worth. As an example of this
metrical prose, we may take the following lines from that
poem :

> " O for the coming of that glorious time
> When, prizing knowledge as her noblest wealth
> And best protection, this Imperial realm,
> While she exacts allegiance, shall admit
> An obligation, on her part, to *teach*
> Them who are born to serve her and obey ;
> Binding herself by statute to secure,
> For all the children whom her soil maintains,
> The rudiments of letters, and inform
> The mind with moral and religious truth."

(2) Restricted
range.

Another obvious defect in Wordsworth is the com-
parative narrowness of his range. He was emphatically

a man of one book. That one book was the Lake
District and the Cumbrian dalesman, who was its image
reflected in human flesh and blood. When he travelled
abroad his heart remained at home; in the Alps and the
Apennines, on Como or Maggiore, he saw only reminiscences of Helvellyn and Windermere; and the
"cottage girls" of Italy and Switzerland whom he celebrated in song are but faint echoes of the Highland lass
whose beauty so fascinated his sister Dorothy and himself. Partly this was constitutional, the outcome of his
close communion with nature as a child; but largely it
was the result of his habitual devotion to the fixed rules
of poetry that he had laid down for his own guidance,
viz. to describe the elementary feelings of humanity in
the actual language of the poor.

Another distinctive limitation of Wordsworth's song is (3) Absence of
the almost entire absence of the element of passionate
love. Wordsworth has written but one love-poem; and
that poem had no reference to his wife. He first visited
Dovedale in company with his future wife, when his
childish friendship for her was beginning to deepen into
conscious love; and he does not appear ever to have
visited it again. That his passion for "Lucy" was a real
one we cannot doubt; but it appears certain that whatever his feeling may have been at the time, he locked it
up unuttered in his breast. But its result was, ten years
later, one of the most perfect in the whole range of
English love-songs, "*She dwelt among the untrodden
ways.*" In speaking of this as Wordsworth's only love-
poem, we take it as representing the set of four
written at Goslar. And this almost entire absence of
love-poetry in Wordsworth is no doubt one main

c

reason of his want of popularity with the ordinary reader.

(4) Want of humour. There is too in Wordsworth an entire lack of humour. The "Prologue" to *Peter Bell* seems intended to be humorous, but so far it is a failure, however instinct it may be otherwise with Wordsworth's happiest characteristics. Not that this is a very serious defect. There is no humour in Milton, and very little in Tennyson. The reason why we regret its absence is that, had Wordsworth possessed this saving quality, he would have been kept from composing much that might have been, with great advantage to his readers, either omitted or wholly modified. Had he possessed a sense of humour, he would have written a much shorter and a far more pathetic tale of Betty Foy's troubles, a story that would have given no opening for Byron's cheap sarcasm :

> "Till all who view the Idiot in his glory
> Conceive the bard the hero of the story."

And no doubt this want of humour contributed largely to that prolixity, stiffness, and heaviness of touch which are the chief faults of Wordsworth's less inspired passages.

(b) Its merits : (1) Purity and simplicity of style. Turning from these defects to the positive merits of Wordsworth's song, we notice first that purity and simplicity of style on behalf of which he so strenuously fought; for which indeed he was really a martyr, since undoubtedly he suffered heavy pecuniary loss and incurred endless obloquy and ridicule by his almost fanatical advocacy of natural and true, as opposed to the conventional poetic diction. How great was the need for this lifelong crusade is perhaps best illustrated by the

fact that even he himself did not wholly free himself from
the stilted phrases of the so-called Classical School. Even
he could write of the "deadly tube" (*Recluse*, i. 277), the
"thundering tube" (*Descriptive Sketches*, 61), where in
either case he simply means a *gun*; or when speaking of
an eclipse of the sun, could call it—

> "the hour
> When Sol was destined to endure
> That darkening of his radiant face ";

or, again, could use the conventional word *numbers* for
"song" or "melody" (*The Solitary Reaper*, 18).

The next, and indeed his most essential characteristic, (2) Austere yet
is his strict truth, his austere and yet vivid naturalness. vivid natural-
Matthew Arnold aptly says of him: "Nature herself ness.
seems to write for him with her own bare, sheer, penetrating power. . . (His expression may often be called
bald, as for instance in the poem of *Resolution and
Independence*, but it is bald as the bare mountain-tops are
bald, with a baldness which is full of grandeur.") We
feel in reading him that his happiest phrases come from
direct out-of-door study of nature; he is as accurate an
observer as Tennyson, though his expression is simpler.
Here are a few examples:

> "The budding twigs spread out their fan
> To catch the breezy air."
> > (*Lines Written in Early Spring*, 17, 18.)

> " That uncertain heaven received
> Into the bosom of the steady lake."
> > (" *There was a boy*," 24, 25.)

> " Thy soul was like a star, and dwelt apart."
> > (*London, 1802*, 9.)

> "Ships, towers, domes, theatres, and temples lie
>
> .   .   .   .
>
> All bright and glittering in the smokeless air."
>
> *(Westminster Bridge,* 6, 8.)

> "The busy dor-hawk chases the white moth
> With burring note."
>
> *("Calm is the fragrant air,"* 22, 23.)

> " —did my boat move on ;
> Leaving behind her still, on either side,
> Small circles, glittering idly in the moon,
> Until they melted all into one track
> Of sparkling light."
>
> *(Influence of Natural Objects,* 7-11.)

> "With the din
> Smitten, the precipices rang aloud ;
> The leafless trees and every icy crag
> Tinkled like iron."
>
> *(Ib.,* 83-86.)

> "Over his own sweet voice the stock-dove broods."
>
> *(Resolution and Independence,* 5.)

> "(the hare) from the plashy earth,
> Raises a mist, that, glittering in the sun,
> Runs with her all the way."
>
> *(Ib.,* 12-14.)

> "A pool bare to the eye of heaven."
>
> *(Ib.,* 54.)

> "The brooks which down their channels fret."
>
> *(Intimations of Immortality,* 193.)

Wordsworth's and Shelley's *Skylark* compared. We may illustrate Wordsworth's vivid naturalness by comparing him with Shelley when their subject is the same. Shelley was to some extent a disciple of Wordsworth ; from the age of twenty-three he had come under his influence, and he wrote *To a Skylark* in the full maturity of his powers when twenty-eight years old

(1820). Wordsworth composed his *Skylark* five years later; and it would appear that he must have been familiar with Shelley's lyric, from several parallelisms of· thought which are found in his lines. Let us refresh our memories with a few of Shelley's stanzas:

> " Hail to thee, blithe spirit !
> Bird thou never wert,
> That from heaven, or near it,
> Pourest thy full heart
> In profuse strains of unpremeditated art.
>
> . . . . . .
>
> Keen as are the arrows
> Of that silver sphere,
> Whose intense lamp narrows
> In the white dawn clear,
> Until we hardly see, we feel that it is there.
>
> . . . . . .
>
> Like a glow-worm golden
> In a dell of dew,
> Scattering unbeholden
> Its aërial hue
> Among the flowers and grass, which screen it from the view.
>
> . . . . . .
>
> Sound of vernal showers
> On the twinkling grass,
> Rain-awakened flowers,
> All that ever was
> Joyous, and clear, and fresh, thy music doth surpass."

Now compare Wordsworth's poem :

> " Ethereal minstrel ! pilgrim of the sky !
> Dost thou despise the earth where cares abound ?
> Or, while the wings aspire, are heart and eye
> Both with thy nest upon the dewy ground ?
> Thy nest which thou canst drop into at will,
> These quivering wings composed, that music still.

> Leave to the nightingale her shady wood ;
> A privacy of glorious light is thine;
> Whence thou dost pour upon the world a flood
> Of harmony, with instinct more divine ;
> Type of the wise who soar, but never roam ;
> True to the kindred points of Heaven and Home !"

We must allow at once that Shelley's lyric is far the more musical of the two; and far more varied in its fanciful imagery. For richness, for luxuriant beauty of expression and of thought, Shelley's is incomparably the superior. His song is to Wordsworth's what the heavy-scented heaped-up profusion of gorgeous exotic bloom in a hothouse is to a bank of primroses and wood-anemones in an English coppice. But when we examine his fidelity to nature, it is different. The stanza describing the appearance of the morning star ("Keen as are the arrows") is indeed as inimitably perfect in accuracy of fact as it is in beauty of expression. So too is the stanza about the glow-worm; and so are the references to a rainbow shower, to April grass, and to flowers opening in the sunlight after rain. But his skylark is in itself little more than a figment of exuberant fancy. It is false to nature at the outset, and hyperbolical all through. "Bird thou never wert" is meaningless. When Wordsworth says, "O Cuckoo, shall I call thee bird, or but a wandering voice?" he admirably expresses the phantom-like ubiquity of that unseen visitor of Spring. Every one living in the country is familiar with the cuckoo's call; not one person in a hundred has ever seen a cuckoo. But it is quite untrue to speak of the skylark as if it were always out of sight. On the contrary it usually is plainly visible, and at no very great height above its nest. It does indeed often soar so high towards the noontide brilliance of the zenith as to become almost or quite invisible; and thus it justifies Wordsworth's exquisite description, "A privacy of glorious light is thine," a single line which expresses simply and naturally a whole stanza of Shelley's, with its imaginatively complicated metaphor. There are five things to be noticed in the skylark: the rapturous joyousness of its song; the spiritual thread which all the while binds the singer to the nest beneath; the rapid vibration of its wings; and the suddenness with which it breaks off its song and drops down into its nest on the ground. Each of these points is reproduced by Wordsworth with exquisite truth and felicity; Shelley, while he enlarges upon the first point, does not even hint at the others. Lastly, Shelley's lyric is wholly non-moral; it does not touch our higher nature, it is purely sensuous; whereas Wordsworth's poem is a true echo of the Great Teacher who bade us consider the lilies and learn the lesson of trust from the birds of the air. Without being in the least degree dull or didactic, it is worth a dozen sermons; and the closing couplet triumphantly vindicates the literal truth of the singer's earlier utterance :

> "One impulse from a vernal wood
> May teach you more of man,
> Of moral evil and of good,
> Than all the sages can."
> (*The Tables Turned*, 21-24.)

We may next notice the seriousness and sanity that (3) Seriousness and sanity. uniformly characterize Wordsworth's work. His poetry reflects himself. He resolutely kept his life and his singing tuned to the keynote of truth and soberness.

There is nothing morbid, sentimental, or sensuous about his verse. Like his own Leechgatherer, his simplest themes are always

"With something of a lofty utterance drest—
Choice word and measured phrase,   .   .   .
.   .   .   .   .   . a stately speech ;
Such as grave livers do in Scotland use,
Religious men, who give to God and man their dues."

(4) Uncom-promising morality. With this quality Wordsworth's stern, uncompromising morality is nearly associated. Here he is in sharp contrast to Byron and Shelley; Byron, the poet of licentious lawlessness, and Shelley, the apostle of revolt against the marriage-law. He seldom touches upon the theme of lawless or unlawful love; and when compelled to do so, he uses all the power of his art to make his readers feel its essential baseness. Like all Englishmen, he reverenced Nelson's patriotism and admired his genius, but he could not pass over the one great blot on his life; and hence while taking Nelson as, in the main, his model for the *Character of the Happy Warrior*, he is careful to tell us that he could not publicly associate Nelson's name with the poem.

(5) Sympathy for man as man. Another prominent characteristic of Wordsworth's poetry is his deep sympathy for man as man. This indeed, as we have already seen, was the avowed aim of his whole poetic career; to dignify the great elementary passions of humanity by an imaginative sympathy which shows them and the external nature which is their background to be parts of one divinely ordered, harmonious whole. The active interest he took in the French Revolution vividly illustrates his enthusiasm for humanity. Other examples of this trait are to be found in *The*

Solitary Reaper, where his whole soul is stirred to its depths by hearing a Highland lass singing in a harvest-field; *Rob Roy's Grave*, where he indignantly contrasts the self-centred ambition of Napoleon with the rough and ready assertion of human freedom as against social tyranny of that "wild chieftain of a savage clan"; and his stirring appeal *To the Men of Kent*:

> "In Britain is one breath ;
> We all are with you now from shore to shore ;
> Ye Men of Kent, 'tis victory or death ! "

Or take again his vivid delineation of a mother's longing for a lost son, *The Affliction of Margaret*, or the beautiful touch in "*Calm is the evening air*," where he listens after sunset to the various sounds of nature:

> " Wheels and the tread of hoofs are heard no more;
> One boat there was, but it will touch the shore
> With the next dipping of its slackened oar ;
> Faint sound, that, for the gayest of the gay,
> Might give to serious thought a moment's sway,
> As the last token of Man's toilsome day."

Or we may note the introduction, in his musings upon the landscape of the Wye valley, of "the burthen of the mystery, the heavy and the weary weight of all this unintelligible world," as parallel to the grief he feels amid the budding tenderness of spring to think "what man has made of man." The Leechgatherer brings home to him the moral dignity that man may still keep amid the dreariest surroundings—a thought which is even more emphatically brought out in *The Old Cumberland Beggar*. For the death of Burns he mourns with a passionate, personal grief, and a large-hearted charity for that poet's failings, which strikes us all the more when we remember his unbending severity towards Nelson.   For there was this great difference between the two : Burns's sins were sins of frailty, confessed and deplored as such ; Nelson's sin, like that of Lancelot and Guinevere in Tennyson's *Idylls of the King*, struck at the very roots of social order, and was therefore to Wordsworth intolerable.   In the close of his poem on the *Feast of Brougham Castle* we find an admirable contrast between the Minstrel's glowing praises of warlike ambition and Wordsworth's own ideal of life as exemplified in the "good Lord Clifford " :

> "How he, long forced in humble walks to go,
> Was softened into feeling, soothed, and tamed.
>
> Love had he found in huts where poor men lie ;
> His daily teachers had been woods and rills,
> The silence that is in the starry sky,
> The sleep that is among the lonely hills. "

His sonnet, again, on the departure of Sir Walter Scott from Abbotsford for Naples is at once a touching illustration of genuine personal friendship and of Wordsworth's peculiar power of realizing an imaginative sympathy between external Nature and Man.

(6) Sympathy for dumb animals.   Closely connected with this human sympathy is Wordsworth's marked tenderness for animal life.   In the *Prelude* he tells us that until he was twenty-three years old external Nature was his supreme passion, and Man merely subordinate, an "accidental grace" to set off her beauty or grandeur.   It was in the period of gloom, consequent upon the crushing of his French Revolution enthusiasms, that he learned to love Man for his own sake and not Nature's.   He adds :

> "Far less had then
> The inferior creatures, beast or bird, attuned
> My spirit to that gentleness of love
> (Though they had long been carefully observed),
> Won from me those minute obeisances
> Of tenderness, which I may number now
> With my first blessings."   (*Prelude*, viii. 356-362.)

In the *Sparrow's Nest* he tells us that it was the early influence of his sister Dorothy (the "Emmeline" of the poem) that taught him this sympathetic reverence for bird-life; and in another poem he describes that influence in vivid contrast with his own boyish thoughtlessness:

> "Oh ! pleasant, pleasant were the days,
> The time, when, in our childish plays,
> My sister Emmeline and I
> Together chased the butterfly !
> A very hunter did I rush
> Upon the prey ;—with leaps and springs
> I followed on from brake to bush ;
> But she, God love her, feared to brush
> The dust from off its wings."
> (*To a Butterfly*, 10-18.)

The story of *Hart-leap Well* repeats this childish contrast on a scale of higher interest, where the poet himself and a shepherd who tells him the story, take the place of Emmeline ; while Sir Walter, who has hunted the hart to death, embodies the ruthless recklessness into which, but for his sister's influence, Wordsworth might himself have grown. In this poem, however, there is an added interest, a deeper solemnity. For Nature mourns for the hunted hart ; and shrinking with horror from its death, as from a foul murder, she does what

she can to show her pity for the animal's cruel fate, and
to punish the unfeeling pride of the man who caused it.
Nature, conceived of as one with the Deity immanent in
clouds and air and leafy grove, loves and cares for all
unoffending creatures; and the poem ends, as Coleridge's companion poem *The Ancient Mariner* does, with
an emphatic plea for humanity towards all living things:

> "Never to blend our pleasure or our pride
> With sorrow of the meanest thing that feels."

(7) Sympathy for vegetable life. Wordsworth even goes further than this, and extends
the lesson of tenderness to everything that lives. He
tells us (*Lines Written in Early Spring*) that it is his faith—

> "that every flower
> Enjoys the air it breathes";

and six lines further on, as if to warn us that this is no
mere fancy, he says of the budding twigs:

> "And I must think, do all I can,
> That there was pleasure there."

Again in *Nutting*, Wordsworth describes how the sight
of broken branches and drooping leaves gave him a
"sense of pain," and warns his sister Dorothy to move
among the hazels gently—

> "with gentle hand
> Touch—for there is a spirit in the woods."

And in his poem *Humanity*, Wordsworth expressly connects humanity to man with humanity to the brutes, and
with a reverent regard even for the brief life of flowers.

(8) Vivid and truthful imagery. Lastly, we may notice the power and truth of Wordsworth's imagery. Seldom does he use mere conventional,
classical comparisons, such as constituted the stock-in-

trade of poets of the pre-Natural school. In one place, indeed, we find him reproducing Milton's archaic astronomy, where blinded Samson complains that for. him the sun is dark—

> "And silent as the moon,
>   When she deserts the night,
>   Hid in her vacant interlunar cave ";

in his lines to *The Moon*—

> "And when thy beauty in the shadowy cave
>   Is hidden, buried in its monthly grave";

and in the somewhat artificial poem addressed to his wife ("*She was a phantom*") the metaphor "pulse of the machine" is both mixed and unhappy, suggesting an odd combination of an anatomist and an automaton-maker. But, broadly speaking, Wordsworth's imagery comes direct from his intense communion with that living world of leaf and stream and sky in which he lived and moved and had his being. The Yew Tree of Lorton Vale is glad to furnish weapons to the Border warriors bred beneath its shade for their forays against the Scot, or their patriotic struggle with France (*Yew-trees*, 4-8). His imagination, fired with martial ardour, gives life even to the weapons and armour hanging in Lord Clifford's castle, and makes them call aloud to their owner to use them once more on the battle-field (*Feast of Brougham Castle*, 142-6). Sometimes Wordsworth's imagination prompts him to felicitous descriptive metaphors, as in the snake-like convolutions of the yew-tree's trunk (*Yew-trees*, 16-18); the tidal "respirations" of the sea (*Excursion*, viii. 141, and *Tour in 1833*, xxxvi. 11); the green moss-grown stones that lie scattered under the shady trees, "like a flock of sheep" (*Nutting*, 35-37); the flocks "gilded "by the sunset, or the "hazy ridges" rising in aërial perspective like a ladder whereon angels may ascend to heaven (*An Evening of Extraordinary Splendour*, 32, and 43-52); the weight of dead Custom which binds us down like "frost" (*Intimations of Immortality*, 128, 129), or the two succeeding lines of that ode where the faculties that still retain traces of their pre-natal spiritual power are compared to the smouldering embers on the hearth which may at any moment be fanned into a flame; or again, that exquisite passage where the delicate grace of a child's pure nature, so easily sullied by the temptations of later life, is compared to the gem-like dewdrop whose rainbow hues vanish the moment it comes in contact with the earth (*To H. C.*, 27-33). Clouds often furnish Wordsworth with his happiest comparisons; the poet himself wanders "lonely as a cloud" (*The Daffodils*, 1); the knight rides "with the slow motion of a summer cloud" (*Hart-leap Well*, 2); kingdoms are to "shift about, like clouds" (*Rob Roy's Grave*, 91); and the decrepit Leechgatherer stands motionless, or else drags his body, his limbs, and his staff painfully one after the other, like a cloud,

> "That heareth not the loud winds when they call;
> And moveth all together, if it move at all."
> (*Resolution and Independence*, 75, 76.)

Sometimes Wordsworth merely plays with his fancy, as when he likens a daisy to a nun, an innocent maid at court, a queen, a starveling, a warlike Cyclops, a fairy's shield, or a star (*To the Daisy*). Sometimes, with more inspired vision, he sees in the long line of dancing daffodils the twinkling stars of the Milky Way; and their gay movement is as the laughter of the rippling waves (*The Daffodils*, 7-14); or he hears the cataracts "blow their trumpets" from the mountain ridges as they fall (*Intimations of Immortality*, 25). Or, again, for him in his intense realization of the all-pervading life of nature, a solitary mountain-peak towers, a grim and awful Phantom, threatening doom (*Influence of Natural Objects*, 21-29); or a grove of yew-trees becomes a pillared temple haunted by ghostly shapes of fear (*Yew-trees*, 20-33). Sometimes, too, he makes a deliberate and well-weighed comparison; as when the old Leech-gatherer, bowed-down and motionless, is pictured by the complementary images of a boulder, perched on some bare hill-top, and a sea-beast crawled forth and basking on the shore (*Resolution and Independence*, 56-62); or where man's ever-shifting apprehension of moral truth is likened to a water-lily floating on the surface of the waves, though rooted below in the "stable earth" (*Excursion*, v. 567-69).

Of the sterling merit of Wordsworth's poetry, both in substance and in style, no better proof perhaps can be given than the fact that he is, next to Shakspere, the great source of popular quotations that have become proverbial, though few perhaps are aware of their authorship. How many have quoted the couplet

> "Alas the gratitude of men
> Hath oftener left me mourning,"

without being aware that they are the closing lines of *Simon Lee, the Old Huntsman*; and how familiar to us all is the vivid picture summoned up by the lines

> "The swan on still St. Mary's Lake
> Float double, swan and shadow";

Wordsworth a source of popular quotations.

and yet probably not one person in a hundred could put
his finger on the quotation, which occurs in the sixth
stanza of *"Yarrow Unvisited."* As further examples,
from these Selections, of quotations that have become
part of the current coin of the language, we may instance
the following :

"And 'tis my faith that every flower
Enjoys the air it breathes."
(Lines Written in Early Spring, 11, 12.)

"O cuckoo ! shall I call thee bird,
Or but a wandering voice?" *(To the Cuckoo,* 3, 4.)

"The river glideth at his own sweet will."
(Westminster Bridge, 12.)

"Thy soul was like a star, and dwelt apart."
(London 1802, 9.)

"The good old rule
.   .   .   .   .   the simple plan,
That they should take who have the power,
And they should keep who can."
(Rob Roy's Grave, 37-40.)

"They flash upon that inward eye
Which is the bliss of solitude."
(The Daffodils, 21, 22.)

"The Child is father of the Man." *(The Rainbow,* 7.)

"A creature not too bright or good
For human nature's daily food."
("She was a phantom," 17, 18.)

"The light that never was, on sea or land."
(Peele Castle, 15.)

"The glory and the freshness of a dream."
(Intimations of Immortality, 5.)

"To me the meanest flower that blows can give
Thoughts that do often lie too deep for tears."
(Ib., 203, 204.)

No survey of Wordworth's poetry would be complete without including some notice of his attitude towards Nature and Science, as contrasted with that of other poets who preceded or followed him.

The foregoing sketch of his life and poetry will have already made it clear that Wordsworth's Nature is a living Presence, the highest and best of all teachers. *The Prelude* is a systematic account of Wordsworth's own moral and spiritual education in Nature's school. All his poems are more or less tinged with this central thought. To Wordsworth's mind complete insensibility to these impressions is the mark of spiritual death—a state set forth in the description of *Peter Bell* :

> " A primrose by the river's brim,
> A yellow primrose was to him,
> And it was nothing more."

To be that is to be reprobate. Even careless, sense wrapped natures are at times touched by the mystic hand and hear the still small voice. The "boy," in "*There was a boy*," whose whole soul is absorbed in the childish delight of challenging the owls to reply to his "mimic hootings"—even he, in some pause of silence, is startled into a spiritual awe by the sound of far-off mountain-torrents, or by the sight of the "solemn imagery" of wood and lake; just as Wordsworth himself (*Influence of Natural Objects*, 21-44), in the midst of his boyish escapade on Esthwaite Lake, was terror-stricken by the apparition of the huge peak of Wetherlam, as it rose above the nearer mountain-ridges; and for days afterwards was troubled with shadowy hauntings of inexplicable dread.

On the other hand, Wordsworth's ideal saint is the

d

being who, from childhood onwards, is habitually
responsive to Nature's touch. To such an one Nature
is all-sufficient; both as a moral law to restrain from
evil and as an inspiration to rouse to active good. This
ideal the poet met, or imagined he met, enshrined in
real flesh and blood in the "Lucy" of his Dovedale
dream, whose education Nature herself is represented
as conducting in the well-known poem, "*Three years
she grew*":

> " The floating clouds their state shall lend
>   To her; for her the willow bend;
>   Nor shall she fail to see,
>   Even in the motions of the storm,
>   Grace that shall mould the Maiden's form
>   By silent sympathy.
>
> The stars of midnight shall be dear
>   To her; and she shall lean her ear
>   In many a secret place
>   Where rivulets dance their wayward round,
>   *And beauty born of murmuring sound*
>   *Shall pass into her face.*"

The two italicised lines have become proverbial; and
the whole poem forms an admirable compendium of
Wordsworth's philosophy.

Here he stands alone, or almost alone. To poets of
the school of Pope, Nature is a convenient storehouse
of conventional images; or, at best, is something that
may become poetical, if sufficiently set off with tricks of
phrase and the paint of metaphor. To Shakspere, and
even to Tennyson, Nature is seldom more than a vividly
sympathetic background for human emotion and human
thought. But with Wordsworth all this is reversed. In
the main body of his poetry Nature comes first and Man

second, subordinated to Nature; though Wordsworth
realised that man himself "half creates," as well
as "perceives," the glory of the universe around him
(*Tintern Abbey*, 105, 106). In *The Prelude*, too, he
admits that the imagination "must give, else never can
receive"; and in *The Excursion* this latter view begins
to predominate, until in the fragmentary *Recluse* it
culminates in the wedding of the "discerning intellect
of Man" to the "goodly universe."

The poet whose attitude towards Nature approaches Shelley's view
of Nature
compared
with Words-
worth's.
nearest to Wordsworth's is Shelley. But there is this
great difference : with Wordsworth, Nature is "both law
and impulse"; with Shelley, she is "impulse" alone,
and sympathises with his chronic attitude of revolt—
his ceaseless and exclusive assertion of individual liberty.
Again, for Wordsworth, Nature is one ; for Shelley she
is virtually many ; and in this respect Wordsworth
resembles the old type of the stern, self-controlled, law-
abiding Jew, with his reverent worship of the one
Jehovah ; while Shelley is the passionate, sensuous, lawless Gentile, with his free, familiar worship of "gods
many and lords many." And from this fundamental
difference between Shelley and Wordsworth there arises
inevitably another, *viz.* that Shelley, in viewing Nature,
perceived only that which appealed vividly to his
sensuous self, as the brilliancy of the morning star or
the tumultuous harmonies of the wind. He had no eyes,
as Wordsworth had, for the homely and the commonplace.

But we must not overlook the obvious limitations in Wordsworth's
optimism.
Wordsworth's attitude towards Nature. The Nature he
communed with was the Nature of the English Lakes.
The burning sirocco, the overwhelming avalanche, the

dreary skeleton-strewn Sahara, the frozen solitudes of
the Pole, the tiger's cruel beauty, and the death-rattle of
the snake—all these, and such as these, he ignores.
Hence arises the tone of complacent optimism that
pervades his poems. He sits amidst the budding loveli-
ness of Spring, and the only thought that damps his joy
is the remembrance of "what man has made of man."
How different are the reflections of the hero of Tennyson's
Maud, seated amid the same beautiful surroundings:

> " For nature is one with rapine, a harm no preacher can heal;
> The Mayfly is torn by the swallow, the sparrow spear'd by the
> shrike,
> And the whole little wood where I sit is a world of plunder and
> prey."

It is for Tennyson, not for Wordsworth, that Nature
"red in tooth and claw with ravine shrieks against his
creed" that Love is the ruling power in the universe.

Wordsworth's attitude towards Science   Of Science Wordsworth knew little or nothing. Coleridge would sometimes entice him to view the marvels
that could be shown with a pocket magnifier or perhaps
a microscope:

> "Glasses he had, that little things display,
> The beetle panoplied in gems and gold,
> A mailèd angel on a battle-day;
> The mysteries that cups of flowers enfold,
> And all the gorgeous sights which fairies do behold."
>> (' *Castle of Indolence*' *Stanzas*, 50-54.)

But his habitual attitude towards the scientist proper
was one of intolerant aversion, as towards—

> " one, all eyes,
> Philosopher! a fingering slave,
> One that would peep and botanise
> Upon his mother's grave." (*A Poet's Epitaph*, 17-20.)

He is indeed more discriminating in his prose preface to a poem composed in 1839, "*This lawn, a carpet all alive.*" It is not, he says, the practice of analysing and dissecting that makes people soulless; that idea has become prevalent chiefly because, as a rule, it is soulless people who take to dissecting. And he adds : "The beauty in form of a plant or an animal is not made less but more apparent as a whole by more accurate insight into its constituent properties and powers. A *Savant* who is not also a poet in soul and a religionist in heart is a feeble and unhappy creature." Still the fact remains that Wordsworth's dominant temper of mind is best expressed in *The Tables Turned* :

"Sweet is the lore which Nature brings ;
Our meddling intellect
Mis-shapes the beauteous forms of things ;—
We murder to dissect.

Enough of Science and of Art ;
Close up those barren leaves ;
Come forth, and bring with you a heart
That watches and receives."

In this respect we must admit that Wordsworth was contrasted with Tennyson's. faulty and one-sided. Nature has secrets that have to be sought. Wordsworth's "wise passiveness" is only one side of the question. Tennyson gives us the other side, in the wide and accurate knowledge of science that his poetry evinces. Hence his greater delicacy of touch and deeper insight in his treatment of the outward manifestations of Nature. The mere meditative gaze of a Wordsworth will never detect those significant little hints which the accurate eye of the man of science notes, trained as he is to the habit of careful dissection and

minute observation—hints which Tennyson often turns
to vivid poetic account. Wordsworth could never have
written such lines as—

> "*Break*, thou deep vase of chilling tears
> That Grief *hath shaken into frost.*"

In one point Tennyson and Wordsworth are wholly
agreed in their view of science. Both deprecate most
strongly the dead agnosticism, the all-pervading materialism, to which a one-sided and absorbing devotion
to physical science is too apt to lead. And it is in the
main his dread of this result that makes Wordsworth so
intolerant towards science. He writes :

> "Science advances with gigantic strides ;
> But are we aught enriched in love and meekness ? "
>
> (*To the Planet Venus*, 7, 8.)

—lines with which may be compared a long passage in
The Excursion (iv. 941 *et seq.*), where he traces the
downward tendency of science to a contemptible self-
centred atheism ; and a similar passage at the close of
Musings near Aquapendente, in *Memorials of a Tour in
Italy.*

Descriptions of Wordsworth. So much for the man and his writings. Of his
personal appearance and habits several word-portraits
have been painted. The two best are one by himself
and one by Carlyle.

By himself. Wordsworth has described himself in *Stanzas* written
in his pocket-copy of Thomson's *Castle of Indolence.*
It is, of course, in a sense, a fancy portrait ; but it
was drawn from the life, and is wonderfully characteristic :

"Out of our valley's limits did he roam :
Full many a time, upon a stormy night,
His voice came to us from the neighbouring height :
Oft could we see him driving full in view
At mid-day when the sun was shining bright ;
What ill was on him, what he had to do,
A mighty wonder bred among our quiet crew.

Ah ! piteous sight it was to see this Man
When he came back to us, a withered flower,—
Or like a sinful creature, pale and wan.
Down would he sit ; and without strength or power
Look at the common grass from hour to hour :
And oftentimes, how long I fear to say,
Where apple-trees in blossom made a bower,
Retired in that sunshiny shade he lay ;
And, like a naked Indian, slept himself away.

    .   .   .   .

Some thought far worse of him, and judged him wrong :
But verse was what he had been wedded to ;
And his own mind did like a tempest strong
Come to him thus, and drove the weary Wight along."

These lines portray Wordsworth, the inspired poet. By Carlyle. Carlyle, who thought little of his poetry, but deeply reverenced the man, has thus described him :—" His face bore marks of much, not always peaceful, meditation : the look of it not bland or benevolent, so much as close, impregnable and hard : a man *multa tacere loquive paraius* in a world where he had experienced no lack of contra- dictions as he strode along ! The eyes were not very brilliant, but they had a quiet clearness : there was enough of brow, and well-shaped ; rather too much of cheek ('horse-face' I have heard satirists say'), face of squarish shape, and decidedly longish, as I think the head itself was (*its* "length" going horizontal) : he was large-boned, lean, but still firmly knit, tall and strong-looking when he stood; a right good old steel-gray figure, with a fine rustic simplicity and dignity about him, and a veracious *strength* looking through him."

Conclusion.   As a poet, competent critics place Wordsworth after Dante, Shakspere, Spenser, and Milton, but inferior only to such masters of song as these. As a man he ranks even higher than as a poet. There are few who have been more typical of the English race at its best than was the great Cumbrian dalesman, combining, as he did, the childlike genius of Nelson with the square-hewn strength of the Iron Duke. With him, as with Wellington, "the path of duty was the way to glory"; and he, too, found

> " the toppling crags of Duty scaled
> Are close upon the shining table-lands
> To which our God Himself is moon and sun."

CHRONOLOGICAL TABLE.

1770. Wordsworth born at Cockermouth, Cumberland, April 7.
1774. Louis XVI. succeeds to the throne of France. Death of Goldsmith.
1775. Commencement of the war between England and her American Colonies.
1776. Declaration of American Independence, July 4.
1780. Rodney defeats the Spanish fleet off Cape St. Vincent. War with Holland.
1782. Close of the American War; recognition of the Independence of the United States.
1789. Commencement of the French Revolution; storming of the Bastille, July 14.
1793. Execution of Louis XVI. France declares war against England.

1795. Death of Burns, July 21.
1797. The troops of Napoleon occupy Venice. Venetian Republic extinguished. Mutinies in the fleet.
1798. Nelson almost destroys the French fleet in the Battle of the Nile.
1799. Napoleon declared First Consul.
1800. Death of Cowper.
1801. Parliamentary Union of Great Britain and Ireland.
1802. Suspension of the war with France by the Treaty of Amiens.
1803. Renewal of the war with France. A French army occupies Switzerland.
1804. Buonaparte becomes Emperor of France under the title of Napoleon I. His preparations for invading England.
1805. Victory of Trafalgar, Oct. 21; death of Nelson. Death of John Wordsworth, Feb. 6.
1808. Commencement of the Peninsular War.
1809. Birth of Tennyson.
1814. Abdication of Napoleon; he retires to the island of Elba.
1815. Escape of Napoleon from Elba. Renewal of the war. Victories of Quatre Bras and Waterloo.
1819. A reform meeting at Manchester dispersed by the soldiery; several persons killed and wounded.
1820. Accession of George IV. Death of Keats.
1822. Death of Shelley.
1824. Death of Byron.
1829. Catholic Emancipation Bill passed.
1830. Accession of William IV.
1832. Reform Bill passed. Death of Sir Walter Scott, Sept. 21.
1833. Abolition of slavery.
1837. Accession of Queen Victoria.
1839. Chartist insurrection.
1846. Corn Laws repealed.
1850. Death of Wordsworth at Rydal Mount, April 23.

SELECTIONS FROM WORDSWORTH

SELECTIONS FROM WORDSWORTH.

PART I.

LINES WRITTEN IN EARLY SPRING.

I HEARD a thousand blended notes,
While in a grove I sate reclined,
In that sweet mood when pleasant thoughts
Bring sad thoughts to the mind.

To her fair works did Nature link   5
The human soul that through me ran ;
And much it grieved my heart to think
What man has made of man.

Through primrose tufts, in that green bower,
The periwinkle trailed its wreaths ;   10
And 'tis my faith that every flower
Enjoys the air it breathes.

The birds around me hopped and played,
Their thoughts I cannot measure :—
But the least motion which they made,   15
It seemed a thrill of pleasure.

The budding twigs spread out their fan,
To catch the breezy air ;
And I must think, do all I can,
That there was pleasure there.   20

If this belief from heaven be sent,
If such be Nature's holy plan,
Have I not reason to lament
What man has made of man?

THERE WAS A BOY.

THERE was a Boy; ye knew him well, ye cliffs
And islands of Winander!—many a time,
At evening, when the earliest stars began
To move along the edges of the hills,
Rising or setting, would he stand alone,   5
Beneath the trees, or by the glimmering lake;
And there, with fingers interwoven, both hands
Pressed closely palm to palm and to his mouth
Uplifted, he, as through an instrument,
Blew mimic hootings to the silent owls,   10
That they might answer him.—And they would shout
Across the watery vale, and shout again,
Responsive to his call,—with quivering peals,
And long halloos, and screams, and echoes loud
Redoubled and redoubled; concourse wild   15
Of jocund din!   And, when there came a pause
Of silence such as baffled his best skill:
Then, sometimes, in that silence, while he hung
Listening, a gentle shock of mild surprise
Has carried far into his heart the voice   20
Of mountain-torrents; or the visible scene
Would enter unawares into his mind
With all its solemn imagery, its rocks,
Its woods, and that uncertain heaven received
Into the bosom of the steady lake.   25
    This boy was taken from his mates, and died
In childhood, ere he was full twelve years old.

Pre-eminent in beauty is the vale
Where he was born and bred : the church-yard hangs
Upon a slope above the village-school ;   30
And, through that church-yard when my way has led
On summer-evenings, I believe that there
A long half-hour together I have stood
Mute—looking at the grave in which he lies !

NUTTING.

                    IT seems a day
(I speak of one from many singled out)
One of those heavenly days that cannot die ;
When, in the eagerness of boyish hope,
I left our cottage threshold, sallying forth   5
With a huge wallet o'er my shoulders slung,
A nutting crook in hand ; and turned my steps
Tow'rd some far-distant wood, a figure quaint,
Tricked out in proud disguise of cast-off weeds
Which for that service had been husbanded,   10
By exhortation of my frugal dame—
Motley accoutrement, of power to smile
At thorns, and brakes, and brambles,—and, in truth,
More raggèd than need was !   O'er pathless rocks,
Through beds of matted fern, and tangled thickets,   15
Forcing my way, I came to one dear nook
Unvisited, where not a broken bough
Drooped with its withered leaves, ungracious sign
Of devastation ; but the hazels rose
Tall and erect, with tempting clusters hung,   20
A virgin scene !—A little while I stood,
Breathing with such suppression of the heart
As joy delights in ; and, with wise restraint
Voluptuous, fearless of a rival, eyed

The banquet ;—or beneath the trees I sate   25
Among the flowers, and with the flowers I played ;
A temper known to those who, after long
And weary expectation, have been blest
With sudden happiness beyond all hope.
Perhaps it was a bower beneath whose leaves   30
The violets of five seasons re-appear
And fade, unseen by any human eye ;
Where fairy water-breaks do murmur on
For ever; and I saw the sparkling foam,
And—with my cheek on one of those green stones   35
That, fleeced with moss, under the shady trees,
Lay round me, scattered like a flock of sheep—
I heard the murmur and the murmuring sound,
In that sweet mood when pleasure loves to pay
Tribute to ease ; and, of its joy secure,   40
The heart luxuriates with indifferent things,
Wasting its kindliness on stocks and stones,
And on the vacant air. Then up I rose,
And dragged to earth both branch and bough, with crash
And merciless ravage : and the shady nook   45
Of hazels, and the green and mossy bower,
Deformèd and sullied, patiently gave up
Their quiet being : and, unless I now
Confound my present feelings with the past ;
Ere from the mutilated bower I turned   50
Exulting, rich beyond the wealth of kings,
I felt a sense of pain when I beheld
The silent trees, and saw the intruding sky.—
Then, dearest maiden, move along these shades
In gentleness of heart ; with gentle hand   55
Touch —for there is a spirit in the woods.

LUCY.

I.

SHE dwelt among the untrodden ways
  Beside the springs of Dove,
A maid whom there were none to praise
  And very few to love :

A violet by a mossy stone   5
  Half hidden from the eye !
—Fair as a star, when only one
  Is shining in the sky.

She lived unknown, and few could know
  When Lucy ceased to be ;   10
But she is in her grave, and, oh,
  The difference to me !

II.

I TRAVELLED among unknown men,
  In lands beyond the sea ;
Nor, England ! did I know till then   15
  What love I bore to thee.

'Tis past, that melancholy dream !
  Nor will I quit thy shore
A second time ; for still I seem
  To love thee more and more.   20

Among thy mountains did I feel
  The joy of my desire ;
And she I cherished turned her wheel
  Beside an English fire.

Thy mornings showed, thy nights concealed   25
    The bowers where Lucy played ;
And thine too is the last green field
    That Lucy's eyes surveyed.

III.

A SLUMBER did my spirit seal ;
    I had no human fears :   30
She seemed a thing that could not feel
    The touch of earthly years.

No motion has she now, no force ;
    She neither hears nor sees ;
Rolled round in earth's diurnal course,   35
    With rocks, and stones, and trees.

HART-LEAP WELL.

THE knight had ridden down from Wensley Moor
With the slow motion of a summer's cloud,
And now, as he approached a vassal's door,
" Bring forth another horse ! " he cried aloud.

" Another horse ! "—That shout the vassal heard   5
And saddled his best steed, a comely grey ;
Sir Walter mounted him ; he was the third
Which he had mounted on that glorious day.

Joy sparkled in the prancing courser's eyes ;
The horse and horseman are a happy pair ;   10
But, though Sir Walter like a falcon flies,
There is a doleful silence in the air.

A rout this morning left Sir Walter's hall,
That as they galloped made the echoes roar ;
But horse and man are vanished, one and all ;   15
Such race, I think, was never seen before.

Sir Walter, restless as a veering wind,
Calls to the few tired dogs that yet remain :
Blanch, Swift, and Music, noblest of their kind,
Follow, and up the weary mountain strain.   20

The knight hallooed, he cheered and chid them on
With suppliant gestures and upbraidings stern ;
But breath and eyesight fail ; and, one by one,
The dogs are stretched among the mountain fern.

Where is the throng, the tumult of the race ?   25
The bugles that so joyfully were blown ?
—This chase it looks not like an earthly chase ;
Sir Walter and the hart are left alone.

The poor hart toils along the mountain-side ;
I will not stop to tell how far he fled,   30
Nor will I mention by what death he died ;
But now the knight beholds him lying dead.

Dismounting, then, he leaned against a thorn ;
He had no follower, dog, nor man, nor boy :
He neither cracked his whip, nor blew his horn,   35
But gazed upon the spoil with silent joy.

Close to the thorn on which Sir Walter leaned,
Stood his dumb partner in this glorious feat ;
Weak as a lamb the hour that it is yeaned ;
And white with foam as if with cleaving sleet.   40

Upon his side the hart was lying stretched :
His nostril touched a spring beneath a hill,
And with the last deep groan his breath had fetched
The waters of the spring were trembling still.

And now, too happy for repose or rest,   45
(Never had living man such joyful lot !)
Sir Walter walked all round, north, south, and west,
And gazed and gazed upon that darling spot.

And climbing up the hill—(it was at least
Four roods of sheer ascent) Sir Walter found   50
Three several hoof-marks which the hunted beast
Had left imprinted on the grassy ground.

Sir Walter wiped his face, and cried, " Till now
Such sight was never seen by human eyes :
Three leaps have borne him from this lofty brow,   55
Down to the very fountain where he lies.

" I'll build a pleasure-house upon this spot,
And a small arbour, made for rural joy ;
'Twill be the traveller's shed, the pilgrim's cot,
A place of love for damsels that are coy.   60

" A cunning artist will I have to frame
A basin for that fountain in the dell !
And they who do make mention of the same,
From this day forth, shall call it HART-LEAP WELL.

" And, gallant stag ! to make thy praises known,   65
Another monument shall here be raised ;
Three several pillars, each a rough-hewn stone,
And planted where thy hoofs the turf have grazed.

" And, in the summer-time when days are long,
I will come hither with my paramour ;   70
And with the dancers and the minstrel's song
We will make merry in that pleasant bower.

" Till the foundations of the mountains fail
My mansion with its arbour shall endure ;—
The joy of them who till the fields of Swale,   75
And them who dwell among the woods of Ure ! "

Then home he went, and left the hart, stone-dead,
With breathless nostrils stretched above the spring.
—Soon did the knight perform what he had said ;
And far and wide the fame thereof did ring.   80

Ere thrice the moon into her port had steered,
A cup of stone received the living well ;
Three pillars of rude stone Sir Walter reared,
And built a house of pleasure in the dell.

And near the fountain, flowers of stature tall   85
With trailing plants and trees were intertwined,—
Which soon composed a little silvan hall,
A leafy shelter from the sun and wind.

And thither, when the summer days were long,
Sir Walter led his wondering paramour ;   90
And with the dancers and the minstrel's song
Made merriment within that pleasant bower.

The knight, Sir Walter, died in course of time,
And his bones lie in his paternal vale.—
But there is matter for a second rhyme,   95
And I to this would add another tale.

PART SECOND.

THE moving accident is not my trade ;
To freeze the blood I have no ready arts :
'Tis my delight, alone in summer shade,
To pipe a simple song for thinking hearts.   100

As I from Hawes to Richmond did repair,
It chanced that I saw standing in a dell
Three aspens at three corners of a square ;
And one, not four yards distant, near a well.

What this imported I could ill divine :   105
And, pulling now the rein my horse to stop,
I saw three pillars standing in a line,—
The last stone pillar on a dark hill-top.

The trees were grey, with neither arms nor head ;
Half wasted the square mound of tawny green ;   110
So that you just might say, as then I said,
" Here in old time the hand of man hath been."

I looked upon the hill both far and near,
More doleful place did never eye survey ;
It seemed as if the spring-time came not here,   115
And Nature here were willing to decay.

I stood in various thoughts and fancies lost,
When one, who was in shepherd's garb attired,
Came up the hollow :—him did I accost,
And what this place might be I then inquired.   120

The shepherd stopped, and that same story told
Which in my former rhyme I have rehearsed.
" A jolly place," said he, " in times of old !
But something ails it now : the spot is curst.

" You see these lifeless stumps of aspen wood—   125
Some say that they are beeches, others elms—
These were the bower ; and here a mansion stood,
The finest palace of a hundred realms !

" The arbour does its own condition tell ;
You see the stones, the fountain, and the stream ;   130
But as to the great lodge ! you might as well
Hunt half a day for a forgotten dream.

" There's neither dog nor heifer, horse nor sheep,
Will wet his lips within that cup of stone ;
And oftentimes, when all are fast asleep,   135
This water doth send forth a dolorous groan.

" Some say that here a murder has been done,
And blood cries out for blood : but, for my part,
I've guessed, when I've been sitting in the sun,
That it was all for that unhappy hart.   140

" What thoughts must through the creature's brain have past !
Even from the topmost stone upon the steep,
Are but three bounds—and look, Sir, at this last—
O Master ! it has been a cruel leap.

" For thirteen hours he ran a desperate race ;   145
And in my simple mind we cannot tell
What cause the hart might have to love this place,
And come and make his death-bed near the well.

" Here on the grass perhaps asleep he sank,
Lulled by the fountain in the summertide ;   150
This water was perhaps the first he drank
When he had wandered from his mother's side.

" In April here beneath the flowering thorn
He heard the birds their morning carols sing ;
And he, perhaps, for aught we know, was born   155
Not half a furlong from that self-same spring.

" Now, here is neither grass nor pleasant shade ;
The sun on drearier hollow never shone ;
So will it be, as I have often said,
Till trees, and stones, and fountain, all are gone."   160

" Grey-headed shepherd, thou hast spoken well ;
Small difference lies between thy creed and mine
This beast not unobserved by Nature fell ;
His death was mourned by sympathy divine.

" The Being, that is in the clouds and air,   165
That is in the green leaves among the groves,
Maintains a deep and reverential care
For the unoffending creatures whom he loves.

"The pleasure-house is dust :—behind, before,
This is no common waste, no common gloom ;   170
But Nature, in due course of time, once more
Shall here put on her beauty and her bloom.

" She leaves these objects to a slow decay,
That what we are, and have been, may be known ;
But at the coming of the milder day,   175
These monuments shall all be overgrown.

" One lesson, shepherd, let us two divide,
Taught both by what she shows, and what conceals ;
Never to blend our pleasure or our pride
With sorrow of the meanest thing that feels."   180

THE SPARROW'S NEST.

Behold, within the leafy shade,
Those bright blue eggs together laid !
On me the chance-discovered sight
Gleamed like a vision of delight.
I started—seeming to espy   5
The home and sheltered bed,
The sparrow's dwelling, which, hard by
My father's house, in wet or dry
My sister Emmeline and I
        Together visited.   10

She looked at it and seemed to fear it ;
Dreading, tho' wishing, to be near it :
Such heart was in her, being then
A little prattler among men.
The blessing of my later years   15
Was with me when a boy :

She gave me eyes, she gave me ears ;
And humble cares, and delicate fears ;
A heart, the fountain of sweet tears ;
    And love, and thought, and joy.   20

TO THE CUCKOO.

O BLITHE new-comer ! I have heard,
  I hear thee and rejoice.
O cuckoo ! shall I call thee bird,
  Or but a wandering voice ?

While I am lying on the grass   5
  Thy twofold shout I hear,
From hill to hill it seems to pass,
  At once far off, and near.

Though babbling only to the vale,
  Of sunshine and of flowers,   10
Thou bringest unto me a tale
  Of visionary hours.

Thrice welcome, darling of the Spring !
  Even yet thou art to me
No bird, but an invisible thing,   15
  A voice, a mystery ;

The same whom in my school-boy days
  I listened to ; that cry
Which made me look a thousand ways
  In bush, and tree, and sky.   20

To seek thee did I often rove
  Through woods and on the green ;
And thou wert still a hope, a love ;
  Still longed for, never seen.

And I can listen to thee yet ;   25
Can lie upon the plain
And listen, till I do beget
That golden time again.

O blessèd bird ! the earth we pace
Again appears to be   30
An unsubstantial, faery place ;
That is fit home for thee !

THE REDBREAST CHASING THE BUTTERFLY

ART thou the bird whom man loves best,
The pious bird with the scarlet breast,
    Our little English Robin ;
The bird that comes about our doors
When Autumn-winds are sobbing ?   5
Art thou the Peter of Norway Boors ?
    Their Thomas in Finland,
    And Russia far inland ?
The bird, that by some name or other
All men who know thee call their brother,   10
The darling of children and men ?
Could Father Adam open his eyes
And see this sight beneath the skies,
He'd wish to close them again.
—If the butterfly knew but his friend,   15
Hither his flight he would bend ;
And find his way to me,
Under the branches of the tree :
In and out, he darts about;
Can this be the bird, to man so good,   20
That, after their bewildering,

Covered with leaves the little children,
    So painfully in the wood ?
What ailed thee, Robin, that thou could'st pursue
    A beautiful creature,   25
That is gentle by nature ?
Beneath the summer sky
From flower to flower let him fly ;
'Tis all that he wishes to do.
The cheerer thou of our in-door sadness,   30
He is the friend of our summer gladness :
What hinders, then, that ye should be
Playmates in the sunny weather,
And fly about in the air together !
His beautiful wings in crimson are drest,   35
A crimson as bright as thine own :
Would'st thou be happy in thy nest,
O pious bird ! whom man loves best,
Love him, or leave him alone !

TO A BUTTERFLY.

I'VE watched you now a full half-hour,
Self-poised upon that yellow flower ;
And, little butterfly ! indeed
I know not if you sleep or feed.
How motionless !—not frozen seas   5
More motionless ! and then
What joy awaits you, when the breeze
Hath found you out among the trees,
And calls you forth again !

This plot of orchard-ground is ours ;   10
My trees they are, my sister's flowers ;
Here rest your wings when they are weary ;
Here lodge as in a sanctuary !

Come often to us, fear no wrong ;
Sit near us on the bough !   15
We'll talk of sunshine and of song,
And summer days, when we were young ;
Sweet childish days that were as long
As twenty days are now.

TO THE SMALL CELANDINE.

PANSIES, lilies, kingcups, daisies,
Let them live upon their praises ;
Long as there's a sun that sets,
Primroses will have their glory ;
Long as there are violets,   5
They will have a place in story :
There's a flower that shall be mine,
'Tis the little celandine.

Eyes of some men travel far
For the finding of a star ;   10
Up and down the heavens they go,
Men that keep a mighty rout !
I'm as great as they, I trow,
Since the day I found thee out,
Little flower !—I'll make a stir,   15
Like a sage astronomer.

Modest, yet withal an elf
Bold, and lavish of thyself ;
Since we needs must first have met
I have seen thee, high and low,   20
Thirty years or more, and yet
'Twas a face I did not know ;
Thou hast now, go where I may,
Fifty greetings in a day.

Ere a leaf is on a bush,   25
In the time before the thrush
Has a thought about her nest,
Thou wilt come with half a call,
Spreading out thy glossy breast
Like a careless prodigal ;   30
Telling tales about the sun,
When we've little warmth, or none.

Poets, vain men in their mood !
Travel with the multitude :
Never heed them ; I aver   35
That they all are wanton wooers ;
But the thrifty cottager,
Who stirs little out of doors,
Joys to spy thee near her home ;
Spring is coming, thou art come !   40

Comfort have thou of thy merit,
Kindly, unassuming spirit !
Careless of thy neighbourhood,
Thou dost show thy pleasant face
On the moor, and in the wood,   45
In the lane ;—there's not a place,
Howsoever mean it be,
But 'tis good enough for thee.

Ill befall the yellow flowers,
Children of the flaring hours !   50
Buttercups, that will be seen,
Whether we will see or no ;
Others, too, of lofty mien ;
They have done as worldlings do,
Taken praise that should be thine,   55
Little, humble celandine !

B

Prophet of delight and mirth,
Ill-requited upon earth ;
Herald of a mighty band,
Of a joyous train ensuing,   60
Serving at my heart's command,
Tasks that are no tasks renewing,
I will sing, as doth behove,
Hymns in praise of what I love !

COMPOSED UPON WESTMINSTER BRIDGE.

EARTH has not anything to show more fair :
Dull would he be of soul who could pass by
A sight so touching in its majesty :
This city now doth, like a garment, wear
The beauty of the morning ; silent, bare,   5
Ships, towers, domes, theatres, and temples lie
Open unto the fields, and to the sky ;
All bright and glittering in the smokeless air.
Never did sun more beautifully steep
In his first splendour, valley, rock, or hill ;   10
Ne'er saw I, never felt, a calm so deep !
The river glideth at his own sweet will :
Dear God ! the very houses seem asleep ;
And all that mighty heart is lying still.

ON THE EXTINCTION OF THE VENETIAN
REPUBLIC.

ONCE did she hold the gorgeous East in fee ;
And was the safeguard of the West : the worth
Of Venice did not fall below her birth,
Venice, the eldest child of Liberty.

She was a maiden city, bright and free ;   5
No guile seduced ; no force could violate ;
And, when she took unto herself a mate,
She must espouse the everlasting sea.
And what if she had seen those glories fade,
Those titles vanish, and that strength decay ;   10
Yet shall some tribute of regret be paid
When her long life hath reached its final day :
Men are we, and must grieve when even the shade
Of that which once was great, is passed away.

LONDON, 1802.

MILTON ! thou should'st be living at this hour :
England hath need of thee : she is a fen
Of stagnant waters : altar, sword, and pen,
Fireside, the heroic wealth of hall and bower,
Have forfeited their ancient English dower   5
Of inward happiness.   We are selfish men ;
Oh ! raise us up, return to us again ;
And give us manners, virtue, freedom, power.
Thy soul was like a star, and dwelt apart :
Thou hadst a voice whose sound was like the sea :   10
Pure as the naked heavens, majestic, free,
So didst thou travel on life's common way,
In cheerful godliness ; and yet thy heart
The lowliest duties on herself did lay.

TO THE DAISY.

WITH little here to do or see
Of things that in the great world be,
Daisy ! again I talk to thee,
    For thou art worthy,

Thou unassuming common-place   5
Of Nature, with that homely face,
And yet with something of a grace,
    Which Love makes for thee !

Oft on the dappled turf at ease
I sit, and play with similes,   10
Loose types of things through all degrees,
    Thoughts of thy raising :
And many a fond and idle name
I give to thee, for praise or blame,
As is the humour of the game,   15
    While I am gazing.

A nun demure of lowly port ;
Or sprightly maiden, of Love's court,
In thy simplicity the sport
    Of all temptations ;   20
A queen in crown of rubies drest ;
A starveling in a scanty vest ;
Are all, as seems to suit thee best,
    Thy appellations.

A little cyclops, with one eye   25
Staring to threaten and defy,
That thought comes next—and instantly
    The freak is over,
The shape will vanish—and behold
A silver shield with boss of gold,   30
That spreads itself, some faery bold
    In fight to cover !

I see thee glittering from afar—
And then thou art a pretty star ;
Not quite so fair as many are   35
    In heaven above thee !

Yet like a star, with glittering crest,
Self-poised in air thou seem'st to rest ;—
May peace come never to his nest,
    Who shall reprove thee !   40

Bright *flower!* for by that name at last,
When all my reveries are past,
I call thee, and to that cleave fast,
    Sweet silent creature !
That breath'st with me in sun and air,   45
Do thou, as thou art wont, repair
My heart with gladness, and a share
    Of thy meek nature !

STEPPING WESTWARD.

" *What, you are stepping westward?*"—" *Yea.*"
—'Twould be a *wildish* destiny,
If we, who thus together roam
In a strange land, and far from home,
Were in this place the guests of Chance :   5
Yet who would stop, or fear to advance,
Though home or shelter he had none,
With such a sky to lead him on ?

The dewy ground was dark and cold ;
Behind all gloomy to behold ;   10
And stepping westward seemed to be
A kind of *heavenly* destiny :
I liked the greeting ; 'twas a sound
Of something without place or bound ;
And seemed to give me spiritual right   15
To travel through that region bright.

The voice was soft, and she who spake
Was walking by her native lake :
The salutation had to me
The very sound of courtesy :   20
Its power was felt ; and while my eye
Was fixed upon the glowing sky,
The echo of the voice enwrought
A human sweetness with the thought
Of travelling through the world that lay   25
Before me in my endless way.

√THE SOLITARY REAPER.

BEHOLD her, single in the field,
Yon solitary Highland lass !
Reaping and singing by herself ;
Stop here, or gently pass !
Alone she cuts and binds the grain,   5
And sings a melancholy strain ;
O listen ! for the vale profound
Is overflowing with the sound.

No nightingale did ever chaunt
More welcome notes to weary bands   10
Of travellers in some shady haunt,
Among Arabian sands :
A voice so thrilling ne'er was heard
In spring-time from the cuckoo-bird,
Breaking the silence of the seas   15
Among the farthest Hebrides.

Will no one tell me what she sings ?—
Perhaps the plaintive numbers flow
For old, unhappy, far-off things,
And battles long ago :   20

Or is it some more humble lay
Familiar matter of to-day ?
Some natural sorrow, loss, or pain,
That has been, and may be again ?

Whate'er the theme, the maiden sang   25
As if her song could have no ending ;
I saw her singing at her work,
And o'er the sickle bending ;—
I listened, motionless and still ;
And, as I mounted up the hill,   30
The music in my heart I bore,
Long after it was heard no more.

ROB ROY'S GRAVE.

A FAMOUS man is Robin Hood,
The English ballad-singer's joy !
And Scotland has a thief as good,
An outlaw of as daring mood ;
She has her brave ROB ROY !   5
Then clear the weeds from off his grave,
And let us chant a passing stave,
In honour of that hero brave !

Heaven gave Rob Roy a dauntless heart,
And wondrous length and strength of arm :   10
Nor craved he more to quell his foes,
    Or keep his friends from harm.

Yet was Rob Roy as *wise* as brave ;
Forgive me if the phrase be strong ;—
A poet worthy of Rob Roy   15
    Must scorn a timid song.

Say, then, that he was wise as brave ;
As wise in thought as bold in deed :
For in the principles of things
    He sought his moral creed.   20

Said generous Rob, " What need of books ?
Burn all the statutes and their shelves :
They stir us up against our kind ;
    And worse, against ourselves.

" We have a passion—make a law,   25
Too false to guide us or control !
And for the law itself we fight
    In bitterness of soul.

" And, puzzled, blinded thus, we lose
Distinctions that are plain and few :   30
These find I graven on my heart :
    That tells me what to do.

" The creatures see of flood and field,
And those that travel on the wind !
With them no strife can last ; they live   35
    In peace, and peace of mind.

" For why ?—because the good old rule
Sufficeth them, the simple plan,
That they should take, who have the power,
    And they should keep who can.   40

" A lesson that is quickly learned,
A signal this which all can see !
Thus nothing here provokes the strong
    To wanton cruelty.

" All freakishness of mind is checked ;   45
He tamed, who foolishly aspires ;
While to the measure of his might
    Each fashions his desires.

" All hinds, and creatures, stand and fall
By strength of prowess or of wit :　　　　　　50
'Tis God's appointment who must sway,
　　And who is to submit.

" Since, then, the rule of right is plain,
And longest life is but a day ;
To have my ends, maintain my rights,　　　55
　　I'll take the shortest way."

And thus among these rocks he lived,
Through summer heat and winter snow :
The eagle, he was lord above,
　　And Rob was lord below.　　　　　　60

So was it—*would*, at least, have been
But through untowardness of fate ;
For Polity was then too strong—
　　He came an age too late ;

Or shall we say an age too soon ?　　　　65
For, were the bold man living *now*,
How might he flourish in his pride,
　　With buds on every bough !

Then rents and factors, rights of chase,
Sheriffs, and lairds and their domains,　　70
Would all have seemed but paltry things,
　　Not worth a moment's pains.

Rob Roy had never lingered here,
To these few meagre vales confined ;
But thought how wide the world, the times　75
　　How fairly to his mind !

And to his sword he would have said,
" Do thou my sovereign will enact
From land to land through half the earth !
　　Judge thou of law and fact !　　　　80

"'Tis fit that we should do our part,
Becoming, that mankind should learn
That we are not to be surpassed
    In fatherly concern.

"Of old things all are over old,   85
Of good things none are good enough :—
We'll show that we can help to frame
    A world of other stuff.

"I, too, will have my kings that take
From me the sign of life and death :   90
Kingdoms shall shift about, like clouds,
    Obedient to my breath."

And, if the word had been fulfilled,
As *might* have been, then, thought of joy !
France would have had her present boast,   95
    And we our own Rob Roy !

Oh ! say not so ; compare them not ;
I would not wrong thee, champion brave !
Would wrong thee nowhere ; least of all
    Here standing by thy grave.   100

For thou, although with some wild thoughts,
Wild chieftain of a savage clan !
Hadst this to boast of : thou didst love
    The *liberty* of man.

And, had it been thy lot to live   105
With us who now behold the light,
Thou would'st have nobly stirred thyself,
    And battled for the right.

For thou wert still the poor man's stay,
The poor man's heart, the poor man's hand ;   110
And all the oppressed, who wanted strength,
    Had thine at their command.

Bear witness many a pensive sigh
Of thoughtful herdsman when he strays
Alone upon Loch Veol's heights,   115
  And by Loch Lomond's braes !

And, far and near, through vale and hill,
Are faces that attest the same ;
The proud heart flashing through the eyes,
  At sound of ROB ROY's name.   120

TO THE MEN OF KENT.

OCTOBER 1803.

VANGUARD of liberty, ye men of Kent,
Ye children of a soil that doth advance
Her haughty brow against the coast of France,
Now is the time to prove your hardiment !
To France be words of invitation sent !   5
They from their fields can see the countenance
Of your fierce war, may ken the glittering lance
And hear you shouting forth your brave intent.
Left single, in bold parley, ye, of yore,
Did from the Norman win a gallant wreath ;   10
Confirmed the charters that were yours before ;—
No parleying now ! In Britain is one breath ;
We all are with you now from shore to shore ;—
Ye men of Kent, 'tis victory or death !

⌐ THE DAFFODILS.

I WANDERED lonely as a cloud
That floats on high o'er vales and hills,
When all at once I saw a crowd,
A host, of golden daffodils ;

Beside the lake, beneath the trees,   5
Fluttering and dancing in the breeze.

Continuous as the stars that shine
And twinkle on the milky way,
They stretched in never-ending line
Along the margin of a bay ;   10
Ten thousand saw I at a glance,
Tossing their heads in sprightly dance.

The waves beside them danced ; but they
Out-did the sparkling waves in glee :
A poet could not but be gay,   15
In such a jocund company :
I gazed—and gazed—but little thought
What wealth the show to me had brought .

For oft, when on my couch I lie
In vacant or in pensive mood,   20
They flash upon that inward eye
Which is the bliss of solitude ;
And then my heart with pleasure fills,
And dances with the daffodils.

THE AFFLICTION OF MARGARET.

I.

WHERE art thou, my beloved son,
Where art thou, worse to me than dead ?
Oh find me, prosperous or undone !
Or, if the grave be now thy bed,
Why am I ignorant of the same   5
That I may rest ; and neither blame
Nor sorrow may attend thy name ?

II.

Seven years, alas ! to have received
No tidings of an only child ;
To have despaired, have hoped, believed,   10
And been for evermore beguiled ;
Sometimes with thoughts of very bliss !
I catch at them, and then I miss ;
Was ever darkness like to this ?

III.

He was among the prime in worth,   15
An object beauteous to behold ;
Well born, well bred ; I sent him forth
Ingenuous, innocent, and bold :
If things ensued that wanted grace,
As hath been said, they were not base ;   20
And never blush was on my face.

IV.

Ah ! little doth the young one dream,
When full of play and childish cares,
What power is in his wildest scream,
Heard by his mother unawares !   25
He knows it not, he cannot guess :
Years to a mother bring distress ;
But do not make her love the less.

V.

Neglect me ! no, I suffered long
From that ill thought ; and, being blind,   30
Said, " Pride shall help me in my wrong ;
Kind mother have I been, as kind
As ever breathed : " and that is true ;
I've wet my path with tears like dew,
Weeping for him when no one knew.   35

VI.

My son, if thou be humbled, poor,
Hopeless of honour and of gain,
Oh ! do not dread thy mother's door ;
Think not of me with grief and pain :
I now can see with better eyes ;   40
And worldly grandeur I despise,
And fortune with her gifts and lies.

VII.

Alas ! the fowls of heaven have wings,
And blasts of heaven will aid their flight ;
They mount—how short a voyage brings   45
The wanderers back to their delight !
Chains tie us down by land and sea ;
And wishes, vain as mine, may be
All that is left to comfort thee.

VIII.

Perhaps some dungeon hears thee groan,   50
Maimed, mangled by inhuman men ;
Or thou upon a desert thrown
Inheritest the lion's den ;
Or hast been summoned to the deep,
Thou, thou and all thy mates, to keep   55
An incommunicable sleep.

IX.

I look for ghosts ; but none will force
Their way to me : 'tis falsely said
That there was ever intercourse
Between the living and the dead ;   60
For, surely, then I should have sight
Of him I wait for day and night,
With love and longings infinite.

X.

My apprehensions come in crowds ;
I dread the rustling of the grass ;   65
The very shadows of the clouds
Have power to shake me as they pass :.
I question things and do not find
One that will answer to my mind ;
And all the world appears unkind.   70

XI.

Beyond participation lie
My troubles, and beyond relief :
If any chance to heave a sigh,
They pity me, and not my grief.
Then come to me, my son, or send   75
Some tidings that my woes may end ;
I have no other earthly friend !

FIDELITY.

A BARKING sound the shepherd hears,
A cry as of a dog or fox ;
He halts—and searches with his eyes
Among the scattered rocks :
And now at distance can discern   5
A stirring in a brake of fern ;
And instantly a dog is seen,
Glancing through that covert green.

The dog is not of mountain breed ;
Its motions, too, are wild and shy ;   10
With something, as the shepherd thinks,
Unusual in its cry :

Nor is there any one in sight
All round, in hollow or on height ;
Nor shout, nor whistle strikes his ear ;   15
What is the creature doing here ?

It was a cove, a huge recess,
That keeps, till June, December's snow ;
A lofty precipice in front,
A silent tarn below !   20
Far in the bosom of Helvellyn,
Remote from public road or dwelling,
Pathway, or cultivated land ;
From trace of human foot or hand.

There sometimes doth a leaping fish   25
Send through the tarn a lonely cheer ;
The crags repeat the raven's croak,
In symphony austere ;
Thither the rainbow comes—the cloud—
And mists that spread the flying shroud ;   30
And sunbeams ; and the sounding blast,
That, if it could, would hurry past ;
But that enormous barrier holds it fast.

Not free from boding thoughts, a while
The shepherd stood ; then makes his way   35
O'er rocks and stones, following the dog
As quickly as he may ;
Nor far had gone before he found
A human skeleton on the ground ;
The appalled discoverer with a sigh   40
Looks round, to learn the history.

From those abrupt and perilous rocks
The man had fallen, that place of fear !
At length upon the shepherd's mind
It breaks, and all is clear :   45

He instantly recalled the name,
And who he was, and whence he came ;
Remembered, too, the very day
On which the traveller passed this way.

But hear a wonder, for whose sake   50
This lamentable tale I tell !
A lasting monument of words
This wonder merits well.
The dog, which still was hovering nigh,
Repeating the same timid cry,   55
This dog, had been through three months' space
A dweller in that savage place.

Yes, proof was plain that, since the day
When this ill-fated traveller died,
The dog had watched about the spot,   60
Or by his master's side :
How nourished here through such long time
He knows, who gave that love sublime ;
And gave that strength of feeling, great
Above all human estimate !   65

TO SLEEP.

A FLOCK of sheep that leisurely pass by,
One after one ; the sound of rain, and bees
Murmuring ; the fall of rivers, winds and seas,
Smooth fields, white sheets of water, and pure sky ;
I have thought of all by turns, and yet do lie ;   5
Sleepless ! and soon the small birds' melodies
Must hear, first uttered from my orchard trees ;
And the first cuckoo's melancholy cry
C

Even thus last night, and two nights more, I lay,
And could not win thee, Sleep, by any stealth !   10
So do not let me wear to-night away :
Without thee what is all the morning's wealth ?
Come, blessed barrier between day and day,
Dear mother of fresh thoughts and joyous health !

THOUGHT OF A BRITON ON THE SUBJUGATION OF SWITZERLAND.

Two voices are there ; one is of the sea,
One of the mountains ; each a mighty voice :
In both from age to age thou didst rejoice,
They were thy chosen music, Liberty !
There came a tyrant, and with holy glee   5
Thou fought'st against him ; but hast vainly striven :
Thou from thy Alpine holds at length art driven,
Where not a torrent murmurs heard by thee.
Of one deep bliss thine ear hath been bereft :
Then cleave, O cleave to that which still is left ;   10
For, high-souled maid, what sorrow would it be
That mountain floods should thunder as before,
And ocean bellow from his rocky shore,
And neither awful voice be heard by thee !

TO A SKY-LARK.

ETHEREAL minstrel ! pilgrim of the sky !
Dost thou despise the earth where cares abound ?
Or, while the wings aspire, are heart and eye
Both with thy nest upon the dewy ground ?
Thy nest which thou canst drop into at will,   5
Those quivering wings composed, that music still !

Leave to the nightingale her shady wood ;
A privacy of glorious light is thine ;
Whence thou dost pour upon the world a flood
Of harmony, with instinct more divine ;   10
Type of the wise who soar, but never roam ;
True to the kindred points of heaven and home !

A MORNING EXERCISE.

HAIL, blest above all kinds !—Supremely skilled
Restless with fixed to balance, high with low,
Thou leav'st the halcyon free her hopes to build
On such forbearance as the deed may show ;
Perpetual flight, unchecked by earthly ties,   5
Leav'st to the wandering bird of paradise.

Faithful, though swift as lightning, the meek dove ;
Yet more hath Nature reconciled in thee ;
So constant with thy downward eye of love,
Yet, in aërial singleness, so free ;   10
So humble, yet so ready to rejoice
In power of wing and never-wearied voice.

To the last point of vision, and beyond,
Mount, daring warbler !—that love-prompted strain,
('Twixt thee and thine a never-failing bond)   15
Thrills not the less the bosom of the plain :
Yet might'st thou seem, proud privilege ! to sing
All independent of the leafy spring.

How would it please old ocean to partake,
With sailors longing for a breeze in vain,   20
The harmony thy notes most gladly make
Where earth resembles most his own domain !
Urania's self might welcome with pleased ear
These matins mounting towards her native sphere.

Chanter by heaven attracted, whom no bars   25
To day-light known deter from that pursuit,
'Tis well that some sage instinct, when the stars
Come forth at evening, keeps thee still and mute ;
For not an eyelid could to sleep incline,
Wert thou among them, singing as they shine !   30

THE PRIMROSE OF THE ROCK.

A ROCK there is whose homely front
    The passing traveller slights ;
Yet there the glow-worms hang their lamps,
    Like stars, at various heights ;
And one coy primrose to that rock   5
    The vernal breeze invites.

What hideous warfare hath been waged,
    What kingdoms overthrown,
Since first I spied that primrose-tuft
    And marked it for my own ;   10
A lasting link in Nature's chain
    From highest heaven let down !

The flowers, still faithful to the stems,
    Their fellowship renew ;
The stems are faithful to the root,   15
    That worketh out of view ;
And to the rock the root adheres
    In every fibre true.

Close clings to earth the living rock,
    Though threatening still to fall ;   20
The earth is constant to her sphere ;
    And God upholds them all :

So blooms this lonely plant, nor dreads
  Her annual funeral.

    *   *   *   *   *

Here closed the meditative strain ;   25
  But air breathed soft that day,
The hoary mountain-heights were cheered,
  The sunny vale looked gay ;
And to the primrose of the rock
  I gave this after-lay.   30

I sang—Let myriads of bright flowers,
  Like thee, in field and grove
Revive unenvied ;—mightier far
  Than tremblings that reprove
Our vernal tendencies to hope,   35
  Is God's redeeming love.

That love which changed—for wan disease,
  For sorrow that had bent
O'er hopeless dust, for withered age---
  Their moral element,   40
And turned the thistles of a curse
  To types beneficent.

Sin-blighted though we are, we too,
  The reasoning sons of men,
From one oblivious winter called   45
  Shall rise, and breathe again ;
And in eternal summer lose
  Our threescore years and ten.

To humbleness of heart descends
  This prescience from on high,   50
The faith that elevates the just,
  Before and when they die ;
And makes each soul a separate heaven,
  A court for Deity.

"CALM IS THE FRAGRANT AIR."

Calm is the fragrant air, and loth to lose
Day's grateful warmth, tho' moist with falling dews.
Look for the stars, you'll say that there are none ;
Look up a second time, and, one by one,
You mark them twinkling out with silvery light,   5
And wonder how they could elude the sight !
The birds, of late so noisy in their bowers,
Warbled a while with faint and fainter powers,
But now are silent as the dim-seen flowers :
Nor does the village church-clock's iron tone   10
The time's and season's influence disown ;
Nine beats distinctly to each other bound
In drowsy sequence—how unlike the sound
That, in rough winter, oft inflicts a fear
On fireside listeners, doubting what they hear !   15
The shepherd, bent on rising with the sun,
Had closed his door before the day was done,
And now with thankful heart to bed doth creep,
And joins his little children in their sleep.
The bat, lured forth where trees the lane o'ershade,   20
Flits and reflits along the close arcade ;
The busy dor-hawk chases the white moth
With burring note, which Industry and Sloth
Might both be pleased with, for it suits them both.
A stream is heard—I see it not, but know   25
By its soft music whence the waters flow :
Wheels and the tread of hoofs are heard no more ;
One boat there was, but it will touch the shore
With the next dipping of its slackened oar ;
Faint sound, that, for the gayest of the gay,   30
Might give to serious thought a moment's sway,
As a last token of man's toilsome day !

COMPOSED BY THE SEASHORE.

WHAT mischief cleaves to unsubdued regret,
How fancy sickens by vague hopes beset ;
How baffled projects on the spirit prey,
And fruitless wishes eat the heart away,
The sailor knows ; he best, whose lot is cast   5
On the relentless sea that holds him fast
On chance dependent, and the fickle star
Of power, through long and melancholy war.
O sad it is, in sight of foreign shores,
Daily to think on old familiar doors,   10
Hearths loved in childhood, and ancestral floors ;
Or, tossed about along a waste of foam,
To ruminate on that delightful home
Which with the dear betrothèd *was* to come ;
Or came and was and is, yet meets the eye   15
Never but in the world of memory ;
Or in a dream recalled, whose smoothest range
Is crossed by knowledge, or by dread, of change,
And if not so, whose perfect joy makes sleep
A thing too bright for breathing man to keep.   20
Hail to the virtues which that perilous life
Extracts from Nature's elemental strife ;
And welcome glory won in battles fought
As bravely as the foe was keenly sought.
But to each gallant captain and his crew   25
A less imperious sympathy is due,
Such as my verse now yields, while moonbeams play
On the mute sea in this unruffled bay ;
Such as will promptly flow from every breast,
Where good men, disappointed in the quest   30
Of wealth and power and honours, long for rest ;
Or, having known the splendours of success,
Sigh for the obscurities of happiness.

SELECTIONS FROM WORDSWORTH.

PART II.

ON REVISITING THE WYE ABOVE TINTERN ABBEY.

FIVE years have past ; five summers, with the length
Of five long winters ! and again I hear
These waters, rolling from their mountain-springs
With a soft inland murmur.—Once again
Do I behold these steep and lofty cliffs,   5
That on a wild secluded scene impress
Thoughts of more deep seclusion ; and connect
The landscape with the quiet of the sky.
The day is come when I again repose
Here, under this dark sycamore, and view   10·
These plots of cottage-ground, these orchard-tufts,
Which at this season, with their unripe fruits,
Are clad in one green hue, and lose themselves
'Mid groves and copses.   Once again I see
These hedge-rows, hardly hedge-rows, little lines   15
Of sportive wood run wild : these pastoral farms,
Green to the very door ; and wreaths of smoke
Sent up, in silence, from among the trees !
With some uncertain notice, as might seem
Of vagrant dwellers in the houseless woods,   20

Or of some hermit's cave, where by his fire
The hermit sits alone.
            These beauteous forms,
Through a long absence, have not been to me
As is a landscape to a blind man's eye :
But oft, in lonely rooms, and 'mid the din   25
Of towns and cities, I have owed to them,
In hours of weariness, sensations sweet,
Felt in the blood, and felt along the heart ;
And passing even into my purer mind,
With tranquil restoration :—feelings too   30
Of unremembered pleasure : such, perhaps,
As have no slight or trivial influence
On that best portion of a good man's life,
His little, nameless, unremembered, acts
Of kindness and of love.   Nor less, I trust,   35
To them I may have owed another gift,
Of aspect more sublime ; that blessed mood,
In which the burthen of the mystery,
In which the heavy and the weary weight
Of all this unintelligible world,   40
Is lightened :—that serene and blessed mood,
In which the affections gently lead us on,—
Until, the breath of this corporeal frame
And even the motion of our human blood
Almost suspended, we are laid asleep   45
In body, and become a living soul :
While with an eye made quiet by the power .
Of harmony, and the deep power of joy,
We see into the life of things.
               If this
Be but a vain belief, yet, oh ! how oft—   50
In darkness and amid the many shapes
Of joyless daylight ; when the fretful stir
Unprofitable, and the fever of the world,
Have hung upon the beatings of my heart—

How oft, in spirit, have I turned to thee,   55
O sylvan Wye ! thou wanderer thro' the woods,
How often has my spirit turned to thee !
  And now, with gleams of half-extinguished thought,
With many recognitions dim and faint,
And somewhat of a sad perplexity,   60
The picture of the mind revives again :
While here I stand, not only with the sense
Of present pleasure, but with pleasing thoughts
That in this moment there is life and food
For future years.   And so I dare to hope,   65
Though changed, no doubt, from what I was when first
I came among these hills ; when like a roe
I bounded o'er the mountains, by the sides
Of the deep rivers, and the lonely streams,
Wherever nature led : more like a man   70
Flying from something that he dreads, than one
Who sought the thing he loved.   For nature then
(The coarser pleasures of my boyish days,
And their glad animal movements all gone by)
To me was all in all.—I cannot paint   75
What then I was.   The sounding cataract
Haunted me like a passion ; the tall rock,
The mountain, and the deep and gloomy wood,
Their colours and their forms, were then to me
An appetite ; a feeling and a love,   80
That had no need of a remoter charm,
By thought supplied, nor any interest
Unborrowed from the eye.—That time is past,
And all its aching joys are now no more,
And all its dizzy raptures.   Not for this   85
Faint I, nor mourn nor murmur ; other gifts
Have followed ; for such loss, I would believe,
Abundant recompence.   For I have learned
To look on nature, not as in the hour
Of thoughtless youth ; but hearing oftentimes   90

The still, sad music of humanity,
Nor harsh nor grating, though of ample power
To chasten and subdue.   And I have felt
A presence that disturbs me with the joy
Of elevated thoughts ; a sense sublime   95
Of something far more deeply interfused,
Whose dwelling is the light of setting suns,
And the round ocean and the living air,
And the blue sky, and in the mind of man ;
A motion and a spirit, that impels   100
All thinking things, all objects of all thought,
And rolls through all things.   Therefore am I still
A lover of the meadows and the woods,
And mountains ; and of all that we behold
From this green earth ; of all the mighty world   105
Of eye, and ear,—both what they half create,
And what perceive ; well pleased to recognise
In nature and the language of the sense,
The anchor of my purest thoughts, the nurse,
The guide, the guardian of my heart, and soul   110
Of all my moral being.
                          Nor perchance,
If I were not thus taught, should I the more
Suffer my genial spirits to decay :
For thou art with me here upon the banks
Of this fair river ; thou my dearest friend,   115
My dear, dear friend ; and in thy voice I catch
The language of my former heart, and read
My former pleasures in the shooting lights
Of thy wild eyes.   Oh ! yet a little while
May I behold in thee what I was once,   120
My dear, dear sister ! and this prayer I make,
Knowing that Nature never did betray
The heart that loved her ; 'tis her privilege,
Through all the years of this our life, to lead
From joy to joy : for she can so inform   125

The mind that is within us, so impress
With quietness and beauty, and so feed
With lofty thoughts, that neither evil tongues,
Rash judgments, nor the sneers of selfish men,
Nor greetings where no kindness is, nor all   130
The dreary intercourse of daily life,
Shall e'er prevail against us, or disturb
Our cheerful faith, that all which we behold
Is full of blessings.   Therefore let the moon
Shine on thee in thy solitary walk ;   135
And let the misty mountain-winds be free
To blow against thee : and, in after years,
When these wild ecstasies shall be matured
Into a sober pleasure ; when thy mind
Shall be a mansion for all lovely forms,   140
Thy memory be as a dwelling-place
For all sweet sounds and harmonies ; oh ! then,
If solitude, or fear, or pain, or grief,
Should be thy portion, with what healing thoughts
Of tender joy wilt thou remember me,   145
And these my exhortations ! Nor, perchance—
If I should be where I no more can hear
Thy voice, nor catch from thy wild eyes these gleams
Of past existence—wilt thou then forget
That on the banks of this delightful stream   150
We stood together ; and that I, so long
A worshipper of Nature, hither came
Unwearied in that service : rather say
With warmer love—oh ! with far deeper zeal
Of holier love.   Nor wilt thou then forget,   155
That after many wanderings, many years
Of absence, these steep woods and lofty cliffs,
And this green pastoral landscape, were to me
More dear, both for themselves and for thy sake !

INFLUENCE OF NATURAL OBJECTS

IN CALLING FORTH AND STRENGTHENING THE IMAGINATION IN BOYHOOD AND EARLY YOUTH.

One summer evening (led by her) I found
A little boat tied to a willow tree
Within a rocky cave, its usual home.
Straight I unloosed her chain, and stepping in
Pushed from the shore. It was an act of stealth   5
And troubled pleasure, nor without the voice
Of mountain-echoes did my boat move on ;
Leaving behind her still, on either side,
Small circles glittering idly in the moon,
Until they melted all into one track   10
Of sparkling light. But now, like one who rows,
Proud of his skill, to reach a chosen point
With an unswerving line, I fixed my view
Upon the summit of a craggy ridge,
The horizon's utmost boundary ; far above   15
Was nothing but the stars and the grey sky.
She was an elfin pinnace ; lustily
I dipped my oars into the silent lake,
And, as I rose upon the stroke, my boat
Went heaving through the water like a swan ;   20
When, from behind that craggy steep till then
The horizon's bound, a huge peak, black and huge,
As if with voluntary power instinct,
Upreared its head. I struck and struck again,
And growing still in stature the grim shape   25
Towered up between me and the stars, and still,
For so it seemed, with purpose of its own
And measured motion like a living thing,
Strode after me. With trembling oars I turned,
And through the silent water stole my way   30
Back to the covert of the willow tree ;

There in her mooring-place I left my bark,—
And through the meadows homeward went, in grave
And serious mood ; but after I had seen
That spectacle, for many days, my brain   35
Worked with a dim and undetermined sense
Of unknown modes of being ; o'er my thoughts
There hung a darkness, call it solitude
Or blank desertion.   No familiar shapes
Remained, no pleasant images of trees,   40
Of sea or sky, no colours of green fields ;
But huge and mighty forms, that do not live
Like living men, moved slowly through the mind
By day, and were a trouble to my dreams.

    Wisdom and Spirit of the universe !   45
Thou Soul that art the eternity of thought !
And giv'st to forms and images a breath
And everlasting motion ! not in vain,
By day or star-light, thus from my first dawn
Of childhood didst thou intertwine for me   50
The passions that build up our human soul ;
Not with the mean and vulgar works of man :
But with high objects, with enduring things,
With life and nature ; purifying thus
The elements of feeling and of thought,   55
And sanctifying by such discipline
Both pain and fear,—until we recognise
A grandeur in the beatings of the heart.
Nor was this fellowship vouchsafed to me
With stinted kindness.   In November days,   60
When vapours rolling down the valley made
A lonely scene more lonesome ; among woods
At noon ; and 'mid the calm of summer nights,
When, by the margin of the trembling lake,
Beneath the gloomy hills homeward I went   65
In solitude, such intercourse was mine :

Mine was it in the fields both day and night,
And by the waters, all the summer long.

   And in the frosty season, when the sun
Was set, and, visible for many a mile,   70
The cottage windows through the twilight blazed,
I heeded not their summons : happy time
It was indeed for all of us ; for me
It was a time of rapture ! Clear and loud
The village clock tolled six,—I wheeled about,   75
Proud and exulting like an untired horse
That cares not for his home.—All shod with steel,
We hissed along the polished ice, in games
Confederate, imitative of the chase
And woodland pleasures,—the resounding horn,   80
The pack loud-chiming, and the hunted hare.
So through the darkness and the cold we flew,
And not a voice was idle : with the din
Smitten, the precipices rang aloud ;
The leafless trees and every icy crag   85
Tinkled like iron ; while far-distant hills
Into the tumult sent an alien sound
Of melancholy not unnoticed, while the stars
Eastward were sparkling clear, and in the west
The orange sky of evening died away.   90
Not seldom from the uproar I retired
Into a silent bay, or sportively
Glanced sideway, leaving the tumultuous throng,
To cut across the reflex of a star ;
Image, that, flying still before me, gleamed   95
Upon the glassy plain : and oftentimes,
When we had given our bodies to the wind,
And all the shadowy banks on either side
Came sweeping through the darkness, spinning still
The rapid line of motion, then at once   100
Have I, reclining back upon my heels,

Stopped short ; yet still the solitary cliffs
Wheeled by me—even as if the earth had rolled
With visible motion her diurnal round !
Behind me did they stretch in solemn train,   105
Feebler and feebler, and I stood and watched
Till all was tranquil as a summer sea.

   Ye presences of Nature in the sky
And on the earth ! Ye visions of the hills !
And souls of lonely places ! can I think   110
A vulgar hope was yours when ye employed
Such ministry, when ye through many a year
Haunting me thus among my boyish sports,
On caves and trees, upon the woods and hills,
Impressed upon all forms the characters   115
Of danger or desire ; and thus did make
The surface of the universal earth
With triumph and delight, with hope and fear,
Work like a sea ?
             Not uselessly employed,
Might I pursue this theme through every change   120
Of exercise and play, to which the year
Did summon us in his delightful round.

THE RAINBOW.

   My heart leaps up when I behold
     A rainbow in the sky :
So was it when my life began ;
So is it now I am a man ;
So be it when I shall grow old,   5
     Or let me die !
The Child is father of the Man ;
And I could wish my days to be
Bound each to each by natural piety.
      D

RESOLUTION AND INDEPENDENCE.

I.

There was a roaring in the wind all night ;
The rain came heavily and fell in floods ;
But now the sun is rising calm and bright ;
The birds are singing in the distant woods ;
Over his own sweet voice the stock-dove broods ;   5
The jay makes answer as the magpie chatters ;
And all the air is filled with pleasant noise of waters.

II.

All things that love the sun are out of doors ;
The sky rejoices in the morning's birth ;
The grass is bright with rain-drops ;—on the moors   10
The hare is running races in her mirth ;
And with her feet she from the plashy earth
Raises a mist, that, glittering in the sun,
Runs with her all the way, wherever she doth run.

III.

I was a traveller then upon the moor,   15
I saw the hare that raced about with joy ;
I heard the woods and distant waters roar ;
Or heard them not, as happy as a boy :
The pleasant season did my heart employ :
My old remembrances went from me wholly ;   20
And all the ways of men, so vain and melancholy.

IV.

But, as it sometimes chanceth, from the might
Of joy in minds that can no further go,
As high as we have mounted in delight
In our dejection do we sink as low ;   25
To me that morning did it happen so ;
And fears and fancies thick upon me came ;
Dim sadness—and blind thoughts, I knew not, nor could
    name.

V.

I heard the sky-lark warbling in the sky ;
And I bethought me of the playful hare :   30
Even such a happy child of earth am I ;
Even as these blissful creatures do I fare ,
Far from the world I walk, and from all care ;
But there may come another day to me—
Solitude, pain of heart, distress, and poverty.   35

VI.

My whole life I have lived in pleasant thought,
As if life's business were a summer mood ;
As if all needful things would come unsought
To genial faith, still rich in genial good ;
But how can he expect that others should   40
Build for him, sow for him, and at his call
Love him, who for himself will take no heed at all ?

VII.

I thought of Chatterton, the marvellous boy,
The sleepless soul that perished in his pride ;
Of him who walked in glory and in joy   45
Following his plough, along the mountain-side :
By our own spirits are we deified :
We poets in our youth begin in gladness ;
But thereof come in the end despondency and madness.

VIII.

Now, whether it were by peculiar grace,   50
A leading from above, a something given,
Yet it befell, that, in this lonely place,
When I with these untoward thoughts had striven,
Beside a pool bare to the eye of heaven
I saw a man before me unawares :   55
The oldest man he seemed that ever wore grey hairs.

IX.

As a huge stone is sometimes seen to lie
Couched on the bald top of an eminence ;
Wonder to all who do the same espy,
By what means it could thither come, and whence ;   60
So that it seems a thing endued with sense :
Like a sea-beast crawled forth, that on a shelf
Of rock or sand reposeth, there to sun itself ;

X.

Such seemed this man, not all alive nor dead,
Nor all asleep—in his extreme old age :   65
His body was bent double, feet and head
Coming together in life's pilgrimage ;
As if some dire constraint of pain, or rage
Of sickness felt by him in times long past,
A more than human weight upon his frame had cast.   70

XI.

Himself he propped, limbs, body, and pale face,
Upon a long grey staff of shaven wood :
And, still as I drew near with gentle pace,
Upon the margin of that moorish flood
Motionless as a cloud the old man stood,   75
That heareth not the loud winds when they call ;
And moveth all together, if it move at all.

XII.

At length, himself unsettling, he the pond
Stirred with his staff, and fixedly did look
Upon the muddy water, which he conned,   80
As if he had been reading in a book :
And now a stranger's privilege I took ;
And, drawing to his side, to him did say,
"This morning gives us promise of a glorious day."

XIII.

A gentle answer did the old man make,			85
In courteous speech which forth he slowly drew :
And him with further words I thus bespake,
" What occupation do you there pursue ?
This is a lonesome place for one like you."
Ere he replied, a flash of mild surprise			90
Broke from the sable orbs of his yet-vivid eyes.

XIV.

His words came feebly, from a feeble chest,
But each in solemn order followed each,
With something of a lofty utterance drest—
Choice word and measured phrase, above the reach	95
Of ordinary men ; a stately speech ;
Such as grave livers do in Scotland use,
Religious men, who give to God and man their dues.

XV.

He told, that to these waters he had come
To gather leeches, being old and poor :			100
Employment hazardous and wearisome !
And he had many hardships to endure :
From pond to pond he roamed, from moor to moor ;
Housing, with God's good help, by choice or chance,
And in this way he gained an honest maintenance.	105

XVI.

The old man still stood talking by my side ;
But now his voice to me was like a stream
Scarce heard ; nor word from word could I divide ;
And the whole body of the man did seem
Like one whom I had met with in a dream ;		110
Or like a man from some far region sent,
To give me human strength, by apt admonishment.

XVII.

My former thoughts returned : the fear that kills ;
And hope that is unwilling to be fed ;
Cold, pain, and labour, and all fleshly ills ;   115
And mighty poets in their misery dead.
—Perplexed, and longing to be comforted,
My question eagerly did I renew,
"How is it that you live, and what is it you do ?"

XVIII.

He with a smile did then his words repeat ;   120
And said, that, gathering leeches, far and wide
He travelled ; stirring thus about his feet
The waters of the pools where they abide.
"Once I could meet with them on every side ;
But they have dwindled long by slow decay ;   125
Yet still I persevere, and find them where I may."

XIX.

While he was talking thus, the lonely place,
The old man's shape, and speech—all troubled me .
In my mind's eye I seemed to see him pace
About the weary moors continually,   130
Wandering about alone and silently.
While I these thoughts within myself pursued,
He, having made a pause, the same discourse renewed.

XX.

And soon with this he other matter blended,
Cheerfully uttered, with demeanour kind,   135
But stately in the main ; and when he ended,
I could have laughed myself to scorn to find
In that decrepit man so firm a mind.
"God," said I, " be my help and stay secure ;
I'll think of the leech-gatherer on the lonely moor !"

"IT IS A BEAUTEOUS EVENING."

It is a beauteous evening, calm and free,
The holy time is quiet as a nun
Breathless with adoration ; the broad sun
Is sinking down in its tranquillity ;
The gentleness of heaven broods o'er the sea :   5
Listen ! the mighty being is awake,
And doth with his eternal motion make
A sound like thunder—everlastingly.
Dear child ! dear girl ! that walkest with me here,
If thou appear untouched by solemn thought,   10
Thy nature is not therefore less divine :
Thou liest in Abraham's bosom all the year ;
And worshipp'st at the Temple's inner shrine,
God being with thee when we know it not.

"WHEN I HAVE BORNE IN MEMORY."

When I have borne in memory what has tamed
Great nations, how ennobling thoughts depart
When men change swords for ledgers, and desert
The student's bower for gold, some fears unnamed
I had, my country !—am I to be blamed ?   5
Now, when I think of thee, and what thou art,
Verily, in the bottom of my heart,
Of those unfilial fears I am ashamed.
For dearly must we prize thee ; we who find
In thee a bulwark for the cause of men :   10
And I by my affection was beguiled :
What wonder if a poet now and then,
Among the many movements of his mind,
Felt for thee as a lover or a child !

TO H. C.

SIX YEARS OLD.

O THOU ! whose fancies from afar are brought ;
Who of thy words dost make a mock apparel,
And fittest to unutterable thought
The breeze-like motion and the self-born carol ;
Thou faery voyager ! that dost float   5
In such clear water, that thy boat
May rather seem
To brood on air than on an earthly stream ;
Suspended in a stream as clear as sky,
Where earth and heaven do make one imagery   10
O blessed vision ! happy child !
Thou art so exquisitely wild,
I think of thee with many fears
For what may be thy lot in future years.

    I thought of times when Pain might be thy guest,   15
Lord of thy house and hospitality ;
And Grief, uneasy lover ! never rest
But when she sate within the touch of thee.
O too industrious folly !
O vain and causeless melancholy !   20
Nature will either end thee quite ;
Or, lengthening out thy season of delight,
Preserve for thee, by individual right,
A young lamb's heart among the full-grown flocks.
What hast thou to do with sorrow,   25
Or the injuries of to-morrow ?
Thou art a dew-drop, which the morn brings forth,
Ill fitted to sustain unkindly shocks,
Or to be trailed along the soiling earth ;
A gem that glitters while it lives,   30
And no forewarning gives ;
But, at the touch of wrong, without a strife
Slips in a moment out of life.

YEW-TREES.

THERE is a yew-tree, pride of Lorton Vale,
Which to this day stands single, in the midst
Of its own darkness, as it stood of yore ;
Not loth to furnish weapons for the bands
Of Umfraville or Percy ere they marched   5
To Scotland's heaths ; or those that crossed the sea
And drew their sounding bows at Azincour,
Perhaps at earlier Crecy, or Poictiers.
Of vast circumference and gloom profound
This solitary tree ! a living thing   10
Produced too slowly ever to decay ;
Of form and aspect too magnificent
To be destroyed.   But worthier still of note
Are those fraternal four of Borrowdale,
Joined in one solemn and capacious grove ;   15
Huge trunks ! and each particular trunk a growth
Of intertwisted fibres serpentine
Up-coiling, and inveterately convolved ;
Nor uninformed with phantasy, and looks
That threaten the profane ;—a pillared shade,   20
Upon whose grassless floor of red-brown hue,
By sheddings from the pining umbrage tinged
Perennially—beneath whose sable roof
Of boughs, as if for festal purpose, decked
With unrejoicing berries—ghostly shapes   25
May meet at noontide ; Fear and trembling Hope,
Silence and Foresight ; Death the skeleton
And Time the shadow ;—there to celebrate,
As in a natural temple scattered o'er
With altars undisturbed of mossy stone,   30
United worship ; or in mute repose
To lie, and listen to the mountain flood
Murmuring from Glaramara's inmost caves.

AT THE GRAVE OF BURNS.

I SHIVER, spirit fierce and bold,
At thought of what I now behold :
As vapours breathed from dungeons cold,
 Strike pleasure dead,
So sadness comes from out the mould   5
 Where Burns is laid.

And have I then thy bones so near.
And thou forbidden to appear ?
As if it were thyself that's here
 I shrink with pain ;   10
And both my wishes and my fear
 Alike are vain.

Off weight—nor press on weight !—away
Dark thoughts !—they came, but not to stay ;
With chastened feelings would I pay   15
 The tribute due
To him, and aught that hides his clay
 From mortal view.

Fresh as the flower, whose modest worth
He sang, his genius "glinted" forth,   20
Rose like a star that touching earth,
 For so it seems,
Doth glorify its humble birth
 With matchless beams.

The piercing eye, the thoughtful brow,   25
The struggling heart, where be they now ?—
Full soon the aspirant of the plough,
 The prompt, the brave,
Slept, with the obscurest, in the low
 And silent grave.   30

I mourned with thousands, but as one
More deeply grieved, for he was gone
Whose light I hailed when first it shone,
    And showed my youth
How verse may build a princely throne   35
    On humble truth.

Alas ! where'er the current tends,
Regret pursues and with it blends,—
Huge Criffel's hoary top ascends
    By Skiddaw seen,—   40
Neighbours we were, and loving friends
    We might have been ;

True friends though diversely inclined ;
But heart with heart and mind with mind,
Where the main fibres are entwined,   45
    Through Nature's skill,
May even by contraries be joined
    More closely still.

The tear will start, and let it flow ;
Thou " poor Inhabitant below,"   50
At this dread moment—even so—
    Might we together
Have sate and talked where gowans blow,
    Or on wild heather.

What treasures would have then been placed   55
Within my reach ; of knowledge graced
By fancy what a rich repast !
    But why go on ?—
Oh ! spare to sweep, thou mournful blast,
    His grave grass-grown.   60

There, too, a son, his joy and pride,
(Not three weeks past the stripling died,)

Lies gathered to his father's side,
    Soul-moving sight !
Yet one to which is not denied   65
    Some sad delight.

For *he* is safe, a quiet bed
Hath early found among the dead,
Harboured where none can be misled,
    Wronged, or distrest ;   70
And surely here it may be said
    That such are blest.

And oh for thee, by pitying grace
Checked oft-times in a devious race,
May He who halloweth the place   75
    Where man is laid
Receive thy spirit in the embrace
    For which it prayed !

Sighing I turned away ; but ere
Night fell I heard, or seemed to hear,   80
Music that sorrow comes not near,
    A ritual hymn,
Chanted in love that casts out fear
    By Seraphim.

"SHE WAS A PHANTOM OF DELIGHT."

She was a phantom of delight
When first she gleamed upon my sight ;
A lovely apparition, sent
To be a moment's ornament ;
Her eyes as stars of twilight fair ;   5
Like twilight's, too, her dusky hair ;
But all things else about her drawn
From May-time and the cheerful dawn ;

A dancing shape, an image gay,
To haunt, to startle, and waylay.   10

I saw her upon nearer view,
A spirit, yet a woman too !
Her household motions light and free,
And steps of virgin liberty ;
A countenance in which did meet   15
Sweet records, promises as sweet ;
A creature not too bright or good
For human nature's daily food ;
For transient sorrows, simple wiles,
Praise, blame, love, kisses, tears, and smiles.   20

And now I see with eye serene
The very pulse of the machine ;
A being breathing thoughtful breath,
A traveller between life and death ;
The reason firm, the temperate will,   25
Endurance, foresight, strength, and skill ;
A perfect woman, nobly planned,
To warn, to comfort, and command ;
And yet a spirit still, and bright
With something of angelic light.   30

ODE TO DUTY.

STERN daughter of the voice of God !
O Duty ! if that name thou love
Who art a light to guide, a rod
To check the erring, and reprove ;
Thou, who art victory and law   5
When empty terrors overawe ;
From vain temptations dost set free ;
And calm'st the weary strife of frail humanity !

There are who ask not if thine eye
Be on them ; who, in love and truth,   10
Where no misgiving is, rely
Upon the genial sense of youth :
Glad hearts ! without reproach or blot ;
Who do thy work, and know it not :
Oh, if through confidence misplaced   15
They fail, thy saving arms, dread power ! around them
    cast.

Serene will be our days and bright,
And happy will our nature be,
When love is an unerring light,
And joy its own security.   20
And they a blissful course may hold
Even now, who, not unwisely bold,
Live in the spirit of this creed ;
Yet seek thy firm support, according to their need.

I, loving freedom, and untried ;   25
No sport of every random gust,
Yet being to myself a guide,
Too blindly have reposed my trust :
And oft, when in my heart was heard
Thy timely mandate, I deferred   30
The task, in smoother walks to stray ;
But thee I now would serve more strictly, if I may.

Through no disturbance of my soul,
Or strong compunction in me wrought,
I supplicate for thy control ;   35
But in the quietness of thought :
Me this unchartered freedom tires ;
I feel the weight of chance-desires :
My hopes no more must change their name,
I long for a repose that ever is the same.   40

Stern lawgiver ! yet thou dost wear
The Godhead's most benignant grace ;
Nor know we anything so fair
As is the smile upon thy face :
Flowers laugh before thee on their beds   45
And fragrance in thy footing treads ;
Thou dost preserve the stars from wrong ;
And the most ancient heavens, through thee, are fresh
    and strong.

To humbler functions, awful power !
I call thee : I myself commend   50
Unto thy guidance from this hour ;
Oh, let my weakness have an end !
Give unto me, made lowly wise,
The spirit of self-sacrifice ;
The confidence of reason give ;   55
And in the light of truth thy bondman let me live !

ON A PICTURE OF PEELE CASTLE IN A STORM.

I was thy neighbour once, thou rugged pile !
Four summer weeks I dwelt in sight of thee :
I saw thee every day ; and all the while
Thy form was sleeping on a glassy sea.

So pure the sky, so quiet was the air !   5
So like, so very like, was day to day !
Whene'er I looked, thy image still was there ;
It trembled, but it never passed away.

How perfect was the calm ! it seemed no sleep ;
No mood, which season takes away, or brings :   10
I could have fancied that the mighty deep
Was even the gentlest of all gentle things.

Ah ! THEN, if mine had been the painter's hand,
To express what then I saw ; and add the gleam,
The light that never was, on sea or land,   15
The consecration, and the poet's dream ;

I would have planted thee, thou hoary pile,
Amid a world how different from this !
Beside a sea that could not cease to smile ;
On tranquil land, beneath a sky of bliss.   20

Thou shouldst have seemed a treasure-house divine
Of peaceful years ; a chronicle of heaven ;—
Of all the sunbeams that did ever shine
The very sweetest had to thee been given.

A picture had it been of lasting ease,   25
Elysian quiet, without toil or strife ;
No motion but the moving tide, a breeze,
Or merely silent Nature's breathing life.

Such, in the fond illusion of my heart,
Such picture would I at that time have made :   30
And seen the soul of truth in every part,
A stedfast peace that might not be betrayed.

So once it would have been,—'tis so no more ;
I have submitted to a new control :
A power is gone, which nothing can restore ;   35
A deep distress hath humanised my soul

Not for a moment could I now behold
A smiling sea, and be what I have been :
The feeling of my loss will ne'er be old ;
This, which I know, I speak with mind serene.   40

Then, Beaumont, friend ! who would have been the friend,
If he had lived, of him whom I deplore,
This work of thine I blame not, but commend ;
This sea in anger, and that dismal shore.

O 'tis a passionate work !—yet wise and well,   45
Well chosen is the spirit that is here ;
That hulk which labours in the deadly swell,
This rueful sky, this pageantry of fear !

And this huge castle, standing here sublime,
I love to see the look with which it braves,   50
Cased in the unfeeling armour of old time,
The lightning, the fierce wind, and trampling waves.

Farewell, farewell the heart that lives alone,
Housed in a dream, at distance from the kind !
Such happiness, wherever it be known,   55
Is to be pitied ; for 'tis surely blind.

But welcome fortitude, and patient cheer,
And frequent sights of what is to be borne !
Such sights, or worse, as are before me here.—
Not without hope we suffer and we mourn.   60

CHARACTER OF THE HAPPY WARRIOR.

Who is the happy warrior ?   Who is he
That every man in arms should wish to be ?
—It is the generous spirit, who, when brought
Among the tasks of real life, hath wrought
Upon the plan that pleased his boyish thought :   5
Whose high endeavours are an inward light
That makes the path before him always bright :
Who, with a natural instinct to discern
What knowledge can perform, is diligent to learn ;
Abides by this resolve, and stops not there,   10
But makes his moral being his prime care ;
Who, doomed to go in company with pain,
And fear, and bloodshed, miserable train !
Turns his necessity to glorious gain ;

E

In face of these doth exercise a power   15
Which is our human nature's highest dower ;
Controls them and subdues, transmutes, bereaves
Of their bad influence, and their good receives :
By objects, which might force the soul to abate
Her feeling, rendered more compassionate ;   20
Is placable—because occasions rise
So often that demand such sacrifice ;
More skilful in self-knowledge, even more pure,
As tempted more ; more able to endure,
As more exposed to suffering and distress ;   25
Thence, also, more alive to tenderness.
—'Tis he whose law is reason ; who depends
Upon that law as on the best of friends ;
Whence, in a state where men are tempted still
To evil for a guard against worse ill,   30
And what in quality or act is best
Doth seldom on a right foundation rest,
He labours good on good to fix, and owes
To virtue every triumph that he knows :
—Who, if he rise to station of command,   35
Rises by open means ; and there will stand
On honourable terms, or else retire,
And in himself possess his own desire ;
Who comprehends his trust, and to the same
Keeps faithful with a singleness of aim ;   40
And therefore does not stoop, nor lie in wait
For wealth, or honours, or for worldly state ;
Whom they must follow ; on whose head must fall,
Like showers of manna, if they come at all :
Whose powers shed round him in the common strife, 45
Or mild concerns of ordinary life,
A constant influence, a peculiar grace ;
But who, if he be called upon to face
Some awful moment to which Heaven has joined
Great issues, good or bad for human kind,   50

Is happy as a lover ; and attired
With sudden brightness, like a man inspired ;
And, through the heat of conflict, keeps the law
In calmness made, and sees what he foresaw ;
Or if an unexpected call succeed,   55
Come when it will, is equal to the need :
—He who, though thus endued as with a sense
And faculty for storm and turbulence,
Is yet a soul whose master-bias leans
To homefelt pleasures and to gentle scenes ; ✓   60
Sweet images ! which, wheresoe'er he be,
Are at his heart ; and such fidelity
It is his darling passion to approve ;
More brave for this, that he hath much to love :—
'Tis, finally, the man, who, lifted high,   65
Conspicuous object in a nation's eye,
Or left unthought-of in obscurity,—
Who, with a toward or untoward lot,
Prosperous or adverse, to his wish or not—
Plays, in the many games of life, that one   70
Where what he most doth value must be won :
Whom neither shape of danger can dismay,
Nor thought of tender happiness betray ;
Who, not content that former worth stand fast,
Looks forward, persevering to the last,   75
From well to better, daily self-surpast :
Who, whether praise of him must walk the earth
For ever, and to noble deeds give birth,
Or he must fall, to sleep without his fame,
And leave a dead unprofitable name—   80
Finds comfort in himself and in his cause ;
And, while the mortal mist is gathering, draws
His breath in confidence of Heaven's applause :
This is the happy warrior ; this is he
That every man in arms should wish to be.   85

THE SONNET.

Nuns fret not at their convent's narrow room ;
And hermits are contented with their cells ;
And students with their pensive citadels ;
Maids at the wheel, the weaver at his loom,
Sit blithe and happy ; bees that soar for bloom,   5
High as the highest peak of Furness-fells,
Will murmur by the hour in foxglove bells :
In truth the prison, unto which we doom
Ourselves, no prison is : and hence for me,
In sundry moods, 'twas pastime to be bound   10
Within the sonnet's scanty plot of ground ;
Pleased if some souls (for such there needs must be)
Who have felt the weight of too much liberty,
Should find brief solace there, as I have found.

PERSONAL TALK.

I.

I am not one who much or oft delight
To season my fireside with personal talk,—
Of friends, who live within an easy walk,
Or neighbours, daily, weekly, in my sight :
And, for my chance-acquaintance, ladies bright,   5
Sons, mothers, maidens withering on the stalk,
These all wear out of me, like forms, with chalk
Painted on rich men's floors, for one feast-night.
Better than such discourse doth silence long,
Long, barren silence, square with my desire ;   10
To sit without emotion, hope, or aim,
In the loved presence of my cottage-fire,
And listen to the flapping of the flame,
Or kettle whispering its faint undersong.

II.

"Yet life," you say, "is life ; we have seen and see,   15
And with a living pleasure we describe ;
And fits of sprightly malice do but bribe
The languid mind into activity.
Sound sense, and love itself, and mirth and glee
Are fostered by the comment and the gibe."   20
Even be it so ; yet still among your tribe,
Our daily world's true worldlings, rank not me !
Children are blest, and powerful ; their world lies
More justly balanced ; partly at their feet,
And part far from them :—sweetest melodies   25
Are those that are by distance made more sweet ;
Whose mind is but the mind of his own eyes,
He is a slave ; the meanest we can meet !

III.

Wings nave we,—and as far as we can go,
We may find pleasure : wilderness and wood,   30
Blank ocean and mere sky, support that mood
Which with the lofty sanctifies the low.
Dreams, books, are each a world ; and books, we know,
Are a substantial world, both pure and good :
Round these, with tendrils strong as flesh and blood,   35
Our pastime and our happiness will grow.
There find I personal themes, a plenteous store,
Matter wherein right voluble I am,
To which I listen with a ready ear ;
Two shall be named, pre-eminently dear,—   40
The gentle lady married to the Moor ;
And heavenly Una with her milk-white lamb.

IV.

Nor can I not believe but that hereby   .
Great gains are mine ; for thus I live remote

From evil-speaking ; rancour, never sought,   45
Comes to me not ; malignant truth, or lie.
Hence have I genial seasons, hence have I
Smooth passions, smooth discourse, and joyous thought :
And thus from day to day my little boat
Rocks in its harbour, lodging peaceably.   50
Blessings be with them—and eternal praise,
Who gave us nobler loves, and nobler cares—
The poets, who on earth have made us heirs
Of truth and pure delight by heavenly lays !
Oh ! might my name be numbered among theirs,   55
Then gladly would I end my mortal days.

ADMONITION.

WELL may'st thou halt—and gaze with brightening eye !
The lovely cottage in the guardian nook
Hath stirred thee deeply ; with its own dear brook,
Its own small pasture, almost its own sky !
But covet not the abode ;—forbear to sigh,   5
As many do, repining while they look ;
Intruders—who would tear from Nature's book
This precious leaf, with harsh impiety.
Think what the home must be if it were thine,
Even thine, though few thy wants !—Roof, window, door, 10
The very flowers are sacred to the poor,
The roses to the porch which they entwine :
Yea, all, that now enchants thee, from the day
On which it should be touched, would melt away.

"THE WORLD IS TOO MUCH WITH US."

THE world is too much with us ; late and soon,
Getting and spending, we lay waste our powers :
Little we see in Nature that is ours ;
We have given our hearts away, a sordid boon !
The sea that bares her bosom to the moon ;　　5
The winds that will be howling at all hours,
And are up-gathered now like sleeping flowers ;
For this, for everything, we are out of tune ;
It moves us not.—Great God ! I'd rather be
A pagan suckled in a creed outworn ;　　10
So might I, standing on this pleasant lea,
Have glimpses that would make me less forlorn ;
Have sight of Proteus rising from the sea ;
Or hear old Triton blow his wreathèd horn.

SONG AT THE FEAST OF BROUGHAM CASTLE.

HIGH in the breathless hall the minstrel sate,
And Emont's murmur mingled with the song.—
The words of ancient time I thus translate,
A festal strain that hath been silent long :—
"From town to town, from tower to tower,　　5
The red rose is a gladsome flower.
Her thirty years of winter past,
The red rose is revived at last ;
She lifts her head for endless spring,
For everlasting blossoming :　　10
Both roses flourish, red and white :
In love and sisterly delight
The two that were at strife are blended,
And all old troubles now are ended.—

Joy! joy to both! but most to her   15
Who is the flower of Lancaster!
Behold her how she smiles to-day
On this great throng, this bright array!
Fair greeting doth she send to all
From every corner of the hall;   20
But chiefly from above the board
Where sits in state our rightful lord,
A Clifford to his own restored!
   They came with banner, spear, and shield;
And it was proved in Bosworth-field.   25
Not long the avenger was withstood—
Earth helped him with the cry of blood:
St. George was for us, and the might
Of blessed angels crowned the right.
Loud voice the land has uttered forth,   30
We loudest in the faithful north:
Our fields rejoice, our mountains ring,
Our streams proclaim a welcoming;
Our strong-abodes and castles see
The glory of their loyalty.   35
   How glad is Skipton at this hour—
Though lonely, a deserted Tower;
Knight, squire, and yeoman, page and groom:
We have them at the feast of Brough'm.
How glad Pendragon—though the sleep   40
Of years be on her!—She shall reap
A taste of this great pleasure, viewing
As in a dream her own renewing.
Rejoiced is Brough, right glad I deem
Beside her little humble stream;   45
And she that keepeth watch and ward
Her statelier Eden's course to guard;
They both are happy at this hour,
Though each is but a lonely tower:—
But here is perfect joy and pride   50

For one fair house by Emont's side,
This day, distinguished without peer
To see her master and to cheer—
Him, and his lady-mother dear !
  Oh ! it was a time forlorn   55
When the fatherless was born—
Give her wings that she may fly,
Or she sees her infant die !
Swords that are with slaughter wild
Hunt the mother and the child.   60
Who will take them from the light ?
—Yonder is a man in sight—
Yonder is a house—but where ?
No, they must not enter there.
To the caves, and to the brooks,   65
To the clouds of heaven she looks ;
She is speechless, but her eyes
Pray in ghostly agonies.
Blissful Mary, mother mild,
Maid and mother undefiled,   70
Save a mother and her child !
  Now who is he that bounds with joy
On Carrock's side, a shepherd-boy ?
No thoughts hath he but thoughts that pass
Light as the wind along the grass.   75
Can this be he who hither came
In secret, like a smothered flame ?
O'er whom such thankful tears were shed
For shelter, and a poor man's bread !
God loves the child ; and God hath willed   80
That those dear words should be fulfilled,
The lady's words, when forced away,
The last she to her babe did say :
'My own, my own, thy fellow-guest
I may not be ; but rest thee, rest,   85
For lowly shepherd's life is best !'

Alas ! when evil men are strong
No life is good, no pleasure long.
The boy must part from Mosedale's groves,
And leave Blencathara's rugged coves,   90
And quit the flowers that summer brings
To Glendermakin's lofty springs ;
Must vanish, and his careless cheer
Be turned to heaviness and fear.
—Give Sir Lancelot Threlkeld praise !   95
Hear it, good man, old in days !
Thou tree of covert and of rest
For this young bird that is distrest ;
Among thy branches safe he lay,
And he was free to sport and play,   100
When falcons were abroad for prey.

A recreant harp, that sings of fear
And heaviness in Clifford's ear !
I said, when evil men are strong,
No life is good, no pleasure long,   105
A weak and cowardly untruth !
Our Clifford was a happy youth,
And thankful through a weary time,
That brought him up to manhood's prime.
—Again he wanders forth at will,   110
And tends a flock from hill to hill :
His garb is humble ; ne'er was seen
Such garb with such a noble mien ;
Among the shepherd grooms no mate
Hath he, a child of strength and state !   115
Yet lacks not friends for simple glee,
Not yet for higher sympathy.
To his side the fallow-deer
Came, and rested without fear ;
The eagle, lord of land and sea,   120
Stooped down to pay him fealty ;
And both the undying fish that swim

Through Bowscale-tarn did wait on him ;
The pair were servants of his eye
In their immortality ;   125
And glancing, gleaming, dark or bright,
Moved to and fro, for his delight.
He knew the rocks which angels haunt
Upon the mountains visitant ;
He hath kenned them taking wing :   130
And into caves where faeries sing
He hath entered ; and been told
By voices how men lived of old.
Among the heavens his eye can see
The face of thing that is to be ;   135
And, if that men report him right,
His tongue could whisper words of might.
—Now another day is come,
Fitter hope, and nobler doom ;
He hath thrown aside his crook,   140
And hath buried deep his book ;
Armour rusting in his halls
On the blood of Clifford calls ;—
'Quell the Scot,' exclaims the lance—
Bear me to the heart of France,   · 145
Is the longing of the shield—
Tell thy name, thou trembling field ;
Field of death, where'er thou be,
Groan thou with our victory !
Happy day, and mighty hour,   150
When our shepherd, in his power,
Mailed and horsed, with lance and sword,
To his ancestors restored
Like a re-appearing star,
Like a glory from afar,   155
First shall head the flock of war ! "

Alas ! the impassioned minstrel did not know
How, by Heaven's grace, this Clifford's heart was framed.

How he, long forced in humble walks to go,
Was softened into feeling, soothed, and tamed.   160

Love had he found in huts where poor men lie ;
His daily teachers had been woods and rills,
The silence that is in the starry sky,
The sleep that is among the lonely hills.

In him the savage virtue of the race,   165
Revenge, and all ferocious thoughts were dead :
Nor did he change ; but kept in lofty place
The wisdom which adversity had bred.

Glad were the vales, and every cottage hearth ;
The shepherd-lord was honoured more and more ;   170
And, ages after he was laid in earth,
"The good Lord Clifford" was the name he bore.

LAODAMIA.

" WITH sacrifice before the rising morn
Vows have I made by fruitless hope inspired ;
And from the infernal gods, 'mid shades forlorn
Of night, my slaughtered lord have I required :
Celestial pity I again implore ;—   5
Restore him to my sight—great Jove, restore !"

So speaking, and by fervent love endowed
With faith, the suppliant heavenward lifts her hands ;
While, like the sun emerging from a cloud,
Her countenance brightens—and her eye expands ;   10
Her bosom heaves and spreads, her stature grows ;
And she expects the issue in repose.

O terror ! what hath she perceived ?—O joy !
What doth she look on ?—whom doth she behold ?
Her hero slain upon the beach of Troy ?   15
His vital presence ? his corporeal mould ?

It is—if sense deceive her not—'tis he !
And a god leads him, wingèd Mercury !

Mild Hermes spake—and touched her with his wand
That calms all fear; "Such grace hath crowned thy prayer,
Laodamía ! that at Jove's command   21
Thy husband walks the paths of upper air :
He comes to tarry with thee three hours' space ;
Accept the gift, behold him face to face ! "

Forth sprang the impassioned queen her lord to clasp ; 25
Again that consummation she essayed ;
But unsubstantial form eludes her grasp
As often as that eager grasp was made.
The phantom parts—but parts to re-unite,
And re-assume his place before her sight.   30

"Protesiláus, lo ! thy guide is gone !
Confirm, I pray, the vision with thy voice :
This is our palace,—yonder is thy throne ;
Speak, and the floor thou tread'st on will rejoice.
Not to appal me have the gods bestowed   35
This precious boon ; and blest a sad abode."

"Great Jove, Laodamía ! doth not leave
His gifts imperfect :—spectre though I be,
I am not sent to scare thee or deceive ;
But in reward of thy fidelity.   40
And something also did my worth obtain ;
For fearless virtue bringeth boundless gain.

"Thou knowest, the Delphic oracle foretold
That the first Greek who touched the Trojan strand
Should die ; but me the threat could not withhold :   45
A generous cause a victim did demand ;
And forth I leapt upon the sandy plain ;
A self-devoted chief—by Hector slain."

"Supreme of heroes—bravest, noblest, best !
Thy matchless courage I bewail no more,   50
Which then, when tens of thousands were deprest
By doubt, propelled thee to the fatal shore ;
Thou found'st—and I forgive thee—here thou art—
A nobler counsellor than my poor heart.

"But thou, though capable of sternest deed,   55
Wert kind as resolute, and good as brave ;
And he, whose power restores thee, hath decreed
Thou should'st elude the malice of the grave :
Redundant are thy locks, thy lips as fair
As when their breath enriched Thessalian air.   60

"No spectre greets me,—no vain shadow this ;
Come, blooming hero, place thee by my side !
Give, on this well-known couch, one nuptial kiss
To me, this day, a second time thy bride !"
Jove frowned in heaven : the conscious Parcæ threw   65
Upon those roseate lips a Stygian hue.

"This visage tells thee that my doom is past :
Nor should the change be mourned, even if the joys
Of sense were able to return as fast
And surely as they vanish.   Earth destroys   70
Those raptures duly—Erebus disdains :
Calm pleasures there abide—majestic pains.

"Be taught, O faithful consort, to control
Rebellious passion : for the gods approve
The depth, and not the tumult, of the soul ;   75
A fervent, not ungovernable, love.
Thy transports moderate ; and meekly mourn
When I depart, for brief is my sojourn—"

"Ah, wherefore ?—Did not Hercules by force
Wrest from the guardian monster of the tomb   80

Alcestis, a reanimated corse,
Given back to dwell on earth in vernal bloom ?
Medea's spells dispersed the weight of years,
And Æson stood a youth 'mid youthful peers.

"The gods to us are merciful—and they 85
Yet further may relent : for mightier far
Than strength of nerve and sinew, or the sway
Of magic potent over sun and star,
Is love, though oft to agony distrest,
And though his favourite seat be feeble woman's breast.

"But if thou goest, I follow—" "Peace !" he said,— 91
She looked upon him and was calmed and cheered ;
The ghastly colour from his lips had fled ;
In his deportment, shape, and mien, appeared
Elysian beauty, melancholy grace, 95
Brought from a pensive though a happy place.

He spake of love, such love as spirits feel
In worlds whose course is equable and pure ;
No fears to beat away—no strife to heal—
The past unsighed for, and the future sure ; 100
Spake of heroic arts in graver mood
Revived, with finer harmony pursued ;

Of all that is most beauteous—imaged there
In happier beauty ; more pellucid streams,
An ampler ether, a diviner air, 105
And fields invested with purpureal gleams ;
Climes which the sun, who sheds the brightest day
Earth knows, is all unworthy to survey.

Yet there the soul shall enter which hath earned
That privilege by virtue.—" Ill," said he, 110
" The end of man's existence I discerned,
Who from ignoble games and revelry

Could draw, when we had parted, vain delight,
While tears were thy best pastime, day and night ;

"And while my youthful peers before my eyes   115
(Each hero following his peculiar bent)
Prepared themselves for glorious enterprise
By martial sports,—or, seated in the tent,
Chieftains and kings in council were detained ;
What time the fleet at Aulis lay enchained.   120

"The wished-for wind was given :—I then revolved
The oracle, upon the silent sea ;
And, if no worthier led the way, resolved
That, of a thousand vessels, mine should be
The foremost prow in pressing to the strand,—   125
Mine the first blood that tinged the Trojan sand.

"Yet bitter, oft-times bitter, was the pang
When of thy loss I thought, belovèd wife !
On thee too fondly did my memory hang,
And on the joys we shared in mortal life,—   130
The paths which we had trod—these fountains, flowers ;
My new-planned cities, and unfinished towers.

"But should suspense permit the foe to cry,
'Behold they tremble !—haughty their array,
Yet of their number no one dares to die ?'   135
In soul I swept the indignity away :
Old frailties then recurred :—but lofty thought,
In act embodied, my deliverance wrought.

"And thou, though strong in love, art all too weak
In reason, in self-government too slow ;   140
I counsel thee by fortitude to seek
Our blest re-union in the shades below.
The invisible world with thee hath sympathised ;
Be the affections raised and solemnised.

"Learn, by a mortal yearning, to ascend—   145
Seeking a higher object.   Love was given,
Encouraged, sanctioned, chiefly for that end;
For this the passion to excess was driven—
That self might be annulled : her bondage prove
The fetters of a dream, opposed to love."——   150

Aloud she shrieked ! for Hermes reappears !
Round the dear shade she would have clung—'tis vain :
The hours are past—too brief had they been years ;
And him no mortal effort can detain :
Swift, toward the realms that know not earthly day,   155
He through the portal takes his silent way,
And on the palace-floor a lifeless corse she lay.

Thus, all in vain exhorted and reproved,
She perished ; and, as for a wilful crime,
By the just gods whom no weak pity moved,   160
Was doomed to wear out her appointed time,
Apart from happy ghosts, that gather flowers
Of blissful quiet 'mid unfading bowers.

—Yet tears to human suffering are due ;
And mortal hopes defeated and o'erthrown   165
Are mourned by man, and not by man alone,
As fondly he believes.—Upon the side
Of Hellespont (such faith was entertained)
A knot of spiry trees for ages grew
From out the tomb of him for whom she died ;   170
And ever, when such stature they had gained
That Ilium's walls were subject to their view,
The trees' tall summits withered at the sight ;
A constant interchange of growth and blight !

COMPOSED UPON AN EVENING OF EXTRA-ORDINARY SPLENDOUR AND BEAUTY.

I.

HAD this effulgence disappeared
With flying haste, I might have sent,
Among the speechless clouds, a look
Of blank astonishment;
But 'tis endued with power to stay,   5
And sanctify one closing day,
That frail mortality may see—
What is?—ah no, but what *can* be!
Time was when field and watery cove
With modulated echoes rang,   10
While choirs of fervent angels sang
Their vespers in the grove;
Or, crowning, star-like, each some sovereign height,
Warbled, for heaven above and earth below,
Strains suitable to both.—Such holy rite,   15
Methinks, if audibly repeated now
From hill or valley, could not move
Sublimer transport, purer love,
Than doth this silent spectacle—the gleam--
The shadow—and the peace supreme!   20

II.

No sound is uttered,—but a deep
And solemn harmony pervades
The hollow vale from steep to steep,
And penetrates the glades.
Far-distant images draw nigh,   25
Called forth by wondrous potency
Of beamy radiance, that imbues
Whate'er it strikes, with gem-like hues!

In vision exquisitely clear,
Herds range along the mountain side ;   30
And glistening antlers are descried ;
And gilded flocks appear.
Thine is the tranquil hour, purpureal Eve !
But long as god-like wish, or hope divine,
Informs my spirit, ne'er can I believe   35
That this magnificence is wholly thine !
—From worlds not quickened by the sun
A portion of the gift is won ;
An intermingling of Heaven's pomp is spread
On ground which British shepherds tread !   40

III.

And, if there be whom broken ties
Afflict, or injuries assail,
Yon hazy ridges to their eyes
Present a glorious scale,
Climbing suffused with sunny air,   45
To stop—no record hath told where !
And tempting Fancy to ascend,
And with immortal Spirits blend !
—Wings at my shoulders seem to play ;
But, rooted here, I stand and gaze   50
On those bright steps that heavenward raise
Their practicable way.
Come forth, ye drooping old men, look abroad,
And see to what fair countries ye are bound !
And if some traveller, weary of his road,   55
Hath slept since noon-tide on the grassy ground,
Ye Genii ! to his covert speed ;
And wake him with such gentle heed
As may attune his soul to meet the dower
Bestowed on this transcendent hour !   60

IV.

Such hues from their celestial urn
Were wont to stream before mine eye,
Where'er it wandered in the morn
Of blissful infancy.
This glimpse of glory, why renewed ?   65
Nay, rather speak with gratitude ;
For, if a vestige of those gleams
Survived, 'twas only in my dreams.
Dread Power ! whom peace and calmness serve
No less than Nature's threatening voice,   70
If aught unworthy be my choice,
From THEE if I would swerve ;
Oh, let thy grace remind me of the light
Full early lost, and fruitlessly deplored ;
Which, at this moment, on my waking sight   75
Appears to shine, by miracle restored ;
My soul, though yet confined to earth,
Rejoices in a second birth !
—'Tis past, the visionary splendour fades ;
And night approaches with her shades.   80

INSIDE OF KING'S COLLEGE CHAPEL,
CAMBRIDGE.

TAX not the royal saint with vain expense,
With ill-matched aims the architect who planned—
Albeit labouring for a scanty band
Of white robed scholars only—this immense
And glorious work of fine intelligence !   5
Give all thou canst ; high Heaven rejects the lore
Of nicely-calculated less or more ;
So deemed the man who fashioned for the sense
These lofty pillars, spread that branching roof

Self-poised, and scooped into ten thousand cells,   10
Where light and shade repose, where music dwells
Lingering—and wandering on as loth to die ;
Like thoughts whose very sweetness yieldeth proof
That they were born for immortality.

"SCORN NOT THE SONNET."

SCORN not the sonnet ; critic, you have frowned,
Mindless of its just honours ; with this key
Shakspeare unlocked his heart ; the melody
Of this small lute gave ease to Petrarch's wound ;
A thousand times this pipe did Tasso sound :   5
With it Camöens soothed an exile's grief ;
The sonnet glittered a gay myrtle leaf
Amid the cypress with which Dante crowned
His visionary brow : a glow-worm lamp,
It cheered mild Spenser, called from Faery-land   10
To struggle through dark ways ; and, when a damp
Fell round the path of Milton, in his hand
The thing became a trumpet ; whence he blew
Soul-animating strains—alas, too few !

ON THE DEPARTURE OF SIR WALTER SCOTT
FROM ABBOTSFORD, FOR NAPLES.

A TROUBLE, not of clouds, or weeping rain,
Nor of the setting sun's pathetic light
Engendered, hangs o'er Eildon's triple height :
Spirits of power, assembled there, complain
For kindred power departing from their sight ;   5
While Tweed, best pleased in chanting a blithe strain,
Saddens his voice again, and yet again.

Lift up your hearts, ye mourners ! for the might
Of the whole world's good wishes with him goes ;
Blessings and prayers, in nobler retinue   10
Than sceptred king or laurelled conqueror knows,
Follow this wondrous potentate.   Be true,
Ye winds of ocean, and the midland sea,
Wafting your charge to soft Parthenope !

ODE. INTIMATIONS OF IMMORTALITY FROM RECOLLECTIONS OF EARLY CHILDHOOD.

I.

THERE was a time when meadow, grove, and stream,
The earth, and every common sight,
   To me did seem
  Apparelled in celestial light,
The glory and the freshness of a dream.   5
It is not now as it hath been of yore ;—
   Turn wheresoe'er I may,
   By night or day,
The things which I have seen I now can see no more.

II.

  The rainbow comes and goes,   10
  And lovely is the rose,
  The moon doth with delight   .
Look round her when the heavens are bare,
  Waters on a starry night
  Are beautiful and fair ;   15
 The sunshine is a glorious birth ;
 But yet I know, where'er I go,
That there hath past away a glory from the earth.

III.

Now, while the birds thus sing a joyous song,
  And while the young lambs bound   20
   As to the tabor's sound,
To me alone there came a thought of grief :
A timely utterance gave that thought relief,
  And I again am strong :
The cataracts blow their trumpets from the steep ;   25
No more shall grief of mine the season wrong ;
I hear the echoes through the mountains throng,
The winds come to me from the fields of sleep,
  And all the earth is gay ;
   Land and sea   30
  Give themselves up to jollity,
   And with the heart of May
  Doth every beast keep holiday ;—
   Thou child of joy,
Shout round me, let me hear thy shouts, thou happy
  shepherd-boy !   35

IV.

Ye blessèd creatures, I have heard the call
  Ye to each other make ; I see
The heavens laugh with you in your jubilee ;
  My heart is at your festival,
  My head hath its coronal,   40
The fulness of your bliss, I feel—I feel it all
  Oh evil day ! if I were sullen
  While earth herself is adorning,
   This sweet May-morning,
  And the children are culling   45
   On every side,
  In a thousand valleys far and wide,
  Fresh flowers ; while the sun shines warm,
And the babe leaps up on his mother's arm :—

I hear, I hear, with joy I hear !　　　　　　　50
—But there's a tree, of many, one,
A single field which I have looked upon,
Both of them speak of something that is gone :
　　The pansy at my feet
　　Doth the same tale repeat :　　　　　　55
Whither is fled the visionary gleam ?
Where is it now, the glory and the dream ?

V.

Our birth is but a sleep and a forgetting :
The soul that rises with us, our life's star,
　　　Hath had elsewhere its setting,　　　60
　　　　And cometh from afar :
　　　Not in entire forgetfulness,
　　　And not in utter nakedness,
But trailing clouds of glory do we come
　　From God, who is our home :　　　　65
Heaven lies about us in our infancy !
Shades of the prison-house begin to close
　　Upon the growing boy,
But he beholds the light, and whence it flows,
　　He sees it in his joy ;　　　　　　70
The youth, who daily farther from the east
　　Must travel, still is Nature's priest,
　　　And by the vision splendid
　　　Is on his way attended ;
At length the man perceives it die away,　　75
And fade into the light of common day.

VI.

Earth fills her lap with pleasures of her own ;
Yearnings she hath in her own natural kind,
And, even with something of a mother's mind,
　　　And no unworthy aim,　　　　　80

The homely nurse doth all she can
To make her foster-child, her inmate man,
    Forget the glories he hath known,
And that imperial palace whence he came.

VII.

Behold the child among his new-born blisses.   85
A six years' darling of a pigmy size !
See, where 'mid work of his own hand he lies,
Fretted by sallies of his mother's kisses,
With light upon him from his father's eyes !
See, at his feet, some little plan or chart,   90
Some fragment from his dream of human life,
Shaped by himself with newly-learned art ;
    A wedding or a festival,
    A mourning or a funeral ;
        And this hath now his heart,   95
    And unto this he frames his song :
        Then will he fit his tongue
To dialogues of business, love, or strife ;
    But it will not be long
    Ere this be thrown aside,   100
    And with new joy and pride
The little actor cons another part ;
Filling from time to time his " humorous stage"
With all the persons, down to palsied age,
That Life brings with her in her equipage ;   105
    As if his whole vocation
    Were endless imitation.

VIII.

Thou, whose exterior semblance doth belie
    Thy soul's immensity ;
Thou best philosopher, who yet dost keep   110
Thy heritage, thou eye among the blind,

That, deaf and silent, read'st the eternal deep,
Haunted for ever by the eternal mind,—
    Mighty prophet ! seer blest !
    On whom those truths do rest,   115
Which we are toiling all our lives to find,
In darkness lost, the darkness of the grave ;
Thou, over whom thy immortality
Broods like the day, a master o'er a slave,
A presence which is not to be put by ;   120
Thou little child, yet glorious in the might
Of heaven-born freedom on thy being's height,
Why with such earnest pains dost thou provoke
The years to bring the inevitable yoke,
Thus blindly with thy blessedness at strife ?   125
Full soon thy soul shall have her earthly freight,
And custom lie upon thee with a weight,
Heavy as frost, and deep almost as life !

IX.

    O joy ! that in our embers
    Is something that doth live,   130
    That nature yet remembers
    What was so fugitive !
The thought of our past years in me doth breed
Perpetual benediction : not indeed
For that which is most worthy to be blest—   135
(Delight and liberty, the simple creed
Of childhood, whether busy or at rest,
With new-fledged hope still fluttering in his breast :—
    Not for these I raise
    The song of thanks and praise) ;   140
    But for those obstinate questionings
    Of sense and outward things,
    Fallings from us, vanishings ;
    Blank misgivings of a creature

Moving about in worlds not realised,   145
High instincts before which our mortal nature
Did tremble like a guilty thing surprised :
    But for those first affections,
    Those shadowy recollections,
  Which, be they what they may,   150
Are yet the fountain light of all our day,
Are yet a master light of all our seeing ;
  Uphold us, cherish, and have power to make
Our noisy years seem moments in the being
Of the eternal silence : truths that wake,   155
    To perish never ;
Which neither listlessness, nor mad endeavour,
    Nor man nor boy,
Nor all that is at enmity with joy,
Can utterly abolish or destroy !   160
    Hence in a season of calm weather
      Though inland far we be,
Our souls have sight of that immortal sea
      Which brought us hither,
    Can in a moment travel thither,   165
And see the children sport upon the shore,
And hear the mighty waters rolling evermore.

.   X.

Then sing, ye birds, sing, sing a joyous song !
    And let the young lambs bound
    As to the tabor's sound ;   170
We in thought will join your throng,
    Ye that pipe and ye that play,
    Ye that through your hearts to-day
    Feel the gladness of the May !
What though the radiance which was once so bright 175
Be now for ever taken from my sight,
    Though nothing can bring back the hour
Of splendour in the grass, of glory in the flower ;

We will grieve not, rather find
Strength in what remains behind ;   180
In the primal sympathy
Which having been must ever be ;
In the soothing thoughts that spring
Out of human suffering ;
In the faith that looks through death,   185
In years that bring the philosophic mind.

XI.

And O, ye fountains, meadows, hills, and groves,
Forebode not any severing of our loves !
Yet in my heart of hearts I feel your might ;
I only have relinquished one delight,   190
To live beneath your more habitual sway.
I love the brooks which down their channels fret,
Even more than when I tripped lightly as they ;
The innocent brightness of a new-born day
        Is lovely yet ;   195
The clouds that gather round the setting sun
Do take a sober colouring from an eye
That hath kept watch o'er man's mortality ;
Another race hath been, and other palms are won.
Thanks to the human heart by which we live,   200
Thanks to its tenderness, its joys, and fears,
To me the meanest flower that blows can give
Thoughts that do often lie too deep for tears.

NOTES TO PART I.

LINES WRITTEN IN EARLY SPRING.

INTRODUCTION.

COMPOSED in 1798 and first published in the same year.

Wordsworth tells us that these lines were written while he was sitting by the side of the brook that runs through the grounds of Alfoxden. "The brook," he continues, "ran down a sloping rock, so as to make a waterfall, ... and across the pool below had fallen a tree ... from which rose perpendicularly boughs in search of the light intercepted by the deep shade above. The boughs bore leaves of green, that for want of sunshine had faded into almost lily-white; and from the under side of this natural sylvan bridge depended long and beautiful tresses of ivy, which waved gently in the breeze, that might, poetically speaking, be called the breath of the waterfall. The motion varied of course in proportion to the power of water in the brook." The holly grove in Alfoxden dell was a trysting-place of Wordsworth, Coleridge, and their friends, and of all the localities round Alfoxden, is the one chiefly associated with Wordsworth.

NOTES.

2. a grove. See Introduction.

3, 4. when ... mind. His happy communings with Nature bring with them a touch of pensive sadness, and thus lead on to the thought of the next stanza.

5-8. To her fair ... of man. While I beheld the beauty and happy order of Nature around me and felt all my sympathies drawn out towards her, I realized with the greater vividness the misery and disorder that man, by the treatment of his fellow-man, has introduced into the world.

8. **What man** etc. Cf. Burns, *Man was made to Mourn*, 55, 56:
" Man's inhumanity to man
Makes countless thousands mourn."

6. **that through me ran**, that filled or permeated me.

10. **The periwinkle** (Lat. *pervinca*, from *vincire*, to bind) is a plant with a rich blue flower and trailing stem covered with glossy green leaves. It is found in moist woodland spots.

11, 12. **every flower ... breathes.** Cf. the *Laws of Manu*, i. 49 : " Vegetables, as well as animals, have internal consciousness, and are sensible of pleasure and pain." In *The Excursion*, i. 189, the poet speaks of " the pure delight of love " diffused by " the silent looks of happy things."

17. **their fan.** The twigs expand from the branches in the form of a fan, so as to secure the greatest amount of air.

19. **do all I can**, in spite of anything to the contrary ; I cannot help thinking.

21-24. See note to ll. 5-8 above.

"THERE WAS A BOY."

INTRODUCTION.

COMPOSED in 1798, in Germany ; and first published in *Lyrical Ballads* in 1800. The lines are included in *The Prelude* (Book v. 364-397). " The Prelude, or, Growth of a Poet's Mind : an Autobiographical Poem " was commenced in 1799 and finished in 1805, but was not published till 1850.

The grave of this ' immortal boy ' cannot be identified. His name, and everything about him except what is here recorded, is unknown ; but he was, in all likelihood, a school companion of Wordsworth at Hawkshead. Wordsworth says : " This practice of making an instrument of their own fingers is known to most boys, though some are more skilful at it than others. William Raincock of Rayrigg, a fine spirited lad, took the lead of all my schoolfellows in this art."

NOTES.

2. **Winander.** ' Windermere ' is a contraction of ' Winander mere.' It is the largest lake in England, and is renowned for its beauty. It lies on the borders of Lancashire and Westmoreland.

3. **earliest stars**, the stars that first appear in the evening sky.

7-9. **hands Pressed ... Uplifted.** Absolute clauses ; ' both hands being pressed ' etc.

10. **mimic hootings.** Owls hoot or "whoop" on a note, a deep A flat, and will readily answer a good imitator of their tone.

15. **concourse wild**, a confused mixture or conglomeration.

17. **baffled his best skill.** When the owls ceased to respond to his "mimic hootings," though he tried his best to induce them.

18. **hung**, remained in suspense.

19. **a gentle shock** etc. The boy, while listening in silence for the owls, was suddenly and deeply impressed by the roar of the cataracts or by the still beauty of the scenery, which came upon him unawares, a new and unexpected revelation to ear and eye. Cf. *Influence of Natural Objects*, 86-88 :

" While far-distant hills
Into the tumult sent an alien sound
Of melancholy not unnoticed."

And *The Prelude*, ii. 342-352, where Wordsworth says that not seldom he
" sate among the woods
Alone upon some jutting eminence,
At the first gleam of dawn-light.
.   .   .   .
Oft in these moments such a holy calm
Would overspread my soul, that bodily eyes
Were utterly forgotten, and what I saw
Appeared like something in myself, a dream,
A prospect in the mind."

And *Ib.* i. 581-588 :
" Thus oft amid those fits of vulgar joy
.   .   .   .   even then I felt
Gleams like the flashing of a shield ;—the earth
And common face of Nature spake to me
Rememberable things."

23. **imagery**, shapes, features.

24, 25. **uncertain heaven ... steady lake.** The sky, vague and indistinct in the twilight, is seen reflected in the still waters of the lake below. Coleridge, writing to Wordsworth, says of this passage, "I should have recognized it anywhere ; and had I met these lines, running wild in the deserts of Arabia, I should have instantly screamed out ' Wordsworth ' ! "

26. **mates**, school-mates, companions.

29. **hangs.** Its situation is so lofty that it almost seems as if it were suspended in the air.

30. **the village-school.** Hawkshead Grammar School, which Wordsworth attended for eight years (1778-1786).

32. I believe. "This qualification," writes Mr. Turner, "is very Wordsworthian, and illustrates at once a power and a weakness in his work—the power of his love of truth, the weakness of a self-possession which can never forget itself, and often leads him to an inartistic description of irrelevant or prosaic details." Cf. a similar qualification in *Nutting*, 48, 49.

NUTTING.

INTRODUCTION.

COMPOSED in 1799, in Germany; and first published in 1800. The poet intended these lines to form part of *The Prelude*, but struck them out as not being wanted there.

He says: "Like most of my schoolfellows I was an impassioned Nutter. For this pleasure, the Vale of Esthwaite, abounding in coppice wood, furnished a very wide range. These verses arose out of the remembrance of feelings I had often had when a boy."

NOTES.

3. heavenly ... die, a day so beautiful that it can never be forgotten.

5. our cottage threshold, the house at which Wordsworth boarded during the time he was at Hawkshead School.

7. A nutting crook (being) in hand. An absolute clause.

8. figure, in apposition to " I " in l. 5.

quaint. The present meaning of *quaint* (O.F. *coint*, Lat. *cognitus*, known) may be traced thus: (1) famous; (2) clever; (3) ingenious; (4) fanciful, odd. Cf. *couth* in *uncouth*.

9. Tricked ... weeds, drest up in fine fashion in old, worn-out clothes. *Weed*, a garment, as in 'widow's weeds,' is from O.E. *wǽd*, from the same root as *weave*. But *weed*, a useless plant, is from O.E. *weód*.

10. for that service, for use on a nutting expedition.

12. Motley accoutrement, a fantastic garb made up of clothes of different colours and materials. *Motley* and *mottled* are both from O.F. *mattelé*, 'curdled,' 'clotted,' and so 'spotted.'

12, 13. of power to smile At, able to defy (because it could not be made more ragged than it was).

21. virgin, unsullied (cf. l. 47), untouched, fresh. Cf. 'a *virgin* fortress,' a fortress that has never been captured. And p. 58.

22. suppression of the heart, repression of the feelings (of delight).

23, 24. wise restraint Voluptuous. This phrase is really a repetition of the previous one, with the addition of the epithet 'wise.' The restraint was wise because it added to his pleasure. For *voluptuous*, cf. "when pleasure loves to pay Tribute to *ease*" (ll. 39, 40).

27. A temper, a mood, a state of feeling. *Temper* is in apposition to the description contained in ll. 21-26.

31. five seasons. *Five* is indefinite. It might be a place so secluded as to be unvisited by any human being for five years together.

33. fairy water-breaks, miniature waves or eddies in the stream, where the brook murmured over the stones. Cf. Tennyson, *The Brook*, 61 :

"With many a silvery *waterbreak*."

36. fleeced. The grey moss, like a fleece, covered the tops of the boulders, which (continuing the image) he compares in the next line to a "flock of sheep." Scattered stones in Wiltshire are called 'grey wethers.' Cf. *roches moutonées,* 'sheep-shaped rocks,' a geological term for rocks rounded by glaciers.

38. the murmur and the murmuring sound. The repetition is an endeavour metrically to represent the ceaseless, monotonous sound of the falling water. Similarly Tennyson, *The Princess*, Canto vii. 206, 207 :

"The moan of doves in immemorial elms,
And murmuring of innumerable bees."

39, 40. when pleasure ... ease, 'when we prefer taking our ease to actively enjoying ourselves.' The active pleasure of gathering the nuts is willingly foregone for the passive pleasure of idly contemplating the scene.

40. secure, sure ; confident in the possession of its joy.

41. luxuriates ... things, 'takes its fill of things that are outside the range of its present feelings.' The boy, sure of the delight of gathering the nuts, temporarily allows his mind to wander to objects that do not concern him. *Indifferent* is used of both persons and things : I may be indifferent to a matter, or a matter may be indifferent to me.

42. Wasting etc. Leaving the matter in hand, it unnecessarily expends its kindly feelings upon extraneous objects.

43. Then up I rose etc. Note the emphatic contrast, both in sense and rhythm, of these lines to the preceding.

47, 48. patiently ... being. Like a victim meekly yielding to the executioner, the bower is represented as unresisting giving itself up to the will of the ravager. This is only one of numerous

G

instances of Wordsworth's attribution of human feelings to natural objects. Cf. *Lines Written in Early Spring*, 11, 12, and note.

48. **unless** etc., 'unless I mistake my present feelings for what I felt then.' For the qualification introduced here, see "*There was a boy*," 32, and note.

53. **silent trees ... intruding sky.** The silent, unresisting trees seemed mutely to reproach him, as well as the sight of the sky peering through the gaps he had made in the broken boughs.

54. **dearest maiden,** his sister Dorothy.

55. **with gentle hand.** Cf. *Humanity*, 105-110 :

> " There are to whom the garden, grove, and field
> Perpetual lessons of forbearance yield ;
> Who would not lightly violate the grace
> The lowliest flower possesses in its place ;
> Nor shorten the sweet life, too fugitive,
> Which nothing less than Infinite Power could give."

56. **a spirit.** For Wordsworth, one divine spirit was diffused through the whole realm of Nature and Man. Cf. *Tintern Abbey*, 100-102 :

> "A motion and a spirit, that impels
> All thinking things, all objects of all thought,
> And rolls through all things."

LUCY.

INTRODUCTION.

THIS and the two following "Lucy" poems were composed at Goslar, in Germany, in 1799, and this and the third were first published in 1800, the second being first published in 1807. Who Lucy was is as unknown as who was the boy of Windermere in "*There was a boy.*"

NOTES.

I.

2. **Dove.** The river Dove is a tributary of the Trent, and with it forms the boundary line between the counties of Derby and Stafford. There is also a small stream of that name in Yorkshire.

II.

22. **The joy of my desire,** the delight of the passion of love.

23. **her wheel**, *i.e.* her spinning-wheel. Till the invention of the spinning jenny in 1767, cotton spinning was performed by the hand spinning-wheel, and was a common occupation for women. Cf. Rogers, *A Wish*, 11, 12 :

> "And Lucy, at her *wheel*, shall sing
> In russet gown and apron blue."

III.

29, 30. **A slumber ... fears.** My mind became insensible to outward events ; fears of death or loss that haunt mankind were gone.

31. **She** is, of course, Lucy.

32. **The touch** etc., the change and decay that Time brings with it.

35, 36. **Rolled ... trees.** She has ceased to have any individual existence, and has become merged in the sublime, impersonal grandeur of nature—the great revolving globe of Earth. Cf. Milton, *Lycidas*, 154-158 :

> "Ay me ! whilst thee the shores, and sounding seas
> Wash far away, where'er thy bones are hurled ;
> Whether beyond the stormy Hebrides,
> Where thou perhaps under the whelming tide
> Visit'st the bottom of the monstrous world."

For a similar, though contrasted, thought, cf. Tennyson's "*Move eastward, happy earth.*"

HART-LEAP WELL.

INTRODUCTION.

COMPOSED at Town-end, Grasmere, in 1800, and first published in the same year. "The first eight stanzas," Wordsworth tells us (1843), "were composed extempore one winter evening in the cottage, when, after having tired myself with labouring at an awkward passage in *The Brothers*, I started with a sudden impulse to this to get rid of the other, and finished it in a day or two. My sister and I had passed the place a few weeks before in our wild winter journey (Dec. 1799) from Sock-burn (Yorkshire) on the banks of the Tees to Grasmere. A peasant, whom we met near the spot, told us the story so far as concerned the name of the Well, and the Hart, and pointed out the Stones. Both the stones and the well are objects that may easily be missed. The tradition by this time (1843) may be extinct in the neighbourhood. The man who related it to us was very old."

"Hart-Leap Well," wrote Wordsworth in 1800, "is a small spring of water, about five miles from Richmond in Yorkshire. ... Its name is derived from a remarkable chace, the memory of which is preserved by the monuments spoken of in the second Part of the following Poem, which monuments do now exist as I have there described them." But, in 1881, the "three aspens" and the "three pillars" had disappeared; though the water still fell into the "cup of stone," and the place—a barren moor for miles around—retained the "doleful" aspect depicted in the poem.

NOTES.

1. **Wensley** is a village on the river Ure, in the north-westerly region of Yorkshire.

2. **With ... cloud.** Cf. *Resolution and Independence*, 75 :
    "Motionless as a cloud the old man stood."
Wordsworth is fond of cloud similes; cf. *The Daffodils*, 1 ; *Rob Roy's Grave*, 91.

13. **A rout,** 'a troop or crowd of people.' The notion of *disorder* attaching to the word in this sense connects it with its primary meaning of 'a defeat' (Lat. *rupta*, broken).

27. **it looks not** etc. A chase in which a hart is pursued by a single lonely horseman seems something weird and supernatural.

33. **a thorn.** Cf. l. 153 below. It appears, however, that the tree was not a Thorn but a Lime.

38. **his dumb partner,** his horse.

39. **yeaned,** brought forth. Cf. *yeanling*, a new-born lamb.

40. **cleaving,** piercing, driving.

46. This line expresses Sir Walter's, not the writer's, thought.

50. **Four roods,** *i.e.* 22 yards. Wordsworth wrote originally 'Nine roods.'

   sheer means lit. 'shining, bright,' and so 'clear, unbroken, abrupt.'

51. **several,** separate, distinct. Cf. l. 67 below.

61. **cunning,** knowing, skilful. Cf. *can* and *ken*. 'Crafty' is a later meaning.

63. **the same.** One of Wordsworth's favourite prosaisms, like "in course of time," l. 93 below. Cf. *Rob Roy's Grave*, 118 ; *The Affliction of Margaret*, 5.

70. **paramour** was originally an adverbial phrase, Fr. *par amour*, 'with love,' 'as a lover'; then, 'a lover, a mistress'; now used only in a bad sense.

75, 76. Swale .. Ure. Two tributaries of the Yorkshire Ouse, between which lies Wensley Moor (l. 1).

81. Ere thrice ... steered, before the moon had completed three of her voyages, *i.e.* within three months' time. The expression seems somewhat far-fetched. We speak of the moon as 'sailing' through the sky, and the crescent moon is sometimes compared to a boat.

97. The moving accident. A reminiscence of Shakspere, *Othello*, I. iii. 134, 135 :

"Wherein I spake of most disastrous chances,
Of *moving accidents* by flood and field."

Moving means 'affecting, pathetic.' Cf. Coleridge, *Love*, st. 6 :
"I sang an old and *moving* story."

98. To freeze the blood, to excite terror. Cf. 'to make the blood run cold,' 'a blood-curdling tale.'

101. Hawes ... Richmond. Hawes stands on the Ure, 15 miles due west of Wensley (l. 1) ; while Richmond, on the Swale, is about 10 miles north of that place.

103-107. Three aspens ... three pillars. See Introduction.

109. arms nor head, branches nor leaves on top. Cf. Ben Jonson :

"Trees have got their *heads*,
The fields their coats."

110. Half wasted, *i.e.* was half wasted or desolated.

117. I stood ... lost. Cf. "*Beloved Vale! I said*," 9 :

"By doubts and thousand petty fancies crost
I stood."

126. Some say etc. The trees were so completely decayed that it was difficult to name them.

129. The arbour ... tell. The aspect of the arbour shows what its present state is.

138. blood cries out for blood. Cf. Bible, *Genesis*, iv. 8 : "The voice of thy brother's *blood crieth* unto me from the ground." And *Brougham Castle*, 27 : "Earth helped him with the *cry* of *blood*."

153. thorn. Cf. l. 33 above, and note.

156. furlong means lit. "furrow-long" (O.E. *furh*, a furrow).

163, 164. This beast ... divine. Cf. Bible, *Matthew*, x. 29 : "Are not two sparrows sold for a farthing? And not one of them shall fall on the ground without your Father."

165. The Being etc. Cf. General Introduction.

171. **But Nature** etc.   Cf. *The White Doe of Rylstone*, 117-119:
> "The gentler work begun
> By Nature, softening and concealing,
> And busy with a hand of healing."

174-176. **She leaves ... overgrown.**   The slow decay of these objects is nature's warning to man against similar acts of cruelty; but when he has learnt the lesson of kindness to dumb animals, these sad memorials will be overgrown and concealed from view.

176. **These monuments ... overgrown.**   Cf. Sonnet *Composed among the Ruins of a Castle in North Wales*, 9-14:
> "Wreck of forgotten wars,
> To winds abandoned and the prying stars,
> Time *loves* thee ! at his call the Seasons twine
> Luxuriant wreaths around thy forehead hoar;
> And, though past pomp no changes can restore,
> A soothing recompense, his gift, is thine !"

178. **what she shows, and what conceals,** what she shows of her beauty (see l. 172), and what she conceals or covers by her growth (see l. 176).

THE SPARROW'S NEST.

INTRODUCTION.

COMPOSED in the orchard, Town-end, Grasmere, in 1801, and first published in 1807 in the series entitled "Moods of my own Mind."

Wordsworth says: "At the end of the garden of my father's house at Cockermouth was a high terrace that commanded a fine view of the river Derwent and Cockermouth Castle. This was our favourite playground. The terrace wall, a low one, was covered with closely-clipt privet and roses, which gave an almost impervious shelter to birds who built their nests there. The latter of these stanzas alludes to one of those nests."

The poet refers to this poem in *A Farewell*, written in the following year, where among "the tales of years gone by" he mentions (ll. 55, 56) that
> "In this bush our sparrow built her nest,
> Of which I sang one song that will not die."

NOTES.

5. **I started** etc.   I was stirred at the sight of this nest, because it reminded me of that other one which my sister and I used to visit.

8. **My father's house.** See Introduction.

in wet or dry (weather). Cf. *Lucy Gray*, st. 16: "O'er *rough* and *smooth* she trips along."

9. **My sister Emmeline.** The poet's only sister, Dorothy. In the MS. sent originally to the printer the line was "My sister Dorothy and I." The name "Emmeline" occurs again in *To a Butterfly*; see note to *To a Butterfly*, 14-17.

11. **She looked** etc. A similar "delicate fear" is recorded of her in *To a Butterfly*, 16-18:

> "I followed on from brake to bush;
> But she, God love her, feared to brush
> The dust from off its wings."

12. **Dreading, tho' wishing.** The reading of 1807 seems superior: "Still wishing, dreading to be near it."

13. **heart,** tenderness of disposition.

being then etc., though she was then only a little child.

19. **A heart...tears,** *i.e.* a heart sensitive and sympathetic. Wordsworth refers to this poem in *The Prelude*, xiv. 233-235:

> "Child of my parents! Sister of my soul!
> Thanks in sincerest verse have been elsewhere
> Poured out for all the early tenderness
> Which I from thee imbibed."

TO THE CUCKOO.

INTRODUCTION.

THE date of the composition of this poem is usually given as 1804, a date assigned it by Wordsworth himself for some years. But two entries in Dorothy Wordsworth's Journal, under March 1802, in which it is mentioned that her brother was "working at *The Cuckoo*," show that the poem belongs to the year 1802, though it may have been recast in 1804. It was first published in 1807.

The cuckoo seems to have been Wordsworth's favourite among the birds (see *The Solitary Reaper*, 13, note), and is as famous in his song as the skylark in Shelley's, or the nightingale in Keats's.

In his preface to the edition of 1815 Wordsworth quotes the two lines

> "Shall I call thee bird,
> Or but a wandering voice?"

as an instance of the exercise of the imagination, and writes: "This concise interrogation characterizes the seeming ubiquity of the voice of the cuckoo, and dispossesses the creature almost of a corporeal existence; the Imagination being tempted to this exertion of her power by a consciousness in the memory that the cuckoo is almost perpetually heard throughout the season of spring, but seldom becomes an object of sight."

NOTES.

1. new-comer. The cuckoo is a migratory bird (see *The Solitary Reaper*, 16, note) and his note is first heard in England in the Spring.

I have heard, I have listened to thee in my boyhood; cf. st. 5.

3. shall I call thee bird. Cf. Shelley, *To a Skylark*, 1, 2:

"Hail to thee, blithe spirit!
Bird thou never wert."

4. a wandering voice. See Introduction. Similarly to Shelley (*ib.*) the skylark was "an unbodied joy." The well-known phrase *Vox et praeterea nihil*, 'A voice and nothing more,' was originally used of the nightingale, because its voice is its main attraction. The poet calls the cuckoo a 'voice,' since, though often heard, it is seldom seen. The cuckoo keeps out of sight, being of a shy, unsocial nature. When seen, too, smaller birds have a way of pursuing the cuckoo, as if he were the hawk he resembles.

6. twofold shout, cry consisting of two notes (*ku-ku*). Cf. *To the Cuckoo*, 3, 4:

"Like the first summons, cuckoo! of thy bill,
With its *twin notes* inseparably paired."

In all known languages the name of the bird is imitative of the sound it makes.

7, 8. In the edition of 1827 Wordsworth altered these lines into

"That seems to fill the whole air's space
As loud far off as near,"

"to record," he said, "a fact observed by himself." At a friend's remonstrance, however, he subsequently restored the present reading.

12. visionary hours, the time of my boyhood when the world seemed imaginary and unreal to me. Cf. st. 8, and *Intimations of Immortality*, 1-5:

'There was a time when meadow, grove, and stream,
The earth, and every common sight,
To me did seem
Apparelled in celestial light,
The glory and the freshness of a dream."

14. **Even yet**, even now that I am a man, and those visionary hours are left behind.

15. **an invisible thing.** See note to l. 4.

27. **beget** etc., reproduce, bring back that old happy time. Cf. *Intimations of Immortality*, 161-164 :

> " Hence in a season of calm weather,
> Though inland far we be,
> Our souls have sight of that immortal sea
> Which brought us hither."

29. **the earth we pace**, the familiar, solid earth.

31. **unsubstantial.** Cf. note to l. 12, and *Intimations of Immortality*, 141-145 :

> " Obstinate questionings
> Of sense and outward things,
>
> . . . . . .
>
> Blank misgivings of a creature
> Moving about in worlds not realized."

32. **for thee,** *i.e.* for thee who art a visionary bird, " a voice, a mystery " (l. 16).

THE REDBREAST CHASING THE BUTTERFLY.

INTRODUCTION.

COMPOSED on April 18, 1802, in the orchard, Town-end, Grasmere, where the incident described was observed by the author ; and first published in 1807. In Dorothy Wordsworth's Journal, under date "Sunday, 18th" we find : "A mild grey morning with rising vapours. We sate in the orchard. William wrote the poem on the Robin and the Butterfly.... W. met me at Rydal with the conclusion of the poem to the Robin. I read it to him in bed. We left out some lines."

The Greek elegiac poet, Euenus, has a charming epigram, in which he similarly remonstrates with a nightingale for preying upon a cicala—the pursuit of one winged songster by another. Cowper's *The Nightingale and the Glowworm* may also be compared with this piece. Among Wordsworth's poems three others celebrate the redbreast : *The Redbreast, To a Redbreast*, and " *I know an aged man constrained to dwell.*"

NOTES.

2. **The pious bird.** See l. 38 below, and cf. Cowley :

> " Robin Redbreasts whom men praise
> For *pious birds*."

In the edition of 1807 the line "Our consecrated Robin !" occurred between ll. 20 and 21 below. The robin has these titles on account of his share in the story referred to in those lines. See note to them, and cf. Gay, *Pastoral* vi. :

> "Their little corpse the robin-redbreast found,
> And strewed with *pious* bill the leaves around."

6, 7. Peter...Thomas. The names by which the bird is known in the countries mentioned. Cf. *The Redbreast*, 58, 59 :

> "Thrice happy creature ! in all lands
> Nurtured by hospitable hands."

6. Boors, peasants. *Boor* means lit. 'a tiller of the soil' (O. E. *búan*, to till), and occurs in 'neigh*bour*.'

12. Could Father Adam etc. In allusion to *Paradise Lost*, xi. 185-203, where Adam points out to Eve the ominous sign of the eagle chasing "two birds of gayest plume," and the gentle hart and hind pursued by the lion.

21-23. That, after...wood. The reference is to the story of The Children in the Wood. The master of Wayland Hall, Norfolk, on his deathbed left his two little ones to the care of their uncle, who was to inherit their property if they died. The children were left in a wood by a ruffian who had been hired to murder them. They died of exposure, and pitying robins came and covered them over with strawberry leaves.

21 bewildering, losing their way. *Bewilder* means lit. 'to lead into a wilderness,' *wilder* being a shortened form of *wildern*, 'a wilderness,' from O. E. *wilder*, a *wild deer* or animal.

23 So painfully, with so much pains or toil. For *painful* in the unusual sense of 'laborious,' cf. Milton, *Par. Lost*, iii. 452 : "painful superstition."

30. in-door sadness. Because the robin appears on our window-sills in the dull, gloomy days of winter.

37. Would'st thou be, *i.e.* if thou would'st be.

TO A BUTTERFLY.

INTRODUCTION.

COMPOSED on April 20, 1802, in the orchard, Town-end, Grasmere, and first published in 1807. Cf. Dorothy Wordsworth's Journal, April 20, 1802 : "William wrote a conclusion to the poem of *The Butterfly*," probably in reference to the poet's previous poem with the same title, written on March 14 of the same year. Both poems refer to the "sweet summer days" of childhood.

NOTES.

5, 6. not...motionless, *i.e.* frozen seas are not more motionless.

. **11. My trees** etc. Some of the trees in the orchard at Dove Cottage were planted by the poet, and many of the flowers by his sister.

13. a sanctuary, a place of refuge, a sacred asylum. From the time of Constantine churches afforded protection to fugitives from the hand of justice. In London the privilege of sanctuary (for debtors) was finally abolished in 1697.

14-17. Come often ... young. Cf. *To a Butterfly*, 5-13:

> "Float near me; do not yet depart!
> Dead times revive in thee.
> .   .   .   .   .   .
> Oh! pleasant, pleasant were the days,
> The time, when, in our childish plays,
> My sister Emmeline and I
> Together chased the butterfly!"

TO THE SMALL CELANDINE.

INTRODUCTION.

COMPOSED on April 30, 1802, at Town-end, Grasmere, and first published in 1807.

Wordsworth says: "It is remarkable that this flower, coming out so early in the spring as it does, and so bright and beautiful, and in such profusion, should not have been noticed earlier in English verse. What adds much to the interest that attends it is its habit of shutting itself up and opening out according to the degree of light and temperature of the air." Dorothy Wordsworth's Journal, April 30, 1802, has: "We came into the orchard directly after breakfast, and sat there. The lake was calm, the sky cloudy. William began to write the poem of *The Celandine* ... I walked backwards and forwards with William. He repeated his poem to me, then he got to work again, and would not give over." Wordsworth wrote a second poem on the same subject on May 1 following, and a third in 1804.

NOTES.

1. kingcups. The name given to a species of crowfoot or buttercup.

8. celandine. The pilewort or lesser celandine (to distinguish it from the *chelidonium majus* or greater celandine) is a flower of the crowfoot tribe, with yellow star-shaped blossoms and shining green leaves. It opens only on bright days, and closes its flowers at dusk.

12. keep a mighty rout, make a great bustle; are full of excitement over their discovery of a new star. Cf. l. 15 below. For *rout*, see *Hart-leap Well*, 13, note.

17. an elf, a little spirit or creature. Cf. l. 42 below.

18. lavish of thyself. Cf. Introduction and ll. 29, 30 below.

28. with half a call, at the slightest inducement; willingly.

31. Telling ... sun, giving notice of the approach of spring. See l. 40 below.

36. wanton wooers, loose, general lovers; men who praise one flower after another, without being constant to any.

41. Comfort etc. Be comforted as regards thy merit; do not think that thou art neglected because thou deservest it.

50. Children etc. Who flaunt themselves in the bright sunshine of spring and summer; whereas thou appearest "when we've little warmth or none" (l. 31).

57. Prophet etc., harbinger of the joys of spring.

59. a mighty band, the coming multitude of flowers, of which thou art the forerunner.

61. Serving ... command, ready to appear when I desire thy presence.

62. Tasks ... renewing, *i.e.* freely and readily opening and shutting thy blossoms from day to day. "Tasks that are no tasks" is like Sophocles's μήτηρ ἀμήτωρ, 'mother that is no mother' (*El.* 1154), ἄδωρα δῶρα, 'gifts that are no gifts' (*Ajax,* 665).

COMPOSED UPON WESTMINSTER BRIDGE.

INTRODUCTION.

COMPOSED on July 31, 1802, and first published in 1807.

On July 31 Wordsworth left London for Dover, on his way to Calais, and this sonnet was written as he travelled towards Dover. Dorothy Wordsworth's Journal has: "Left London between five and six o'clock of the morning outside the Dover coach. A beautiful morning. The city, St. Paul's, with the river—a multitude of little boats, made a beautiful sight as we crossed

Westminster Bridge ; the houses not overhung by their clouds of smoke, and were hung out endlessly ; yet the sun shone so brightly, with such a pure light, that there was something like the purity of one of Nature's own grand spectacles." A passage from a letter by Mr. R. Spence Watson may be given in illustration of this sonnet : " Many years ago I chanced to be passing over Waterloo Bridge at half-past three on a lovely June morning. It was broad daylight, and I was alone. Never when alone in the remotest recesses of the Alps, with nothing around me but the mountains, or upon the plains of Africa, alone with the wonderful glory of the southern night, have I seen anything to approach the solemnity—the soothing solemnity—of the city, sleeping under the early sun :

> ' Earth has not anything to show more fair.'

How simply, yet how perfectly, Wordsworth has interpreted it ! "

Westminster Bridge crosses the Thames in the neighbourhood of Westminster Abbey, the Houses of Parliament, and Whitehall.

Notes.

4. like a garment. A frequent Biblical image ; see *Psalms,* civ. 2 : " Who coverest thyself with light as with a garment." Cf. *Intimations of Immortality,* 4 : " *Apparelled* in celestial light."

5. bare, clear, distinct, undimmed by smoke ; see l. 18 below. Cf. *London, 1802,* 11, and note.

6. temples is used as indicating a less narrow and more general notion than *churches.*

7. Open etc. London, as he sees its outspread panorama in its early morning brightness and purity, seems to him at one with the silent beauty of the nature he loves. In its midday smoke and noise, London is cut off from all community with the green fields around and the blue sky above.

12. The river is, of course, the Thames, as the "city" (l. 4) is London.

at his own sweet will, with the repose that is natural to it ; undisturbed by oar or paddle-wheel.

13. Dear God! an exclamation of strong feeling—here of mingled awe and wonder. Cf. note to *The Affliction of Margaret,* 61 ; and " *The world is too much with us,*" 9 : "*Great God. I'd rather be,*" etc.

14. that mighty heart, the energies and activities of the great city.

ON THE EXTINCTION OF THE VENETIAN REPUBLIC.

INTRODUCTION.

COMPOSED in August, 1802, and first published in 1807.   This, along with the sonnets *To the Men of Kent* (p. 27) and *Thought of a Briton on the Subjugation of Switzerland* (p. 34), Wordsworth included among the "Sonnets dedicated to Liberty," a title he subsequently (1845) changed to "Poems dedicated to National Independence and Liberty."

NOTES.

1. Once ... fee.   The Venetians assisted the Franks of Syria in the reduction of the sea-coast, and shared with them the sovereignty of Tyre.   Afterwards, in 1202, they joined the French in the fourth crusade, and, under the leadership of the Doge Dandolo, twice besieged and captured Constantinople, then a Greek city.   The conquerors divided the Greek empire among them, Venice receiving three-eighths of the conquered city, together with Roumania and parts of Greece and Thessaly, and many of the Byzantine cities.   Cf. Byron, *Childe Harold*, iv. 2 :

> "Her daughters had their dowers
> From spoils of nations, and the exhaustless East
> Pour'd in her lap all gems in sparkling showers."

"The gorgeous East" occurs in Milton, *Par. Lost*, ii. 3.

in fee, in possession.   *Fee* is O.E. *feoh*, cattle, property. Cf. Spenser, *Faery Queene*, VI. x. 21 :

> "All those Ladies, which thou sawest late,
> Are Venus Damzels, all within her *fee.*"

And Milton, *Sonnet VII.* 6, 7 :

> "Latona's twin-born progeny (Apollo and Diana),
> Which after held the sun and moon in *fee.*"

2. the safeguard of the West.   Owing to her naval power and great wealth, Venice took a prominent part in the crusades, and powerfully resisted the encroachments of the Turks, whom she helped to defeat at Lepanto in 1571, and whom she worsted in sea fights at Scio and in the Dardanelles a hundred years later. Cf. Byron, *Childe Harold*, iv. 14, who calls her "Europe's bulwark 'gainst the Ottomite."

4. the eldest child of Liberty.   When Attila invaded Italy, A.D. 452, Venice was founded by families who fled before the invader from the mainland to the chain of islands at the head of the Adriatic.   There they gradually coalesced into a republic, and, lying on the verge of two empires, the Latin and the Greek, "the Venetians exult in the belief of primitive and perpetual independence," and "the freedom of domestic government was fortified by the independence of foreign dominion" (Gibbon).

5. **a maiden city**, a city that had never been conquered; cf. 'a *maiden* fortress.' Cf. *Nutting*, 21, and note.

8. **She must ... sea.** Pope Alexander III., in return for the services rendered him by Venice in 1177 against the German emperor, presented the Doge Liani with a ring, with which he told him to wed the Adriatic, that posterity might know that the sea was subject to Venice, "as a bride is to her husband." This "marriage" was celebrated annually, the ring being dropt into the sea at a great state ceremonial. Cf. Byron, *Childe Harold*, iv. 11:

" The spouseless Adriatic mourns her lord ;
And, annual marriage now no more renew'd—"

9. **And what if etc.** In 1797 the troops of Napoleon occupied Venice, and on October 17 he concluded the treaty of Campo Formio with Austria, which extinguished the old Venetian Republic. Austria received Istria, Dalmatia, and Venice itself; while the rest of her territory and the Ionian islands were annexed to the Cisalpine Republic. When the ex-doge Luigi Manin was to take the oath of allegiance to Austria, he fell senseless to the ground. In 1866 Venetia was finally transferred to Italy. Cf Shelley, *Euganean Hills* (Oct. 1818):

" Sun-girt City, thou hast been
.Ocean's child, and then his queen ;
Now is come a darker day."

12. **her long life.** The Venetian Republic under the Doges or Dukes dates from 697 to 1797, or 1100 years.

13. **Men are we etc.** Cf. Terence, *The Self-Tormentor*, I. i. 25: *Homo sum* : *humani nil a. me alienum puto*, ' I am a man, and nothing that concerns man do I deem a matter of indifference to me.' Also Vergil, i. 462: *Sunt lacrimæ rerum et mentem mortalia tangunt*, "the sense of tears in mortal things," and *Laodamia*, 163-165:

" Tears to human suffering are due ;
And mortal hopes defeated and o'erthrown
Are mourned by man."

the shade. The power of Venice reached its height at the close of the 15th century. The discovery of America (1492) and of the Cape passage to India (1497) much decreased her commerce, and after the beginning of the 16th century her greatness gradually declined. She was nearly ruined by the League of Cambray in 1508.

LONDON, 1802.

INTRODUCTION.

COMPOSED in September 1802, and first published in 1807.

The state of England in 1802 was one that might well fill a nature like Wordsworth's with dismay. The wealth of the country had greatly increased, but so had the population; the rate of wages was thus kept down, and the rise in the price of wheat, owing to the war, while it enriched the landowner and the farmer, terribly impoverished the labouring classes. The amount of the poor-rate was doubled, and with the increase of poverty came the increase of crime. "It is indeed from these fatal years that we must date that war of classes, that social severance between employers and employed, which still forms the main difficulty of English politics" (Green's *History of the English People*). In politics it was an age of coalitions and time-serving expedients; there was little or no progressive movement, rather a reaction. In 1785 Pitt had been compelled by the selfish opposition of trading members of the House of Commons to abandon his wise and liberal measures for giving Ireland commercial freedom; and in the same year his motion for Reform, involving the disfranchisement of thirty-six rotten boroughs, was thrown out by a large majority. Two other parliamentary Reform Bills, in 1793 and 1797, met with still less success, and in 1801 the failure of Pitt's measure for the Relief of the Catholics caused his resignation, and the succession of the feeble Addington ministry. In 1797 occurred the Mutinies in the fleet, at Spithead and at the Nore, and in 1802 the hollow and short-lived Peace of Amiens with Napoleon was signed, a treaty which was regarded by many as both mischievous and disgraceful.

Wordsworth has another sonnet, *Written in London, September 1802*, in the same strain. In reference to it, as well as to *London, 1802*, he says: "This was written immediately after my return from France to London, when I could not but be struck, as here described, with the vanity and parade of our own country, especially in great towns and cities, as contrasted with the quiet, and I may say the desolation, that the Revolution had produced in France. This must be borne in mind, or else the reader may think that in this and the succeeding Sonnets I have exaggerated the mischief engendered and fostered among us by undisturbed wealth." Wordsworth stayed in London from August 30 to September 22, 1802.

NOTES.

2, 3. a fen ... waters, *i.e.* men's hearts seem dull and dead to noble aims and efforts. Contrast the image in *Written in London, September 1802*, 5, 6, where "show" is stigmatized:

' We must run glittering like a brook
　In the open sunshine, or we are unblest.''

3-6. altar ... happiness. The Church, the Army, Literature,
the Family, and Society have lost what our fore-fathers of Milton's
day possessed—the happiness that is independent of mere outward things and that rests in the inner consciousness of duty
done.

3. pen perhaps includes the notion of all the learned pro-
fessions.

4. heroic wealth. *Wealth* is put for 'wealthy men,' so that
the heroic wealth of hall and bower means the wealthy upper
classes of noble lineage.

hall and bower. In the old castle the *hall* was the principal room, where meals were taken etc. ; the *bower* was the
inner apartment set aside for ladies. Hence in the older literature ' in hall and bower ' is used as equivalent to ' among both
lords and ladies.' Cf. Scott, *Lady of the Lake,* II. vi. 31, 32 :

"" For of his clan, in *hall* and *bower,*
　Young Malcolm Græme was held the flower."

7. raise us up etc. In his own day Milton was famous rather
as the literary champion of English liberty and the right of the
individual to think and act for himself than as a poet. As
Secretary to the Council of State he was at the centre of political
affairs, and as the author of *Areopagitica,* of *Defensio pro Populo
Anglicano* (" Defence for the People of England "), and of *Eikono-
clastes* (" Image-Breaker," a reply to the famous *Eikon Basilike,*
the " Kings Book "), he stamped his own strong personality
upon the minds and events of his time.

8. manners. The word is used in its higher sense of that
lofty independence and self-respect which guides our behaviour
towards others by what we feel is due to ourselves. Cf. the
old Winchester School motto, "*Manners* makyth man," and the
Lat. *mores.*

9. Thy soul ... apart. Milton's lofty personal character, and
his strong independence, coupled with his tenacious adherence to
his political beliefs, set him apart from the men of his time. In
the face of the wild Royalist enthusiasm of 1660 he alone refused
to be silent, and in his *Ready and Easy Way to Establish a
Free Commonwealth* he remained the ardent defender of a lost
cause.

10. Thou ... sea. The simile is justified by the power of his
arguments, the boldness of his utterance, and the majestic dignity
of his style.

11. the naked heavens, the clear unclouded firmament ; cf.
Intimations of Immortality, 13 : " When the heavens are bare " ;

H

and *bare* in *Westminster Bridge,* 5. *Pure* is in syntactical agree-
ment with *thou* in l. 6.

13. and yet, *i.e.* though thou wast so unique and majestic a
figure.

14. The lowliest duties. Upon his return to England in 1639
Milton occupied himself for seven years in teaching private pupils,
showing them "an example of hard study and spare diet."
Johnson's sneer at such "lowly duties," which he calls "vapour-
ing away his patriotism in a private boarding-school," will be
remembered. Cf. Milton's *Sonnet on his Blindness,* 14 : "They
also serve who only stand and wait."

TO THE DAISY.

INTRODUCTION.

COMPOSED in 1802, in the orchard, Town-end, Grasmere, and first
published in 1807. Wordsworth wrote two other poems on this
subject in the same year and in the same metre, and a third (an
elegy on his brother John), differing in metre, in 1805. The
poet characterizes these two as "overflowings of the mind in
composing the one which stands first." To this he prefixed the
following extract from Wither, *The Shepherd's Hunting,* Ecl. iv.
368-380 :

> "Her (his Muse's) divine skill taught me this,
> That from every thing I saw
> I could some invention draw,
> And raise pleasure to her height
> Through the meanest object's sight.
> By the murmur of a spring,
> Or the least bough's rustelling ;
> By a Daisy whose leaves spread
> Shut when Titan goes to bed ;
> Or a shady bush or tree ;
> She could more infuse in me
> Than all Nature's beauties can
> In some other wiser man."

NOTES.

3. again. Referring to the first poem, *To the Daisy* ; see
Introduction.

7. And yet etc., *i.e.* thou art beautiful to those who love thee.

9. **dappled**, spotted with daisies. *Dapple* is Norwegian *depel*, a pool, a splash of water or other liquid.

11. **through all degrees.** Thus the type or analogue is at one time a queen (l. 21), at another, a starveling (l. 22).

13. **fond and idle**, foolish and vain.

25. **cyclops.** Greek for 'round-eyed,' the name of a giant in Greek legend with a single circular eye in the middle of the forehead.

31. **faery.** A better spelling than the more common *fairy*, as if connected with *fair*. *Faery* properly means 'enchantment'; the correct name for the elf is *fay*.

39, 40. **his nest Who** is equivalent to 'the nest (or abode) of him who.'

46. **repair**, heal, refresh, recruit.

STEPPING WESTWARD.

INTRODUCTION.

COMPOSED between 1803 and 1805, and first published in 1807.

Dorothy Wordsworth in her *Recollections of a Tour made in Scotland*, 1803, writes : "Sunday, Sept. 11th.—We have never had a more delightful walk than this evening. ... The sun had been set for some time, when, being within a quarter of a mile of the ferry-man's hut, our path having led us close to the shore of the calm lake, we met two neatly-dressed women, without hats, who had probably been taking their Sunday evening's walk. One of them said to us in a friendly, soft tone of voice, 'What, you are stepping westward?' I cannot describe how affecting this simple expression was in that remote place, with the western sky in front, yet glowing with the departed sun. William wrote the following poem long after, in remembrance of his feelings and mine."

The points of the compass are much more freely utilized in Scotland than elsewhere; every cottage has its east room and its west room, and people speak of sitting north. or south of one another at table.

NOTES. •

2. **wildish.** The italics draw attention to the fact that the word in this form (with -*ish* suffix) is rather colloquial than literary.

3. **If we** etc. The vagueness of the expression *westward* might seem to imply that they were homeless wanderers, travelling

through a strange land as chance might direct them, without any definite place or object in view.

8-10. With such a sky ... behold. Cf. *Lines written while Sailing in a Boat at Evening*, 1-5:

"How richly glows the water's breast
Before us, tinged with evening hues,
While, facing thus the crimson west,
The boat her silent course pursues!
And see how dark the backward stream!"

10. all gloomy, *i.e.* all was gloomy. *To behold* = 'for beholding'—the gerundial infinitive, as in 'fair *to see*' (Burns), 'long *to tell*' (Milton). Cf. *The Affliction of Margaret*, 16.

12. heavenly destiny, a destiny or future course invited and sanctioned, as it were, by the glowing heavens that lay before them.

13. I liked the greeting etc. "The sense of sudden fellowship, and the quaint greeting beneath the glowing sky, seem to link man's momentary wanderings with the cosmic spectacles of heaven" (Myers's *Wordsworth*).

15. spiritual right. *Spiritual* is opposed to *legal* or *moral*; it was a right that lay beyond and apart from all earthly considerations. The sympathetic greeting is conceived of as a kind of passport of admission to the bright region beyond.

18. her native lake. Loch Katrine, situated in the south-west corner of Perthshire.

24. A human sweetness. The aloofness of a "heavenly destiny" and of a pilgrimage into unknown space was softened and sweetened by the human element of the woman's voice that speeded them on their imaginary journey.

25, 26. travelling ... endless way. For the sentiment—the charm and mystery of the Beyond, cf. "*Where lies the land to which yon ship must go?*" 6-8:

"Let her travel where she may,
She finds familiar names, a beaten way
Ever before her, and a wind to blow."

And Tennyson, *The Voyage*, 7, 8:

"We knew the merry world was round,
And we might sail for evermore."

Also *Id.*, *Ulysses*, 59-61:

"For my purpose holds
To sail beyond the sunset, and the baths
Of all the western stars, until I die.'

THE SOLITARY REAPER.

INTRODUCTION.

COMPOSED between 1803 and 1805, and first published in 1807. It forms one among a group of poems entitled "Memorials of a Tour in Scotland" (1827), a tour that was made by the poet with his sister and Coleridge in the autumn of 1803. In Dorothy Wordsworth's *Recollections* of the Tour, September 13, 1803, we find: "As we descended, the scene became more fertile. ... It was harvest-time, and the fields were quietly—might I be allowed to say pensively?—enlivened by small companies of reapers. It is not uncommon in the more lonely parts of the Highlands to see a single person so employed."

Wordsworth appended the following note to this poem: "This Poem was suggested by a beautiful sentence in a MS. 'Tour in Scotland,' written by a friend, the last line being taken from it *verbatim*." The sentence referred to occurs in Wilkinson's *Tours to the British Mountains*: "Passed a female who was reaping alone: she sung in Erse, as she bended over her sickle; the sweetest human voice I ever heard: her strains were tenderly melancholy, and felt delicious, long after they were heard no more."

NOTES.

4. **gently**, quietly, without disturbing her.

6. **melancholy.** See Introduction.

8. **overflowing.** Cf. Tennyson, *The Dying Swan*, iii.:

"And the creeping mosses and clambering weeds

. . . . . .

Were *flooded over* with echoing song."

9. **nightingale** (O.E. *nightegale*, from *nihte*, 'of right,' and *gale*, 'singer') means lit. 'singer of the night,' the bird that sings by night.

11. **shady haunt**, oasis in the desert.

13. **A voice so thrilling.** Cf. *To the Cuckoo*, 1-3:

"Not the whole warbling grove in concert heard
When sunshine follows shower, the breast can *thrill*
Like the first summons, Cuckoo! of thy bill."

In Wordsworth's poems there are frequent references to this bird. In one place he refers to the "thousand delightful feelings connected in his mind with the voice of the cuckoo."

15. **the silence of the seas.** Cf. Coleridge, *Ancient Mariner*, Part ii. st. 6:

"And we did speak only to break
The *silence of the sea*."

16. farthest Hebrides. This expression seems to be a reminiscence of Vergil's *Ultima Thule*, 'farthest Thule,' Thule probably standing for one of the Shetland Islands, reckoned as the northern limit of the world. The Hebrides are a group of islands on the north-west of Scotland. The cuckoo is a migratory bird, and arrives in northern Europe in April or May. Cf. *On the Power of Sound*, ii. :

> "Shout, cuckoo !—let the vernal soul
> Go with thee to the frozen zone."

18. numbers (Lat. *numeri*, verses; *numerus*, musical measure), for poetry or poetic rhythm, was a common 'poetical' word in the so-called 'classical' period of English poetry, and is therefore one that we should hardly expect from Wordsworth's pen. See General Introduction.

19. things, *i.e.* events. Cf. *Artegal and Elidure*, 12 : "The marvellous current of forgotten *things*."

23. natural, belonging to the natural course of things ; such as might be expected ; ordinary. Cf. Milton, *Par. Lost*, xii. 645 : "Some *natural* tears they dropp'd, but wip'd them soon "; and *The Rainbow*, 8 : "*natural* piety."

29. The original line was more simply : 'I listen'd till I had my fill.' For *motionless*, cf. l. 4 : "Stop here."

31. in my heart I bore. Wordsworth's memory was a "dwelling-place" for all sweet sounds and lovely sights. The former he bears away with him in his heart, and the latter

> "flash upon that inward eye
> Which is the bliss of solitude" (*The Daffodils*, 21, 22).

ROB ROY'S GRAVE.

INTRODUCTION.

COMPOSED between 1803 and 1805, and first published in 1807.

Robert Macgregor, the famous Scottish outlaw, nicknamed Rob Roy, *i.e.* Robert the Red, from his red hair, was born in 1671. His own designation was of Inversnaid, but he acquired the ownership of Craig Royston, a domain of rock and forest on the east side of Loch Lomond, and engaged in cattle-dealing. In 1712 he was evicted and outlawed on a charge of embezzlement, and became a Highland freebooter ; and under the protection of the Duke of Argyll levied blackmail on the Scottish gentry for many years. He died in his own house at Balquhidder in Perthshire, and was buried at the eastern end of the old church, where his grave, marked by a sculptured stone, lies between the tombs of his wife and eldest son.

In person Rob Roy was not tall, but remarkably strong and compact. "The greatest peculiarities of his frame," writes Scott in his Introduction to *Rob Roy*, "were the breadth of his shoulders, and the great and almost disproportioned length of his arms ; so remarkable, indeed, that it was said he could, without stooping, tie the garters of his Highland hose, which are placed two inches below the knee. His countenance was open, manly, stern at periods of danger, but frank and cheerful in his hours of festivity .... To these personal qualifications must be added a masterly use of the Highland sword, in which his length of arm gave him great advantage. In character he was for the most part humane, avoiding unnecessary bloodshed. His schemes of plunder were contrived and executed with equal boldness and sagacity, and were almost universally successful, from the skill with which they were laid, and the secresy and rapidity with which they were executed. Like Robin Hood of England, he was a kind and gentle robber, and while he took from the rich, was liberal in relieving the poor. This might in part be policy ; but the universal tradition of the country speaks it to have arisen from a better motive."

NOTES.

1. **Robin Hood.** A traditional English outlaw and popular hero, said to have flourished in the reign of Richard I. He lived in the woods with his band, Friar Tuck, Little John, etc., where he robbed the rich, though he was kind to the poor. According to some he was the outlawed Earl of Huntingdon.

2. **The English ... joy.** There are numerous English ballads relating to Robin Hood, such as *Robin Hood and Guy of Gisborne* in Percy's "Reliques," and *Robin Hood rescuing the Widow's Three Sons, Robin Hood's Death and Burial* in " Robin Hood's Garland."

6. **his grave.** See Introduction. Wordsworth was misinformed as to Rob Roy's burial place, which he places near the head of Loch Katrine.

7. **stave,** stanza, verse.

10. **wondrous ... arm.** See Introduction.

19. **the principles of things.** Rob Roy's final principle or guiding rule of life and conduct is formulated in ll. 39, 40, viz. force, physical or mental.

21. **generous Rob.** The epithet is partly ironical. Rob "liberally" dispensed with all statute law.

24. **against ourselves.** The obligation to obey the law opposes our natural impulse that might is right.

25. We have a passion etc. In order to curb our violent instincts we make laws, which are unable to control us, because they are not founded upon true principles; and then we fight for this idol of the law we have made, with envenomed bitterness against our opponents.

30. Distinctions, *i.e.* not between right and wrong, but between strength and weakness only.

42. A signal, a token, a guiding principle.

43. here, in such a state of things. No wanton cruelty is excited, because the weak recognize their position and do not resist the strong.

53. the rule of right, *i.e.* the rule (of l. 37) that shows us what is right.

63. Polity etc. The State—Law and Order—was too strong for him, and prevented him from realizing his theories.

67. How might he etc. If Rob Roy had lived in our days he would have been a lawless conqueror like Napoleon, overriding all opposition.

69. factors, estate-managers.

rights of chase. Equivalent to 'game laws.' *Chase* is a noun, and signifies a small deer-forest held by a private individual.

84. fatherly concern. The phrase is ironical. We will be a "father" to our subjects, mankind, by imposing our rule upon them—which is the best thing for them.

85. over old. And therefore ready to be superseded by something else.

89. I, too etc. As Napoleon had his puppet kings. Thus after the [battle of Austerlitz (1805), about the time that this poem was written, he made his brother Joseph King of Naples and his brother Louis King of Holland.

91. like clouds. See *Hart-leap Well,* 2, and note.

94. thought of joy! Said ironically.

95. France would etc. We, like France, should have had, in the shape of Rob Roy, our Napoleon to be proud of.

102. chieftain, in the Highland acceptation, signifies the head of a particular branch of a clan, in opposition to *Chief,* who is the leader of the whole clan.

clan. The clan Macgregor. The clan was outlawed in 1603 and the name abolished. Hence Rob Roy's assumption of the name of Campbell.

109. thou wert still etc. See Introduction.

110. heart ... hand. One to encourage the poor man and to act in his behalf.

115. **Loch Veol**, or Loch Voil, and Loch Lomond lie on the border of the counties of Perth and Stirling. Balquhidder (see Introduction) stands upon Loch Voil, and Inversnaid (*ib.*) on Loch Lomond.

116. **braes**, hill-sides.

118. **attest the same.** See *Hart-leap Well*, 63, and note. Scott writes: "All whom I have conversed with, and I have in my youth seen some who know Rob Roy personally, gave him the character of a benevolent and humane man 'in his way.'"

119. **The proud heart** etc. An absolute clause. Cf. Dorothy Wordsworth's *Recollections* of the Scotch Tour: "Aug. 27, 1803. —We mentioned Rob Roy, and the eyes of all glistened; even the lady of the house, who was very diffident, and no great talker, exclaimed, 'He was a good man, Rob Roy!'"
This line is a striking improvement upon the reading of the 1807 edition, "And kindle, like a fire new stirr'd."

TO THE MEN OF KENT.

INTRODUCTION.

COMPOSED in October 1803, and first published in 1807. See Introduction to *On the Extinction of the Venetian Republic.*
The Treaty of Amiens, signed in March 1802, lasted only till the following May, when war was again declared between England and France. Napoleon showed his rancour against this country by the immediate arrest of nearly 10,000 English persons travelling or resident in France, and proceeded to the develop-ment of his plan for the invasion of England. In pursuance of this design, in January 1804, he assembled at Boulogne a vast flotilla of light vessels and flat-bottomed craft to convey his army across the channel. The warlike excitement in England was intense at the time when this sonnet was written, and 300,000 volunteers had been enrolled for the national defence by the 10th of August; while the whole male population of the kingdom from 17 to 55 years of age were divided into classes to be successively armed and drilled. Wordsworth wrote three other sonnets at this date in reference to this expected invasion.

NOTES.

1. **Vanguard … Kent.** Cf. Drayton, *Baron's Wars*, i. :
"Then those of Kent, unconquered of the rest,
That to this day maintain their ancient right."

4. **hardiment,** 'courage,' is found in Chaucer, Spenser, and Shakspere, but is now archaic.

5. **invitation,** *i.e.* challenge.

6. **can see** etc. An excusable poetic exaggeration, since the chalk cliffs of Dover are readily discernible from France on a clear day.

9. **Left single** etc. The reference appears to be the Peasants' Revolt in 1381, when, after the dispersal of the men of Essex and Hertfordshire, 30,000 Kentish-men, under the leadership of Wat Tyler, in conference with King Richard II. at Smithfield, obtained from him charters of emancipation. These, however, were subsequently declared null and void.

14. **'tis victory or death.** Cf. "*It is not to be thought of,*" 11-13 :

> "*We must be free or die,* who speak the tongue
> That Shakspeare spake ; the faith and morals hold
> Which Milton held."

THE DAFFODILS.

INTRODUCTION.

COMPOSED at Town-end, Grasmere, in 1804, and first published in 1807 in the series "Moods of my own Mind."

In Dorothy Wordsworth's Journal, under date April 15, 1802, we find : "When we were in the woods beyond Gowbarrow Park, we saw a few daffodils close to the water side ... As we went along there were more, and yet more ; and, at last, under the boughs of the trees, we saw that there was a long belt of them along the shore, about the breadth of a country turnpike road. I never saw daffodils so beautiful. They grew among the mossy stones, about and above them ; some rested their heads upon these stones, as on a pillow for weariness ; and the rest tossed and reeled and danced, and seemed as if they verily laughed with the wind that blew upon them over the lake. They looked so gay, ever glancing, ever changing."

NOTES.

1. **as a cloud.** See *Hart-leap Well*, 2, and note. His human loneliness was suddenly broken in upon by a "crowd"—"a jocund company "—of natural objects. For a similar sentiment, cf. *Intimations of Immortality*, 25, 26 :

"The cataracts blow their trumpets from the steep;
No more shall grief of mine the season wrong."
And *ib.* ll. 42-50.

4. **daffodils.** The initial *d* is properly no part of this word, the M.E. form being *affodille*, Lat. *asphodelus*, Eng. *asphodel*.

20. **vacant,** idle, unoccupied.

21, 22. **They flash … solitude.** These two lines—according to Wordsworth, the two best lines in the poem—were composed by his wife. Upon someone's once remarking that this piece was "a fine morsel for the Reviewers," the poet observed that "there were *two lines* in that little poem which, if thoroughly felt, would annihilate nine-tenths of the reviews of the kingdom, as they would find no readers." With the sentiment compare J. Montgomery, *The Little Cloud*:

"Bliss in possession will not last:
Remembered joys are never past:
At once the fountain, stream, and sea,
They were—they are—they yet shall be."
And *Tintern Abbey*, 139-142:
"When thy mind
Shall be a mansion for all lovely forms,
Thy memory be as a dwelling-place
For all sweet sounds and harmonies."

THE AFFLICTION OF MARGARET.

INTRODUCTION.

COMPOSED in 1804, at Town-end, Grasmere, and first published in 1807.

Wordsworth says : "This was taken from the case of a poor widow who lived in the town of Penrith. Her sorrow was well known to Mrs. Wordsworth, to my sister, and, I believe, to the whole town. She kept a shop, and when she saw a stranger passing by, she was in the habit of going out into the street to enquire of him after her son."

NOTES.

5. **of the same.** See *Hart-leap Well*, 63, and note.

6. **neither blame** etc., so long as I know not whether thou art alive or dead, I blame and grieve over thy non-return to me.

8. **years** is to be parsed as an adverbial objective of duration of time, as in 'I stayed there a *week*.'

8. to have received, an instance of the infinitive used absolutely in exclamation, as in ' *To think* that it should come to this ! '

12. very bliss, true bliss, the greatest bliss ; because she feels sure he will come back to her.

16. beauteous to behold. Cf. *Stepping Westward*, 10, and note.

19. things ... that wanted grace, wild and thoughtless actions.

24. wildest scream. The child, at play, heedlessly screams in fun, little thinking what a shock it is to his mother to hear him.

25. unawares, 'ignorant of the cause '; a genitival adverb, like *needs*.

27. Years ... distress. The mother's anxieties and misgivings increase with the child's growth.

31. Pride ... wrong. I will be too proud to complain, and will bear myself as if I did not mind his neglect of me.

35. Weeping etc. Mark the deep pathos of this line.

39. with grief and pain, as if I were too indifferent or disappointed to welcome my son home again.

40. with better eyes. Cf. Tennyson, *In Memoriam*, li. 14-16 :

" Ye (the dead) watch, like God, the rolling hours
    With *larger other eyes* than ours,
To make allowance for us all."

47. us is emphatic ; ' us men,' as opposed to the birds.

53. Inheritest etc. Perhaps thou art driven to take shelter in a lion's den, left to thee by its occupant.

54. summoned. The word implies an invisible power which leads him on. So that " something mysterious and awful is added to his fate " (Myers's *Wordsworth*).

to the deep etc., *i.e.* perhaps thou hast been shipwrecked and drowned at sea.

56. incommunicable. Employed here, by poetic license, in the unusual sense of ' incapable of being communicated with,' ' cutting off all communication '; so that " to keep an incommunicable sleep " is a periphrasis for " to lie dead." Cf. Tennyson, *In Memoriam*, lxxxii. st. 4 :

" For this alone on Death I wreak
    The wrath that garners in my heart ;
    He put our lives so far apart
We cannot hear each other speak."

61. For, surely, then etc. Cf. Tennyson, *Maud*, Part II. iv. 3 :

"Ah Christ, that it were possible
    For one short hour to see
The souls we loved, that they might tell us
    What and where they be."

67. to shake me, to make me tremble.

FIDELITY.

INTRODUCTION.

COMPOSED in 1805, and first published in 1807.

The young man whose death gave occasion to this poem was named Charles Gough, who had come early in the spring to Patterdale for the sake of angling. While attempting to cross over Helvellyn to Grasmere, he slipped from a steep part of the rock where the ice was not thawed, and perished. This was early in April, and his body was not found till July 22, 1805.

Scott heard of the accident and also wrote a poem, in admiration of the dog's fidelity, entitled *Helvellyn*, to which Wordsworth refers as containing "a most beautiful stanza:

' How long did'st thou think that his silence was slumber ?
When the wind waved his garment, how oft did'st thou start?'"

He adds that "the sentiment in the last four lines of the last stanza of my verses was uttered by a shepherd with such exactness, that a traveller, who afterwards reported his account in print, was induced to question the man whether he had read them, which he had not." The poet told Henry Crabb Robinson that "he purposely made the narrative as prosaic as possible, in order that no discredit might be thrown on the truth of the incident." The unadorned simplicity of Wordsworth's version are in striking contrast to the more ambitious setting Scott has given to the incident.

NOTES.

6. **a brake,** a thicket ; a spot overgrown with ferns.

8. **Glancing,** rapidly appearing and disappearing ; visible for an instant. Cf. *Influence of Natural Objects*, 49 : "I ... *glanced* sideway,*" where the word means 'darted,' and Whittier, *Mogg Megone*, ii. : "With birchen boat and *glancing* oars."

19, 20. **A lofty ... below.** The tarn, or small mountain lake, referred to is Red Tarn, under Helvellyn, to the east. Cf. Scott, *Helvellyn*, st. 1 :

" On the right, Striden-edge round the Red-tarn was bending,

. . . .

One huge nameless rock in the front was ascending,
When I marked the sad spot where the wanderer had died."

21. **Helvellyn** is a mountain on the border of Cumberland and Westmoreland, 3118 feet high.

26. **a lonely cheer,** a cheerfulness in which the feeling of loneliness is still present. The occasional signs of life that cheer the

solitude do not make it seem the less lonesome. Cf. *The White Doe of Rylstone*, 329 (of the doe): "Haunting the spots with lonely cheer." And *The Prelude*, v. 439-442:

> "Meanwhile the calm lake
> Grew dark with all the shadows on its breast,
> And, now and then, a fish up-leaping snapped
> The breathless stillness."

27. **The crags ... croak.** In *The Excursion*, iv. 1175-1187, Wordsworth enlarges upon the effect produced by the raven's croak, at evening, echoed by the surrounding mountains.

28. **In symphony austere,** 'with accordant sternness.' Dorothy Wordsworth, describing such an echo (*Journal*, July 27, 1800), says that it was a "musical, bell-like" sound that "answered to the bird's hoarse voice"; so that it is to the solemnity rather than to the harshness of the sound that the poet seems to refer here.

30. **mists ... shroud.** The rising mists are driven along by the wind and envelop everything.

33. **barrier,** the "lofty precipice" of l. 19.

45. **It,** *i.e.* what had happened.

50. **whose** is here the possessive of *what.* The prose construction would be 'for the use *of which.*'

52. **A lasting monument.** Cf. Horace (*Carm.* iii. 30) of his own Odes: *Exegi monumentum aere perennius,* 'I have completed a monument more lasting than bronze.'

63. **He knows, who** etc., *i.e.* of course, God.

TO SLEEP.

INTRODUCTION.

COMPOSED in 1806, and first published in 1807, and classed by Wordsworth, along with two other sonnets with the same title, among the "Miscellaneous Sonnets."

With this piece should be compared William Drummond's sonnet *To Sleep,* beginning

> "Sleep, silence' child, sweet father of soft rest,"

and the address to sleep in Shakspere, *Henry IV.* Part II. III. i. 5 *et seq.* :

> "O sleep, O gentle sleep,
> Nature's soft nurse, how have I frighted thee,
> That thou no more wilt weigh my eyelids down
> And steep my senses in forgetfulness?" etc.

NOTES

1. **A flock of sheep** etc. The notion is that to fix the mind upon the soothing monotony of continuous sights or sounds (sheep passing singly through a gate, the steady patter of rain, the murmur of bees or of water-falls, the sighing of the wind, the dull roar of the waves) or of vague, indefinite spaces (expanses of meadow, water, or sky) clears it of exciting topics of thought and induces sleep.

2, 3. **rain ... bees ... fall of rivers, winds.** Cf. Spenser, *Faery Queene*, I. i. 41 :

"And more to lulle him in his slumber soft,
A trickling streame from high rock tumbling downe,
And ever-drizling raine upon the loft,
Mixt with a murmuring winde, much like the sowne
Of swarming bees, did cast him in a swowne."

8. **melancholy cry.** So to the sleepless man sounds the note of the once "blithe new-comer" (*To the Cuckoo*, 1).

12. **wealth**, all the good things that the morning brings. Cf. Southey, *To Sleep*, 21-24 :

"Freely thou roam'st o'er hill and vale,
Thy presence none control,
But whomsoe'er thou visit'st not,
Heaven save the wretched soul !"

13, 14. **Come ... health.** Cf. Shaks. *Macbeth*, II. ii. 37-40 :

"Sleep that knits up the ravell'd sleave of care,
The death of each day's life, sore labour's bath,
Balm of hurt minds, great nature's second course,
Chief nourisher in life's feast."

THE SUBJUGATION OF SWITZERLAND.

INTRODUCTION.

COMPOSED in 1807, and first published in the same year. See Introduction to *On the Extinction of the Venetian Republic.* Wordsworth says : "This was composed while pacing to and fro between the hall of Coleorton, then rebuilding, and the principal farm-house of the estate, in which we lived for nine or ten months."

In 1798 the French Directory found an excuse for interfering in the affairs of the Swiss Confederation, which, after a three centuries' struggle for freedom, had been recognized as independent since 1648. First Berne and then the mountain or "forest" cantons were overwhelmed by numbers after a desperate resistance, and "the men of Uri, of Unterwalden, and of Schwytz bowed for the first time to a foreign conqueror." On the ruins of the Confederation was set up the so-called Helvetic Republic, but in 1803 a French army again occupied Switzerland, and from this time to the collapse of Napoleon's power she was in effect a province of France.

NOTES.

1. **one is of the sea.** Cf. *On a High Part of Cumberland*, 11 : "The earth-*voice* of a mighty sea."

3. **In both ... rejoice.** Islands and mountainous countries (of which Great Britain and Switzerland are the types), as being difficult of invasion, have ever been the chosen seats of liberty. Cf. "*Advance—come forth*" (a sonnet written in 1809), 1-3 :

> Advance—come forth from thy Tyrolean ground,
> Dear Liberty ! stern nymph of soul untamed ;
> Sweet nymph, O rightly of the mountains named ! "

and Bryant, *William Tell*, 1-4 :

> ' Chains may subdue the feeble spirit, but thee,
> Tell, of the iron heart ! they could not tame !
> For thou wert of the mountains ; they proclaim
> The everlasting creed of liberty."

5. **a tyrant**, Napoleon Buonaparte.

6. **Thou fought'st** etc. See Introduction.

10. **cleave ... left.** Let not Great Britain share the fate of Switzerland. For Napoleon's projected invasion of England, see Introduction to *To the Men of Kent*, p. 68.

TO A SKY-LARK.

INTRODUCTION.

COMPOSED in 1825, and first published in 1827. Wordsworth says of this piece : "Written at Rydal Mount, where there are 10 sky-larks, but the Poet is everywhere." He had composed an earlier poem with the same title in 1805, and was no doubt acquainted with Shelley's famous lyric, which was written in 1820. The third stanza of the succeeding poem, *A Morning Exercise* (see the Introduction to that poem), was, from 1827 to 1843, the second stanza of this one.

NOTES.

1. pilgrim of the sky, lone traveller up into the sky. *Pilgrim* is O.F. *pelerin*, for *pelegrin*, Lat. *peregrinus*, a stranger, foreigner.

2. despise the earth. Cf. Shelley, *To a Skylark*, st. 20: "Thou scorner of the ground." So Horace, *Carm.* III. ii. 24, of Virtue : *Spernit humum fugiente penna*, "She scorns the ground with fugitive wing."

3, 4. Or while ... ground. Cf. J. Hogg, *The Skylark*, 10-12:
> "Where, on thy dewy wing,
> Where art thou journeying?
> *Thy lay is in heaven, thy love is on earth.*"

6. Those ... still. Both clauses are in the absolute construction—'Those quivering wings being composed (*i.e.* folded), that music being still.'

7. nightingale. See note to *The Solitary Reaper*, 9.

her. It is the male bird that is the singer, though the poets almost universally make it female, *philomela* (nightingale) being a feminine noun in Latin.

8. A privacy .. thine. The bird soars so high, that the open light of heaven is for her a secluded spot. Cf. Shelley, *Ib.* st. 8:
> "Like a poet hidden
> In the light of thought."

9. thou dost pour etc. Cf. Shelley, *Ib.* st. 7: "From thy presence showers a rain of melody."

10. instinct refers to the following couplet. The nightingale, like the lark, is true to her nest; but, unlike the lark, she does not soar. Hence the lark's "diviner instinct."

11, 12. who soar .. home. The wise, while they do not neglect the lowlier duties of everyday life, cultivate at the same time higher and holier interests. They harmoniously combine the two inter-related aims. Cf. *A Morning Exercise*, st. 1 and 2. A comparison is implied between this steadfastness of the wise and the constancy with which the magnetic needle points to the north and south poles.

A MORNING EXERCISE.

INTRODUCTION.

THIS poem, of which only the last five stanzas are given here, was, with the exception of the third stanza (see Introduction to

To a Sky-lark), composed in 1828 and first published in 1832. It is of these five stanzas that Wordsworth says he "could wish them to be read with the poem addressed to the sky-lark."

NOTES.

1. Hail. The poet is addressing the sky-lark.

2. Restless with fixed. In the lark the restlessness of its upward flight is counterbalanced by his fixed faithfulness to its nest. Cf. *To a Sky-lark*, 11, 12.

3–6. The kingfisher cares only for its nest, the bird of paradise only for being on the wing; whereas the lark unites both characteristics.

3. halcyon. The Greek name for the kingfisher. This bird was fabled to lay its eggs in nests that floated on the sea for fourteen days, before the winter solstice, during which time the weather was always calm and the sea smooth. Hence 'halcyon days' means days of peace and tranquillity.

5. Perpetual flight. The *Paradisea apoda* (footless bird of paradise) was so called from the fable that it was always on the wing and had no feet.

8. more ... thee. Though the dove also is both faithful to its nest and swift of flight, yet nature has combined the two characteristics more fully and strikingly in the lark.

9. downward eye. Cf. *To a Sky-lark*, 3, 4.

10. in aërial etc. So unconfined in thy solitary flight in mid air. Cf. *To a Sky-lark*, 8.

12. wing ... voice. Cf. Shelley, *To a Sky-lark*, st. 2: "And singing still dost soar, and soaring ever singest."

17. Yet might'st thou seem etc. So far from earth thou soarest, that thy song, unlike that of all other birds, might seem not to be inspired by the advent of spring.

22. Where ... domain. The lark soars and sings above broad open commons and meadow land, resembling the expanse of ocean.

23. Urania. Among the Greeks, the Muse who presided over astronomy; but used here rather in Milton's sense (see *Par. Lost*, vii. 1–39) of the heavenly Muse, the inspirer of heavenly song.

30. Singing as they shine. A reminiscence of the last line but one of Addison's hymn in *Spectator*, No. 465: "For ever singing as they shine."

THE PRIMROSE OF THE ROCK.

INTRODUCTION.

COMPOSED in 1831 at Rydal Mount, and first published in 1835. Wordsworth says : "The rock stands on the right hand a little way leading up the middle road from Rydal to Grasmere. We have been in the habit of calling it the glow-worm rock from the number of glow-worms we have often seen hanging on it as described. The tuft of primrose has, I fear, been washed away by the heavy rains."

The primrose has disappeared, and glow-worms have now almost deserted the district; but the rock remains one of the most interesting objects connected with Wordsworth in the Lake district.

NOTES.

3. **the glow-worms.** See Introduction.

7, 8. **What hideous ... overthrown.** Between 1802 (see the following note) and 1831 had occurred the battles of Austerlitz (1805), Jena (1806), Friedland (1807), Wagram (1809), Borodino (1812), Lützen (1813), Leipzig (1813), Waterloo (1815), wars between England and the United States (1812), the Nepalese war (1813), the Greek insurrection (1821), and war between Russia and Turkey (1828); the dissolution of the Holy Roman Empire (1806), the overthrow of the Spanish monarchy (1808), the flight of Louis XVIII. from France (1815), and the second French Revolution (1830).

9, 10. **Since first ... own.** Cf. the following in Dorothy Wordsworth's Grasmere *Journal*: "April 24, 1802.—We walked in the evening to Rydal. Coleridge and I lingered behind. We all stood to look at Glowworm Rock—a primrose that grew there, and just looked out on the road from its own sheltered bower."

11. **Nature's chain.** In relation to the primrose, this chain or succession of causes, of which God is the great final link or First Cause, is described in the two following stanzas. Bacon (*Advancement of Learning*, I. i. 3), in allusion to Homer's "golden chain" (*Il.* viii. 19), uses the same metaphor to indicate that the series of natural phenomena is directed by God: "When a man ... seeth the dependence of causes, and the works of Providence, then, according to the allegory of the poets, he will easily believe that the highest link of nature's chain must needs be tied to the foot of Jupiter's chair." See *To* ——, 49, 50:

"The filial chain let down
From his everlasting throne."

Cf. Spenser, *Faery Queene*, I. v. 25, 4–6 :
> "But who can turn the stream of destiny,
> Or break the chain of strong necessity,
> Which fast is tied to Jove's eternal seat ?"

And Browne, *Religio Medici*, Part I. § 18 : "There is a nearer way to heaven than Homer's chain ; an easy logic may conjoin a heaven and earth in one argument, and, with less than a sorites, resolve all things to God. For though we christen effects by their most sensible and nearest causes, yet is God the true and infallible cause of all."

13. faithful to, holding fast to. Cf. "*When haughty expectations,*" 6-9, of snowdrops that "together cling," when smitten by the blast :
> "Observe the *faithful* flowers ! "

14. renew. By reblossoming year after year.

21. her sphere, her orbit.

31. I sang etc. Mankind need not envy the flowers their annual revival ; for, though our hopes of a future resurrection are often clouded by fears, God's redeeming love is far mightier than those fears. Hood (*Ode to Melancholy*) writes in a less hopeful strain :
> "The roses bud and bloom again,
> But Love may haunt the grave of Love,
> And watch the mould in vain."

37-42. That love ... beneficent. Through God's love, our standpoint in regard to disease, bereavement, and old age is altered ; what to us were once merely the penalties of sin have now become pledges of a future resurrection (since the introduction of death into the world brought with it the promise of immortality) ; and even the thistles, which the curse upon man's disobedience inflicted, are now for us, in their annual reblossoming, types of our own resurrection.

38, 39. sorrow ... dust. The sorrow with which we bent over the graves of dear ones was hopeless, apart from God's redeeming love. Cf. Bible, 1 *Thess.* iv. 13 : "Concerning them that fall asleep (*i.e.* die), that ye sorrow not, even as the rest, which have no hope."

41. thistles of a curse. Cf. God's words to Adam after his disobedience, *Genesis* iii. 17, 18 : "Cursed is the ground for thy sake ; in sorrow shalt thou eat of it all the days of thy life · thorns also and thistles shall it bring forth to thee."

43. Sin-blighted etc. Contrast J. Sylvester, *Spectacles*, 11 :
> "After Winter, Spring (in order)
> Comes again ; but earthly thing
> Rotting here, not rooting further,
> Can thy Winter hope a Spring ? "

44. reasoning. As opposed to the reasonless plants.

45. oblivious winter, *i.e.* the oblivion of death. *Oblivious* means here 'causing oblivion'; cf. Milton's "oblivious pool" (*Par. Lost*, i. 266).

47. eternal summer, *i.e.* the life immortal, in which our brief human existence will be merged. The Bible reckons the average human life at seventy years; see *Psalms*, xc. 10: "The days of our years are three score years and ten."

50. This prescience, this prevision of a resurrection to immortality.

51. elevates, exalts, animates.

53. And makes etc. Each soul, in virtue of its individual immortality, becomes the dwelling-place of the Divine Spirit. Cf. Bible, 1 *Cor.* iii. 16: "Know ye not that ye are the temple of God, and that the Spirit of God dwelleth in you?"

"CALM IS THE FRAGRANT AIR."

INTRODUCTION

COMPOSED in 1832 and first published in 1835. It forms one of Wordsworth's "Evening Voluntaries"—poetic records of impressions made upon his mind by evening sights or sounds—of which his ode, *Composed upon an Evening of Extraordinary Splendour and Beauty,* is the crowning example. The term "Voluntary" is adopted by the poet in reference to its use in church music, to denote an organ solo performed before, during, or after church service. It was so called because it was originally *extemporized* by the organist, unrestricted by formal rules of composition. Similarly these poems are spontaneous outpourings of some special mood of the poet.

NOTES.

1. loth, in the older spelling *loath,* is an adjective, with verb derivative *loathe.*

12. Nine ... bound. The air is so clear and calm that each separate stroke is heard distinctly, as the nine drowsily follow one another in regular succession.

13. how unlike etc. Whereas in the stormy weather of winter the clock-beats are confusedly heard, and startle listeners, who perhaps mistake them for the notes of an alarm-bell.

22. dor-hawk. A local name for the common goat-sucker or night-jar.

24. it suits them both. Since it unites the notions both of activity and of monotony.

COMPOSED BY THE SEASHORE.

INTRODUCTION.

COMPOSED in 1834 and first published in 1845. It forms one of the "Evening Voluntaries"; see the Introduction to the preceding poem.

Wordsworth says: "These lines were suggested during my residence under my son's roof at Moresby, on the coast near Whitehaven, at the time when I was composing those verses among the "Evening Voluntaries" that have reference to the sea. It was in that neighbourhood I first became acquainted with the ocean and its appearances and movements. My infancy and early childhood were passed at Cockermouth, about eight miles from the coast, and I well remember that mysterious awe with which I used to listen to anything said about storms and shipwrecks."

NOTES.

7, 8. the fickle star Of power, the shifting fortunes of men in power. *Star* is used in reference to the old notion of the influence of the stars upon human destiny. Cf. *disastrous, jovial, saturnine.*

14. Which ... come. Which was intended to be his home upon his marriage.

17, 18. whose ... change. Into the midst of the pleasantest dream comes the remembrance that a change has taken place, or the fear that it will. *Smoothest range* = most untroubled course.

19, 20. whose ... keep. The greatness of the joy overwhelms and awakes the sleeper.

20. breathing man, mortal man, weak man.

22. elemental, of the elements, of winds and waves.

26. A less imperious etc. But our sympathy for the captains and crews of vessels no longer tossed about at sea, but lying at anchor in this calm bay, is of a gentler character.

30. Where good men etc., *i.e.* we readily sympathize with the longings of good men for rest. *Where* = in cases where.

33. the obscurities of happiness, the happiness that is found in retirement and seclusion.

NOTES TO PART II.

TINTERN ABBEY.

INTRODUCTION.

COMPOSED in July 1798, and first published in *Lyrical Ballads* the same year. Wordsworth says: "No poem of mine was composed under circumstances more pleasant for me to remember than this. I began it upon leaving Tintern, after crossing the Wye, and concluded it just as I was entering Bristol in the evening, after a ramble of four or five days, with my sister. Not a line of it was altered, and not any part of it written down till I reached Bristol." The previous visit, referred to at the commencement of the poem, was made alone and on foot in 1793 in the course of a journey from Salisbury Plain to Wales.

NOTES.

1. **Five years.** See Introduction.
4. **soft inland murmur.** Cf. *The Brothers*, 48, 49:

> "The tones of waterfalls, and *inland sounds*
> Of caves and trees."

The bed of the Wye is so steep that the river is not affected by the tides a few miles above Tintern, a distance of only ten miles from where it flows into the Severn. Cf. Tennyson, *In Memoriam*, xix. :

> "There twice a day the Severn fills ;
> The salt sea-water passes by,
> And hushes half the babbling Wye,
> And makes a silence in the hills.
>
> . . . . . .
>
> The tide flows down, the wave again
> Is vocal in its wooded walls."

135

5. cliffs, the wooded hills that overhang the Wye on both sides between Monmouth and Chepstow.

6-8. That on a wild ... sky. The eye follows the steep cliffs upwards to the sky, whose perfect calm thus seems to mingle with and deepen the seclusion of the valley below. Cf. *Poems on the Naming of Places,* iii. 5-8:

> "This Peak, so high
> Above us, and so distant in its height,
> Is visible; and often seems to send
> Its own deep quiet to restore our hearts."

11. orchard-tufts. *Tuft* or *toft* means a plantation or a green knoll, and is distinct from *tuft,* a cluster, a crest. Cf. *The Green Linnet,* 25: "Yon *tuft* of hazel trees"; and Shaks. *As You Like It,* III. v. 75: "The *tuft* of olives."

13. one green hue, 'a uniform hue of green.' Since their fruits are unripe and green, the fruit-trees are undistinguishable from other trees. In the 1798 edition Wordsworth wrote:

> "With their unripe fruits,
> Among the woods and copses lose themselves,
> Nor with their green and simple hue, disturb
> The wild green landscape."

16. sportive wood. The hedge-rows are not formal hedges, but strips of coppice that has, as it were, playfully spread itself in lines.

17. wreaths of smoke etc. Cf. "*Not Love, not War,*" 7, 8:

> "Watching the twilight smoke of cot or grange,
> Skyward ascending from a woody dell."

18. in silence. There is no sound or sign of human life except the smoke; so that the spectator might imagine it to come from a gypsy camp or a hermit's cave.

23. Through, *i.e.* throughout, during.

24. As is a landscape etc., *i.e.* I retained every detail in my mental vision, which he could not do.

28, 29. Felt in the blood ... mind. Not only were my bodily senses and mental feelings refreshed, but my intellectual powers also.

30, 31. feelings ... pleasure, pleasurable feelings, which, though the occasion of them be forgotten, have an unconscious influence upon our lives, prompting us to kind actions. Cf. *The Prelude,* Book ii. 315-318:

> "The soul
> Remembering how she felt, but what she felt
> Remembering not, retains an obscure sense
> Of possible sublimity."

37. Of aspect more sublime, of a higher quality.

38-49. In which ... things. In this mood, the sense of depression caused by things in this world that we cannot understand, such as the presence of evil and suffering, is relieved ; and under the guidance of our higher emotions, our vital functions and animal nature are for the time suppressed, and we become all spirit : and so, with our mental vision calmed by the confidence that harmony and not chaos governs the world, and by the joy that comes from this state of spiritual exaltation, we are able to see things in their true aspect and to discern their inner meanings. Cf. *The Prelude*, ii. 299-302 :

> "Difference
> Perceived in things, where, to the unwatchful eye,
> No difference is, and hence, from the same source,
> Sublimer joy."

39. weary, wearisome, irksome.

47. eye made quiet. Cf. *A Poet's Epitaph*, 51 : "The harvest of a *quiet eye.*"

51. shapes, manifestations, experiences.

52. the fretful stir etc. There seems to be a reminiscence of two passages from Shakspere here ; cf. *Hamlet*, I. ii. 133, 134 :

> "How weary, stale, flat and *unprofitable*
> Seem to me all the uses of this world ! "

And *Macbeth*, III. ii. 23 :

> "After life's fitful *fever* he (Duncan) sleeps well."

And cf. *The Prelude*, i. 278-281 (of the river Derwent) :

> "Giving me
> Amid the fretful dwellings of mankind
> A foretaste, a dim earnest, of the calm
> That Nature breathes among the hills and groves."

A'so *Ib.* ii. 440-447 :

> "If, in this time
> Of dereliction and dismay, I yet
> Despair not of our nature .   .   .
>   .   .   .   the gift is yours
> Ye winds and sounding cataracts ! 'tis yours
> Ye mountains ! thine, O Nature ! "

And ll. 128-134 below.

54. hung ... heart, weighed my heart down ; oppressed my feelings.

55. turned to thee, *i.e.* for relief and healing.

58. with gleams etc. The sight of the old scene awakens recollections of the past, as dying embers are stirred into a blaze.

60. sad perplexity. These recollections are somewhat confused, and therefore sad.

61. The picture of the mind, the mental picture that he had carried away with him five years before ; see l. 1.

65. so, *i.e.* that it will be so.

67. like a roe etc. A Biblical image. Some of David's warriors (1 *Chron.* xii. 8) were "as swift as the *roes* upon the mountains." Cf. " *Three years she grew,*" 13-15 :

> "She shall be as sportive as the *fawn*
> That, wild with glee, across the lawn
> Or up the mountain springs."

73. coarser pleasures. Such as bathing, boating, skating, bird-nesting (see *Prelude,* Book i.).

74. animal movements, mere bodily activity and enjoyment of nature, as opposed to the deeper impression she produced upon his mind in later life.

75. To me was all in all. Cf. *The Prelude,* viii. 346 :

> "Nature, prized
> For her own sake, became my joy, even then."

77. a passion, an object of intense desire.

80. An appetite, things that he hungered for. The words "passion, appetite" indicate the sensuousness of his attitude towards nature at this time, as opposed to the contemplativeness of later years. The mere outward colours and forms of scenery satisfied him. In his Preface to the edition of 1815, Wordsworth quotes this passage as "representing implicitly some of the features of a youthful mind, at a time when images of nature supplied to it the place of thought, sentiment, and almost of action."

84. aching joys. Cf. Shelley, *With a Guitar, to Jane,* 6-8 :

> "Make the delighted spirit glow,
> Till joy denies itself again,
> And, *too intense, is turned to pain.*"

And *The Excursion,* i. 282-286 :

> " He was o'erpowered
> By Nature ; by the turbulence subdued
> Of his own mind ; by mystery and hope
> And the first virgin passion of a soul
> Communing with the glorious universe."

Also *Ib.* iv. 111-122.

86. Faint I etc. Cf. ll. 137-139, and *Intimations of Immortality,* 179-186.

91. The still ... humanity. Cf. *Ib.* 183, 184 ; 196-198. To the worshipper of nature, lightened of "the weary weight of all this unintelligible world " (ll. 39, 40), and able to "see into the life of things " (l. 49), even human sorrow and suffering is part of one harmonious whole, and so, though their contemplation sobers him, it does not fret him.

94. A presence, *i.e.* something present in Nature. Cf. p. 144.

disturbs me. Cf. Coleridge, *Love*, st. 17 :

> "My faltering voice and pausing harp
> *Disturbed* her soul with pity !"

95-102. a sense ... all things. In Wordsworth's mind, animate and inanimate objects, God and Nature, were so closely connected and interwoven, that he could feel the presence of one divine spirit diffused and working through the whole realm of Nature and Man. Cf. *The Prelude*, ii. 401-409 :

> "I felt the sentiment of Being spread
> O'er all that moves and all that seemeth still ;
> O'er all that " etc.

And *The Excursion*, ix. 1-15, where "an active Principle " is said to "subsist in all things," and is

> "Spirit that knows no insulated spot,
> No chasm, no solitude ; from link to link
> It circulates, the Soul of all the worlds."

105, 106. the mighty world Of eye and ear, the world as it is revealed to us through sight and hearing.

106. what they half create. Wordsworth noted the resemblance of this line to one of Young's, who (*Night*, vi. 427) says that the senses "half create the wondrous world they see." Part of the influence of a scene in nature is subjective and derived from the seer himself.

108. the language of the sense, the interpretation (of nature) by the senses ; my sense-perceptions of natural objects.

109-111. The anchor ... being. The contemplation of nature through the senses helped me to retain my hold upon my highest and purest conceptions ; cherished, directed, and strengthened my feelings ; and formed the mainspring of my conscience and will. Cf. *The Prelude*, ii. 447-451 :

> "O Nature ! thou hast fed
> My lofty speculations ; and in thee,
> For this uneasy heart of ours, I find
> A never-failing principle of joy
> And purest passion."

113. my genial spirits, my natural cheerfulness. Cf. Milton, *Samson Agonistes*, 594 :

> "So much I feel my *genial spirits* droop."

114. thou, his sister Dorothy.

116. in thy voice etc.   You have now the same feelings towards nature that I had then.

117, 118. read My former pleasures.   Cf. ll. 148, 149.

122, 123. Nature ... loved her.   Nature was never found wanting to those who loved her.   The lovers of nature always have their love amply rewarded.

125. inform, mould by internal forces, inspire with life.   Cf. *Yew Trees,* 19; *An Evening of Extraordinary Splendour,* 35; and Milton, *Par. Lost,* iii. 593, 594 (of the sun):

> " Not all parts like, but all alike *inform'd*
> With radiant light, as glowing iron with fire."

Also Dryden, *Absalom and Achitophel,* Part I. 156-158:

> " A fiery soul, which working out its way
> Fretted the pigmy body to decay
> And o'er-*informed* the tenement of clay."

126, 127. impress ... beauty.   Cf. " *Three years she grew,*' st. 3, where Nature says of Lucy :

> " And hers shall be the breathing balm,
>   And hers the silence and the calm
>   Of mute insensate things."

134. Therefore, *i.e.* since this early simple delight in nature will be succeeded (as in my own case) by a higher, if more chastened, joy.   Cf. Wordsworth's lines *To a Young Lady,* beginning " Dear child of Nature."

138. wild ecstasies, the "aching joys " and " dizzy raptures " of ll. 84, 85.

139. a sober pleasure.   Cf. note to l. 90.

when thy mind etc.   Cf. *The Daffodils,* 21, 22:

> " They flash upon that inward eye
>   Which is the bliss of solitude."

143. If solitude etc.   It was so.   Dorothy Wordsworth's last years were spent in a condition of physical and mental decay. Cf. *To H. C.* 13, 14, and note.

148, 149. catch ... existence.   See ll. 116-119, and notes.

159. for thy sake, *i.e.* because thou wert with me ; cf. ll. 111-115.

INFLUENCE OF NATURAL OBJECTS.

INTRODUCTION.

COMPOSED at Goslar, in Germany, in 1799.   The passage comprising ll. 45-107 was first published in *The Friend,* Dec. 28, 1809, with the title " Growth of Genius from the Influences of

Natural Objects on the Imagination, in Boyhood and Early Youth," and was afterwards included in *The Prelude*, a biographical poem composed 1799-1805, but not published till 1850. The remaining lines (1-44 and 108-122) are those that, in *The Prelude*, precede and follow this passage, and are added here because they help to illustrate it and explain its bearing.

NOTES.

1. **by her,** *i.e.* by Nature.

3. **cave.** Perhaps *cove* is the true reading. "Rocky cave" sounds tautological; and how could the boat be tied to a tree, if it were in a cave? Cf. ll. 31, 32.

17. **an elfin pinnace,** a very light boat. *Elfin* (= *elf-en*) is the adjective form of *elf*, a sprite, a faery. *Pinnace* is from Lat. *pinus*, a pine, because made of pine-wood.

22. **a huge peak.** There have been different attempts to localize this peak and the "craggy steep." Professor Knight's opinion is that the latter is the ridge of Ironkeld, and the former is either the summit of Wetherlam or of the Pike o' Blisco. The lake on which he rowed is Esthwaite, near those of Coniston and Windermere.

23. **with ... instinct.** As if it were a living thing, endued with the power of will and action.

24. **I struck,** *i.e.* struck the water with my oars; rowed.

30. **stole my way,** 'stealthily made my way.' An instance of a verb with a cognate object, in which the verb and the noun are not co-extensive in meaning. Similarly 'to steal a look' = 'to stealthily look a look.'

37. **unknown modes of being.** I dimly and vaguely felt that there were existences outside the range of my own consciousness—mysterious forms which haunted my mind to the exclusion of the living world around me.

In these lines (ll. 21-44), "the boy's mind is represented as passing through precisely the train of emotion which we may imagine to be at the root of the theology of many barbarous peoples. This passage might fairly be cited as an example of the manner in which those objects, or those powers, can impress the mind with that awe which is the foundation of savage creeds" (Myers's *Wordsworth*).

✗ 46-48. **Thou Soul ... motion.** Wordsworth conceived that a divine Spirit animated and so rendered ideally immortal all objects. Cf. *Tintern Abbey*, 100, and note to l. 95; *Nutting*, 56: "There is a spirit in the woods."

50. **for me,** in my case. Cf. ll. 116-119.

52-54. Not with ... nature, *i.e.* thou didst not intertwine my human passions or feelings with things of mere human production (such as a factory chimney or a railway train), but with higher. lasting, natural objects (such as a yew tree or a mountain peak).

54. purifying relates to " Soul," l. 2.

55. elements, first principles, sources.

56, 57. sanctifying . fear. Nature by her teaching makes even the feelings of pain and fear have a salutary effect upon the mind and character. Cf. l. 118 : " With hope and fear " ; and *Intimations of Immortality,* 183, 184, and note.

58. A grandeur etc. It is thus that nature reveals to us that a lofty teaching is to be found in the mere play of the emotions.

59. fellowship, communion with nature.

64. trembling, sparkling and quivering in the dim light.

68. all the summer long, ' for the whole length of summer. *Long* is an adverb, and *summer* is an adverbial objective modifying it. Layamon uses, convertibly, the two forms þene longe dæi (*Brut.* vol. iii. p. 131) and þene dæi longe (*ib.* p. 62), *longe* being in each case an adjective agreeing with *dæi* in the accusative case. In later English the latter form of the phrase appears to have been adopted, and we get " (all) day long," with *long* used adverbially.

71. through the twilight blazed. The poet altered this, forty-nine years later, in *The Prelude* version, into " blazed through twilight gloom." The alteration, a doubtful improvement, has the drawback of repeating the expression (" gloomy ") of l. 65.

72. their summons, *i.e.* to go home. Cf. l. 33.

75. village clock. The village of Hawkshead.

77. shod with steel, *i.e.* wearing skates. *All* is an adverb.

79. Confederate, uniting in games.

81. loud-chiming. Cf. Shakspere, *Midsummer-Night's Dream,* IV. i. 120-123, where Theseus describes his hounds as

" Match'd in mouth like bells
Each under each. A cry more tuneable
Was never holla'd to, nor cheer'd with horn.

The original reading was, less happily, ' loud-bellowing.'

83-86. with the din ... iron. With the remarkable sound-effect of this passage cf. that of Tennyson, *Morte d'Arthur,* 186-190 :

" Dry clash'd his harness in the icy caves
And barren chasms, and all to left and right
The bare black cliff clang'd round him, as he based
His feet on juts of slippery crag that rang
Sharp-smitten with the dint of armed heels."

And S. T. Coleridge, *The Friend,* vol. ii. p. 325 : " When **very** many are skating together, the sounds and the noises give an impulse to the icy trees, and the woods all round the lake *tinkle*."

87. an alien sound, *i.e.* an echo, which seems something aloof and apart from the 'tumult' which produced it. It is this sense of the majestic aloofness of nature that prompts the feeling of melancholy.

88. not unnoticed. Cf. " *There was a boy*," 18-21 :

"Then, sometimes, in that silence, while he hung
  Listening, a gentle shock of mild surprise
  Has carried far into his heart the voice
  Of mountain-torrents,"

where also the voice of nature makes itself heard in a pause of "jocund mirth and din."

93. Glanced, darted, sped. Cf. *Fidelity*, 8, 9 :

" A dog is seen
  Glancing through that covert green."

94. To cut across the reflex, 'to skate over the reflection.' The reading of 1809 was 'To cut across the image,' altered in the edition of 1820 to 'To cross the bright reflection.' Tennyson (*In Memoriam*, cviii. 3) has " The *reflex* of a human face."

95. The *Prelude* version has : "That fled, and, flying still before me, gleamed," with no stop after "star."

99, 100. spinning ... motion. The banks continued to whirl swiftly past him, as he sped onwards between them. Mr. Turner remarks : "The banks on either side would seem to have a circling motion towards the skater, due to the nearer part of each bank seeming to move past him faster than the parts further off." But I doubt whether the poet meant more than that the banks "spun," *i.e.* moved rapidly, past him on either side.

101. reclining etc. A skater can stop himself abruptly by leaning backwards, and so digging the sharp heels of his skates into the ice.

103. Wheeled by me. The brain is retentive of the sensation of movement for some time after the movement that excited it has ceased. Thus we feel a ship's rolling for days after a voyage is over.

104. With visible motion etc. The emphasis is on 'visible.' It seemed as though he could *see* the earth revolving. *Round* is cognate object to *rolled*. Cf. " *Three years she grew*," st. 5 : "Where rivulets *dance* their wayward *round*." And l. 30 and note.

106. Feebler and feebler, moving or seeming to move more and more slowly (as the sense of the motion passed from the brain).

107. a summer sea. Wordsworth altered this in the *Prelude* version into "a dreamless sleep."

108. presences, manifestations; the inspired "forms and images" of l. 47. Cf. *Tintern Abbey*, 94.

110. souls of lonely places. Cf. *Nutting*, 56: "There is a *spirit* in the woods."

115, 116. Impressed ... desire, made all objects, even inanimate ones, seem dangerous (as in the case of the "huge peak" of l. 22) or desirable—awful or beautiful.

118. triumph and delight refers to "desire," as *hope and fear* refers to "danger."

119. Work like a sea. Under the influence of these feelings the earth's surface became to me like the sea's surface—full of change and agitation.

Not uselessly employed, *i.e.* I should not be uselessly employed.

THE RAINBOW.

INTRODUCTION.

COMPOSED at Town-end, Grasmere, in 1802, and first published in 1807.

Coleridge writes in *The Friend*, i. p. 58: "Men laugh at the falsehoods imposed on them during their childhood, because they are not good and wise enough to contemplate the past in the present, and so to produce that continuity in their self-consciousness, which Nature has made the law of their animal life. Men are ungrateful to others, only when they have ceased to look back on their former selves with joy and tenderness. They exist in fragments." And again in *Biographia Lit.* iv. : "To carry on the feelings of childhood into the powers of manhood; to combine the child's sense of wonder and novelty with the appearances which every day perhaps for forty years have made familiar,—this is the character and privilege of genius." Compare also *The Excursion*, ix. 36-44 :

> "Ah ! why in age
> Do we revert so fondly to the walks
> Of childhood—but that there the soul discerns
> The dear memorial footsteps unimpaired
> Of her own native vigour ; thence can hear
> Reverberations ; and a choral song
> Commingling with the incense that ascends,
> Undaunted, toward the imperishable heavens,
> From her own lonely altar ?"

And *The Prelude,* v. 507-511 :
> " Our childhood sits
> Our simple childhood, sits upon a throne
> That hath more power than all the elements.
> I guess not what this tells of being past,
> Nor what it augurs of the life to come."

NOTES.

7. The Child ... Man. *Child* is the emphatic word here. It is to what he was as a child—to his childhood's instincts and desires, that the individual owes the better and nobler part of his nature in manhood. Cf. Introduction. Coleridge says of the critic who should despise this thought as puerile : "Not willingly in his presence would I behold the sun setting behind our mountains." Cf. also Milton, *Par. Regained,* iv. 220, 221 :
> " The childhood shews the man,
> As morning shews the day."

And Dryden, *All for Love,* iv. 1 : " Men are but children of a larger growth."

8, 9. And I could ... piety. *Piety* is used here in its Latin sense (see *Laodamia,* Introduction) of 'dutiful affection and reverence,' and the sequence of thought is : 'Since the Child is *father* to the Man, the Man naturally ought to love and reverence the Child, as a son does his father, by cherishing, as he grows older, the simple feelings of his childhood and youth, and thus preventing any breach of continuity in his spiritual development.' Cf. Pope, *Essay on Man,* iv. 175 : "The Boy and Man an individual makes"; and Introduction.

In the light of the above explanation, we can understand the propriety of the adoption of lines 6-8 by Wordsworth as a motto to his *Intimations of Immortality,* begun in the following year.

RESOLUTION AND INDEPENDENCE.

INTRODUCTION.

COMPOSED at Town-end, Grasmere, in 1802, and first published in 1807.

"This old man," Wordsworth says, "I met a few hundred yards from my cottage ; and the account of him is taken from his own mouth. I was in the state of feeling described in the beginning of the poem, while crossing over Barton Fell, at the foot of Ullswater, towards Askam. The image of the hare I then observed on the ridge of the Fell." In

K

Dorothy Wordsworth's Journal of Oct. 3, 1800, we find: "We met an old man almost double. He had on a coat thrown over his shoulders above his waistcoat. Under this he carried a bundle, and had an apron on, and a nightcap. His face was interesting. He had dark eyes and a long nose. ... His trade was to gather leeches ; but now leeches were scarce, and he had not strength for it."

A letter of Wordsworth's refers to this poem : "I will explain to you, in prose, my feelings in writing that poem. I describe myself as having been exalted to the highest pitch of delight by the joyousness and beauty of nature ; and then as depressed, even in the midst of these beautiful objects, to the lowest dejection and despair. A young poet in the midst of the happiness of nature is described as overwhelmed by the thoughts of the miserable reverses which have befallen the happiest of all men, viz. poets. I think of this till I am so deeply impressed with it, that I consider the manner in which I was rescued from my dejection and despair almost as an inter-position of Providence. A person reading the poem with feelings like mine will have been awed and controlled, expecting some-thing spiritual and supernatural. What is brought forward? A lonely place, a pond, by which an old man *was*, far from all house or home : not *stood*, nor *sat*, but was—the figure presented in the most naked simplicity possible. This feeling of spirituality or supernaturalness is again referred to as being strong in my mind in this passage. How came he here ? thought I, or what can he be doing ? I then describe him, whether ill or well is not for me to judge with perfect confidence ; but this I *can* con-fidently affirm, that though I believe God has given me a strong imagination, I cannot conceive a figure more impressive than that of an old man like this, the survivor of a wife and ten children, travelling alone among the mountains and all lonely places, carrying with him his own fortitude and the necessities which an unjust state of society has laid upon him. ... But, good heavens ! such a figure, in such a place ; a pious, self-respecting, miserably infirm and pleased old man telling such a tale !"

"Two trains of ideas form the substance of the poem : the interaction, namely, of the moods of Nature with the moods of the human mind ; and the dignity and interest of man as man, depicted with no complex background of social or political life, but set amid the primary affections and sorrows, and the wild aspects of the external world " (Myers's *Wordsworth*).

NOTES.

5. Over ... broods. In his Preface to the edition of 1815, Wordsworth remarks upon this line : " The stock-dove is said to coo, a sound well imitating the note of the bird ; but by the intervention of the metaphor *broods*, the affections are called in by the imagination to assist in marking the manner in which the bird reiterates and prolongs her soft note, as if herself delighting to listen to it, and participating of a still and quiet satisfaction, like that which may be supposed inseparable from the continuous process of incubation."

18. **Or heard them not,** *i.e.* whether I listened to them or not, I was happy.

28. **Dim sadness ... blind thoughts.** The epithets point to the vague and unintelligible nature of his sad feelings.

31. **child of earth.** Similarly the poet addresses "A Young Lady who had been reproached for taking long walks in the country " as " Dear child of Nature !"

33. **I walk,** 'I take my way in life, I live.' This indefinite meaning is common in the Bible; cf. *Romans,* xiii. 13 : "Let us *walk* honestly "; and *Feast of Brougham Castle,* 159.

36. **My whole life** etc. Cf. Wordsworth's description of himself in *Stanzas written in Thomson's ' Castle of Indolence,'* 3-7 :

> " For never sun on living creature shone
> Who more devout enjoyment with us took :
> Here on his hours he hung as on a book,
> On his own time here would he float away,
> As doth a fly upon a summer brook."

Stanza 3 of the same poem points to the same terrible reaction of spirit, following his joyous hours of insight and inspiration, that is delineated in stanzas 4-7 of this poem.

43. **Chatterton.** A poet of precocious genius, born at Bristol in 1752. With wonderful skill he palmed upon the world sundry professed ancient manuscripts as the poems of Rowley, a Bristol priest of the 15th century. In 1769 he went to London, trusting to literature for a livelihood. But this resource failing him, he fell into deep despondency, caused by absolute want, and poisoned himself at the age of eighteen.

44. **sleepless,** unresting, eager, full of literary enthusiasm.

45. **him who walked** etc. The reference is to the poet Burns, who writes of himself (*A Bard's Epitaph*) as one who "runs himself life's mad career, Wild as the wave," and whose "thoughtless follies laid him low And stained his name." See Introduction to *At the Grave of Burns.*

46. **Following his plough.** Cf. *At the Grave of Burns,* 27.

47. **By our ... deified.** We poets imagine ourselves to be as gods, exalted above the ordinary human destiny of suffering and misfortune.

49. **madness.** The poet's early enthusiasm is dashed by a hard world, and ends in melancholy and insanity. Shakspere (*Mid-*

summer-Night's Dream, v. i. 7) classes together the lunatic and the poet; and cf. Dryden, *Absalom and Achitophel*, Part I., 163, 164:

> " Great wits are sure to madness near allied,
> And thin partitions do their bounds divide."

50. **by peculiar grace** etc. See Wordsworth's letter in the Introduction.

54. **bare to the eye of heaven.** Cf. " *The world is too much with us*," 5; and *Stray Pleasures*, 16: " In the broad open eye of the solitary sky."

47. **As a huge stone** etc. On these images Wordsworth remarks: "The stone is endowed with something of the power of life to approximate it to the sea-beast; and the sea-beast stripped of some of its vital qualities to assimilate it to the stone; which intermediate image is thus treated for the purpose of bringing the original image, that of the stone, to a nearer resemblance to the figure and condition of the aged man, who is divested of so much of the indications of life and motion as to bring him to the point where the two objects unite and coalesce in just comparison."

For a similar image, cf. *Nutting*, 35-37:

> " Green stones
> That, fleeced with moss, under the shady trees
> Lay round me, scattered like a flock of sheep."

These boulders, which are found all over England, are relics of glacial action. They were deposited by icebergs that floated southwards in the glacial epoch.

59. **the same.** One of Wordsworth's favourite prosaisms; cf. *Hart-leap Well*, 63; *Rob Roy's Grave*, 118; *The Affliction of Margaret*, 5.

68. **constraint of pain** etc. Dorothy Wordsworth (*Journal*) tells us that the old man "had been hurt in driving a cart, his leg broken, his body driven over, his skull fractured."

70. **more than human,** greater than man can support.

75. **Motionless as a cloud.** Cf. *Hart-leap Well*, 2: " With the slow motion of a summer's cloud." The poet is fond of cloud-similes; cf. *Daffodils*, 1: " I wandered lonely as a cloud "; *Rob Roy's Grave*, 91: " Kingdoms shall shift about like clouds."

78. **himself unsettling,** *i.e.* stirring from his fixed and motionless posture.

91. **yet-vivid,** *i.e.* vivid, or bright and piercing, though he was so old. Cf. *The Excursion*, i. 426-428: " Time ... had not tamed his eye."

94. a lofty utterance etc. Wordsworth said of the leech-gatherer to a friend that "he gave to his poetic character powers of mind which his original did not possess."

104. Housing, finding a lodging for himself. Cf. *Peele Castle*, 54.

114. hope ... fed, hope that does not expect its fulfilment.

122. about his feet. That the leeches might fasten on to them.

125. they have dwindled. Cf. Dorothy Wordsworth's Journal: " He said leeches were very scarce, partly owing to this dry season ; but many years they had been scarce. He supposed it was owing to their being much sought after ; that they did not breed fast ; and were of slow growth. Leeches were formerly 2s. 6d. the 100 ; now they were 30s."

136. stately in the main. Cf. ll. 93-95.

138. decrepit is from Lat. *decrepitus*, 'that makes no noise' ; hence, 'creeping about noiselessly like an old man,' 'broken down with age.'

"IT IS A BEAUTEOUS EVENING."

INTRODUCTION.

COMPOSED on the beach near Calais in August 1802, and first published in 1807.

It has been thought that the "girl" addressed in line 9 was Dorothy Wordsworth, but it is more probable that the reference is to the girl Caroline mentioned in her Journal : "We arrived at Calais at four o'clock on Sunday morning, the 3rd of July ... We found out Annette and C. at Madame Avril's in the Rue de la Tête d'or. The weather was very hot. We walked by the shore almost every evening with Annette and Caroline, or William and I alone ... It was beautiful on the calm hot night to see the little boats row out of harbour with wings of fire, and the sail-boats with the fiery track which they cut as they went along, and which closed up after them with a hundred thousand sparkles and streams of glowworm light. Caroline was delighted." It is not known who Annette and Caroline were.

NOTES.

1. **free,** fresh, pleasant. In the older English poetry *free*, especially in the phrase 'fair and free,' is often used without any special significance.

3. **Breathless.** So rapt in adoration as scarcely to breathe.

broad. Not a conventional epithet. At evening the sun

appears larger—an optical illusion caused by the refraction of his rays passing very obliquely through the atmosphere. Cf. Tennyson, *The Princess*, iii. 345, 346 :

> "The sun
> Grew *broader* toward his death."

9. **Dear child !** etc. See Introduction.

12-14. **Thou liest ... not.** It is the privilege of childhood to live all the year round in a spiritual atmosphere, and to be admitted into intimate communion with the Unseen ; the child being ever under divine influence, though we may fail to recognize that it is so. Cf. *Intimations of Immortality*, 66-74 ; and *The Prelude*, v. 506-509 :

> " Dumb yearnings, hidden appetites, are ours,
> And *they must* have their food. Our childhood sits
> Our simple childhood, sits upon a throne
> That hath more power than all the elements."

The term " Abraham's bosom " is used in the Bible for heaven ; cf. *Luke*, xvi. 22 : " The beggar died, and was carried by the angels into Abraham's bosom." The " Temple's inner shrine " refers to the " Holy of Holies," or most holy place of Solomon's temple, into which only the High Priest was allowed to enter once a year.

"WHEN I HAVE BORNE IN MEMORY."

INTRODUCTION.

COMPOSED in September 1802, and first published in 1807. This sonnet was printed previously in *The Morning Post*, Sept. 17, 1802, under the title *England.* S. T. Coleridge has prefixed it as a motto to his " Poems occasioned by Political Events."

Two other sonnets of Wordsworth, commencing " O Friend ! I know not which way I must look " and " Milton ! thou should'st be living at this hour," were also written in Sept. 1802, shortly after his return from France to London, when, as he tells us, he " could not but be struck with the vanity and parade of our own country, especially in great towns and cities," and " the mischief engendered and fostered among us by undisturbed wealth." A fourth sonnet, " *It is not to be thought of,*" also composed in Sept. 1802, seems to indicate the turning of the tide, as it were, of Wordsworth's thoughts on this subject :

> " We must be free or die, who speak the tongue
> That Shakespeare spake ; " etc.

And in the present sonnet, the flood sets in the opposite direction to that of the first two sonnets, and he finds in England "a bulwark for the cause of men."

NOTES.

3, 4. When men ... gold. Cf. *Written in London, Sept. 1802*, 7 :
" The wealthiest man among us is the best," and 9-11 :

" Rapine, avarice, expense,
This is idolatry ; and these we adore :
Plain living and high thinking are no more. "

And " *The world is too much with us*," 2, 4. Also Tennyson, *Maud*, Part I. i. 6 : " Why do they prate of the blessings of Peace ? we have made them a curse " with " lust of gain," in times " when only the ledger lives. "

4. bower, chamber ; O.E. *búr*, from *buan*, to dwell. In *London, 1812*, 4, *bower* is used in the medieval sense of 'lady's apartment'; in *Hart-leap Well*, 92, it is used in the modern sense of ' arbour.'

10. a bulwark etc. In allusion to England's efforts in the cause of liberty against the Napoleonic tyranny.

11. I by my ... beguiled. My affection for my country misled me into cherishing fears on her account.

14. As a lover or a child. I felt on her account the jealous, causeless fears that lovers feel for each other, or that a parent feels about his child.

TO H. C.

INTRODUCTION.

COMPOSED in 1802, and first published in 1807.

Hartley Coleridge, to whom these verses were addressed, was the eldest son of Samuel Taylor Coleridge, and was born at Clevedon in 1796. He entered at Oxford and became fellow of Oriel College, but lost his fellowship chiefly through a habit of intemperance, and his fortunes were blighted. He afterwards became a school-master, but failed at that occupation, and spent his remaining years in literary labours. Many of his poems are of great excellence. He died at Rydal in 1849.

An extract from a letter of his father's, dated July 25, 1800, well illustrates this poem : " Hartley is a spirit that dances on an aspen leaf ; the air that yonder sallow-faced and yawning tourist is breathing, is to my babe a perpetual nitrous oxide. Never was more joyous creature born. Pain with him is so wholly trans-substantiated by the joys that had rolled on before, and rushed on after, that oftentimes five minutes after his mother has whipt him, he has gone up and asked her to whip him again. "

1. from afar. His fancies are strange and unfamiliar, as though he had brought them with him from some far-off state of existence. Cf. *Personal Talk*, 25; *Intimations of Immortality*, 61; and Tennyson, *Far—far—away*, st. 3, 4, 5:

> " What vague world-whisper, mystic pain or joy,
> Thro' those three words would haunt him when a boy,
> > Far—far—away?
>
> A whisper from his dawn of life? a breath
> From some fair dawn beyond the doors of death
> > Far—far—away?
>
> Far, far, how far? from o'er the gates of Birth,
> The faint horizons, all the bounds of earth,
> > Far—far—away?"

2-4. Who ... carol. Whose childish speech, to us seemingly irrelevant, forms the disguise of thought too profound to be uttered; which is thus brought into harmony with the light, airy movements and spontaneous songfulness of childhood.

5. Thou faery voyager! etc. The child is of so buoyant and ethereal a disposition, that he seems to the poet a sort of vision-ary child, a creature of the air rather than of the earth.

8. To brood on air. Wordsworth's note refers the reader to " Carver's description of his situation upon one of the lakes of America."

10. Where earth etc. His temperament is a blending of the earthly and the ethereal, of the real and the visionary.

13, 14. I think ... years. This sad presentiment was borne out by Hartley Coleridge's subsequent career; see Introduction. Compare a similar conjecture, also realized, in the case of Dorothy Wordsworth; see *Tintern Abbey*, 143, and note. Words-worth tells us that the lines

> " Or strayed
> From hope and promise, self-betrayed,"

in *Written in a Blank Leaf of Macpherson's Ossian*, were " sug-gested from apprehensions of the fate of his friend, H. C."; and adds that " the piece to ' Memory ' arose out of similar feelings."

16. thy house, the house of thy mind. For a similar meta-phor, cf. *Tintern Abbey*, 140, 141.

19. too industrious folly. It is foolish of me to occupy myself so unnecessarily with such thoughts.

23. Preserve for thee etc. Thou wilt retain, as thy special prerogative, the simplicity and purity of childhood when thou reachest manhood. Among grown-up men thou wilt be still a child.

27. **Thou art a dew-drop** etc., *i.e.* thy nature is too delicate and ethereal to sustain the rough contact of hardship or misfortune. Thou wilt either escape earthly sorrow, or be annihilated by it.

YEW-TREES.

INTRODUCTION.

COMPOSED at Grasmere in 1803, and first published in 1815.

Of the yew-trees described, "the pride of Lorton vale" was a mere ruin in 1880, and has since disappeared; but "the fraternal four of Borrowdale" stood firm and strong till December 1883, when the great gale of the 11th of that month uprooted one bodily and completely wrecked the others.

Ruskin (*Modern Painters*) remarks upon "the real and high action of the imagination in Wordsworth's *Yew-trees* (perhaps the most vigorous and solemn bit of forest landscape ever painted). ... The reader should refer to it : let him note especially, if painter, that pure touch of colour, 'by sheddings from the pining umbrage tinged.'" Mr. Stopford Brooke writes (*Theology in the English Poets*) that the poet's description suggests "an ideal grove, in which the ghostly masters of mankind meet, and sleep, and offer worship to the Destiny that abides above them, while the mountain flood, as if from another world, makes music to which they dimly listen."

NOTES.

1. **Lorton Vale** lies about four miles south of Cockermouth, in Cumberland, while some five miles further south is Borrowdale (l. 14).

3. **its own darkness**, the gloom that it makes for itself with its huge, overshadowing boughs. The foliage of the yew is thick and dark. Cf. l. 9, and note to l. 14. Also Tennyson, *In Memoriam*, ii. : "the *dusk* of thee" (the yew).

of yore. *Yore* is the genitive plural of O.E. *geár*, a year, so that 'of yore' = of years, *i.e.* in years past. Cf. 'of a day,' 'of a morning,' and Shaks. *Hamlet*, I. v. 60 : "My custom always *of the afternoon.*" See p. 198.

4. **Not loth to furnish.** An instance of the 'pathetic fallacy,' the meaning being that the tree frequently furnished etc. Cf. *Feast of Brougham Castle*, 142, and note.

5. **Of Umfraville or Percy.** The reference is to the old border frays, such as the Battle of Otterbourne, in 1838, between Percy on the English side and Douglas on the Scotch. There are

several Umfravilles mentioned in Scotch history as fighting
against the Scots at Bannockburn and elsewhere. The weapon,
both of these and of the English soldiers who fought in the
French battle-fields mentioned below, was the bow, made of the
wood of the yew-tree. It was the English archers with their
yew bows that won the battles of Crecy and Poitiers. Chaucer
(*Parliament of Fowles*, 180) calls the tree "the shooter yew";
and cf. Drayton, *The Ballad of Agincourt*, st. 10 :

> " With Spanish yew so strong,
> Arrows a cloth-yard long,
> That like to serpents stung,
> Piercing the weather."

The 'long bow' was six feet long, and the arrow three feet.

7. **Azincour** or Agincourt is a village in the north of France,
about forty miles south of Calais. It was here that Henry V.,
on Oct. 15, 1415, defeated the French army, though four times
more numerous than his own.

8. **Crecy, or Poictiers.** Crecy is in the department of the
Somme, about ten miles south-west of Agincourt. Poitiers is in
the department of Vienne, one of the western departments of
France, south of the Loire. In the battle of Crecy, fought on
Aug. 26, 1846, Edward III. defeated Philip of Valois whose
army numbered 120,000, or more than three times the number of
the English. The battle of Poitiers was fought on Sept. 19,
1356, between the Black Prince and King John, whose army
was five times more numerous.

9. **Of vast circumference.** Prof. Knight quotes from a friend's
letter, dated May 1880 : " The tree in outline expanded towards
the root considerably : then, at about two feet from the ground,
the trunk began to separate into huge limbs, spreading in all
directions. I once measured this trunk at its least circumference,
and found it 23 feet 10 inches."

11. **Produced too slowly etc.** Yew trees are of very slow
growth, especially in rocky situations, and attain an age of
many centuries.

14. **those fraternal four.** Cf. *The Excursion*, i. 29, 30 :

> " The gloom
> Spread by a *brotherhood* of lofty elms."

And *Sonnet at —— Castle*, 6 :

> "A *brotherhood* of venerable trees."

17, 18. **serpentine Up-coiling.** Cf. Tennyson, *The Last Tourna-
ment*, 12-14 :

> "A stump of oak half-dead,
> From roots like some *black coil of carven snakes*
> Clutch'd at the crag."

18. **inveterately convolved**, inextricably twisted together or

entangled. Cf. Tennyson, *Gareth and Lynette*, 221-224, of the Gate of Camelot, upon which

> " Were Arthur's wars in weird devices done,
> New things and old *co-twisted*, as if Time
> Were nothing, so *inveterately*, that men
> Were giddy gazing there."

Inveterate (from Lat. *vetus*, old) is applied to what has become fixed and established through long continuance; as, 'an *inveterate* habit,' ' an *inveterate* talker.'

19. **Nor uninformed with phantasy.** The tree has a weird influence, arising from its fantastic appearance. To *inform*, in this connection, means ' to mould internally, to inspire.' Cf. *Tintern Abbey*, 125, and note.

20. **a pillared shade,** hence forming a "natural temple" (l. 29). Cf. Tennyson, *Arabian Nights*, 39 : "Imbower'd vaults of *pillar'd* palm." Similarly Cowper (*The Poplar Field*, 2) calls a plantation of poplars a " colonnade," lit. ' a row of columns.'

21. **grassless.** Because no grass will grow under so thick a shade.

22. **By sheddings** etc., by the fall of withered leaves.

23. **Perennially** (Lat. *per*, through, *annus*, year) means ' all through the year,' or ' through many years, unceasingly.' The former sense suits the yew, since it is an evergreen, and sheds its leaves all the year round.

25. **unrejoicing berries,** cheerless, obnoxious berries. The berries as well as the leaves of the yew are highly poisonous.

ghostly shapes etc. This loftily imaginative passage is a fine example of the new Romantic movement, marked, as it is, by a complete detachment from the real and the actual, and culminating in a dreamy suggestiveness. A similar picture occurs in Vergil, *Æneid*, vi. 273-284. Rapt in contemplation of this spot of overshadowing gloom, the poet's imagination peoples it with appropriate presences. It is a place fitted to rouse the feelings of fear and of hope that is almost despair ; it is a place for silence and for musing upon the future ; it is a place where thoughts of death and the shortness of human life naturally occur to the mind. To the poet these abstract ideas transmute themselves into ghostly shapes ; these column-like trunks supporting a roof of shade become their temple ; these scattered stones, their altars ; and he imagines them as either holding solemn festival there together, or as dimly listening to the roar of the neighbouring cataract.

28. **Time the shadow.** Life in the Bible is frequently compared to a shadow ; cf. *Psalms*, cii. 11 : "My days are like a shadow that declineth."

33. **Glaramara** is one of the mountains enclosing Borrowdale.

AT THE GRAVE OF BURNS.

INTRODUCTION.

COMPOSED in 1803, and first published in 1842.

In Dorothy Wordsworth's Journal of a Tour in Scotland we find: "Thursday, August 18th.—Went to the churchyard where Burns is buried. A bookseller accompanied us. He showed us the outside of Burns's house, where he had lived the last three years of his life, and where he died. It has a mean appearance, and is in a bye situation, white-washed. ... Went on to visit his grave. He lies at a corner of the churchyard, and his second son, Francis Wallace, beside him. There is no stone to mark the spot; but a hundred guineas have been collected, to be expended on some sort of monument."

Robert Burns was born in Ayrshire in 1759 of very poor parents, and worked on a farm taken by himself and his brother. In 1786 he published a volume of poems, was invited to Edinburgh, and welcomed and flattered by the highest society of the capital. After this he could no longer content himself without indulgence in sensual and exciting pleasures, which were followed by embarrassments, depression, and broken health. He died at Dumfries, July 21, 1795.

NOTES.

11. **my wishes and my fear,** *i.e.* my wish that thou could'st appear, and my shrinking with pain at thy tomb.

13. **Off weight ... weight!** Away with grief! Let me not pile grief on grief that is there already!

15. **chastened,** sober, calm.

19. **Fresh as the flower** etc. Cf. Burns, *To a Mountain Daisy,* 13-16 :

> " Cauld blew the bitter-biting north
> Upon thy early, humble birth ;
> Yet cheerfully thou *glinted* forth
>   Amid the storm."

Glinted means ' glanced, gleamed.'

whose modest worth. Burns's poem begins : " Wee, *modest,* crimson-tippéd flow'r."

21. **like a star** etc. As a star shines down upon the spot from whence it rose, so Burns's genius glorified its humble origin.

27. **the aspirant of the plough,** ' the aspiring ploughman. Burns died at the age of 37 ; hence " full soon."

31. **but as one,** *i.e.* while I mourned his death with many others, I had a deeper grief of my own.

35, 36. **How verse ... truth.** How poetry treating of the humble actualities of life may yet be dignified and inspired. *Truth*—not mere literal truth, but truth informed and spiritualized by the imagination—was, for Wordsworth, the first law of poetry.

37. **the current,** the current of my thoughts.

39. **Huge Criffel's** etc. Criffel, a mountain on the shores of Solway Firth, a short distance south of Dumfries, where Burns lived, is visible from Skiddaw in Cumberland, which is not far from Wordsworth's residence at Grasmere,—so that Burns and he were neighbours, and he is pursued with regret that they had not been also friends. Dorothy Wordsworth (*Journal*) says: "We saw the Cumberland mountains, within half a mile of Ellisland, Burns's house. ... We talked of Burns, and of the prospect he must have had, perhaps from his own door, of Skiddaw and his companions, including ourselves in the fancy that we *might* have been personally known to each other."

45. **Where the main** etc. Where two persons' characters are in the main congenial, nature has the skill to utilize minor differences to bring them closer together.

49. **The tear will start.** Cf. Burns, *A Bard's Epitaph*, 17, 18:
> "Here pause—and, thro' the *starting tear,*
> Survey this grave."

50. **"poor Inhabitant below."** A quotation from the same poem, l. 19:
> "The *poor Inhabitant below*
> Was quick to learn and wise to know," etc.

Cf. *Resolution and Independence*, 45, and note. Dorothy Wordsworth (*Journal*) writes: "We looked at the grave with melancholy and painful reflections, repeating to each other his own verses" (from *A Bard's Epitaph*).

53. **gowans,** daisies.

61. **a son.** Francis Wallace; see Introduction.

70. **here.** At the grave of Burns, who was misled etc.

78. **For which it prayed.** Though giving the verses a different application, Wordsworth apparently refers to Burns's ode *To Ruin*, 25-28:
> "I court, I beg thy friendly aid,
> To close this scene of care!
> .   .   .   .   .   .
> No fear more, no tear more,
> To stain my lifeless face
> Enclasped, and grasped
> Within thy cold embrace!'

In Wordsworth's MS. a different version of this stanza formed the third of the poem. It ran :

> " But wherefore tremble ? 'tis no place
> Of pain and sorrow, but of grace,
> Of shelter, and of silent peace
>   And ' friendly aid ' ;
> Grasped is he now in that embrace
> For which he prayed."

—where clearly the reference is to the ode *To Ruin*.

79. Sighing I turned etc.   With this stanza compare the last of Mr. William Watson's splendid ode, *The Tomb of Burns* :

> " While, plumed for flight, the Soul deplores
> The cage that foils the wing that soars ;
> And while, through adamantine doors,
>   In dreams flung wide,
> We hear resound on mortal shores
>   The immortal tide."

80. I heard ... hear.   Cf. Vergil, *Æneid*, vi. 454 : *Aut videt aut vidisse putat*, ' He sees or thinks he sees ' ; and Milton, *Par. Lost*, i. 713 : " Sees or dreams he sees."

82. ritual, ceremonial, solemn.

83. love that casts out fear.   Cf. Bible, *1 John*, iv. 18 : " There is no fear in love : but perfect love casteth out fear."

" SHE WAS A PHANTOM."

INTRODUCTION.

COMPOSED at Town-end, Grasmere, in 1804, and first published in 1807.   Wordsworth says : " The germ of this poem was four lines composed as part of the verses on the *Highland Girl*. Though beginning in this way, it was written from my heart, as is sufficiently obvious."   It is doubtful what were the four lines referred to.   They can hardly be lines written at first for the *Highland Girl*, but afterwards transferred to this poem, because the *Highland Girl* is in the second person, while the subject of " *She was a phantom* " is in the third.   It appears probable that they are ll. 15-18 of *To a Highland Girl*.   In that poem, after telling us that the girl and her surroundings seem

> " Like something fashioned in a dream ;
> Such forms as from their covert peep
> When earthly cares are laid asleep ! "

the poet continues (ll. 15-18) :

> " But O fair creature ! in the light
> Of common day, so heavenly bright,
> I bless thee, vision as thou art,
> I bless thee with a human heart."

These four lines might well suggest to Wordsworth the present poem, the keynote of which is that the " phantom of delight" is " a spirit, yet a woman too."

That the subject of this poem is his wife Mary, is certain both from a statement made by Wordsworth to the late Hon. Justice Coleridge, and from a conversation with Henry Crabb Robinson, in which the poet said that the pieces " ' Our walk was far among the ancient trees,' then ' She was a phantom of delight,' and finally the two sonnets ' To a Painter,' should be read in succession as exhibiting the different phases of his affection to his wife."

If other proof were needed, both Wordsworth's remarks, quoted above, about this poem, and his obvious allusion to it in *The Prelude*, in verses written in 1805 that refer to his future wife, point in the same direction. See *The Prelude*, xiv. 268-271 :

> " She came, no more a phantom to adorn
> A moment, but an inmate of the heart,
> And yet a spirit, there for me enshrined
> To penetrate the lofty and the low."

NOTES.

1. a phantom of delight. Cf. *The Prelude*, vi. 224-227 :

> " Another maid there was, who also shed
> A gladness o'er that season, then to me,
> By her exulting outside look of youth
> And placid under-countenance, first endeared."

The three stanzas of this poem represent woman under three aspects. In the first, she is depicted as an ideally beautiful and entrancing object in man's eyes ; in the second, as the pleasant companion of his every-day life ; in the third, as an intellectual and moral being, fitted to be his adviser and comforter.

4. To be ... ornament, to give a mere momentary pleasure, and then to disappear.

5, 6. Her eyes ... hair. Cf. Byron, *" She walks in beauty,"* st. 1, which reads like an expansion of these two lines :

> " She walks in beauty, like the night
> Of cloudless climes and starry skies ;
> And all that's best of dark and bright
> Meet in her aspect and her eyes :
> Thus mellowed to that tender light
> Which heaven to gaudy day denies."

6. Like twilight's. Cf. Milton's " the raven down Of Darkness " (*Comus*, 251, 252). Her eyes and hair were dark ; but her complexion was fair and clear, and her disposition gay and cheerful. Cf. " her exulting outside look of youth " quoted above.

13. household motions. Movements made in the performance of household occupations.

14. steps of virgin liberty. The light tread of the maiden, free as yet from the cares and responsibilities of married life.

16. records, promises. A countenance whose expression told of a happy and blameless past, and betokened as happy and blameless a future. Cf. Byron, "*She walks in beauty,*" 15, 16 :

> " The smiles that win, the tints that glow,
> But tell of days in goodness spent."

17. A creature etc. Cf. Wordsworth's lines addressed to his wife :

> " Let other bards of angels sing,
> Bright suns without a spot ;
> But thou art no such perfect thing :
> Rejoice that thou art not ! "

And "*Her only pilot,*" 12-14 :

> " While here sits one whose brightness owes its hues
> To flesh and blood ; no goddess from above,
> No fleeting spirit, but my own true love ! "

18. human ... food. She was not too superfine to satisfy the common wants of human nature in every-day life. Cf. *The Prelude*, v. 411, 412 :

> " A race of real children ; not too wise,
> Too learned, or too good."

22. pulse of the machine. The inner workings of this intricate piece of mechanism, *i.e.* the directing forces of her whole nature and disposition. Cf. *The Waggoner*, iv. 802, 803 :

> " I had been
> On friendly terms with this *machine.*"

And Shaks. *Hamlet*, ii. ii. 124 : " Thine evermore, most dear lady, whilst this *machine* is to him, Hamlet."

24. A traveller .. death. One who passes through life with a sense of its duties and responsibilities.

ODE TO DUTY.

INTRODUCTION.

COMPOSED in 1805, and first published in 1807.

In the edition of 1837 Wordsworth prefaced this poem with

the motto : " Jam non consilio bonus, sed more eò perductus, ut non tantum rectè facere possim, sed nisi rectè facere non possim "; ' No longer good by resolve, but reaching by habit this goal— that not only can I do right, but that I cannot do otherwise than right.' " This ode," says Wordsworth, " is on the model of Gray's *Ode to Adversity*, which is copied from Horace's *Ode to Fortune*. Many and many a time have I been twitted by my wife and sister for having forgotten this dedication of myself to the stern lawgiver. Transgressor indeed I have been from hour to hour, from day to day : I would fain hope, however, not more flagrantly, or in a worse way, than most of my tuneful brethren. But these last words are in a wrong strain. We should be rigorous to ourselves, and forbearing, if not indulgent, to others ; and, if we make comparison at all, it ought to be with those who have morally excelled us."

NOTES.

1-8. Duty is a God-given rule of conduct under whose guid-ance and support the struggle between right and wrong in the human breast is ended and peace is attained.

1. **Stern ... God !** Cf. Gray's *Ode*, who addresses Adversity as "Daughter of Jove, relentless Power," and "Stern rugged Nurse." The sense of Duty is implanted by God in the human heart ; it is an emanation of the Divine Will.

2. **if that name thou love,** *i.e.* the name of "Duty." So Milton (*P. L.*, iii. 6) addressing Light : "Or hear'st thou rather pure ethereal stream ; *i.e.* ' Dost thou prefer to be called ? '

5, 6. **Thou, who ... overawe.** Under thy guidance we gain the victory over groundless terrors, since the only thing we have to fear is disobedience to thy commands.

7. **vain temptations.** If we are influenced solely by Duty, nothing has power to tempt us to do wrong.

vain, foolish, worldly. Cf. *The Somnambulist*, 149, 150.

> " In hermit's weeds repose he found,
> From *vain temptations* free."

8. **strife,** the inner struggle between right and wrong. Cf. Bible, *Romans*, vii. 23 : " I see another law in my members (*i.e.* body), warring against the law of my mind."

9-16. There are some happy souls who follow Duty merely from a natural impulse towards what is right, but who yet may need her help.

9. **There are who,** ' there are those who '; an imitation of the Latin idiom *sunt qui.*

L

9. **ask not** etc.　Cf. Cowper, *Task*, ii. 788-793 :

> " Some minds are tempered happily,　.　　.
> .　.　.　.　.　they thirst
> With such a zeal to be what they approve,
> That no restraints can circumscribe them more
> Than they themselves by choice, for wisdom's sake. "

And Patmore, *The Angel in the House*, x. i. 37-40 :

> " Souls, found here and there,
> Oases in our waste of sin,
> Where everything is well and fair,
> And Heav'n remits its discipline. "

10. **in love and truth**, in their love of what is right and sincerity in following it.　Such persons are troubled by no doubts as to their conduct.

12. **the genial sense of youth**, the warm and kindly impulses that belong to the time of youth.　Cf. " *It is a beauteous evening,*" 9-14 ; *Intimations of Immortality*, 66.

13. **without reproach or blot**, free from blame and from the stain of wrong-doing.

14. **and know it not**, without knowing that they do it.

15. **confidence misplaced.**　A confidence in their own virtuous instincts, which turns out to be misplaced.

17-24. Blessed is the state of those who can completely rely upon love and joy to guide them ; and happy too are they who make such reliance the rule of their life, but supplement it by the support of Duty.

18. **happy will our nature be.**　Our nature will contain no jarring elements ; all our feelings and inclinations will be in happy harmony with one another.

19. **unerring light.**　*Unerring* is emphatic ; ' a light upon which we can rely never to lead us astray.'

20. **joy its own security.**　Our happiness guarantees itself ; our possession of happiness proves this happiness to be well-founded, and therefore permanent.

22. **Even now**, even under present conditions ; in this world.

Not unwisely bold, bold without being unwise ; combining boldness with discretion.　Cf. l. 53, *lowly wise*, ' wise and at the same time humble.'

23. **Live in ... this creed**, rely upon love and joy to guide them right.

25-32. I, however, through inexperience and too much self-confidence, have often disobeyed the commands of Duty ; but I would do so no longer.

25. loving freedom. Cf. *Inscriptions*, i. 17, 18 :

> ' What is truth ?—a staff rejected ;
> Duty ?—*an unwelcome clog.*"

And *The Prelude*, vi. 32-35 ;

> " That overlove
> Of freedom which encouraged me to turn
> From regulations even of my own
> As from restraints and bonds."

26. No sport ... gust, although not carried away by wild gusts of passion.

28. reposed my trust, been self-confident.

29. when in my heart etc., when Duty uttered its bidding through the Conscience. *Timely,* opportune.

31. smoother walks, the easier paths of self-indulgence, as opposed to the rugged and difficult path of Duty. So Tennyson (*Wellington Ode*, 212, etc.) speaks of "the path of duty" as climbed "with toil of heart and knees and hands," and of its "toppling crags."

33-40. This desire is not the outcome of strong feeling, but of a longing for rest in my soul—for a mental and moral equilibrium.

33. disturbance, perturbation, agitation. Cf. Coleridge, *Love,* 68 :

> " My faltering voice and pausing harp
> *Disturbed* her soul with pity ! "

34. wrought, produced. *Wrought* is the archaic past participle of *work*.

36. thought. The meditative mood, as opposed to the mood of passion.

37. unchartered. *Chartered* means exercising freedom under certain provisions, as those of the famous Magna Charta. Cf. Churchill, *Gotham*, i. 49 : "An Englishman in *chartered freedom* born." Hence *unchartered* means exercising freedom without any such provisions, unconditionally free, unbridled, anarchical. Cf. Shaks. *As You Like It*, II. vii. 47-8 :

> " I must have liberty
> Withal, as large a charter as the wind."

38. weight, burden. Cf. *The Sonnet*, 13.

chance, casual ; cf. *random*, l. 26.

39. change their name, be variable and discordant.

41. The aspect of Duty, though severe, is kind ; for from her emanates not only moral but physical law—the beauty of nature and the order of the universe.

41. Stern, *i.e.* though thou art stern ; cf. l. 1.

41-44. thou dost wear ... upon thy face. Cf. Tennyson, *Wellington Ode*, 203, etc. :

> " He that walks it (the path of Duty)
> .   .   . before his journey closes,
> He shall find the stubborn thistle bursting
> Into glossy purples, which outredden
> All voluptuous garden roses."

46. fragrance ... treads. Cf. *Laodamia,* 34, and note. And Tennyson, *Maud,* Part I. xii. 5 :

> " I know the way she went
> Home with her maiden posy,
> For her feet have touched the meadows
> And left the daisies rosy."

And *Ib. Œnone,* 94 :

> "At their (the goddesses') feet the crocus brake like fire.'

And B. Jonson, *The Sad Shepherd,* I. i. 8, 9 :

> " And where she went, the flowers took thickest root,
> As she had sow'd them with her odorous foot."

Also Persius, *Sat.* ii. 38 : *Quidquid calcaverit hic, rosa fiat !* 'May whatever he treads become a rose !' And Hesiod, *Theogony,* 194, 195 ; ἀμφὶ δὲ ποίη Ποσσὶν ὕπο ῥαδινοῖσιν ἀέξατο, 'Thick sprouted the grass beneath the slender feet (of the goddess).'

47-8. Thou dost ... strong. Natural law and moral law both emanate from the same source, the Deity, and are but two applications of the same principle. Hence Duty, the moral sanction, is really one with the great physical law that directs and preserves the order of the universe. Cf. *Gypsies,* 21-24 ·

> " Oh better wrong and strife
> (By nature transient) than this torpid life ;
> *Life which the very stars reprove*
> *As on their silent tasks they move.*"

And Mr. Wm. Watson, *The Things that are more Excellent,* st. 4 :

> " The stars of heaven are free because
> In amplitude of liberty
> Their joy is to obey the laws."

Cf. also Ulysses's speech in Shaks. *Troilus and Cressida,* I. iii. 83 etc., where 'Degree' (*i.e.* the due arrangement or subordination of things) is an allied notion to Duty, and where physical as well as moral order are shown to depend upon its observance. *Wrong,* injury. *Most ancient, i.e.* in spite of their great antiquity.

49-56. Henceforth I place myself under the guidance of Duty. May she enable me to give up my old foolish self-confidence and become her obedient and enlightened servant !

53 lowly wise. See note to l. 22.

54. **self-sacrifice**, a readiness to give up "straying in smoother walks" (l. 31).

55. **The confidence of reason**, confidence based upon reasonable grounds, as opposed to the "misplaced" confidence of l. 15.

56. **In the light of truth**, enlightened as to my true position. The phrase is opposed to the "blindly" of l. 28.

bondman. Cf. "thee I now would serve" (l. 31).

PEELE CASTLE IN A STORM.

INTRODUCTION.

COMPOSED in 1805, and first published in 1807.

The poem was suggested by a picture painted by Sir George Beaumont, a friend of the poet, and a landscape painter of some repute. He died in 1827. Wordsworth says: "Sir George Beaumont painted two pictures of this subject, one of which he gave to Mrs. Wordsworth, saying she ought to have it; but Lady Beaumont interfered, and after Sir George's death she gave it to Sir Uvedale Price, at whose house at Foxley I have seen it." The other is still in the Beaumont Gallery at Coleorton Hall, Essex, the seat of the artist.

There are two Peele Castles: one is on a rocky islet close to the town of Peele, on the west coast of the Isle of Man, separated from it by a narrow channel; the other, known as Piel Castle, is near Barrow-in-Furness, on the Lancashire coast. There is little doubt that this poem refers to the latter. For the poet spent four weeks (see ll. 1, 2) of a summer vacation in 1794 with his cousin, Mr. Barker, whose house was at Rampside, the village opposite Piel; and, from a comparison with the picture, it is apparent that it was this, and not Peele Castle in the Isle of Man, that the artist painted. Piel Castle was built by the Abbot of Furness in the first year of Edward III.'s reign.

Wordsworth headed this poem *Elegiac Stanzas*, in allusion to its reference to the loss of his brother John Wordsworth, captain of the *Abergavenny*, East Indiaman, which sprung a leak off St. Alban's Head, and went down with all on board on Feb. 6, 1805. He alludes to his death in *The Prelude*, xiv. 419-424:

> "A private grief
> Keen and enduring, which the mind and heart
>   .   .   .   needs must make me feel
> More deeply, yet enable me to bear
> More firmly."

Other poems relating to this event are *To the Daisy* and *Elegiac Verses in Memory of my Brother*. All three were placed by the poet among his "Epitaphs and Elegiac Pieces."

NOTES.

4. sleeping, *i.e.* it was reflected on the calm, still surface of the water. Cf. Shaks. *Merchant of Venice,* v. i. 54: "How sweet the moonlight *sleeps* upon this bank!"

8. It trembled etc., *i.e.* the sea was occasionally ruffled by a breeze, but never sufficiently to efface the image.

9. no sleep. The calm seemed a permanent one, and not, like sleep, temporary and liable to interruption.

10. No mood etc. It did not seem to be a state dependent on the weather or the time of year. *Season* is used here in a *general* sense, and so dispenses with the article.

14-16. the gleam ... dream. 'An ideal beauty, such as never actually existed, but is conceived of in the mind of the Poet and the Artist, and hallows their work.' Cf. *The Excursion,* i. 79: "The vision and the faculty divine." For *dream,* cf. *Intimations of Immortality,* 5, and note. In the editions of 1820 and 1827 these lines were altered to

"And add a gleam,
The lustre, known to neither sea or land,
But borrowed from the youthful Poet's dream."

Afterwards the original and far superior text was returned to.

15. that never was etc. Cf. Gray, *The Progress of Poetry,* 120: "Orient hues, unborrowed of the sun."

21, 22. a treasure-house ... years. A spot full of perfect, unending tranquillity.

22. a chronicle of heaven. A place whose history was a record of a more than earthly happiness.

25. had it been, *i.e.* it should have been.

26. Elysian quiet. See note to *Laodamia,* 95, and cf. ll. 97, 108 of that poem. Also Shaks. *Two Gent. of Verona,* II. vii. 37, 38:

"And there I'll rest, as after much turmoil
A blessed soul doth in Elysium."

28. silent ... life. The activities of nature noiselessly fulfilling their functions around us. Cf. *Lines written in Early Spring,* 3, 5; and *The Excursion,* 188: "The silent looks of happy things."

31. the soul of truth, 'complete truth or accuracy.' To my feelings at that time there would have been nothing fallacious in the picture.

32. betrayed, 'tampered with, impaired, lost.' This line originally ran:

"A faith, a trust that could not be betray'd."

35. A power. The power of perceiving things in their ideal aspect, apart from the disillusioning influences of daily life. Cf. *Intimations of Immortality*, st. 1 and 2 ; ll. 53-57 ; ll. 175, 176.

36. A deep distress etc. My brother's death has put an end to the old exaltation of feeling and brought me down to the level of my ordinary fellow-men, and into fuller sympathy with them. Cf. *Intimations of Immortality*, 183, 184.

39, 40. The feeling ... serene. The sense of the loss that I have sustained in my brother's death will always be fresh ; but I can speak with calmness and composure of the new experience which that sorrow has brought with it.

45. a passionate work etc. It is a picture that shows strong feeling in the artist, yet there are no exaggerated or ill-selected effects.

47. hulk, the dismasted ship represented in the painting.

. **50. I love to see etc.** He could regard the castle as emblematical of the "fortitude and patient cheer" that he welcomed. Its attitude is emphasized by the strong contrast of the labouring hulk beside it.

51. Cased ... time. Like a knight in armour of proof, the castle is represented as defying the attack of the elements with its stubborn, time-worn walls.

53. the hcart that lives alone etc. Cf. the lesson of Tennyson's *Palace of Art*, where the Soul that has isolated herself from human sympathy, eventually comes to loathe her solitude.

54. Housed in a dream, living in a world that it has idealized for itself. Cf. *housing,* p. 149.

the kind, *i.e.* its own kind, the human race.

57. cheer, cheerfulness, courage. Cf. *Fidelity,* 26 : " A lonely *cheer.*"

60. Not without hope. Cf. *Intimations of Immortality,* 179, 180 etc.

THE HAPPY WARRIOR.

INTRODUCTION.

COMPOSED early in 1806, and first published in 1807. Wordsworth tells us that these verses were written soon after tidings had been received of the death of Lord Nelson (on Oct. 21, 1805), which event directed his thoughts to the subject. "But," he continues, "his (Nelson's) public life was stained with ono great crime, so that though many passages of these lines were suggested by what was generally known as excellent in his conduct, I have not been able to connect his name with the poem as I could wish, or even to think of him with satisfaction in reference to the idea of what a warrior ought to be." He adds that many elements of the character here portrayed were found in his brother John. "His messmates used to call him the Philosopher, from which it must be inferred that the qualities and dispositions I allude to had not escaped their notice. ... He greatly valued moral and religious instruction for youth, as tending to make good sailors."

Mr. F. W. H. Myers (*Wordsworth*) remarks upon this poem : "Between these two men, so different in outward fates,— between 'the adored, the incomparable Nelson' and the homely poet, 'retired as noontide dew,'—there was a moral likeness so profound that the ideal of the recluse was realised in the public life of the hero, and, on the other hand, the hero himself is only seen as completely heroic when his impetuous life stands out for us from the solemn background of the poet's calm. ... For indeed this short poem is in itself a manual of greatness; there is a Roman majesty in its simple and weighty speech."

Notes.

3-5. who, when brought ... thought, who carries with him into the active duties of his manhood the fresh enthusiasm and single-heartedness of his boyhood. Cf. Patmore, *The Angel in the House*, x. i. 14-16 :

> "Youth, impatient to disown
> Those visions high, which to forget
> Were worse than never to have known."

6, 7. Whose high ... bright, who makes a noble purpose the guiding motive of all his actions.

9. This line is an Alexandrine ; cf. *Laodamia*, 90, and note.

11. But makes etc. He is not content with mere intellectual culture, but is careful to train and develop his moral character.

14. Turns his necessity etc. This is "one of the lessons which Wordsworth is never tired of enforcing, the lesson that virtue grows by the strenuousness of its exercise, that it gains strength as it wrestles with pain and difficulty, and converts the shocks of circumstance into an energy of its proper glow" (Myers). Cf. Cowper, *Table Talk*, 77, 78 :

> "To touch the sword with conscientious awe,
> Nor draw it, but when Duty bids him draw."

19. By objects etc. The frequent sight of pain and bloodshed, instead of making him callous to suffering, makes him the more compassionate ; see l. 26. Cf. Nelson's prayer before the battle of Trafalgar : " May humanity after victory be the predominant feature in the British fleet ! "—a humanity shown by himself in face of the blazing *Orient,* and in the harbour at Teneriffe.

22. **such sacrifice,** *i.e.* the sacrifice of his own feelings that prompt him to severity.

23. **More skilful in self-knowledge.** The more temptations he meets with, the better he learns to scan his own motives and principles of action.

29. **a state,** a situation, a condition of affairs.

30. **To evil** etc. Cf. Bible, *Romans,* iii. 8 : " Some affirm that we say, Let us do evil that good may come, whose condemnation is just."

34. **To virtue.** These words are emphatic—' to virtue, not to evil employed as a preventive against worse evil ' (l. 30).

38. **in himself,** etc., rest satisfied with his own conduct, without regretting the loss of office.

43, 44. **Whom ... at all.** Cf. Pope, *Temple of Fame,* 513, 514 :
    "Nor Fame I slight, nor for her favours call ;
    She comes unlook'd for, if she comes at all."
And Carew, *Epistle to the Countess of Anglesie,* 57, 58 :
    "He chose not in the active stream to swim,
    Nor hunted Honour, which yet hunted him."

44. **Like showers of manna.** Because manna was the *free gift* of God to the Israelites in the desert—food which they had not to labour to produce.

45. **powers,** moral force of character.

48. **But who** etc. Cf. Capt. Mahan, *Life of Nelson* : " For success in war, the indispensable complement of intellectual grasp and insight is a moral power, which enables a man to trust the inner light, a power which dominates hesitation, and sustains action, in the most tremendous emergencies. ... The two elements— mental and moral power—are often found separately, rarely in due combination. In Nelson they met."

51, 52. **Is happy ... inspired.** Confident in the purity of his aims, he can face a great crisis without being weighed down by a sense of responsibility. Cf. Southey, *Life of Nelson,* chap. vii., before the battle of Copenhagen : " No sooner was he in battle, where his squadron was received with the fire of more than a thousand guns, than, as if that artillery, like music, had driven away all care and painful thoughts, his countenance brightened, and his conversation became joyous, animated, elevated, and delightful."

53. **through the heat** etc. In the excitement of the struggle he keeps to the course of action that he had laid down for him-

self beforehand. "Clemency" Canning is a good instance in point.

54. **sees what he foresaw.** His anticipations are justified by the event.

56. **is equal to the need.** Cf. Tennyson, of the Duke of Wellington, *Ode*, 37 :

"O iron nerve to true occasion true !'

57. For the change of tone here, cf. the Introduction to *Brougham Castle*.

60. **homefelt pleasures** etc. Cf. the *Wellington Ode*, 236, 237

"One about whose patriarchal knee
Late the little children clung."

And " *I grieved for Buonaparte,*" 6-8 :

"The Governor who must be wise and good,
And temper with the sternness of the brain
Thoughts motherly, and weak as womanhood."

We have here " Nelson's womanly tenderness, his constant craving for the green earth and home affections in the midst of storm and war " (Myers).

62, 63. **such fidelity ... approve.** His most cherished aim is to show himself loyal to these gentler influences.

64. **More brave** etc. Cf. Tennyson's Song in *The Princess*, " *Thy voice is heard thro' rolling drums* " :

"A moment, while the trumpets blow,
He sees his brood about thy knee ;
The next, like fire he meets the foe,
And strikes him dead for thine and thee."

In reference to which Mr. P. M. Wallace points to "the vital truth that in all noble endeavour man's energy is inspired and his arm strengthened by the recollection of those whom he loves."

70, 71. **Plays .. won.** He chooses his course of action in life, not with a view to earthly honours or rewards, but because it will bring with it the " testimony of a good conscience."

73. The thought of home ties—of wife and children—makes some men shrink in the hour of trial.

76. **From well to better.** Adapted from Chaucer, *The Floure and the Leafe*, 571-573 :

"For knightes ever should be *persevering*,
To seeke honour without feintese or slouth,
Fro wele to better in all manner thinge."

self-surpast. To ' surpass oneself' means to go beyond any previous effort.

78. **to noble deeds give birth.** Cf. Goldsmith, *The Taking of Quebec*, 11, 12 (of Wolfe) :

"Yet shall they know thou conquerest, though dead !
Since from thy tomb a thousand heroes rise !"
And Trench, *The Alma*, 37-40 :
"And our sons unborn shall nerve them
For some great deed to be done,
By that twentieth of September,
When the Alma's heights were won."

79. his fame, the fame that was his due.

82. the mortal mist. Cf. Tennyson's " *Tears, idle tears*," in *The Princess* :
" When unto dying eyes
The casement slowly grows a glimmering square."

THE SONNET.

INTRODUCTION.

COMPOSED in 1806, and first published in 1807.

It is in reference to this sonnet that Wordsworth tells us how much he was struck by the sonnets of Milton when they were read to him by his sister one day in May 1802. "I took fire," he adds, "if I may be allowed to say so, and produced three sonnets the same afternoon."

This sonnet was originally entitled *Prefatory Sonnet*, as being introductory to the series of " Miscellaneous Sonnets."

NOTES.

3. pensive citadels, ' their studies.' The student shuts himself up in his study from the outer world (like beleaguered soldiers in the citadel of a castle) that he may be alone with his own thoughts ("pensive"). So Milton (*Il Penseroso*, 86) places the pensive man in "some high lonely tower." And cf. " *When I have borne in memory*," 4 : " the student's bower."

4. the wheel, *i.e.* the spinning-wheel. Till the invention of the spinning jenny in 1767, cotton-spinning was performed by the hand spinning-wheel, and was a common occupation for women. Cf. " *I travelled among unknown men*," 11, 12
" And she I cherished turned her *wheel*
Beside an English fire."

at his loom. The steam-loom was introduced in 1807, but in 1825 there were still 250,000 hand-looms in Great Britain. Their use is now almost extinct.

6. Furness-fells. Furness is an extensive mountainous district in the north-west of Lancashire, including the lofty Coniston fells or hills and those of Yewdale and Tilberthwaite.

8. In truth, the prison etc. When we imprison ourselves voluntarily, such imprisonment is not irksome. For the sentiment, cf. Lovelace, *To Althea ; from Prison*, 25-28 :

> "Stone walls do not a prison make,
>   Nor iron bars a cage ;
> Minds innocent and quiet take
>   That for a hermitage."

11. the sonnet's scanty plot. The sonnet is limited to fourteen lines, divided into two groups of eight and six lines each. In the first group (the octave), lines 1, 4, 5, 8, and lines 2, 3, 6, 7 rhyme together respectively; in the second (the sestet), the lines rhyme alternately, though (as in this sonnet) the order of the rhymes is often varied. The sonnet should be the expression of a single thought or sentiment.

13. the weight of too much liberty. Cf. *Ode to Duty*, 37, 38.

PERSONAL TALK.

INTRODUCTION.

COMPOSED at Town-end, Grasmere, in 1806, and first published in 1807.

Four lines from Sonnet IV. (ll. 51-54) have been placed by Dean Stanley underneath the statue of Wordsworth in the Baptistery of Westminster Abbey. This sonnet-sequence was classed among the "Poems of Sentiment and Reflection."

NOTES.

2. To season my fireside etc., to flavour the conversation at my fireside with an intermixture of gossip about friends and neighbours.

6. maidens ... stalk, maidens that grow old without being married, like flowers that wither unplucked. Cf. Shaks. *Mid. Night's Dream*, I. i. 76-78 :

> "But earthlier happy is the rose distill'd,
>   That that which *withering on the virgin thorn*
> Grows, lives, and dies in single blessedness."

7. wear out of me, fade from my recollection.

11. **To sit without emotion** etc. Cf. Cowper, *Task*, iv. 277-297:

"Not undelightful is an hour to me
So spent in parlour twilight; such a gloom
Suits well the thoughtful or unthinking mind,
The mind contemplative, with some new theme
Pregnant, or indisposed alike to all.

.   .   .   .

'Tis thus the understanding takes repose
In indolent vacuity of thought."

12. **In the loved** etc. Wordsworth says that this line "stood, at first, better and more characteristically, thus:

'By my half-kitchen and half-parlour fire.'

My sister and I were in the habit of having the tea-kettle in our little sitting-room: and we toasted the bread ourselves." The present reading was adopted in the edition of 1815. The "cottage" was Dove Cottage.

23. **Children are blest** etc. People who take pleasure in gossip and scandal are "true worldlings," since they care only for worldly matters; whereas it is the blessedness and the strength of childhood that its interest is divided between the real world that lies around them and the ideal world of imagination that is far removed from the actual and the present. Cf. *To H. C.* 1; *Intimations of Immortality*, 61.

25, 26. **sweetest ... sweet.** The best things are those that lie beyond the range of our senses. Cf. Collins, *The Passions*, 60: "In notes by distance made more sweet," an expression quoted by Wordsworth in *An Evening Walk*, 236, 237:

"Yon isle, which feels not even the milkmaid's feet,
Yet hears her song, 'by distance made more sweet.'"

27. **Whose mind** etc. The man who cares only for mere material objects and shuts out the world of thought and fancy from his view, is in the worst bondage, the bondage of the senses. Cf. *The Prelude*, xii. 151-153:

"I knew a maid,
A young enthusiast who escaped these bonds;
Her eye was not the mistress of her heart."

29. **Wings.** Powers of thought and feeling.

30-32. **wilderness ... low.** The influence of ordinary natural objects upon our minds, by the emotional state that it cherishes, exalts alike the greatest and the commonest thing of life. Cf. *Ib.* 171-173:

"God delights
In such a being; for her common thoughts
Are piety."

For *sanctify*, cf. *An Evening of Extraordinary Splendour*, 6.

33. **Dreams**, musings, excursions of the imagination.

34. **substantial.** As opposed to the ideal world of dreams.

41. **lady...Moor.** Desdemona, the wife of Othello; see Shakspere's *Othello*. Wordsworth said on one occasion that he thought *Othello*, the close of the *Phaedo*, and Walton's *Life of George Herbert*, the three " most pathetic " writings in the world.

42. **heavenly Una.** See Spenser, *Faery Queene*, i. 4, where the Red Cross Knight, representing reformed England, is accompanied by "a lovely ladie," Una, or Truth ; "And by her in a line a milke white lambe she lad," representing Innocence.

45. **rancour** is from Lat. *rancor*, ' rancidness, sourness,' and so, ' spite.'

50. **Rocks in its harbour.** My life is peaceful without being dull and insipid.

52. **Who gave us** etc. Cf. Wordsworth's account (Letter to Lady Beaumont, May 1807) of the purpose of his poetry : " To console the afflicted ; to add sunshine to daylight by making the happy happier ; to teach the young and the gracious of every age to see, to think, and feel, and therefore to become more actively and securely virtuous."

ADMONITION.

INTRODUCTION.

COMPOSED in 1806, and first published in 1807. Wordsworth gave it the heading : " Intended more particularly for the perusal of those who may have happened to be enamoured of some beautiful place of retreat in the country of the Lakes." It is possible that Dove Cottage, the poet's residence at Town-end, Grasmere, may have been in his mind when he wrote this sonnet.

NOTES.

4. **its own sky.** Cf. *Peter Bell*, 228-230 :

> " Where deep and low the hamlets lie
> Beneath *their little patch of sky*
> And little lot of stars."

7, 8. **who would ... impiety,** who would desecrate this specimen of nature's beautiful handiwork by living here themselves. A similar feeling finds expression in *Nutting*, 43-56.

11. **sacred to the poor.** The cottage and its surroundings derive their congruity and significance from their being a poor man's abode. The unity and beauty of the scene would be marred by the touch of a richer hand.

"THE WORLD IS TOO MUCH WITH US."

INTRODUCTION.

COMPOSED in 1806, and first published in 1807. It formed one of the " Miscellaneous Sonnets."

The idea of the poem is that when once we lose touch with nature, and have no eye or ear for her beauty or grandeur, we have no spiritual life, and our religion is but a sham. Better the old Greek's deification of the powers of nature than the empty materialism of modern days. Better a living faith in Pantheism than the dead and callous formalism of the worldly man's Christianity. Compare Tennyson's *The Higher Pantheism* :

" The sun, the moon, the stars, the seas, the hills, and the
      plains—
Are not these, O Soul, the Vision of Him who reigns ?

. . . .

And the ear of man cannot hear, and the eye of man cannot
      see ;
But if we could see and hear, this Vision—were it not He ? "

NOTES.

1. **The world**, *i.e.* worldliness, the pursuit of wealth and pleasure, to the exclusion of higher and nobler aims.

late and soon. Cf. Bible, *Psalms*, cxxvii. 2 : "It is vain for you to rise up early, to sit up late, to eat the bread of sorrows."

2. **we lay waste our powers.** We dissipate our higher spiritual energies.

3, 4. **Little ... boon.** Wordsworth's belief was that we all have an inward spiritual love which enables us to understand nature, even as a babe its mother ; see *Prelude*, ii. 260-263 :

" Such, verily, is the first
Poetic spirit of our human life,
By uniform control of after years,
In most, abated or suppressed."

The mind trained in business, science, or social activities loses this sympathetic instinct, and can see in nature nothing but the merely external. Thus we are like Esau ; we have bartered our spiritual birthright ; this inner sympathy ("our heart") we have given away for a mess of pottage, mere worldly success.

Boon is O. E. *bén*, Scand. *bón*, a prayer ; hence the answer to a prayer, a favour, a gift. " A sordid boon " = a mean, mercenary bargain.

5-7. The sea ... flowers. Nature is full of sympathy ("The sea that bares her bosom to the moon") and of spiritual voices, as "The winds that will be howling," which, even when motionless, Wordsworth thinks of as still living, only asleep, like flowers with petals folded at night.

7. up-gathered, composed to rest.

sleeping flowers. In the absence of sunlight some flowers close their petals, *e.g.* the pimpernel ; and most flowers do so at night ; the delicate stamens and seed-organs being thus protected from the cold and dew of night. Cf. Keble, *Christian Year, 15th Sunday after Trinity,* 55 : "Go sleep like closing flowers at night."

8. For this, for sympathy with the sea, the winds—nature in general.

we are out of tune. And so we (1) make a discord with nature, and (2) fail to vibrate sympathetically with nature. Two musical instruments perfectly in tune with each other can set each other in motion, if either be played upon.

9. It moves us not. It stirs no responsive emotion within us.

Great God ! An exclamation of strong feeling. Cf. *Westminster Bridge,* 13 : "*Dear God !* the very houses seem asleep."

I'd rather be etc. Cf. *The Excursion,* iv. 613-621 :

" Yet rather would I instantly decline
To the traditionary sympathies
Of a most rustic ignorance, and take
A fearful apprehension from the owl
Or death-watch : and as readily rejoice,
If two auspicious magpies crossed my way ;—
To this would rather bend than see and hear
The repetitions wearisome of sense,
Where soul is dead, and feeling hath no place."

10. pagan, a heathen. Lat. *paganus,* 'a villager' ; since the country-folk adhered to their heathen superstitions after Christianity had become the accepted religion of the city-folk.

11. So might I, if so (*i.e.* by being a pagan) I might.

on this pleasant lea. The particular spot is unknown. *Lea,* a meadow or grassy plain, is found in local names, as Brom-*ley,* Had-*leigh.*

12. forlorn, O.E. *forloren,* p.p. of *forleósan,* means 'utterly lost.' Here the sense is 'forsaken, left solitary.' To us, spoiled by civilization, nature is dead : in her presence we find ourselves solitary, unfriended. The heathen were better off : for them every tree had its wood-nymph, every stream its Naiad ; every form of nature might give chance "glimpses" of some indwelling spirit.

13. **Proteus.** A mythological sea-deity (son of Oceanus and Tethys), an old man of the sea. He tended the seal-flocks of the sea-god Poseidon or Neptune. If any one caught him in his mid-day sleep on the shore of his dwelling (the island of Carpathos, between Crete and Rhodes), and then held him fast, undaunted by the weird shapes into which he transformed himself, Proteus would finally resume his proper personality and reveal the unknown secret to his questioner. Cf. Milton, *Par. Lost*, iii. 603, 604, of philosophers who

> "call up unbound
> In various shapes old Proteus from the sea."

13, 14. **sight ... hear.** Line 13, answering to l. 5, represents a *sight* of nature, as l. 14, answering to l. 6, represents a *sound*.

14. **Triton.** A son of Poseidon and Amphitrite; figured as a man with a dolphin's tail, who, as an attendant on the sea-god, calms the waves by blowing on his conch or spiral shell ("wreathèd horn"). Cf. Spenser, *Colin Clout's come Home again*,

> Triton, blowing loud his wreathèd horne."

FEAST OF BROUGHAM CASTLE.

INTRODUCTION.

COMPOSED in 1807, and first published in the same year. Words-worth says : "This poem was composed at Coleorton while I was walking to and fro along the path that led from Sir George Beaumont's farmhouse, where we resided, to the Hall, which was building at that time."

Henry, Lord Clifford, the subject of this poem, was the son of John, Lord Clifford, who was killed at Ferrybridge, the day before the battle of Towton. It was this John who slew the young Earl of Rutland, son of the Duke of York, after the battle of Wakefield ; and, besides this act, the family of Clifford had done enough to draw upon them the vehement hatred of the House of York : so that after the battle of Towton there was no hope for them but in flight and concealment. Accordingly the child Henry was carried off to the northern wilds, and remained de-prived of his estate and honours during the space of twenty-four years ; all which time he lived as a shepherd in Yorkshire, or in Cumberland, where the estate of his father-in-law (Sir Lancelot Threlkeld) lay. He was restored to his dignities in the first year of Henry VII. It is recorded that "when called to Parliament, he behaved nobly and wisely ; but otherwise came seldom to London or the Court ; and rather delighted to live in the country, where he repaired several of his castles, which had

M

gone to decay during the late troubles." There is a tradition current in the village of Threlkeld and its neighbourhood, his principal retreat, that, in the course of his shepherd life, he acquired great astronomical knowledge. He died in 1523, and was buried in Bolton Priory.

The following is the substance of Sara Coleridge's criticism of this poem: "The ode commences in a tone of festivity. The Clifford is restored to the home of his ancestors. Then it falls away to the remembrance of times of war and flight and distress, when the Clifford was brought, a little child, to the shelter of a northern valley. After a while it gradually rises into a strain of elevated tranquillity and contemplative rapture; through the power of the imagination, the beautiful and impressive aspects of nature are represented as gladdening and exalting the lonely man's spirit, whilst they keep it 'pure and unspotted from the world.' Suddenly the poet returns to the point whence he started, and flings himself back into the tide of stirring life. All is to come over again, struggle and triumph and overthrow. I know nothing, in lyric poetry, more affecting than the final transition from this part of the ode, with its rapid metre, to the slow elegaic stanzas at the end, when from warlike fervour the poet passes back into the sublime silence and solemn tenderness of Nature." A similar change of tone occurs in the *Happy Warrior*, from the "heat of conflict" (l. 53) to "homefelt pleasures" and "gentle scenes" (l. 60).

NOTES.

1. **breathless hall**, *i.e.* hall full of breathless listeners.

2. **Emont's murmur.** The river Emont flows past Brougham Castle, which is in Westmoreland, two miles south of Penrith. It is now a ruin.

7. **Her thirty years** etc. The thirty years of adversity for the House of Lancaster date from its defeat in the first battle of St. Albans, 1455, to its triumph in the battle of Bosworth, 1485, and the accession of Henry VII. For *winter*, cf. Shaks. *Richard III.* I. i. 1: "the *winter* of our discontent."

9. **She lifts** etc. Cf. Butler, *Hudibras*, II. i. 567, 568:
" That shall infuse eternal spring,
And *everlasting flourishing.*"

11. **Both roses flourish.** By the marriage of the Lancastrian, Henry VII., with Elizabeth of York, which united the two Houses.

15. **to both,** *i.e.* to Henry and his mother.

to her, Lady Margaret, the wife of John, Lord Clifford, and Henry's mother; see l. 54.

20. From every corner etc. The lady does not "keep her state," but passes round among the guests with words and looks of welcome.

21. above the board, *i.e.* on the dais or platform, where stood the "high table" at which the family and distinguished guests sat.

24. They, the combatants.

25. it was proved, proof was made ; the affair was settled.

Bosworth-field. Bosworth is in Leicestershire. The battle was fought on Aug. 22, 1485.

26. the avenger. Henry VII., Earl of Richmond, last scion of the House of Lancaster, who avenged the misfortunes of his line and the crimes of Richard III., by his defeat and death at the battle of Bosworth.

27. Earth helped etc. Wordsworth adapted this line from Sir John Beaumont's *The Battle of Bosworth Field* : "The earth assists thee with the cry of blood." Cf. God's words to Cain after his murder of Abel, Bible, *Genesis*, iv. 10 : "What hast thou done? the voice of thy brother's blood crieth unto me from the ground." The "cry of blood" here is Richard's murder of the young princes in the Tower.

28. St. George, the patron saint of England from very early times. He was martyred in Diocletian's persecution in 303.

30. Loud voice, etc., *i.e.* all England rejoices.

35. The glory, *i.e.* the glorious result.

36. Skipton. The Castle of Skipton in Yorkshire was the chief residence of the Cliffords. It was a " deserted tower " because its inmates, "knight, squire," etc., had come to the feast of Brougham Castle.

40. Pendragon. Pendragon Castle stands on the borders of Westmoreland, near the source of the river Eden. It was said to have been built by Uter or Uther Pendragon, the British king who preceded Arthur.

though the sleep etc., 'though she has been for many years in ruins.' The castle had been burned by Scottish raiders in 1341, and long remained in a ruinous state.

44. Brough. The Castle of Brough, or Brough-under-Stanmore, stands on the Hillbeck, a small tributary of the Eden.

46. she that etc. Appleby Castle, on the Eden.

49. lonely. For the same reason that Skipton was a "deserted tower " (l. 37).

51. one fair house. Brougham Castle.

54. his lady-mother. See note to l. 15.

56. the fatherless. Henry's father, John, Lord Clifford, having been slain at Ferrybridge, near Knottingley in Yorkshire, in 1461.

61. from the light, from publicity and discovery.

67, 68. her eyes Pray. Cf. Tennyson, *In Memorian*, xxxii.: " Her eyes are homes of silent prayer."

68. ghostly agonies, agonies of spirit.

69. Mary. The Virgin mother of Jesus Christ.

72. who is he. " He " is, of course, Henry, the "shepherd-lord."

73. Carrock's side. Carrock-fell is in Cumberland.

89. The boy must part etc. To escape pursuit, he had to leave these parts and conceal himself, disguised as a shepherd-boy, on Sir Lancelot Threlkeld's estates in Cumberland. The old hall of Threlkeld has long been a ruin.

 Mosedale's groves. North of Blencathara, or Saddleback, in the Lake District.

92. Glendermakin is a river that rises on the high ground to the north of Blencathara.

93. cheer, cheerfulness, happiness. Cf. *Peele Castle*, 57.

95. Sir Lancelot Threlkeld. See Introduction.

97. Thou tree of covert etc. Cf. *The Waggoner*, 628-639.

108. a weary time. Twenty-four years ; see Introduction.

114. grooms. Here used in the older and wider sense of 'servants, lads.'

122. the undying fish etc. It is imagined by the people of the country that there are two immortal fish, inhabitants of this tarn, which lies to the north of Blencathara, not far from Threlkeld.

131. where faeries sing. Cf. *The White Doe of Rylstone*, 267-271 :

> " The gracious fairy,
> Who loved the Shepherd-lord to meet
> In his wanderings solitary :
> Wild notes she in his hearing sang,
> A song of Nature's hidden powers."

134. Among the heavens. Alluding to his astronomical or astrological studies. See Introduction.

135. The face ... to be. Cf. *The White Doe*, 238-288 :

> " And hence, when he, with spear and shield,
> Rode full of years to Flodden-field,
> His eye could see the hidden spring,
> And how the current was to flow ;
> The fatal end of Scotland's king,
> And all that hopeless overthrow."

141. buried deep his book, his book of magic ("words of might," l. 137). Cf. Shaks. *The Tempest*, v. i. 54-57 (of Prospero, abjuring his magical arts):

> "I'll break my staff,
> Bury it certain fathoms in the earth,
> And deeper than did ever plummet sound
> I'll drown my book."

And Scott, *Lay of the Last Minstrel*, II. xv.:

> "I swore to bury his Mighty Book,
> That never mortal might therein look."

142-146. Armour ... shield. The weapons are represented as sympathizing with the purpose for which they are intended. Cf. *Yew-trees*, 4.

143. On the blood ... calls. The martial character of the Cliffords is well known. The four immediate progenitors of Henry, Lord Clifford, died in the field of battle.

148. Field of death etc. Perhaps in prophetic allusion to Flodden-field, a battle in which Henry was appointed to a principal command; see note to l. 135.

156. the flock of war, an army in the field. *Flock* is in allusion to his previous employment as a shepherd.

160. Was softened etc. After his restoration to his ancestral estates, he lived to a large extent in retirement at Barden Tower, with a small retinue, where he found a retreat equally favourable to taste, to study, and to devotion. The narrow limits of his residence and the smallness of his train show that he had learnt to despise the pomp of greatness.

161. Love had he found etc., *i.e.* during the time that he had lived as a shepherd-boy among the wilds of Cumberland and Yorkshire.

164. The sleep etc., the perfect stillness that broods, like a sleep, over the lonely mountains. Cf. *On Westminster Bridge*, 13: "Dear God! the very houses seem *asleep*"; and *Written in March*, 5: "The green fields *sleep* in the sun."

165. the savage virtue. Cf. *The Borderers*, iii. 56: "They say, Lord Clifford is a savage man." And see note to l. 143.

LAODAMIA.

INTRODUCTION.

COMPOSED in 1814 at Rydal Mount, after re-reading Vergil with his son, and first published in 1815.

Wordsworth says: "The incident of the trees growing and

withering put the subject into my thoughts, and I wrote with the hope of giving it a loftier tone than, so far as I know, has been given to it by any of the ancients who have treated of it. It cost me more trouble than almost anything of equal length I have ever written."

This poem is remarkable for its sympathy with the spirit of antiquity in its great moral and religious ideas, especially as expressed and interpreted by Vergil. "The idea," writes the Rev. W. A. Heard, "that underlies the poem is the same conception of 'piety' which Vergil has embodied in the *Æneid*. 'Piety' embraces all the duties of life that are based upon the affections —love of home and parents and children, love of the gods of our fathers, and a reverence for that great order of things in which man finds himself a part. The pious man believes in a destiny, or order transcending his own will: to exalt any passion, however innocent, above this, is a rebellion ; to intensify any passion, so as to disturb the appropriate calm of resignation, is to act irreverently against the gods. Lesser duties must give way to greater : love of wife must give way to love of country, and the sorrow of bereavement must not obscure the larger issues of life. Thus, not only did Laodamia's yearning for the restoration of her husband to life show a failure to recognise the fixity of eternal laws, but her death was 'ὑπὲρ μόρον' ('a transgression of the ordinance of destiny') and in reason's spite ; it was, after all, self-will, and could not win the favour of heaven."

The poem reflects also the Platonic notion of the inferiority of sensuous and material existence. "This life is only a discipline under imperfect conditions, and to be set free from the passion and fretfulness of existence is the choice and longing of the wise."

NOTES.

1. **sacrifice … morn.** Sacrifices to the infernal gods were made between midnight and sunrise. Cf. Vergil, *Æneid*, vi. 252: "Tum Stygio regi *nocturnas* inchoat aras," 'Then he begins a *nocturnal* sacrifice to the Stygian king'; and Silius Ital. *Pun.* xiii. 404-406 : "Mactare repostis Mos umbris, inquit, consueta piacula nigras *Sub lucem* pecudes," 'It is customary (said the priestess) to sacrifice to the buried shades the usual expiations of black sheep *on the verge of dawn.*'

2. **have I made.** Laodamia is speaking. She was the daughter of Acastus and the wife of Protesilaus, a Thessalian king, who accompanied the rest of the Greeks to the Trojan war. The Greek who first set foot on the Trojan shore was doomed by the Delphic oracle to death, a fate to which Protesilaus devoted himself, being slain by Hector. Laodamia grieved over his loss with such constancy that the gods allowed him to come back to

earth from the lower world and revisit his wife for three hours. She killed herself, or, according to Wordsworth, died of a broken heart, upon his return to the shades.

3. infernal gods. The *di inferi*, or gods of the lower world, as opposed to the *di superi*, or Olympian deities.

4. required. Used here in its Latin sense of 'asked back.'

7, 8. by fervent ... faith. Cf. Bible, *Galatians*, v. 6 : "Faith which worketh by love."

8. suppliant, lit. 'bending under' (Lat. *sub*, under, and *plicare*, to fold, bend), hence 'submissive,' and so 'earnestly entreating.'

heavenward ... hands. Vergil's (*Æneid*, i. 93) "duplices tendens ad sidera palmas," 'stretching both hands to the stars.' There are many classical reminiscences in this poem.

10, 11. Her countenance ... grows. Cf. Vergil, *Æn.* vi. 47-49 (of the Sybil): "Non voltus, non color unus ... sed pectus anhelum, ... majorque videri," 'Neither face nor hue remained the same, but her bosom heaves, and she is ampler to behold.'

12. expects. In its Latin sense of 'awaits'; cf. note to l. 4.

15. Her hero, Protesilaus; see note to l. 2.

16. presence ... corporeal. Cf. "*I saw the figure of a lovely maid*" (Wordsworth's dream of his daughter), 9 : "The bright corporeal presence."

18. wingèd Mercury. Mercury, the Greek Hermes, was termed ψυχαγωγός, the 'conductor of souls' to and from the lower regions (cf. l. 151), and was the messenger of the gods. He wore winged sandals ('talaria') and a winged cap ('petasus'), and carried a wand entwined at one end with serpents ('caduceus'). Cf. Vergil, *Æn.* iv. 239-243.

20. That calms all fear. Cf. Vergil, *Æn.* iv. 244 : "Dat somnos adimitque," 'He gives and takes away sleep' (with his wand).

Such grace ... prayer, thy prayer hath received such a gracious fulfilment.

25. impassioned. This word is a key-note of the poem ; see Introduction.

26. Again etc., 'again she tried to attain that crowning-point of her desire.' The expression has been accused of turgidity, but is in keeping with the stately, deliberate style of the narrative.

27, 28. But ... made. Cf. Vergil, *Æn.* vi. 700-702 (of Æneas trying to embrace his father's ghost): "Ter conatus" etc., 'Thrice then he tried to cast his arms around his neck ; thrice grasped in vain, the phantom escaped his hands, as unsubstantial as the fleeting winds and winged sleep.'

34. the floor ... rejoice. For a similar notion, cf. *Ode to Duty*, 46, and note.

40, 41. thy fidelity ... my worth. The wife's constancy and the husband's devotion to duty are both included in Vergil's 'piety.' Cf. *Æn.* vi. 688 : "Vicit iter durum *pietas*?" 'Has thy *piety* prevailed over the difficulties of the journey' (of Æneas to Hades)?

43. Thou knowest etc. So Ovid, *Her.* xiii. 93, 94 : "Sors quoque nescio quem fato designat iniquo, Qui primus Danaum Troada tangat humum," 'An oracle too destines to a cruel doom him, whoever he be, who first touches Trojan soil.'

the Delphic oracle. The famous oracle at the temple of Apollo at Delphi, a town of Phocis.

46. A generous cause, a noble, worthy cause. *Generous* (from Lat. *genus, generis,* race) means lit. 'high-bred,' 'of a noble nature.'

48. self-devoted. "Devovere se diis," 'to devote oneself to the gods below,' was used among the Romans of those who, like Curtius or the first Decius Mus, voluntarily sacrificed themselves for some patriotic object.

53, 54. Thou found'st ... heart. 'Thy courage that bade thee die taught thee nobler conduct than my weak affection which wanted to keep thee alive ; and I forgive your seeming unkindness, for are you not restored to me?' Ovid (*Her.* xiii. 95) represents Laodamia as warning her husband to be the last rather than the first to disembark.

58. elude. It is noticeable that the poet substituted this word for "cheat" ("that thou should'st cheat") of the 1815 edition, as more in harmony with the dignity of the style. See note to l. 26.

60. As when etc., as when thou wert alive at home in thy native Thessaly.

62. place thee. *Thee, him,* etc., for *thyself, himself,* etc., are common in older English, as they are still in poetry ; cf. Keble, "Mark she how close she veils *her* round." We still say 'He looked about *him.*'

63. Give etc. So Ovid (*Her.* xiii. 117) makes Laodamia ask when would be the time that he should share the couch and recount to her his warlike achievements.

65. the conscious Parcæ, 'the Parcæ who were conscious of what was happening.' The Parcæ were three goddesses who presided over human life : named Clotho, whose province was the moment of birth, and who held a distaff ; Lachesis, who spun the thread of human life ; and Atropos, who cut it.

66. a Stygian hue, a hue of the lower world, *i.e.* a pallid or livid hue. The Styx (from Greek στυγεῖν, to hate) was one of the rivers of the lower regions.

67. This visage etc. The pallor of my countenance shows thee that I am a denizen of the lower world, and can never come back again to the enjoyments of earth.

68-70. Nor should ... vanish. We ought not to mourn the loss of sensuous pleasures, since they are fleeting and uncertain ; but even if we could recover them, they are in themselves not worth having. See Introduction.

70-72. Earth ... pains. Earthly life, bringing old age, in due course puts an end to the delights of sense ; but in the life of the lower world such delights are not merely ended, but despised : grave and temperate are the pleasures and pains that inhabit there. *Erebus* was the son of Chaos and Darkness and the husband of Night, by whom he had Day. The word was often used, as here, to signify the lower world itself.

74. the gods approve etc. See Introduction.

77. meekly is emphatic—'mourn with meekness, not with passion.'

78. sojourn is here accented, by poetic license, on the second syllable. *Sojourn* is from French *sojourner, séjourner, so* or *se* representing the Latin *sub,* and *journer* the low Latin *diurnare,* to stay, from *diurnus,* daily.

79. "Ah, wherefore etc." Laodamia here breaks in.

Hercules. This hero's twelfth and last labour was to bring up from the lower world Cerberus, the three-headed dog which guarded the entrance to Hades ; and, in connexion with this adventure, he rescued and brought back with him Alcestis, the wife of Admetus, who had voluntarily laid down her life to save her husband from death. Alcestis, being sister to Acastus, was aunt to Laodamia, so that Alcestis's story would naturally occur to her.

80. the guardian monster. This should refer to Θανατος, or Death, with whom Euripides, in his drama of *Alcestis,* represents Hercules as struggling for the possession of Alcestis ; though the phrase "guardian monster" seems to indicate that Wordsworth had Cerberus in his mind.

81, 82. reanimated ... vernal bloom. These expressions are emphatic. Alcestis came back to earth not as a spectre, but as a young, fresh, living person.

83. Medea's spells etc. The witch Medea restored her husband, Jason's aged father Æson, to youthful vigour by drawing away the blood from his veins and filling them with the juice of certain herbs. The daughters of Pelias, who, encouraged by this success, were treacherously induced by Medea to cut up and boil their aged father, were Laodamia's aunts, so that here again she would naturally be familiar with the story of Medea and Æson.

84. **a youth** etc.   He was grown young again, and could share the sports of youthful companions.   The words *youth* and *youthful* are emphatic; see note to ll. 80, 81 above.   *Peer* is from Lat. *par, parem,* 'equal,' as in *peerless,* 'having no equal,' 'matchless.'

87, 88. **Than strength ... star.**   Than the force of Hercules or the spells of Medea.

87. **nerve,** muscle.   'Strength of nerve' would generally mean firmness or courage.

88. **sun and star.**   Witches were supposed to have power to cause eclipses, and to draw the moon and stars from their courses.

89. **to agony,** to the pitch of agony; so much distrest as to reach the point of agony.   So Keats: "Though I *to dimness* gaze."

90.   This line is an Alexandrine, containing six feet.   Line 157 is another; the rest of the poem is in the regular five-foot measure.

91. **if thou goest, I follow.**   If thou goest back to Hades, I will kill myself and so follow thee.

95, 96. **Elysian ... place.**   These lines well reflect the tone of tender yet dignified sadness that marks the Sixth *Æneid.* Elysium, or the Elysian Fields, was the place in the lower regions where the souls of the virtuous abode after death.   Cf. *Peele Castle,* 26.

98. **whose course is equable.**   Where the course of existence is even and calm.

99. **No fears,** *i.e.* with no fears to be subdued.

101, 102. **heroic arts ... pursued.**   In Hades heroes renewed their favourite pursuits with calmer feelings than on earth, and practised them with a more perfect congruity of aim.   Their nature was purged of all discordant elements.   Vergil (*Æn.* vi. 651-655) represented the shades of the heroes as still taking delight in chariots and armour, and in pasturing their glossy steeds.

103. **Of all,** *i.e.* he spake of all.

imaged.   Things below were images or reflections of earthly objects.   Vergil's spectral heroes had spectral chariots ("currus inanes").

105. **An ampler ether** etc.   The description is taken from Vergil, *Æn.* vi. 640, 641: "Largior hic campos æther et lumine vestit Purpureo, solemque suum, sua sidera norunt," 'Here an ampler ether spreads over the plains and clothes them in purple

(*i.e.* bright and beautiful) light, and they have a sun of their own and their own stars.' In Latin, *æther*, the pure upper air, was opposed to *aer*, the lower atmospheric air. *Purpureal* recurs in *An Evening of Extraordinary Splendour*, 33.

109. **Yet,** *i.e.* though it is so superior to Earth.

111. **The end,** the object, purpose.

112. **Who,** *i.e.* in that I.

116. The line is an absolute clause. *Bent* = inclination.

120. **What time,** 'at the time at which.' *Time* is here in the adverbial objective case.

At Aulis. Aulis was a town on the sea coast of Bœotia, where the Greek fleet, assembled to sail against Troy, was detained by contrary winds, through the anger of Artemis, whom Agamemnon, the Greek general, had offended. To appease the goddess, Agamemnon sacrificed his daughter Iphigenia, and a favourable wind was given.

122. **the silent sea.** The quiet of the voyage was conducive to meditation.

124. **of a thousand vessels** etc. A reversal of Laodamia's warning to her husband, Ovid, *Her.* xiii. 97 : "Inter mille rates tua sit millesima puppis," 'Among a thousand vessels let thy prow be the thousandth and last.'

132. **unfinished towers.** Homer (*Iliad*, ii. 701) represents Protesilaus as leaving behind him his "palace half-finished" (δόμος ἡμιτελής).

133. **suspense,** hesitation on our part.

136. **In soul** etc., I drove the shameful thought from my mind.

137, 138. **Old ... wrought.** My former weakness again made me shrink from the sacrifice ; but, by putting my noble resolve into action, I was saved from yielding to that weakness.

143, 144. **The invisible ... solemnised.** The invisible world hath shown its sympathy with thee by allowing me to revisit thee in answer to thy prayers ; do thou accordingly cultivate greater loftiness and calmness of feeling, and so become still more in sympathy with the serene inhabitants of that unseen world.

145-150. **Learn ... love.** 'Let an earthly, sensuous love teach thee to rise to something higher—an immortal and passionless affection ; for it was mainly with this object that love was given to mankind and its growth encouraged and sanctioned. Nay, the passion of love was allowed to become violent and excessive, in order that it might lift men completely out of themselves, and that the thraldom of selfishness, when pitted against love, might show itself as weak as mere imaginary bonds.' Love was given to eradicate selfish desires and so lead men up to higher things than the joys of sense. Cf. Tennyson, *Locksley Hall*, **33, 34 :**

" Love took up the harp of Life and smote on all the chords with
        might ;
Smote the chord of Self, that, trembling, pass'd in music out
        of sight."

151. **Hermes.** See note to l. 18 above.

153. **The hours.** The three hours permitted ; see l. 23.

158-162. The original reading was :

" Ah, judge her gently who so deeply loved !
Her, who, in reason's spite, yet without crime, ·
Was in a trance of passion thus removed ;
Delivered from the galling yoke of time
And these frail elements—to gather flowers " etc.

Upon this version the poet remarked : " As at first written, the
heroine was dismissed to happiness in Elysium. To what purpose then the mission of Protesilaus? He exhorts her to moderate
her passions ; the exhortation is fruitless, and no punishment
follows. So it stood : at present she is placed among unhappy
ghosts for disregard of the exhortation. Vergil also places her
there." See _Æneid_, vi. 440-449, where those who died of love
(and Laodamia among them) are placed in the 'lugentes campi'
(the 'plains of mourning') in the outer regions of Hades.

159. **as for a wilful crime.** Her crime was passive rather than
active—weakness rather than self-will.

164-166. **Yet tears ... mourned by man.** A reminiscence of
Vergil, _Æn._ i. 462 : "Sunt lacrimæ rerum et mentem mortalia
tangunt," 'There are events that claim our tears, and human
woes touch the heart.'

167. **As ... believes.** 'Men foolishly believed that sympathy
can exist only between man and man, whereas nature also
sympathizes with man.' Note that it was this instance of
nature's sympathy that suggested the poem to Wordsworth ; see
Introduction. A similar thought forms the _motif_ of _Hart-leap Well_.

168. **Hellespont.** The modern Dardanelles, the narrow strait
between the Ægean Sea and the Sea of Marmora. Ilium, or
Troy, stood on its southern shore.

173. **at the sight,** i.e. at the sight of Ilium, the scene of Protesilaus's death and the cause of his wife's sorrowful fate. Cf.
Pliny, _Hist. Nat._ xvi. 44 : "Sunt hodie ex adverso Iliensium
urbe," etc., 'Opposite to Ilium and close to the Hellespont there
are to this day on Protesilaus's tomb trees, which ever as soon as
they have grown high enough to have Ilium in view, wither away
and again shoot up.' Also the _Greek Anthology_, vii. 141-144,
σᾶμα δέ τοι, κ.τ.λ., 'Right opposite hated Ilium the Nymphs shroud
thy tomb with thick-leaved elms, trees visited by heavy wrath ;
and if ever they see the walls of Troy, they shed their withering
foliage.'

AN EVENING OF EXTRAORDINARY SPLENDOUR.

INTRODUCTION.

COMPOSED in 1818, and published in 1820. Wordsworth says that this poem was "felt, and a great measure composed, upon the little mount in front of our abode at Rydal."

It forms one of his 'Evening Voluntaries "—poetic records of impressions made upon his mind by evening sights or sounds. *Calm is the Fragrant Air* and *Composed by the Sea-shore* are other instances of this type of composition. The term "Voluntary" is adopted by the poet in reference to its use in church music, to denote an organ solo performed before, during, or after church service. It was so called because it was originally *extemporized* by the organist, unrestricted by formal rules of composition. Similarly these poems are spontaneous outpourings of some special mood of the poet.

This ode, writes Mr. Myers, is "the last considerable production of Wordsworth's genius." It is a great symbolical spectacle, a solemn farewell, with which his poetic life closes. In it "we recognize the peculiar gift of reproducing with magical simplicity as it were, the inmost virtue of natural phenomena."

NOTES.

1. **this effulgence.** An MS. copy of this poem bears the title, "Composed during a sunset of transcendent Beauty, in the summer of 1817."

6. **sanctify.** Cf. *Personal Talk*, 32; *Influence of Natural Objects*, 56.

9. **Time was when** etc. Cf. Milton, *Par. Lost*, iv. 680-684, where Adam says:

" ' How often from the steep
Of echoing hill or thicket have we heard
Celestial voices to the midnight air,
Sole, or responsive each to other's note,
Singing their great Creator ! ' "

10. **modulated echoes.** Echoes not of confused but of modulated sounds ; musical, harmonious echoes.

31. **antlers.** There used to be fallow deer in the park at Rydal Hall.

33. **purpureal Eve.** So S. Johnson : " Evening now with *purple* wings." *Purpureal* occurs in *Laodamia*, 106.

35. **Informs,** quickens, animates, inspires. Cf. *Tintern Abbey*, 125, and note.

37. not quickened by the sun. Cf. Gray, *The Progress of Poetry*, 119, 120 :

> " Such forms, as glitter in the Muse's ray,
>   With Orient hues, *unborrowed of the sun.*"

And *Peele Castle*, 15. The poet declares that he must believe there is something supernatural and divine about such extraordinary splendour.

39. Heaven's is emphatic ; opposed to the earthly " ground " of the next line.

41. broken ties. As alienated friendship, or bereavement caused by death.

43. hazy ridges. Wordsworth's note tells us that the multiplication of mountain-ridges, here described as a kind of Jacob's Ladder, leading to heaven, is produced either by watery vapours, or sunny haze ;—in the present instance by the latter cause.

44. scale is the Latin *scala*, a ladder. The *scale* of a fish and the *scale* of a balance are of English derivation.

47. to ascend. Like Jacob's angels. See Bible, *Genesis*, xxviii. 12 : "And he (Jacob) dreamed, and behold a ladder set up on the earth, and the top of it reached to heaven : and behold the angels of God ascending and descending on it."

49. Wings at my shoulders etc. ' I feel within myself as if I too could mount on angel wings.' The " sense of belonging at once to two worlds " again comes home to the poet, and he seems to be almost "lifted to the golden doors." It is this same feeling that breathes through *Stepping Westward*, " where the sense of sudden fellowship, and the quaint greeting beneath the glowing sky, seem to link man's momentary wanderings with the cosmic spectacles of heaven " (Myers).

In a note to these lines Wordsworth acknowledges his indebtedness to a picture entitled " Jacob's Dream," by Mr. Washington Allston, an American painter, to whom in gratitude he sent a MS. copy of this poem. Probably something in the picture gave definite form to observations of natural phenomena the significance of which the poet had not immediately noted.

52. practicable. The " bright steps " are so clearly defined that it looks as if one could actually climb them.

57. Genii. Disembodied spirits, fabled to influence mankind in various ways.

59. the dower, the rich gift of splendour. Cf. *London, 1802*, 5.

61-64. Such hues ... infancy. Cf. *Intimations of Immortality*, 1-5.

69, 70. whom peace ... voice. Nature's calmer aspects, no less than the thunder and the storm, are Thy ministers. The MS. copy ran :

> "Dread Power ! whom clouds and darkness serve,
>   The thunder, or the still small voice,"

in allusion to Bible, *Psalms*, xcvii. 2 : "Clouds and darkness are round about him" (God); and *1 Kings*, xix. 11, 12, where, when "the Lord passed by," there is a wind, an earthquake, and a fire, and "after the fire a still small voice."

74. **Full early lost**, etc. Cf. *Intimations of Immortality*, 17-22 ; 53-57 ; 175-178.

78. **a second birth**, a complete revival ; a renewal of her old powers.

KING'S COLLEGE CHAPEL.

INTRODUCTION.

COMPOSED in 1821, and first published in 1822. This is one of the "Ecclesiastical Sonnets," and is the 43rd of Part III., which is headed "From the Restoration to the Present Times." The whole series of 132 sonnets are intended to embody a History of the Church of England, both previous and subsequent to the Reformation. The sonnet preceding this one is entitled "Cathedrals etc.," and concludes :

> "And ye, whose splendours cheer
> Isis and Cam, to patient Science dear ! "

—thus introducing the subject of the present sonnet, a subject which is continued in the two sonnets that succeed it.

NOTES.

1. **the royal saint.** King Henry VI., who founded King's College, Cambridge.

2. **ill-matched aims.** In planning so gorgeous a building for a society of poor scholars.

6, 7. **the lore .. more,** the careful calculation of the exact amount that will suffice.

9. **These lofty pillars** etc. King's College Chapel is a pre-eminent example of the Perpendicular or Florid style of architecture. Floor alone excepted, the whole is one mass of panelling. The roof is composed entirely of arches of the most airy construction, covered with exquisite fan-like tracery. Decoration runs riot everywhere, and the sense aches again at the beauty and splendour and variety that everywhere meet the gaze.

10. **Self-poised.** The "lofty pillars" form part of the walls, and the arched roof is thrown from wall to wall, unsupported by any intermediate columns.

11, 12. **where music ... die.** Cf. the succeeding sonnet, 4-7 :
" But, from the arms of silence—list ! O list !
The music bursteth into second life ;
The notes luxuriate, every stone is kissed
By sound, or ghost of sound, in mazy strife."

"SCORN NOT THE SONNET."

INTRODUCTION.

COMPOSED in 1827, and first published in 1827. This sonnet was composed, Wordsworth tell us, "almost extempore, in a short walk on the western side of Rydal Lake." It formed one of the " Miscellaneous Sonnets."

NOTES.

3. **unlocked his heart.** Of Shakspere's sonnets the first 126 are addressed to a friend, and the last 28 to a woman ; but who these persons were is unknown, though many conjectures have been made as to the identity of the mysterious "Mr. W. H." of the dedication. But there seems little doubt that they express Shakspere's own feelings in his own person, and that many of them are autobiographical.

4. **Petrarch's wound.** Petrarch, the great Italian poet, was born at Arezzo, in 1304. His hopeless love for the beautiful Laura found solace and expression in his exquisite sonnets.

5. **Tasso.** Torquato Tasso, also a great Italian poet, was born at Sorrento, in 1544. His works include two volumes of sonnets, addressed to the Princess Eleanora, sister of Alfonso, duke of Ferrara. But his chief work is an epic, the " Jerusalem Delivered."

6. **Camöens,** the celebrated Portuguese poet, was born at Lisbon, in 1517. In 1556, for a satire that he wrote, he was banished to Macao, a Portuguese settlement in China, where he wrote many sonnets and lyrics, as well as his great poem, the " Lusiad."

8. **Dante,** the greatest poet of Italy, was born at Florence, in 1265. His *Vita Nuova,* a treatise which he appears to have written about his twenty-eighth year, is plentifully interspersed with sonnets, often relating to his beloved Beatrice. Thus these poems were composed at a comparatively happy time of his life ("a gay myrtle leaf"), before the year 1300, when his misfortunes and wanderings began (" the cypress "). The myrtle is emblematical of joy, as the cypress is of mourning.

9. **visionary** refers to his "Divine Comedy," which, in the form of a vision, sets forth the mysteries of the invisible world.

10. **Spenser** was born in London, in 1553. Besides his well-known *Faerie Queene*, he wrote 88 *Amoretti* or love sonnets on his wife Elizabeth, and four other occasional sonnets.

> **called from Faery-land.** Cf. his Sonnet lxxx.:
>
> "After so long a race that I have run
> Through Faery land, which these six books compile,
> Give leave to rest me, being half foredone,
> And gather to myself new breath awhile.
>
> .   .   .   .
>
> Till then give leave to me, in pleasant mew
> To sport my Muse, and sing my Love's sweet praise."

These sonnets were written in 1592 and 1593, and published in 1595.

11. **dark ways.** This refers to Spenser's Irish experiences. In 1586 he received a grant of land in the county of Cork, where he resided, at Kilcolman; and in 1596 we find him Clerk of the Council of the Province of Munster. There, exiled from London and his literary associates, he felt himself a banished man; nor does he appear to have lived happily with his neighbours, with whom he had quarrels about land.

> **when a damp** etc. Milton's 23 sonnets, of which six are in Italian, were written at intervals between 1630 and 1658, when his political duties forced other poetry into abeyance. His last 16 sonnets, says Prof. Masson, "are the few occasional strains that connect, as by intermittent trumpet-blasts through twenty years, the rich minor poetry of his youth and early manhood with the greater poetry of his declining age." Thus in times of depression's "damp" he would have recourse to sonnet composition.

14. **Soul-animating strains.** Cf. especially the sonnets *To Cromwell, On the Late Massacre in Piedmont,* and *On his Blindness.*

ON THE DEPARTURE OF SIR WALTER SCOTT.

INTRODUCTION.

COMPOSED in 1831, and first published in 1835.

Wordsworth tells us that he first became acquainted with Sir Walter Scott in 1803, when he and his sister, making a tour in Scotland, were hospitably received by Scott in Lasswade upon the banks of the Esk, where he was then living. In the autumn of 1831, he and his daughter left Rydal to visit Sir Walter at

N

Abbotsford before his departure for Italy. On the day after their arrival he accompanied them and others of the party to Newark Castle on the Yarrow. "On our return in the afternoon we had to cross the Tweed directly opposite Abbotsford. The wheels of our carriage grated upon the pebbles in the bed of the stream that there flows somewhat rapidly ; a rich but sad light of rather a purple than a golden hue was spread over the Eildon Hills at that moment ; and, thinking it probable that it might be the last time Sir Walter would cross the stream, I was not a little moved, and expressed some of my feelings in the sonnet beginning—'A trouble, not of clouds, or weeping rain.'" Wordsworth sent Scott this sonnet before his departure from England.

NOTES.

2. pathetic light. See Introduction :—"a rich but sad light."

3. Eildon's. See Introduction. For "triple height," cf. Scott, *Lay of the Last Minstrel*, II. xiii. :

"I could say to thee
The words that cleft Eildon hills in three."

According to the legend, Michael Scott ordered a troublesome demon to divide Eildon hill, which was then a uniform cone, into the three picturesque peaks which it now bears.

4. Spirits of power etc. Nature, in the person of the genii of the mountain, is represented as mourning the departure of the great poet, endowed with a creative power akin to hers. Cf. *Yew-trees*, 23-26. For a similar portrayal of Nature sympathizing with man, cf. Milton, *Par. Lost*, ix. 1002-1004 :

"Sky lower'd, and muttering thunder, some sad drops
Wept at completing of the mortal sin
Original."

5. power departing. Cf. *On the Expected Death of Fox*, 17 : "A power is passing from the earth."

6. Tweed. This river flows past Abbotsford, on the borders of Roxburgh and Selkirk, into the North Sea at Berwick.

11. laurelled conqueror. Among the Romans, victorious generals, in triumphal processions, wore laurel crowns on their heads, and carried laurel branches in their hands, while their lictors' *fasces*, or bundles of rods, were bound with laurel. Hence, in modern literature, the laurel is regarded as the symbol of victory. Cf. Cowper, *Heroism*, 77 : "Laurelled heroes"; and *The Russian Fugitive*, Part III. st. 2 :

"Conquerors thanked the Gods,
With laurel chaplets crowned."

12. Be true etc. Compare Horace's address to the ship that was carrying the poet Vergil to Greece. "May the stars and winds prosper thee," he writes, "till thou deliver thy trust in safety" (*Odes*, i. 3).

13. **midland sea.** The Mediterranean.

14. **soft Parthenope.** The ancient name of Naples was Parthenope, the name of one of the Sirens. According to the legend, it was so called because the Siren's body was found on the sea-shore there. *Soft* alludes to the mildness of its climate.

In 1831 Scott's physicians recommended an excursion to Italy for the benefit of his health, and he reached Naples on Dec. 27. Feeling, however, that his strength was rapidly decreasing, he returned in July 1832 to Abbotsford, where he died on Sept. 21 of the same year.

INTIMATIONS OF IMMORTALITY.

INTRODUCTION.

COMPOSED at Town-end, Grasmere, between 1803 and 1806, "two years at least," says Wordsworth, "passing between the writing of the four first stanzas and the remaining part." It was first published in 1807.

"Nothing," the poet tells us, "was more difficult for me in childhood than to admit the notion of death as a state applicable to my own being ... With a feeling congenial to this, I was often unable to think of external things as having external existence, and I communed with all that I saw as something not apart from, but inherent in, my own immaterial nature. Many times while going to school have I grasped at a wall or tree to recall myself from this abyss of idealism to the reality." And again: "There was a time in my life when I had to push against something that resisted, to be sure that there was anything outside of me. I was sure of my own mind; everything else *fell away*, *and vanished* (see l. 143) into thought."

As regards the doctrine of pre-existence, Wordsworth remarks: "To that dream-like vividness and splendour which invests objects of sight in childhood, every one, I believe, if he would look back, could bear testimony ... It is far too shadowy a notion to be recommended to faith, as more than an element in our instincts of immortality. But let us bear in mind that, though the idea is not advanced in revelation, there is nothing there to contradict it, and the fall of man presents an analogy in its favour. Accordingly, a pre-existent state has entered into the popular creeds of many nations; and is an ingredient in Platonic philosophy." There are, however, some differences in the way in which the idea commended itself to Plato and to

Wordsworth. The stress was laid by Wordsworth on the effect of terrestrial life in putting the higher faculties to sleep, and making us "forget the glories we have known." Plato, on the other hand, looked upon the mingled experiences of mundane life as introducing a gradual but slow remembrance (ἀνάμνησις) of the past.

Some passages in Bishop Earle's *Microcosmographie*, published in 1628, seem to foreshadow the present poem : "A child is a man in a small letter. ... He is nature's fresh picture newly drawn in oil, which time and much handling dims and defaces. His soul is yet a white paper unscribbled with observations of the world, wherewith at length it becomes a blurr'd notebook. ... His hardest labour is his tongue, as if he were loath to use so deceitful an organ; and he is best company when he can but prattle. ... His father hath writ him as his own little story, wherein he reads those days of his life that he cannot remember, and sighs to see what innocence he has outlived. ... The elder he grows, he is a stair lower from God, and, like his first father, much worse in his breeches."

It is probable, however, that Wordsworth found the germ of his ode in Henry Vaughan's "The Retreat," from *Silex Scintillans* :

> "Happy those early days when I
> Shined in my Angel-infancy !
> Before I understood this place
> Appointed for my second race,
> Or taught my soul to fancy ought
> But a white celestial thought ;
> When yet I had not walk'd above
> A mile or two from my first Love,
> And looking back, at that short space,
> Could see a glimpse of his bright face ;
> When on some gilded cloud or flower
> My gazing soul would gaze an hour,
> And in those weaker glories spy
> Some shadows of eternity ;
>   .   .   .   .   .   .
> But felt through all this fleshly dress
> Bright shoots of everlastingness.
> O how I long to travel back,
> And tread again that ancient track !
> That I might once more reach that plain
> Where first I left my glorious train ;
>   .   .   .   .   .   .
> Some men a forward motion love,
> But I by backward steps would move ;
> And when this dust falls to the urn,
> In that state I came, return."

Compare too the same author's *Corruption* :

> "Sure it was so. Man in those early days
> Was not all stone and earth ;
> He shined a little, and, by those weak rays,
> Had some glimpse of his birth.
> He saw Heaven o'er his head, and knew from whence
> He came condemned hither,
> And, as first Love draws strongest, so from hence
> His mind sure progressed thither."

Also his *Childhood* ; M. Arnold's *To a Gipsy Child* and *In Utrumque Paratus* ; and Tennyson's *The Two Voices* and *Far—far—away.* See also Wordsworth's Ecclesiastical Sonnet xvi., *Persuasion.*

The metre of the poem is irregular ; the lines vary in length from the Alexandrine to the line with two accents, forming a kind of ebb and flow in the tide of song. Perhaps the most remarkable thing in its structure is the frequent change of the keynote, and the skill and delicacy with which the transitions are made. For the motto Wordsworth prefixed to this poem, see *The Rainbow*, note to ll. 8, 9. Compare also the Introduction to that poem.

NOTES.

1-9. In my childhood all nature had a freshness and beauty for me which I no longer possess the faculty of seeing.

1. **There was a time** etc. Cf. *Tintern Abbey*, 76-83 ; *An Evening of Extraordinary Splendour*, 37, 38 ; 61-64 ; and *To the Cuckoo*, ii. 12 :

> "Thou bringest unto me a tale
> Of visionary hours."

2. **every common sight.** Cf. *Personal Talk*, 30-32.

4. **Apparelled in celestial light.** Cf. Bible, *Psalms*, civ. 2 : "Who (*i.e.* God) coverest thyself with light as with a garment"; also *Westminster Bridge*, 4, 5 :

> "This city now doth, like a garment, wear
> The beauty of the morning."

Celestial is emphatic ; it was "a light that never was, on sea or land" (*Peele Castle*, 15). Cf. *Maternal Grief*, 16-19 :

> "The child . . . . . partook
> Reflected beams of that *celestial light*
> To all the little-ones on sinful earth
> Not unvouchsafed."

5. **freshness of a dream.** The phrase combines the ideas of imaginative vividness and transitoriness. It is a "visionary

gleam" (l. 57).   Cf. *Peele Castle*, 16; and *The Excursion*, i. 142-147 :

> "And, being still unsatisfied with aught
> Of dimmer character, he thence attained
> An active power to fasten images
> Upon his brain ; and on their pictured lines
> Intensely brooded, even till they acquired
> *The liveliness of dreams.*"

6. **of yore** is a double genitival adverb, since *yore* = O. E. *geára*, ' of years ' (like ' of course,' ' of right '). See page 153.

10-18. The outward shows of nature are still fair ; but the old splendour is gone.

10. **The rainbow.**   Cf. *The Rainbow*, 1-4.

12, 13. **The moon ... are bare.**   A characteristic instance of Wordsworth's bold personification of natural objects—the outcome, in his case, not so much of poetic feeling as of personal sympathy with nature.   A similarly bold image occurs in l. 25. *Bare* = cloudless.   Cf. *London, 1802*, 11 : " Pure as the *naked* heavens."

16. **birth,** ' thing born '; abstract for concrete.

19-35. It is true that, in spite of my joyful surroundings, a private grief made me melancholy ; but I have got rid of that feeling and can now fully appreciate earth's spring-tide rejoicings.

21. **tabor,** a small drum.   The word is of imitative origin, like *tap* and *pat*.

22. **To me alone** etc.   The " thought of grief " is for the glory that has passed away.   It has been supposed to refer to the death of his brother John (see Introduction to *Peele Castle*); but the fact that this stanza was composed not later than 1804 (see Introduction), whereas his brother's death occurred in 1805, forbids this supposition.

23. **A timely utterance,** *i.e.* stanzas I. and II.   Cf. Bible, *Psalms*, xxxix. 2, 3 : " I was dumb with silence, I held my peace, even from good ; and my sorrow was stirred.   My heart was hot within me, while I was musing the fire kindled : then spake I with my tongue."   And Shaks. *Macbeth*, IV. iii. 209, 210 :

> "Give sorrow words : the grief that does not speak
> Whispers the o'er-fraught heart and bids it break."

24. **I again am strong.**   Cf. *Peele Castle*, 57.

25. **their trumpets.**   See note to ll. 12, 13 ; and cf. Tennyson, *Merlin and the Gleam*, iv. : " Cataract music of falling torrents."

26. **the season wrong.**   My grief would show ingratitude to the joy-giving season of spring.   Cf. Tennyson, *The Two Voices*, st. 152 :

"The woods were fill'd so full with song,
There seem'd no room for sense of wrong."

28. **the fields of sleep.** The fresh morning breeze blows upon me from the fields after their night's repose.

32. **with the heart of May,** with the joyous feelings inspired by spring.

36-57. I am determined to sympathize with the general joy; and yet each well-known object around me reminds me that the old glory is departed.

36. **blessèd,** innocent and happy.

38. **jubilee,** a season of rejoicing; Hebrew *yóbel,* 'a shout of joy.' This is a different word from *jubilation, jubilant,* which are from Lat. *jubilum,* a joyful cry.

40. **coronal,** garland. An illusion to the old Roman custom of crowning the head with flowers at feasts. Cf. *The Idle Shepherd-boys,* 28-30:

" Both earth and sky
Keep *jubilee,* and more than all,
Those boys with their green *coronal.*"

51. **But there's a tree** etc. The power of natural scenery to awaken old associations, referred to here, is enlarged upon in "*'Tis said that some have died for love.*" Cf. R. Browning, *May and Death,* 13-20:

" Only, one little sight, one plant,
Woods have in May, that starts up green.

.   .   .   .   .   .

. That, they might spare ; a certain wood
Might miss the plant ; their loss were small:
But I,—whene'er the leaf grows there
Its drop comes from my heart, that's all."

And Tennyson, *Early Spring,* vi. :

" Past, Future glimpse and fade
Thro' some slight spell,
A gleam from yonder vale,
Some far blue fell."

And the "single elm-tree bright" in M. Arnold's *Thyrsis.*

54. **pansy,** heart's-ease (French *pensée,* a thought), the flower of thought or remembrance. Cf. Shaks. *Hamlet,* IV. v. 176: " There is pansies, that's for thoughts."

57. **the glory and the dream.** Cf. l. 5, and note.

58-76. The poet now proceeds to trace the origin of this feeling of loss. We were born into this world from a previous state of existence. Coming from God, we bring with us vestiges of our old heavenly surroundings, which mark our infancy, but gradually fade till they are lost in manhood.

58. Our birth is but a sleep etc. When we were born into this life we lost consciousness of a previous state of existence, which was then forgotten or but dimly remembered. For Plato's doctrine of pre-existence, see Introduction.

59-61. The soul that rises ... from afar. As a star disappears below the horizon of one hemisphere before it can appear above the horizon of another, so our soul (the guiding star of our life) ceased to inhabit a previous state before it accompanied us into the present life.

61. from afar. Cf. *To H. C.* 1, and note.

63. in utter nakedness, bare of all traces of its glorious past.

64. trailing clouds of glory. The soul, as it rises above the earthly horizon (*i.e.* in infancy), is represented as accompanied by the rosy clouds of dawn—a " vision splendid " (l. 73) which still follows its progress to the period of youth. When the zenith of manhood is reached, these early golden hues "fade into the light of common day " (l. 76). Cf. " My glorious train " (*i.e.* the glory that attended me) in l. 20 of Vaughan's *Retreat*, quoted in the Introduction.

65. From God. Cf. *The Excursion*, iv. 83-86 :

" Thou, who did'st wrap the cloud
Of infancy around us, that thyself,
Therein, with our simplicity awhile
Mightst hold, on earth, communion undisturbed."

who is our home. Man is a lodger in this world (cf. " her inmate man," l. 82); Heaven is his true home. Cf. Cowper, *Task*, iv. 912-914 (of the happy man) ;

"One
Content indeed to sojourn while he must
Below the skies, but having there his home."

66. Heaven ... infancy. Cf. Mrs. Browning, *A Rhapsody of Life's Progress*, 1-6 :

" We are born into life—it is sweet, it is strange !
We lie still on the knee of a mild mystery,
Which smiles with a change !
But we doubt not of changes, we know not of spaces,
The heavens seem as near as our own mother's face is,
And we think we could touch all the stars that we see."

And Hood, " *I remember, I remember*," st. 4 :

" I remember, I remember
The fir trees dark and high ;
I used to think their slender tops
Were close against the sky :

> It was a childish ignorance,
> But now 'tis little joy
> To know I'm further off from heaven
> Than when I was a boy."

67. Shades of the prison-house, the cares and interests of earthly existence. The image (see note to l. 64) is slightly varied here. For *prison-house*, cf. Shaks. *Hamlet*, i. v. 14, where the Ghost says he is forbid "to tell the secrets of his prison-house"; and Cowper, *Task*, ii. 661:

> "So fare we in this prison-house the world."

71, 72. who daily ... Must travel, *i.e.* although he must daily travel further away from the Eastern horizon (see note to l. 64).

72. Nature's priest, a devout worshipper at the shrine of nature; in close communion with her divine beauty and splendour. Cf. *Tintern Abbey*, 152: "I, so long A worshipper of Nature."

73. And by the vision etc. Cf. Bacon, *Essays*, xlii.: "A certain rabbin, upon the text, *Your young men shall see visions, and your old men shall dream dreams*, inferreth that young men are admitted nearer to God than old, because vision is a clearer revelation than a dream."

75. the man etc. Cf. Tennyson, *In Memoriam*, xliv.:

> "How fares it with the happy dead?
> For here *the man is more and more*;
> But he forgets the days before
> God shut the doorways of his head.
>
> The days have vanish'd, tone and tint,
> - And yet perhaps the hoarding sense
> Gives out at times (he knows not whence)
> A little flash, a mystic hint."

die away. Cf. the sonnet, "*Dark and more dark,*" 13, 14:

> " They are of the sky,
> And from our earthly memory fade away."

77-84. Earthly pleasures and pursuits all tend to make us forget our former glorious state.

77. fills her lap, *i.e.* for the amusement of her "foster-child" man.

78. Yearnings ... natural kind. Man being a native of heaven (which is his "home," l. 65), Earth is represented throughout this stanza as his foster-mother or nurse, who, though not his real mother, still has a strong natural affection for the child entrusted to her care.

80. no unworthy aim. Because, being born into this world, it is right that we should take an interest in its pleasures and pursuits. We are not meant to be ascetics.

81. homely, plain, conventional. This "homely" is opposed to the "glories" of l. 83, just as "common day" is opposed to "clouds of glory" in the previous stanza.

82. inmate. See note to l. 65.

84. imperial palace. Observe the grand sound-effect produced by the double consonantal alliteration combined with vowel alliteration—"imperial palace."

85-107. Thus the child, happy in his home life, is soon taken up with earthly things, and occupies himself in continually imitating the actions and pursuits of his elders.

85. the child. Wordsworth probably had the little Hartley, son to S. T. Coleridge, in his thoughts; see *To H. C. Six Years Old*.

New-born blisses, newly-tasted earthly pleasures.

. **86. six years'**, *i.e.* six years old. Cf. 'a two-foot (long) rule,' 'a three-ounce (heavy) weight.'

pigmy, or *pygmy*, from Greek Πυγμαῖοι, the pygmies, a fabulous race of dwarfs, whose height was the length from the elbow to the *fist* (Gr. πυγμή).

88. Fretted, beset. See note to l. 192.

sallies, sudden attacks, outbursts; Lat. *salire*, to leap. Cf. Tennyson's "Check every outflash, every ruder *sally*."

89. light, beaming looks of affection. Cf. "the love-light in her eye" (H. Coleridge, *The Light of Love*, 10), and "love-darting eyes" (Milton, *Comus*, 753).

90. some little plan or chart. The child, picturing to himself human life as he imagines it, arranges his toys or dolls in imitation of a marriage ceremony or a funeral procession.

96. frames his song. Some particular object or pursuit attracts him, and he makes it the subject of his merry childish prattle.

97. fit, apply.

98. dialogues, imaginary conversations relating to business, etc. Thus children play at "keeping shop."

102. cons, studies, learns. *Con* is a form of *can*, O.E. *cunnan*, to know.

103. his "humorous stage," the stage on which he sets forth the moods and caprices of mankind. The child imitates all the characters ("persons") that he sees around him, at one time playing at being a school-boy, at another, an old man, and so on. The words marked as a quotation occur in the *Musophilus* of S. Daniel, a poet much admired by Wordsworth. There is an evident reference to the well-known passage in Shaks. *As You Like It*, II. vii. 139 etc. : "All the world's a stage," etc.

humorous. According to the old medical theory, the body contained four "humours" (Lat. *humor*, moisture), upon the due admixture of which the moral and physical health depended. These "humours" were based upon the four corresponding elements. Thus we have :—

Blood (sanguine)	Phlegm (phlegmatic)	Choler (choleric)	Melancholy (melancholic)
Air (moist)	Water (cold)	Fire (hot)	Earth (dry)

An undue preponderance of one humour made a person "humorous" (or a "humorist"), *i.e.* eccentric or whimsical, whence came the later meaning of witty.

104. **palsied age,** the paralytic old man, Shakspere's "last scene of all," which he describes as "second childishness and mere oblivion." *Palsy* = M.E. *palsey* = Fr. *paralysie*, paralysis.

105. **equipage,** equipment, array, surroundings. *Equip* is from Icel. *skipa*, to arrange, from the same root as *shape*.

108-128. Alas that the child, in his most glorious state of being, and blest with these divine intuitions, should be so eager to anticipate the dull round of earthly existence, which comes of itself too soon.

108. **exterior semblance.** He is small and weak in outward appearance, which thus belies or misrepresents the greatness of his soul.

110. **yet,** as yet, up to the present.

112. **deaf and silent,** though deaf and silent; *i.e.* though unconscious of thy innate powers and giving no sign of their possession. Note the catachresis, or describing one sense in terms of another, and cf. *Airey-Force Valley*, 14 : "A soft *eye-music* of slow-waving boughs"; and Milton, *Lycidas*, 119 : "blind mouths."

read'st the eternal deep, dost clearly understand the secret of an eternal state of being.

113. **Haunted ... by the eternal mind,** continually visited by divine inspirations. Cf. l. 120.

114. **prophet.** Because the child is an unconscious declarer of the truth. The Greek πρό (pro-) has the two meanings of 'forth, publicly' and of 'before'; so that *prophet* = (1) one who expounds, (2) one who predicts.

115. **rest,** remain without effort on his part.

117. **the darkness of the grave,** *i.e.* utter, deadly darkness.

119. **Broods ... slave.** The sense of his previous state of immortal existence embraces and encompasses the child (as light

does an object) with a dominant and overpowering influence.
The word *slave* denotes here absolute, not servile subjection.
Cf. *Ode to Duty*, 56: "thy *bondman* let me live!"

120. **not to be put by.** Cf. l. 113. *Put by* = put aside, got
rid of.

121. **yet.** See note to l. 110.

122. **freedom.** Subjection (see l. 119) to an ennobling influence
is true freedom. Cf. the English Prayer Book: "Whose (God's)
service is perfect freedom."

on thy being's height. From the poet's point of view,
childhood, not manhood, is the highest and noblest stage of
existence.

124. **yoke,** bondage to worldly pursuits.

126. **earthly freight,** burden of earthly cares.

127. **custom,** conventionalism; the dull routine of everyday
life. Cf. *The Excursion*, iv. 205-207:

> "Alas! the endowment of immortal power
> Is matched unequally with *custom*, time,
> And domineering faculties of sense."

128. **Heavy .. life,** subduing thee, as frost does the soil, and
penetrating thy whole being, like the vital principle.

129-167. Yet I delight to think that something of the old
glory of childhood remains; not merely its freedom and
simplicity, but its sense of the unreality of its earthly surroundings—a feeling which has a guiding, strengthening, and tran-
quillizing power over us, and which never can be wholly quenched.
Hence it is that we are able sometimes to realize once more that
immortal state of existence from which we came.

129. **O joy! that,** how delightful it is that. *That* in ll. 129,
131 is a conjunction, not a relative.

in our embers. Cf. Gray, *Elegy*, 92:

> "Ev'n in our ashes live their wonted fires."

And Chaucer, *Reeve's Prologue*, 28:

> "Yet in our ashen cold is fire i-reke" (I reckon).

135. **most worthy,** very worthy.

136, 137. **the simple ... at rest,** the innocent faith of the child,
in all his moods, whether full of eager curiosity or calmly
receptive. *Creed* is coordinate with, not descriptive of "delight,
and liberty."

141. **obstinate questionings.** See Introduction.

142. **outward things.** Cf. *To the Cuckoo*, 29-31:

" The earth we pace
Again appears to me
An unsubstantial, faery place. "

143. **Fallings from us, vanishings,** the feeling we have that external objects, visible and tangible, seem to fall away from us, as unreal, and vanish in unsubstantiality. See Introduction ; and *The Prelude,* ii. 349-352 :

" Bodily eyes
Were utterly forgotten, and what I saw
Appeared like something in myself, a dream,
A prospect of the mind."

144. **Blank misgivings,** vague, baffling doubts.

146. **High instincts** etc. Cf. *The Prelude,* xii. 221-225 :

" How
The mind is lord and master—outward sense
The obedient servant of her will.   Such moments
Are scattered everywhere, taking their date
From our first childhood."

147. **Did tremble ... surprised.**   An echo of Shaks. *Hamlet,* I. i. 148, 149 :

" And then it started like a guilty thing
Upon a fearful summons."

149. **Those shadowy recollections.**   Plato's ἀνάμνησις ; see Introduction.   Cf. Tennyson, *The Two Voices,* 127, 128 :

" Moreover, something is or seems,
That touches me with mystic gleams,
Like glimpses of forgotten dreams—

Of something felt, like something here ;
Of something done, I know not where ;
Such as no language may declare."

And *The Prelude,* i. 631-635 :

" Those recollected hours that have the charm
Of visionary things, those lovely forms
And sweet sensations that throw back our life,
And almost make remotest infancy
A visible scene."

151, 152. **the fountain light ... a master light.**   These recollections of a previous immortal existence are the prime source of all our truest happiness and the chief guiding influence to direct our lives aright.

154, 155. **Our noisy years ... silence.**   As we contemplate that calm eternity from which we came and to which we go, our human life, with its turmoil and excitement, seems but a momentary interval lying between the two eternities. Cf. *On the Power of Sound,* xiv. :

> " O Silence ! are Man's noisy years
> No more than moments of thy life ? "

158. man nor boy, manhood nor boyhood.

161-167. Hence in a season ... evermore. Wordsworth represents the soul as borne by the ocean of eternity to the shore of this world and landing upon it at its human birth. As we grow older, we travel further and further inland, away from "that immortal sea"; but, under the influence of these recollections, we may yet at once retrace our steps and so recover and feel once more in sympathy with those old "high instincts" of childhood. So, on the other hand, Tennyson in *Crossing the Bar* pictures himself at death as "putting out to sea," "embarking" upon the ocean of eternity, to be carried by it away from earth—"our bourne of Time and Place." Cf. *A Tradition of Oker Hill,* 13, 14 :

> " The sea
> That to itself takes all, Eternity."

168-186. Therefore we can still join in the spring-tide rejoicings of nature. For though the old splendour is gone, the early sympathy with nature remains, and with riper years come strength and calm after sorrow, and faith in a future life.

168. Then sing etc. See lines 19-21.

171. in thought, not actively, but in sympathetic feeling.

181. the primal sympathy, childhood's intuitive sympathy and communion with nature—an instinct which is never lost.

183, 184. In the soothing ... suffering. Our experience of the sorrows of human life brings with it the exercise of patience and sympathy for others which have a softening effect upon our minds. Cf. *Peele Castle,* 35, 57-60 ; and *The Excursion,* iv. 1058-1077 : "Within the soul a faculty abides" etc.

185. through death, *i.e.* to the immortal life beyond the grave. This thought is illustrated by *The Primrose of the Rock.*

186. the philosophic mind, calmness and self-control, which we acquire as we grow older. Cf. R. Browning, *James Lee's Wife,* vi. 10 :

> " For kind
> Calm years, exacting their account
> Of pain, mature the mind."

And *The Prelude,* i. 235-237 :

> " With trust
> That mellower years will bring a riper mind
> And clearer insight."

187-203. Nay, I love nature as much or even more than before, though my love is now chastened by my experience of the frailty and the changes of human life—an experience, however, which has given me rich human sympathies, so that the humblest natural object can for me be suggestive of the deepest pathos.

188. **our loves.** Nature, as it were, requited his love for her by her revelation of herself to him. Cf. *Tintern Abbey*, 122, 123.

190, 191. **one delight ... sway.** I have lost one particular delight (the "visionary gleam" of l. 56), with the result of living in more continual communion with nature.

192. **fret** is O.E. *fretan,* a contraction of *for-etan*, to eat away; hence, to chafe, to be in commotion or agitation.

194. **innocent brightness.** The beautiful epithet "innocent" (*i.e.* pure) harmonizes with the subsequent "new-born." Day is compared to an innocent new-born infant.

196-198. **The clouds ... mortality.** Such an aspect of nature as a sunset, beautiful as it is, has a tinge of melancholy for my maturer vision, for it presents to my mind a type of human decay.

197. **a sober colouring.** Cf. *Tintern Abbey*, 138-140.

199. **Another race ... are won.** 'A new course of strenuous self-discipline has been gone through, and has brought me new spiritual gains to balance the loss I have sustained.' Cf. *Peele Castle*, 34, and *Tintern Abbey*, 87-89. For *race*, cf. Bible, *1 Cor.* ix. 24 : "Know ye not that they which run in a race run all, but one receiveth the prize? So run, that ye may obtain." For "palms are won," cf. *The Prelude*, iii. 505 : "Whatever palms are won"; and *Ib.* v. 8 : "those palms achieved."

Prof. Dowden, however, explains the line thus : "It is a sunset reflection, natural to one who has 'kept watch o'er man's mortality': the day is closing, as human lives have closed; the sun went forth out of his chamber as a strong man to run a race, and now the race is over and the palm has been won; all things have their hour of fulfilment " (see Bible, *Psalms*, xix. 4, 5).

It seems just possible that "another race " may be in allusion to " my second race " in l. 4 of Vaughan's *Retreat*, quoted in the Introduction.

200. **the human heart,** our human sympathy, which is the mainstay of our moral being. Cf. *Peele Castle*, 53, 54.

203. **Thoughts that ... tears.** Just as a sunset (l. 196) may suggest thoughts of human decay, so a humble flower may give rise to feelings that are too deep and intense to find expression in tears. Cf. *The Tables Turned*, st. 6 :

> " One impulse from a vernal wood
> May teach you more of man,
> Of moral evil and of good,
> Than all the sages can."

And *The Excursion*, i. 942-952:

> " I well remember that those very plumes,
> Those weeds, and the high spear-grass on that wall,
> By mist and silent rain-drops silvered o'er,
> As once I passed, into my heart conveyed
> So still an image of tranquillity,
>
> . . . .
>
> That what we feel of sorrow and despair
>
> . . . . . .
>
> Appeared an idle dream."

And *Peter Bell*, Part i. st. 12:

> " A primrose by the river's brim
> A yellow primrose was to him,
> And it was nothing more."

203. **too deep for tears.** Cf. Thucydides, vii. 75 : μείξω ἢ κατὰ δάκρυα, "(misfortunes) too great for tears."

INDEX TO NOTES.

[The references are to the pages. Italics denote subjects.]

Abraham's bosom, 150.
Absolute clause, 94, 96, 121, 187.
Absolute infinitive, 124.
Aching joys, 138, 140.
Addison, 130.
Adverbial objective, 123.
Alexandrine, 168, 186, 197.
Alfoxden, 93.
Alien sound, An, 143.
All the summer long, 142.
Alliteration, 202.
Altar, 113.
Ampler ether, An, 186.
Animal movements, 220.
Apparelled, 197.
Appetite, An, 220.
Arms nor head, 101.
Arnold, M., 197, 199.
Attila, 110.
Aulis, 187.
Azincour, 154.

Bacon, 131, 201.
Bare, 109, 113, 148, 198.
Beaumont, Sir G., 165, 177.
Beget, 105.
Bent, 187.
Betrayed, 166.
Better eyes, 124.

Bewilder, 106.
Bible, 101, 132, 133, 138, 150,
    155, 158, 161, 169, 175, 183,
    191, 197, 198, 207.
Bird of Paradise, 130.
Birth, 198.
Blank misgivings, 205.
Blessèd, 199.
Bondman, 165, 204.
Book (of magic), 181.
Boon, 175.
Boor, 106.
Bosworth, 179.
Bower, 113, 151.
Braes, 121.
Brake, 125.
Breathing man, 134.
Breathless, 149, 178.
Broad (sun), 149.
Broods, 203.
Brooke, Mr. S., 153.
Brough, 179.
Browne, 132.
Browning, R., 199, 206.
Browning, Mrs., 200.
Bryant, 128.
Burns, 94, 116, 147, 156, 157.
Butler, 178.
Byron, 110, 111, 159, 160.

o   209

Camöens, 192.
Canning, 170.
Carew, 169.
Carrock, 180.
Catachresis, 203.
Cave, 141.
Celandine, 108.
Celestial, 197.
Chase, 120.
Chastened, 156.
Chatterton, 147.
Chaucer, 122, 154, 170, 204.
Cheer, 125.
Chieftain, 120.
Child of earth, 147.
Children in the Wood, The, 106.
Chronicle of heaven, 166.
Churchill, 163.
Clan, 120.
Cloud similes, 100, 120, 122, 148.
Clouds of glory, 200, 202.
Cockermouth, 102, 134.
Cognate object, 141, 143.
Coleorton, 127, 165, 177.
Coleridge, Hartley, 151, 152, 202.
Coleridge, S. T., 93, 95, 117, 131, 139, 142, 144, 145, 150, 151, 163, 202.
Coleridge, Sara, 178.
Coleridge, Hon. Justice, 159.
Collins, 173.
Con, 202.
Concourse wild, 95.
Confederate, 142.
Confidence of reason, The, 165.
Coronal, 199.
Cowper, 105, 155, 162, 168, 173, 194, 200, 201.
Crecy, 154.
Creed, 204.
Criffel, 157.
Cry of blood, 101, 179.
Cuckoo, 104, 117, 118, 127.
Cunning, 100.
Custom, 204.
Cyclops, 115.

Daffodil, 123.
Daniel, S., 202.
Dante, 192.
Dappled, 115.
Dark ways, 193.
Darkness of the grave, The, 203.
Deaf and silent, 203.
Dear God, 109.
Decrepit, 149.
Delphic oracle, The, 184.
Disturbance, 163.
Do all I can, 94.
Dor-hawk, 134.
Dove (river), 98.
Dove Cottage, 173, 174.
Dore cottage, 107.
Dowden, Prof., 207.
Dower, 190.
Drayton, 121, 154.
Dream, 166, 174, 197, 199.
Drummond, 126.
Dryden, 140, 145, 148.

Earle, 196.
Earliest stars, 94.
Earthly freight, 204.
Ecclesiastical Sonnets, 191.
Eildon, 194.
Eldest child of Liberty, 110.
Elemental, 134.
Elevates, 133.
Elf, 108, 115.
Elfin, 141.
Elude, 184.
Elysian, 166, 186.
Emmeline, 103.
Embers, 204.
Emont, 178.
Equipage, 203.
Erebus, 185.
Esthwaite, 96.
Eternal deep, The, 203.
Eternal mind, The, 203.
Eternal summer, 133.
Euenus, 105.
Evening Voluntaries, 133, 134, 189.

Excursion, The, 94, 126, 138, 139, 144, 148, 154, 166, 176, 198, 200, 204, 206, 208.
Expects, 183.
Exterior semblance, 203.

Factors, 120.
Faery, 115, 180, 193.
Faery voyager, 152.
Fairy, 97.
Faithful, 132.
Fallings from us, 205.
Fan, 94.
Fatherly concern, 120.
Fay, 115.
Fee, 110.
Fen, 112.
Field of death, 181.
Five seasons, 97.
Fleeced, 97.
Flock of war, The, 181.
Flodden, 181.
Forlorn, 176.
Fountain light, 205.
Fraternal four, Those, 154.
Free, 149.
Freedom, 204.
Freeze the blood, 101.
Fret, 202, 207.
Fretful stir, The, 137.
From afar, 152, 200.
From well to better, 170.
Furlong, 101.
Furness-fells, 172.

Gay, 106.
Generous, 184.
Genial, 139, 162.
Genii, 190.
Genitival adverb, 124.
Gerundial infinitive, 116.
Ghostly agonies, 180.
Ghostly shapes, 155.
Glanced, 143.
Glancing, 125.
Glaramara, 155.
Gleam, 137, 166, 207.

Glendermakin, 180.
Glinted, 156.
Goldsmith, 128, 170.
Goslar, 98, 140.
Gowans, 157.
Gray, 161, 166, 199, 204.
Great God, 176.·
Greek Anthology, 188.
Green's History, 112.
Grooms, 180.
Guardian monster, The, 185.

Halcyon, 130.
Half a call, 108.
Half create, 139.
Hall and bower, 113.
Hardiment, 122.
Hawes, 101.
Hawkshead, 94, 142.
Hawkshead Grammar School, 95, 96.
Hazy ridges, 190.
Heard, Rev. W. A., 182.
Heart of May, 199.
Heavenly destiny, 116.
Heavy as frost, 204.
Hebrides, 118.
Helvellyn, 125.
Hellespont, 188.
Hercules, 185, 186.
Heroic arts, 186.
Heroic wealth, 113.
Hesiod, 164.
Hogg, J., 129.
High instincts, 205, 206.
Homefelt pleasures, 170.
Homely, 202.
Homer, 131, 187.
Hood, 132, 200.
Horace, 129, 161, 194.
House (verb), 149, 167.
Household motions, 160.
Hulk, 167.
Human heart, The, 207.
Human sweetness, A, 116.
Humorous, 202, 203.
Humours, Four, 203.

Ill-matched aims, 191.
Imaged, 186.
Images, 97, 100, 113, 148, 201.
Immortal sea, 206.
Impassioned, 183.
Imperial palace, 202.
Incommunicable, 124.
Indifferent, 97.
Indoor sadness, 106.
Infernal gods, 183.
Inform, 140, 155, 189.
Inheritest, 124.
Inland murmur, 135.
Inmate, 202.
Innocent brightness, 207.
Instinct, 129.
Inveterate, 155.

Jonson, Ben, 101, 164.
Jubilee, 199.

Keats, 103, 186.
Keble, 176, 184.
Kent, 121.
Kingcups, 107.
Knight, Prof., 141, 154.

Language of the sense, 139.
Lasting monument, A, 126.
Late and soon, 175.
Laurelled, 194.
Laws of Manu, 94.
Layamon, 142.
Lea, 176.
Like a garment, 109.
Like a roe, 138.
Loch Veol, 121.
London, 107, 109.
Long (adv.), 142.
Loom, 171.
Lorton Vale, 153.
Loth, 133, 153.
Loud-chiming, 142.
Lovelace, 172.
Lowliest duties, The, 114..
Lowly wise, 164.
Luxuriates, 97.

Machine, 160.
Madness, 147.
Mahan, Capt., 169.
Maiden city, A, 111.
Man nor boy, 206.
Manna, 169.
Manners, 113.
Mary, 180.
Masson, Prof., 193.
Master light, 205.
Medea, 185, 186.
Meekly, 185.
Mercury, 183.
Midland sea, 195.
Mighty heart, 109.
Milton, 99, 106, 110, 113, 114,
    116, 118, 122, 133, 139, 140,
    145, 158, 159, 161, 171, 177,
    189, 193, 194, 202, 203.
Mimic hootings, 95.
Modulated echoes, 189.
Montgomery, J., 123.
Mortality, 207.
Mosedale, 188.
Most ancient, 164.
Motley, 96.
Moves, 176.
Moving, 101.
Murmur, 97.
Myers, Mr., 116, 124, 141, 146,
    168, 170, 189, 190.

Naked heavens, The, 113.
Napoleon, 111, 112, 120, 121,
    128.
Natural, 118.
Nature, 93, 95, 98, 102, 138, 139,
    140, 141, 142, 143, 176, 190,
    194, 199, 201, 207.
Nature's chain, 131.
Nature's priest, 201.
Nelson, 167, 168, 169, 170.
Nerve, 186.
New-born blisses, 202.
New-comer, 104, 127.
Nightingale, 104, 117, 129.
Noisy years, 205.
Numbers, 118.

Oblivious, 133.
Obscurities of happiness, 134.
Obstinate questionings, 204.
Of yore, 153, 198.
One green hue, 136.
Othello, 174.
Out of tune, 176.
Outward things, 204.
Overflowing, 117.
Overgrown, 102.
Ovid, 184, 187.

Pagan, 176.
Painful, 106.
Palms, 207.
Palsy, 203.
Pansy, 199.
Paramour, 100.
Parca, 184.
Parthenope, 195.
Passion, A, 138.
Passionate work, A, 167.
'*Pathetic Fallacy*,' *The*, 153, 181.
Patmore, 162, 168.
Peer, 186.
Pen, 113.
Pendragon, 179.
Pensive citadels, 171.
Perennially, 155.
Percy, 119, 153.
Periwinkle, 94.
Persius, 164.
Petrarch, 192.
Phantom of delight, A, 159.
Philosophic mind, The, 206.
Piety, 145.
Pigmy, 202.
Pilgrim, 129.
Pillared shade, A, 155.
Pinnace, 141.
Pious bird, The, 105.
Plato, 182, 195, 196, 200, 205.
Pliny, 188.
Poitiers, 154.
Polity, 120.
Pope, 145, 169.
Practicable, 190.

Prayer Book, 204.
Prelude, The, 94, 95, 96, 103, 126, 136, 137, 138, 139, 141, 142, 143, 144, 145, 150, 159, 160, 163, 165, 173, 175, 205, 206, 207.
Prescience, 133.
Presence, A, 139, 144.
Primal sympathy, 206.
Prison-house, 201.
Privacy, 129.
Promises, 160.
Prophet, 203.
Proteus, 177.
Purpureal, 187, 189.
Put by, 204.

Quaint, 96.

Race, 207.
Rancour, 174.
Readings, Various, 100, 103, 104, 118, 121, 136, 142, 143, 144, 158, 166, 173, 188.
Reasoning, 133.
Records, 160.
Redbreast, 105, 106.
Reflex, 143.
Repair, 115.
Required, 183.
Richmond, 100, 101.
Rob Roy, 118, 119, 120, 121.
Robin Hood, 119.
Robinson, H. Crabb, 125, 159.
Rout, 100, 108.
Royal saint, The, 191.
Rule of right, The, 120.
Ruskin, 153.
Rydal, 105, 128, 131, 151, 181, 189, 192, 193.

Sacred to the poor, 174.
Safeguard of the West, 110.
Sallies, 202.
Same, The, 100, 121, 123, 148.
Sanctify, 142, 173, 189.
Sanctuary, 107.
Scale, 190.

Scott, 100, 125, 181, 193, 194, 195.
Season, 166.
Second birth, A, 191.
Secure, 97.
Self-devoted, 184.
Self-poised, 191.
Self-sacrifice, 165.
Self-surpast, 170.
Serpentine up-coiling, 154.
Several, 100.
Shady haunt, 117.
Shake, 124.
Shakspere, 101, 122, 126, 127, 136, 137, 142, 147, 153, 160, 163, 164, 166, 172, 174, 178, 181, 192, 198, 199, 201, 202, 203, 205.
Sheer, 100.
Shelley, 103, 104, 111, 128, 129, 130, 138.
Shod with steel, 142.
Silence of the seas, 117.
Silius Ital., 182.
Singing as they shine, 130.
Skipton, 179.
Slave, 204.
Sleep, 181, 199, 200.
Sleeping flowers, 176.
Sleepless, 147.
Smoother walks, 163.
Smoothest range, 134.
Sober colouring, A, 207.
Sojourn, 185.
Sonnet, The, 172.
Sophocles, 108.
Southey, 127, 169.
Sordid boon, A, 175.
Soul of truth, The, 166.
Sound-effect, 142.
Spenser, 110, 122, 127, 132, 174, 177, 193.
Sphere, 132.
Spirits of power, 194.
Spiritual right, 116.
Sportive wood, 136.
St. George, 179.
Stanley, Dean, 172.

Star, 134.
Stave, 119.
Stole my way, 141.
Stygian, 184.
Substantial, 174.
Summoned, 124.
Suppliant, 183.
Swale, 101.
Sweet will, 109.
Sylvester, 132.
Symphony austere, 126.

Tabor, 198.
Tarn, 125.
Tasks that are no tasks, 108.
Tasso, 192.
Temper, 97.
Temples, 109.
Tennyson, 97, 99, 116, 117, 124, 135, 142, 143, 150, 151, 152, 153, 154, 155, 163, 164, 167, 170, 171, 175, 180, 187, 197, 198, 199, 201, 205, 206.
Terence, 111.
Thames, 109.
There are who, 161.
Thistles of a curse, 132.
Threlkeld, Sir L., 177, 180.
Timely, 163, 198.
To agony, 186.
To behold, 116, 124.
Too deep for tears, 207, 208.
Touch, 99.
Town-end, 99, 102, 105, 106, 107, 114, 122, 123, 144, 145, 158, 172, 174, 195.
Treasure-house, 166.
Treaty of Amiens, 112, 121.
Trench, 171.
Triton, 177.
Tuft, 136.
Turner, Mr., 96, 143.
Tweed, 194.
Twofold shout, 104.
Types beneficent, 132.

Umbraville, 153.
Una, 174.

Uncertain heaven, 95.
Unchartered, 163.
Undying fish, The, 180.
Unerring light, 162.
Unfinished towers, 187.
Unsubstantial, 105.
Up-gathered, 176.
Urania, 130.
Ure, 101.

Vacant, 123.
Vain temptations, 161.
Vanishings, 205.
Vaughan, H., 196, 200. 207.
Vergil, 111, 118, 155, 158, 181, 182, 183, 184, 186, 188, 195.
Venice, 110, 111.
Very bliss, 124.
Victory or death, 122.
Virgin, 96.
Visible motion, 143.
Vision splendid, 200, 201.
Visionary, 193, 207.
Visionary hours, 104.
Voluptuous, 97.

Walk, 147.
Wallace, Mr., 170.
Wandering voice, A, 104.
Wanton wooers, 108.
Wat Tyler, 122.
Waterbreak, 97.
Watson, Mr. R. S., 109.
Watson, Mr. Wm., 158, 164.
Wealth, 127.

Weeds, 96.
Wensley, 100, 101.
Wet or dry, 103.
What time, 187.
Wheel, 99, 171.
Whittier, 125.
Wild ecstasies, 140.
Wildish, 115.
Wilful crime, A, 188.
Wilkinson, 117.
Winander, 94.
Wise restraint, 97.
Wither, 114.
Wordsworth, Dorothy, 98, 103, 117, 139, 140, 149, 152, 193.
    Journals, 103, 105, 106, 107, 108, 115, 117, 122, 146, 148, 149, 156, 157.
Wordsworth, John, 114, 165, 168, 198.
Wordsworth, Mary, 123, 159.
Wordsworth, W., *classicisms*, 118.
    criticisms, 117, 138, 139, 146, 148, 149, 152, 173, 174.
    prosaisms, 96, 100, 148.
    qualifications, 96, 98.
World, The, 175.
Wrought, 163.
Wye, 136, 136.

Yeaned, 100.
Yet-vivid, 148.
Yoke, 204.
Young, 139.

GLASGOW: PRINTED AT THE UNIVERSITY PRESS BY ROBERT MACLEHOSE AND CO.

MACMILLAN'S
ENGLISH CLASSICS:.
A SERIES OF SELECTIONS FROM THE
WORKS OF THE GREAT ENGLISH WRITERS,
WITH INTRODUCTION AND NOTES.

The following Volumes, Globe 8vo, are ready or in preparation.

ADDISON—Selections from the Spectator. By K. Deighton. 2s. 6d.

ADDISON AND STEELE—Coverley Papers from the Spectator. Edited by K. Deighton. 1s. 9d.

ARNOLD—Selections. By G. C. Macaulay. [*In the Press.*

BACON—Essays. By F. G. Selby, M.A. 3s. ; sewed, 2s. 6d.
The *Schoolmaster*—"A handy and serviceable edition of a famous English classical work, one that can never lose its freshness and its truth."

—The Advancement of Learning. By F. G. Selby, M.A. Book I., 2s. ; Book II., 4s. 6d.

BURKE—Reflections on the French Revolution. By F. G. Selby, M.A. 5s.
Scotsman—"Contains many notes which will make the book valuable beyond the circle to which it is immediately addressed."
Schoolmaster—"A very good book whether for examination or for independent reading and study."
Glasgow Herald—"The book is remarkably well edited."

—Speeches on American Taxation ; on Conciliation with America ; Letter to the Sheriffs of Bristol. By F. G. Selby, M.A. 3s. 6d.

BYRON—Childe Harold. Edited by Edward E. Morris, M.A. [*In Preparation.*

CAMPBELL—Selections. By W. T. Webb, M.A. [*In Preparation.*

CHAUCER—Selections from Canterbury Tales. By H. Corson. 4s. 6d.

CHOSEN ENGLISH—Selections from Wordsworth, Byron, Shelley, Lamb, and Scott. With short biographies and notes by A. Ellis, B.A. 2s. 6d.

COWPER—The Task, Book IV. By W. T. Webb, M.A. Sewed, 1s.

—Letters, Selections from. By W. T. Webb, M.A. 2s. 6d.

—Shorter Poems. Edited by W. T. Webb, M.A. 2s. 6d.

DRYDEN—Select Satires—Absalom and Achitophel ; The Medal ; Mac Flecknoe. By J. Churton Collins, M.A. 1s. 9d.

GOLDSMITH—The Traveller and The Deserted Village. By Arthur Barrett, B.A. 1s. 9d. The Traveller (separately), sewed, 1s. The Deserted Village (separately), sewed, 1s.

—Vicar of Wakefield. By Michael Macmillan, B.A. [*In Preparation.*
The *Scotsman*—"It has a short critical and biographical introduction, and a very full series of capital notes."

MACMILLAN AND CO., LIMITED, LONDON.

GOLDEN TREASURY OF SONGS AND LYRICS. Book Second. By W. BELL, M.A. 3s. 6d.

GRAY—POEMS. By JOHN BRADSHAW, LL.D. 1s. 9d.

Dublin Evening Mail—"The Introduction and Notes are all that can be desired. We believe that this will rightly become the standard school edition of Gray."

Schoolmaster—"One of the best school editions of Gray's poems we have seen."

HELPS—ESSAYS WRITTEN IN THE INTERVALS OF BUSINESS. By F. J. ROWE, M.A., and W. T. WEBB, M.A. 1s. 9d.

The *Literary World*—"These essays are, indeed, too good to be forgotten." The *Guardian*—"A welcome addition to our school classics. The introduction, though brief, is full of point."

JOHNSON—LIFE OF MILTON. By K. DEIGHTON. 1s. 9d.

LAMB—THE ESSAYS OF ELIA. First Series. Edited by N. L. HALLWARD, M.A., and S. C. HILL, B.A. 3s.; sewed, 2s. 6d.

MACAULAY—ESSAY ON ADDISON. By J. W. HALES, M.A. [*In the Press.*]

—ESSAY ON WARREN HASTINGS. Ed. by K. DEIGHTON. 2s. 6d.

—LIFE OF DRYDEN. By P. PETERSON. [*In the Press.*]

—LIFE OF POPE. By P. PETERSON. [*In the Press.*]

—LORD CLIVE. Edited by K. DEIGHTON. 2s.

—ESSAY ON BOSWELL'S LIFE OF JOHNSON. Edited by R. F. WINCH, M.A. 2s. 6d.

MALORY—MORTE D'ARTHUR. Edited by A. T. MARTIN, M.A. [*In the Press.*]

MILTON—PARADISE LOST, BOOKS I. and II. By MICHAEL MAC-MILLAN, B.A. 1s. 9d. Books I.-IV. separately, 1s. 3d. each; sewed, 1s. each.

The *Times of India*—"The notes of course occupy the editor's chief attention, and form the most valuable part of the volume. They are clear, concise, and to the point, . . . while at the same time they are simple enough for the comprehension of students to whom Milton without annotation must needs be a mystery."

The *Schoolmaster*—"The volume is admirably adapted for use in upper classes of English Schools."

The *Educational News*—"For higher classes there can be no better book for reading, analysis, and grammar, and the issue of these books of Paradise Lost must be regarded as a great inducement to teachers to introduce higher literature into their classes."

—L'ALLEGRO, IL PENSEROSO, LYCIDAS, ARCADES, SONNETS, &c. By WILLIAM BELL, M.A. 1s. 9d.

The *Glasgow Herald*—"A careful study of this book will be as educative as that of any of our best critics on Aeschylus or Sophocles."

—COMUS. By the same. 1s. 3d.; sewed, 1s.

The *Dublin Evening Mail*—"The introduction is well done, and contains much sound criticism."

The *Practical Teacher*—"The notes include everything a student could reasonably desire in the way of the elucidations of the text, and at the same time are presented in so clear and distinct a fashion, that they are likely to attract the reader instead of repelling him."

—SAMSON AGONISTES. By H. M. PERCIVAL, M.A. 2s.; sewed, 1s. 9d.

The *Guardian*—"His notes are always of real literary value. . . . His introduction is equally masterly, and touches all that can be said about the poem."

MACMILLAN AND CO., LIMITED, LONDON.

MILTON—TRACTATE OF EDUCATION. By E. E. MORRIS, M.A. 1s. 9d.

POEMS OF ENGLAND. A Selection of English Patriotic Poetry, with notes by HEREFORD B. GEORGE, M.A., and ARTHUR SIDGWICK, M.A. 2s. 6d.

POPE—ESSAY ON MAN. Epistles I.-IV. Edited by EDWARD E. MORRIS, M.A. 1s. 9d.

—ESSAY ON CRITICISM. Edited by J. C. COLLINS, M.A. *[In the Press.*

SCOTT—THE LADY OF THE LAKE. By G. H. STUART, M.A. 2s. 6d. ; sewed, 2s. Canto I., sewed, 9d.

—THE LAY OF THE LAST MINSTREL. By G. H. STUART, M.A., and E. H. ELLIOT, B.A. 2s. Canto I., sewed, 9d. Cantos I.-III., and IV.-VI., 1s. 3d. each; sewed, 1s. each.

The *Journal of Education*—"The text is well printed, and the notes, wherever we have tested them, have proved at once scholarly and simple."

—MARMION. By MICHAEL MACMILLAN, B.A. 3s.; sewed, 2s. 6d.

The *Spectator*—" . . . His introduction is admirable, alike for point and brevity."

The *Indian Daily News*—"The present volume contains the poem in 200 pages, with more than 100 pages of notes, which seem to meet every possible difficulty."

—ROKEBY. By the same. 3s.; sewed, 2s. 6d.

The *Guardian*—"The introduction is excellent, and the notes show much care and research."

SHAKESPEARE—THE TEMPEST. By K. DEIGHTON. 1s. 9d.

The *Guardian*—"Speaking generally of Macmillan's Series we may say that they approach more nearly than any other edition we know to the ideal school Shakespeare. The introductory remarks are not too much burdened with controversial matter; the notes are abundant and to the point, scarcely any difficulty being passed over without some explanation, either by a paraphrase or by etymological and grammatical notes."

—MUCH ADO ABOUT NOTHING. By the same. 2s.

The *Schoolmaster*—" The notes on words and phrases are full and clear."

—A MIDSUMMER-NIGHT'S DREAM. By the same. 1s. 9d.

—THE MERCHANT OF VENICE. By the same. 1s. 9d.

—AS YOU LIKE IT. By the same. 1s. 9d.

—TWELFTH NIGHT. By the same. 1s. 9d.

The *Educational News*—"This is an excellent edition of a good play."

—THE WINTER'S TALE. By the same. 2s.

—KING JOHN. By the same. 1s. 9d.

—RICHARD II. By the same. 1s. 9d.

—HENRY IV., Part I. By the same. 2s. 6d.; sewed, 2s.

—HENRY IV., Part II. By the same. 2s. 6d.; sewed, 2s.

—HENRY V. By the same. 1s. 9d.

—RICHARD III. By C. H. TAWNEY, M.A. 2s. 6d.; sewed, 2s.

The *School Guardian*—"Of Mr. Tawney's work as an annotator we can speak in terms of commendation. His notes are full and always to the point."

—HENRY VIII. By K. DEIGHTON. 1s. 9d.

MACMILLAN AND CO., LIMITED, LONDON.

SHAKESPEARE — CORIOLANUS. By K. DEIGHTON. 2s. 6d.; sewed, 2s.

—ROMEO AND JULIET. By the same. 2s. 6d.; sewed, 2s.

—JULIUS CAESAR. By the same. 1s. 9d.

—HAMLET. By the same. 2s. 6d.; sewed, 2s.

—MACBETH. By the same. 1s. 9d.

The *Educational Review*—"This is an excellent edition for the student. The notes are suggestive, . . . and the vivid character sketches of Macbeth and Lady Macbeth are excellent."

—KING LEAR. By the same. 1s. 9d.

—OTHELLO. By the same. 2s.

—ANTONY AND CLEOPATRA. By the same. 2s. 6d.; sewed, 2s.

—CYMBELINE. By the same. 2s. 6d.; sewed, 2s.

The *Scotsman*—"Mr. Deighton has adapted his commentary, both in *Othello* and in *Cymbeline*, with great skill to the requirements and capacities of the readers to whom the series is addressed."

SOUTHEY—LIFE OF NELSON. By MICHAEL MACMILLAN, B.A. 3s.; sewed, 2s. 6d.

SPENSER—THE FAERIE QUEENE. Book I. By H. M. PERCIVAL, M.A. 3s.; sewed, 2s. 6d.

—THE SHEPHEARD'S CALENDER. By C. H. HERFORD, Litt.D. 2s. 6d.

STEELE—SELECTIONS. By L. E. STEELE, M.A. 1s. 9d.

TENNYSON—SELECTIONS. By F. J. ROWE, M.A., and W. T. WEBB, M.A. 3s. 6d. Also in two Parts, 2s. 6d. each. Part I. Recollections of the Arabian Nights, The Lady of Shalott, The Lotos-Eaters, Dora, Ulysses, Tithonus, The Lord of Burleigh, The Brook, Ode on the Death of the Duke of Wellington, The Revenge.—Part II. Oenone, The Palace of Art, A Dream of Fair Women, Morte d'Arthur, Sir Galahad, The Voyage, and Demeter and Persephone.

The *Journal of Education*—"It should find a wide circulation in English schools. . . . . The notes give just the requisite amount of help for understanding Tennyson, explanations of the allusions with which his poems teem, and illustrations by means of parallel passages. A short critical introduction gives the salient features of his style with apt examples."

The *Literary World*—"The book is very complete, and will be a good introduction to the study of Tennyson's works generally."

—MORTE D'ARTHUR. By the same. Sewed, 1s.

—ENOCH ARDEN. By W. T. WEBB, M.A. 2s. 6d.

—AYLMER'S FIELD. By W. T. WEBB, M.A. 2s. 6d.

—THE PRINCESS. By P. M. WALLACE, M.A. 3s. 6d.

—THE COMING OF ARTHUR; THE PASSING OF ARTHUR. By F. J. ROWE, M.A. 2s. 6d.

—GARETH AND LYNETTE. By G. C. MACAULAY, M.A. 2s. 6d.

—THE MARRIAGE OF GERAINT; GERAINT AND ENID. By G. C. MACAULAY, M.A. 2s. 6d.

—LANCELOT AND ELAINE. By F. J. ROWE, M.A. 2s. 6d.

—THE HOLY GRAIL. By G. C. MACAULAY, M.A. 2s. 6d.

—GUINEVERE. By G. C. MACAULAY, M.A. 2s. 6d.

WORDSWORTH—SELECTIONS. By F. J. ROWE, M.A., and W. T. WEBB, M.A. [*In preparation.*

MACMILLAN AND CO., LIMITED, LONDON.

10.12.96.

www.ingramcontent.com/pod-product-compliance
Lightning Source LLC
Chambersburg PA
CBHW020343030726
47496CB00007B/1983